Praise for *The White Devil*

‘Want a good Englis[illegible] cold winter night? [*The White Devil*] gathers you in lov[illegible] then takes you in a strangler’s grip with its escalating horrors’

Stephen King

‘Done beautifully well. Evans, an American who spent a year at Harrow himself, is a masterly conjuror of mood’ *Daily Express*

‘Demonic possession, the provocative topic of Justin Evans’s first novel, *A Good and Happy Child*, takes on a literary twist and a sexual jolt in *The White Devil* . . . Evans heaps an assortment of gothic embellishments onto this coming-of-age narrative’

New York Times Book Review

‘Have Andrew’s Byronic good looks conjured up this malevolent wraith? The Byronic storyline has some intriguing moments’

Daily Mail

‘*The White Devil* is an intelligent, bristling ghost story with a stunning sense of place, a uniquely frightful spirit, and a band of absolutely charming heroes – Byronic and otherwise. You’ll dread reaching the end while flipping the pages furiously’

Gillian Flynn, author of *Dark Places* and *Gone Girl*

Justin Evans grew up in Lexington, Virginia, and attended Columbia University with a graduate MBA in finance from NYU. After university, he worked at the *New York Times* as well as being a film scout for Paramount Pictures. When not writing, he's a strategy executive at social media company The Pluck Corporation and lives in New York City with his wife and son.

By Justin Evans

A Good and Happy Child
The White Devil

THE WHITE DEVIL

A Ghost Story

JUSTIN EVANS

A PHOENIX PAPERBACK

First published in Great Britain in 2011
by Weidenfeld & Nicolson
This paperback edition published in 2012
by Phoenix,
an imprint of Orion Books Ltd,
Orion House, 5 Upper St Martin's Lane,
London WC2H 9EA

An Hachette UK company

1 3 5 7 9 10 8 6 4 2

All the characters in this book are fictitious, and any resemblance to actual persons, living or dead, is purely coincidental.

A CIP catalogue record for this book is available from the British Library.

ISBN 978-1-7802-2026-0

Typeset by Input Data Services Ltd, Bridgwater, Somerset

Printed and bound in Great Britain by Clays Ltd, St Ives plc

The Orion Publishing Group's policy is to use papers that are natural, renewable and recyclable products and made from wood grown in sustainable forests. The logging and manufacturing processes are expected to conform to the environmental regulations of the country of origin.

www.orionbooks.co.uk

For Phoebe and for my mother

The white devil is worse than the black

ENGLISH PROVERB

OUTSIDE A COOL evening awaited. The perspiration on his back and neck turned icy. He staggered through the darkness, his breathing heavy. It had seized him, like a beast, a monkey sinking fangs into him, clinging to him and weighing him down, waiting for him to tire; a predator making a kill.

Get as far from people as you can.

He climbed the stairs. When he reached the top, he stumbled forward. He pulled up a trouser leg and found his calves and ankles had swollen: taut, puffy; dragging beneath him like bags of fluid.

What was happening to him?

He was enduring the journey from life to death. The force he was confronting was taking its revenge on him. He was experiencing in the space of an hour what might otherwise be a slow, consuming decline.

He reached up and touched his face; felt the ridge of his own cheekbone, traced it with his fingertip. The fat had melted away. The sores grew in his mouth. The fever burned his cheeks. He was plummeting quickly through the expected symptoms. He realized he had very little time left.

It was going to kill him.

It was going to kill all of them.

PART I

What exile from himself can flee?

1

Gap Year

ANDREW TAYLOR STOOD alone before a gate. The growl of his taxi pulling away had long since faded. A sky, whipped by winds, changing preternaturally, galloped overhead: clouds, sun, low-slung fog, in rapid succession. So this was English weather. The place felt wet. A smoky smell (bracken, burnt by gardeners) stung his nose. From somewhere close, a church bell rang. He was on a high hilltop, a few miles to the north-west in the swirl of suburbia flung off by London. The taxi had dropped him on the High Street, a twist of road lined with whitewashed shops, three-storey town houses, and weary-looking trees leaning out of holes cut in the pavement. There were views to the north, more hills, rolling away, each stamped with a chain link of identical suburban homes: brown brick, chimney, walled yard. Until he saw the gate, and the eccentric building that would be his new home, he thought he might have come to the wrong place. This was supposed to be a school for England's elite. That's what his father had told him. *You don't know how lucky you are*, he had said – repeatedly. But Andrew had attended schools for the elite. And in his experience, they were sprawling green *campuses*, with golf courses and big gymnasiums and gleaming dining centres ... not buildings distributed along a *street*. Yet here he was. Twenty-five High Street, Harrow-on-the-Hill, Middlesex. Same address as on the welcome packet, on the brochure, on the welcome letter from his housemaster. And it looked like a fucking time warp.

First, there was the name. *The Lot.* It bore the funk of English eccentricity. Andrew already felt allergic to it. Back at Frederick Williams Academy, in Connecticut, the houses were named after donors. Andrew had been two years in Davidson, two in Griswold, and his senior year – the most decadent by far, in a large double room, perfumed by bong water and unwashed clothes – in Noel House. But *the Lot* rose before him now, a shambling Victorian mansion, ascending four storeys to an old-fashioned cross-gabled roof. It was constructed of mouldering red brick, with triangular nooks and attic rooms pointing upward, arrow-like, in various spots, while over the door – and elsewhere, wherever a lintel presented a broad hunk of brick – there were carvings on agricultural themes. Hay and scythes. Sunshine and tilling. Moss, soot and old grit competed for residence in the thin lines of mortar. A low wall, of the same red brick, encircled the place. Between the wall and the house lay a driveway of beige gravel, like a pebbly moat. The arms of the wall met in a gate: two square brick posterns, topped by cast-iron lanterns. Andrew felt his heart sink. This place was dank, cramped, old. The year he would stay here suddenly seemed wearingly long.

I don't want to hear a word of complaint out of you. I moved mountains to get you in there.

Andrew's father's voice entered his head, unbidden. As it had a tendency to do. Fierce, southern-accented, accusatory. When Andrew was younger he used to hear it in the shower, arising from the babble of the water pounding the bathtub. He would stop the shower, get out, dripping, and stand in the doorway calling *Yes? Yes, Daddy?* when it had been nothing. Just the guilt; the internal clock telling him it had been several hours since he had heard the hammer and tongs of that voice. And Andrew had heard the voice plenty this past summer.

I sold the last of Grandfather's shares for this. Sold them for pennies, in this market, to get your sorry ass out of trouble. What a waste, his father had ranted. *What a failure for us all. Ah, me*, he would groan. *I never thought I would see this happen. Never.*

That was the speech designed to stamp out any complaints about the school. Harrow School. The brochure had made it look like a miniseries on PBS. Scrubbed British schoolboys in jackets and ties and odd, tidy straw hats, which, his father informed him with some relish, were the tradition of the school. Choirboys. Andrew knew the school was prestigious. He knew he was lucky – sort of. But he couldn't forget that he wasn't here because he wanted to be here; not even because he deserved to be. Far from it. It was to get him out of sight, quickly. Off, across the Atlantic, to some cross between reform school and finishing school. So that his college applications would have a new listing at the top. So he would have a new set of teachers and administrators to write recs. So the last five years at Frederick Williams Academy would be just a footnote. *I went to the prestigious Harrow School . . . and oh, yes, the equally prestigious Frederick Williams Academy. But the less said about that, the better.* Maybe, with college applications bragging international experience, the gap between his ninetieth-percentile SATs and his C grades would stand out less. Maybe phrases like *doesn't apply himself . . . tests well, but lazy* . . . and most recently, the packed euphemism *discipline issues* would seem less prominent.

Despite the urgent circumstances, the welcome packet for Harrow School had impressed his father. There was the school crest: a prancing lion, heraldic symbols, a Latin motto. Bragging rights: seven prime ministers had attended the school, including Winston Churchill. Andrew's father had puffed with pride. The Taylors, in his view, were aristocrats. There had been the family plantations in Louisiana. There had been the great-great-uncle, the Civil War admiral, with a battleship named for him (every few years they got hats from some pal of his dad's in the navy – dark blue with orange stitching: *U.S.S. Taylor*). And grandfather

Taylor had been president of a contact lens manufacturer, Hirsch & Long, had made a small fortune in stock, and had been quite a grandee in Killingworth, Connecticut, living in a lovingly restored farmhouse – a landmark – with stone walls around a generous property. Never mind that Andrew's father had floundered for years at American Express, bridling that he'd risen to be no more than a mere vice president, passed over for promotion to executive rank (due, no doubt, to his temper, and his poorly concealed snobbery); or that Hirsch & Long stock had foundered since the introduction of laser surgery and cheap Chinese imports; or that Andrew, the grandson, was now a certified screw-up. Never mind that there was no fortune or prestigious career to raise them to the upper echelon of Connecticut or New York society. They would be damned if they were middle class. They were American aristocrats, Andrew's father thought. They had the stamp of quality. The Taylors *deserved* Harrow School. In the eyes of his father, this was a homecoming, not an exile.

But all his son could see was rules. Infantilizing, seemingly infinite rules. A tiny, prim pamphlet Andrew received, titled 'New Boys' Guide', helpfully pointed them out.

No drinking.

No smoking.

No eating in the street.

No leaving the Hill without a chit. (Whatever that was.)

Boys must wear their Harrow hat to classes.

Boys must wear school uniform at all times. Except on Sundays, when Sunday dress is mandatory.

No wearing light-coloured raincoats to school meetings. (This one left him speechless.)

No food in the rooms.

Boys must 'cap' the masters when passing on the street – raise one finger to the brim of the Harrow hat.

For ladies or the Headmaster, boys must raise the Harrow hat.

Then there was the copious supply of precious, arcane jargon – cute nicknames, presumably developed over centuries, referring to every aspect of the school. The New Boys' Guide offered a lexicon.

Shell = boy in first form. (Eighth grade, Andrew retranslated.)

Remove = boy in second form.

Eccer = exercise.

Bluer = boys' school jacket, made of blue wool.

Greyers = boys' school trousers, made of grey wool.

Beak = master (Teacher, Andrew retranslated.)

And so it went. Andrew felt the claws of claustrophobia on him, sinking deeper with every repetition of the word *boy*.

An all-boys' school.

He felt awkward in guy groups. Remote and prickly, he was stung by the joshing of sporty types. His subjugation to his father made him hate bullies, and provided fuel for outbursts of violent temper when confronted with casual cruelty in the dormitory halls. And generally wasting time with friends made him anxious. It seemed inefficient. He could waste time so much better on his own.

On the contrary, he liked girls. They sought him out at parties and at school socials – that is, when he deigned to go. He would hang back and make sarcastic remarks or sneak off smoking, or better yet make plans to have a bottle of liquor available and get plastered with some small side group. Most Saturdays, by ten o'clock check-in, he would be untangling himself from some girl's bra and licking the Southern Comfort and punch that had been deposited, second-hand, around the rim of his mouth. The bohemian girls – the dancers, the hippie chicks – thought he was *one of them*, with his black T-shirts and angry rebellious questions in class and citations of obscure or otherwise cool literary figures (*Mr Wheeler, why can't we read any Brautigan? Or Bukowksi?*); and the preppie girls – the ones inclined to slum with the druggie kids – would sometimes venture his way as well. Summers, back at home in Killingworth, it was another story altogether. Girls with big hair and obvious perfume bought the package of Boarding School and Long Luxurious Black Hair. They would drink two or three beers and let him do what he wanted to them.

To get locked away on a hilltop with a few hundred boys made him nervous in a way he couldn't completely comprehend. What happened when the girls, the sunshine and the warmth were on the outside and you were on the inside, chilly, English and isolated? It would be like passing a year in a meat locker.

Andrew squatted and gripped his heavy bags, and heaved one of them over his shoulder. He stood but he did not advance; he could not cross, not yet. The lanterns stared at him balefully; dirty and unlit. He felt that if he crossed that threshold, he would step into the nineteenth century and be lost there. *You'd better get every damn thing right*, his father's voice came to him. *Low profile. No rock bands* (a reference to Andrew's band, the One-Eyed Bandits, a favourite excuse for all-weekend bacchanals; cases of cheap beer and jam sessions until daylight). *No school plays* (Andrew had been busted for smoking outside rehearsals – twice). *No party weekends* (plenty of stories there). *Homework and home. That's your mantra. You make this good or we're through with you.* Andrew sensed the seriousness in his father's voice. The anger in the eyes. The desperation. *We're through with you.* Could his father really mean it? Cut him off? Throw him out of the house? Not pay for college? Andrew did not think of himself as spoiled, but the consequences of his parents being *through with him*, at seventeen, seemed hard. He knew the kids from Killingworth who never left the small town. Who worked in retail, or ended up as contractors – painters, landscapers, the guys who drove around in vans, eyes red from the joints they passed … *We're through with you.* Did he want to test his father's resolve? To find out what *through* meant? He was jet-lagged, sleep-deprived, hungry … no. Not today he didn't.

He breathed deep and took his first step on to Harrow School property. Squelch. Into a puddle.

Fuck. Figures.

He shuffled across the gravel, trying not to drop a bag.

APPARENTLY HE WAS early.

'You're not due till five,' snapped the woman who opened the door. She had frosted hair, over-mascara'd lashes, and icy blue eyes that might have once been pretty. Now she was all bosom and belly. She wiped her hand on a towel. Off to the right, through the vestibule, Andrew could see a door opened to a small apartment; a lunch tray; the glow of a television.

'I'm supposed to live here now,' he said emphatically. 'I don't have anywhere else to go.'

'American,' she observed, glaring at him. 'Everything on your own time.'

'Unfortunately there weren't any flights to Heathrow scheduled to land *when the maid was ready*.'

'Maid?' She drew herself up, angrily. 'I am Matron.'

Was this a name, or a title? She announced it with ontological pride, as if Matron were an element in the periodic table, and she were made of it.

'And *I've* been travelling since last night. May I please come in?'

Matron – the Matron? – took a theatrical step to one side and let him through with a resigned sigh.

THE LOT, IN keeping with its appearance, was something of a mess inside. Old glossy paint; battered bulletin boards; an overall dimness. The fumes of a disinfectant hung about, as if the place had been mopped in a hurry to prepare for the incoming boarders. Stairwells and passages spun outward from the main foyer. Up three flights of stairs – made of heavy slate, worn in the centre by many years' use – Matron led Andrew to his room. It shared a short corridor with three other rooms – all Sixth Formers, Matron told him (*seniors*, he silently translated). Its ceiling was slanted, giving it a cosy feel.

'I suppose you'd like a tour,' grumbled Matron.

The Lot, she said, bustling up to the next storey, was really two houses: this one – the original, with all the character – and a new one, constructed on to the back of the original. She whirled him along passages and hallways. The house held sixty boys, Shells to Sixth Form. Wooden plaques with the names of the house's former residents carved into them (*Gascoigne, M.B.H.*; *Lodge, J.O.M. The Hon*; *Podmore, H.J.T.*) lined the walls of the longer corridors; upstairs there were common rooms with satellite TV and kitchenettes. Downstairs there was a snooker room, music rooms, shower and baths. (*Snooker?* he wondered.) They passed a filthy brick pit with a net covering that Matron referred to as the *yarder* – clearly a place to play, blow off steam in bad weather. A few abandoned balls were trapped in its webbing like inedible flies.

Then they descended a narrow stair into a warren of tight passages and low ceilings.

'This the basement?' Andrew asked. He felt a chill crawl up his arms. 'It's cold. Feels like someone left the fridge door open.'

Matron shot him a look of annoyance. 'You must have caught something on the plane.'

He began to respond – *Hey, I wasn't criticizing* – but stopped. There was something different about the basement. It was as if all the crumbling and decrepit parts of the house had been banished down here. The ceiling showed bare beams with bee-hived plaster and old bent nails, like somebody's attic. The walls bared their brickwork like the layers of an archaeological dig: in one place, herringboned, cathedral-like; in another, ranged in crude verticals, chewed by age, the survivor of a poorer, cruder era. Along the walls, older name-plaques stood stacked against the walls, gathering dust like ancient shields in some neglected treasure room. They were not the warmer, walnut-coloured ones hanging on the walls upstairs; the blackness of their lettering merged into stained and sooty wood, as if the old plates themselves were forgetting the names carved into them. A dull, almost drugged sensation came over Andrew. His mind went into slow motion, taking all this in. Maybe he *had* caught something on the plane. The place seemed to throb. *Here is where they hide the history*.

They walked over to the shower stalls, a long, rectangular box of terracotta tile, lined with shower heads and soap trays. *You can fight your way for a spot through all the naked boys*, Matron was wryly saying, and as she spoke the words, she conjured the pictures, bare white figures twisting to bathe and scrub themselves through a scrim of steam. Andrew shook off the image. It was as if it had materialized, then vanished, of its own accord.

'I don't like it down here,' Matron continued. 'Gives me the creepy-crawlies. There's a ghost in the Lot, you know. Boys tease that it's up in the rooms. I think it's down here.'

'Ghost?' he said.

'If you believe that sort of thing.'

'Not really,' he drawled.

*

THEY COMPLETED THE tour, Matron chattering about the rules of the house. Andrew, at last, could not take any more in. His face screwed up, his eyes tightened. Matron caught his expression.

'You're tired,' she said.

Without another word, she led him to his room and withdrew quickly, knowing from years of experience what was coming next.

Andrew flung himself on the bare mattress, and, to his shame, found himself crying. He plunged his face into the starchy, uncased pillow, not wanting Matron to hear. It all piled on top of him suddenly, on his hazy, jet-lagged brain. The long journey. The crummy loneliness of the place. That vertigo underpinning everything: *How did I end up here. How can I last a year here.* It lasted for two short minutes. Then he fell into a stupor.

SMEARING DROOL FROM his chin, Andrew awoke to a soft knock and the whoosh of his door opening. *You need a minute?* came a voice. His eyes focused and Andrew saw his first Harrovian. Small-framed, and far from being a sickly boy cased in a wool uniform, a young man stood who was forged from sunshine: his clothes were colourful, stylish, expensive, unfamiliar – no fusty Brooks Brothers stuff here, but a purple shirt with a splayed collar and fitted, unpleated trousers and a suede jacket. His hair made tight yellow curls along his forehead; his eyes were deep-set and sympathetic. He was lean, athletic. The tendons around his neck quivered when he moved, his chest smooth and tanned a rich gold. Andrew gazed at him as if he were dreaming. Was this what they were like at Harrow? He felt soft, and pale, and ... American. The specimen grinned at Andrew.

'You're the American,' he stated. 'I'm Theo Ryder, next door.' Andrew caught a different accent here: *Nixt dooh*. 'Matron told me you might need a bit of an introduction to the place.'

'Did she?'

Theo laughed. 'Not exactly warm and fuzzy, is she? You get used to it.'

'Oh, so this isn't your first year at Harrow?'

'I've been here since I was twelve. I was one of these Shells. Crying for my mummy into my pillow every night.'

Andrew flushed and wondered whether his tears had left visible tracks.

'Have you got your kit?' Theo continued.

'My . . .'

'Ties, boater, so forth.'

'No, I've got to get a boater.'

'*Godda gedda boaterr*,' Theo said with a grin, imitating his accent. 'You don't have anything? No greyers, nothing?' Andrew shook his head. 'We have work to do. Come on. Let's get you to Pags & Lemmon.'

THEY STROLLED TO a dusty outfitter's, where a white-haired man with a wall eye (*Hieronymus Pags*, Andrew read on a business card on the counter) measured his chest, neck and head and produced a heap of clothing: greyers, bluers, Harrow hat and Harrow ties. His outfit for a year. *The Harrow tie is black*, Mr Pags explained with a simper, *in mourning for Queen Victoria*.

Andrew stood in the mirror. He looked like a half-tamed animal, packed into the confining clothing, his wild black hair spilling out of the top.

But he could not – or would not – tie the tie. It was the final submission. The dog collar. Theo laughed and climbed behind Andrew, standing on a chair and facing the mirror so he could see the gestures from his own perspective. His hands twisted around Andrew's neck; Andrew squirmed; but Theo affably tugged and yanked until the job was done. He patted Andrew on the shoulder.

'No escape now, mate. You're one of us.'

*

THEO WAS AGAIN his guide on the way to the dining hall – a low, 1970s structure, accessible through an unlabelled arch on the High Street.

This was a good thing, because anarchy awaited inside: a steamy, low-ceilinged room of brown brick, ababble with hundreds of boys' voices. Two food lines stretched back from the kitchens. To amuse themselves, two huge boys had started pushing at the end of the lines, putting their shoulders to their companions and knocking them forward, like flexible dominoes. *Oi*, went up the aggrieved shout. Faces crinkled in annoyance. Monitors appeared – nervous in their roles as rising Sixth Formers, exercising their authority for the first time – and strained to hold the boys back like Security at a rock concert. Andrew eventually received a white plate with two fried eggs and a ladleful of beans. He was pleasantly surprised. It wasn't gruel. He followed Theo across the room – weaving through boys in bluers and past an enormous toast station, heaped with grainy bread and lined with a half-dozen toasters and bowls of red jelly; these boys would live on toast, Andrew was to discover – towards a long, heavy wooden table against the window. This was the Lot's Sixth Form table. The lower forms ate at their own tables, perpendicular to this one.

Theo introduced him.

'Oi, everyone: Andrew, from America. Say hello like human beings.'

'Go fuck yourself, Ryder.'

'Yeah, go fuck yourself.'

'Fuck you too, Yank.'

'Yeah, piss off.'

There was sniggering at this.

'Eat shit, assholes,' snarled Andrew.

The crew looked up, somewhat startled that Andrew had not taken their remarks in fun.

'Charming.'

'That how they say hello in America?'

'Is *that* how you say hello in England?' Andrew snapped back.

'It's English humour, man,' piped up one stocky boy with tight brown curls. 'Americans don't understand English humour.'

'Let's try this again,' said Theo wearily. 'Andrew is a new student. He's here on his gap year.'

'You're spending your gap year . . . *here*?'

'You must be insane to come to this place.'

'What's a gap year?' asked Andrew.

'What's a gap year?' sputtered the stocky boy again. 'Were you born yesterday?'

'Year for travel, before university,' Theo explained, then gestured to the stocky boy. 'May I introduce Roddy Binns.'

'Total freak,' added the freckled boy next to Roddy, as if this were Roddy's subtitle.

'Fucking loser,' added another farther down the table, who threw a bunched-up napkin at Roddy.

'You'll have to excuse them. I seem to be the only one with any manners around here.' Roddy stood and shook Andrew's hand.

Roddy was the house oddball, Theo later confided; the others referred to him as *nouveau*, as in nouveau riche, because his father owned a chain of fast-food restaurants in London; Roddy was addicted to comics and spent most of his time in his room. He was a lightning rod for abuse, Theo explained, shaking his head.

'Oh, sit down, you git,' barked the napkin thrower in disgust.

That, Theo told Andrew, in an aside, was St. John Tooley. Tan, with high cheekbones and a bored, slack manner, his father, Theo whispered, was one of the hundred richest men in England. Tooley, as in Tooley, Inc., the global temp placement firm. As in Sir Howard Tooley.

A boy named Hugh was introduced: he was over six feet tall with long features and a willowy manner. He was greeted with a volley of insinuating cat sounds, a kind of *Mrrrowww.* Hugh's eyes went dark. This, Andrew realized, must be the term of abuse for suspected homosexuals. Real subtle.

And so it went. Andrew had the sensation of having crashed someone else's family vacation – all the squabbles and petty hatreds of prolonged cohabitation were here in evidence. Epithets, embarrassing anecdotes; alliances and animosities. In succession each of them spilled bits and pieces to Andrew. He quickly realized this group had started together as Shells, and were desperate for someone new to tell their stories to.

'So what's the deal with the ghost?' he ventured, during a lull.

Shhhh, he was told.

'New boys,' someone stage-whispered. 'We'll tell one of them tonight.'

'Tell them what?'

'We pick someone,' explained a boy named Rhys, who, it turned out, was head of house; a stocky, genial guy with straw-blond hair from Wales who was studying agriculture. 'And tell him his room is haunted.'

'*Someone died in that very room*,' offered someone in a spooky tone.

'Then later we come in and completely abuse him.'

'Soak him.'

'Scream.'

'Remember the year they dumped Pat out of bed?'

'The poor bastard thinks it's the ghost and loses it,' explained Rhys. 'It's totally wet.'

'Fuck it is, it's funny.'

'It's a Lot tradition.'

'How'd you get hold of that, on your first day?' someone asked him.

'I thought I felt a chill in the basement.'

A questioning glance was passed around the table.

'Matron mentioned it,' he explained to fill the awkward silence.

'So why are you here?' asked a large, muscular boy next to

St. John. This, Theo explained, was Cam: short for Cameron Findlay. Scot. His family held a patent on wind-turbine technology, Theo whispered, and Cam knew more about science than most masters. Andrew found this hard to believe: Cam was a thickset boy of enormous size; arms, legs, body all rounded and heavy as slabs of meat. (*He's an undefeated boxer*, Theo explained. He had a square nose, a thrusting chin, and a face spread wide and flat across a football-shaped skull, with watchful, squinting eyes and short red hair in a Roman cut. He looked like a menacing and steroidal version of Ernie from *Sesame Street*. Cam seemed to speak rarely, except to add to a communal joke, but when he did, the others paused to listen. St. John's every jerky movement seemed designed to amuse Cam.

'Don't ask him that,' protested Theo. 'It's his business.'

'Why not? You never see new boys in Sixth Form. There must be a reason.'

'Yeah, why are you here, Yank?' demanded St. John.

The table went quiet. Andrew hesitated.

'Uh-oh, he's going to tell us to eat shit again.'

General laughter.

'My father thought it would be a good idea to take a year abroad,' said Andrew, carefully.

'*Mrrrowww*, dad-dy,' came the catcalls.

'Your dad? Why?'

'What do you mean, why?' Andrew parried, stalling for time. 'To get my grades up. And reapply to colleges. Universities.'

'Are you taking A-Levels?' persisted Cam.

Andrew paused. 'What are A-Levels?'

Pandemonium ensued. Roddy especially could barely stay in his seat. *You don't know what A-Levels are? Are you mentally retarded? Do you even* have *schools in America?* And so forth. It turned out A-Levels were big exams at the year's end; everything in the whole school year led up to them. Whoops. Exploded by Andrew's outrageous lack of knowledge, the conversation took different turns, and Andrew was out of the hot seat. But he caught Cam eyeing him. No one who'd crossed the ocean to better his grades would not know what A-Levels were, and Cam knew it. So what was Andrew the American hiding?

A BRIEF HOUSE meeting followed, where the boys crowded on to benches in a long common room. Andrew stared at the framed photographs lining the walls: house photos. Rows of boys lined up in the garden in tailcoats. First in colour, then, as the dates stretched back to the 1960s, in black-and-white. For one of the years the picture had bleached out. In place of faces was a white-hot, radioactive glow. Andrew was forced to stop looking when the boys on one end of his bench tried shoving the last guy off the other end.

Then came a scramble, and smirks: the housemaster had arrived, late. *Fawkes*, they whispered. Piers Fawkes swept in in his black beak's robes, a slim, slightly stooped forty-five, his light brown hair boyish and uncombed, and his large eyes bulging slightly, giving him the placid, somewhat clownish expression of someone who'd been caught napping at his own birthday party. *Drunk and useless*, Rhys told him, shaking his head. *Who arrives late to the first house meeting?* Then added a single word – *Poet* – as if that explained everything.

AFTERWARDS, ANDREW STAGGERED to his room. He could not absorb any more. Theo stopped him in the corridor.

'All right, mate?'

'My brain is mush.'

'It'll come. Want a lager?'

'What?'

'Beer.'

'You sneak them in?'

'Sneak? I don't sneak anything. It's my beer allowance.'

Andrew blinked. 'From home?'

'From the bloody housemaster. God, you *are* tired. Come on. Beer?'

Andrew hesitated. His father's voice materialized again. *You make this good or we're through with you.*

'It's been a long day.'

'Don't worry about those wankers.' He nodded towards the rest of the house. 'That's just the way they are.'

'I get it. Rain check on that beer.'

Puzzled look. 'Rain jacket?'

'Never mind. Goodnight.'

SLEEP CAME LIKE a whirlwind, more frenetic than the stone drop of that afternoon's nap. He had travelling dreams: aeroplanes, escalators, passport lines, non-stop images flashing like some endless video game. These combined with a relentless review of all the new language he'd been exposed to, as if his subconscious mind were scribbling it down for an exam: questions that rose in the middle, not the end of the sentence (*have you ever BEEN there?*); new idioms (*lift, brilliant, jumper*) and pronunciations (*hoff* for *half*, *chizz* for *cheers* – what does *cheers* mean anyway?). Then the images sped up, reached nauseating speeds.

The bleached-out faces from the common room photographs.

X-rays. White hair and black faces.

Uniforms. Black clothes. Straw hats.

The face of a single Harrow boy with white hair came into view. Then whipped around and around, a repeating frame in a feverish slide show.

The face came closer with each pass. It pulsed with raw intensity. He knew, in his dream, that the face belonged to someone intensely exciting. Andrew grew aroused. He felt his heart beating, felt himself simultaneously panic and thrill.

He woke with a start. He was sweating. Disoriented in the dark.

School, he breathed. *England. Dorm room*. Then: *sleep*.

He drifted to murkier depths, free at last of word and image. He slumbered until his travel alarm woke him, at seven, with its merciless electric whine.

2

A Wrong Turn

ANDREW HAD LITTLE time the next morning to reflect upon his dream. Only in the in-between moments. Pulling on his socks, standing in line for eggs and kippers (*They really serve kippers here*, he observed in surprise; they were fried, brown and oily; not tempting). His anxiety came at him, obliquely, as anxieties do, and therefore all the more distressing; not with a bold proposition (*One night in a boys' school and you have become gay*) but with an insinuation (*Theo stood very close to you yesterday, shepherded you, tied your tie; Theo is good-looking, tan, stylish ... then you have that dream*). Andrew would not have admitted it, but his previous boarding school, Frederick Williams, had been a coddling place. Its faculty consisted of baby boomers who oozed liberal virtues and tried to force these on to their pupils in the form of self-congratulatory fund-raising for Haiti, or a Diversity Day that included a handful of brave 'out' senior boys and girls identifying themselves as officers of the student group Pride. Tolerance for homosexuality was not only officially demanded; it in fact took root; so while Andrew rebelled against his school (in a Holden Caulfield way, believing its leafy opulence was really somehow oppressive to its students), he had internalized these American cultural sensitivities. Back home, he could have (cautiously) cornered a friend or a teacher and *talked about* his apprehensions, his *experience*. He had wit enough now to look around him and realize that in his current environment – the taut English faces, the centuries-old traditions of dress and name (Churchill songs, Churchill buildings; every house named after some long-dead Ur-beak) – such sensitivities were not shared; or at least, not outwardly. *Look at the way they abuse Hugh.* He sensed, rightly, that in an all-boys' school homosexuality was the greatest sin. The more convenient the transgression, the more potent the taboo. He would keep the vivid dream to himself.

He had no chance to reflect or talk anyhow. He had overslept. He nearly missed breakfast. He arrived two minutes late to class – *lessons* – dishevelled, unwashed and breathless.

THE CLASSROOM WAS small and square. Individual desks were arrayed in a phalanx. (At FW there had been round tables – so egalitarian.) Here a dais stood at the front (so hierarchical). A beak sat waiting there, legs crossed, a kind of statue. This was Andrew's first Harrow class. For this beak, it was his thousandth. Mr Montague. Silver-haired. Skin mottled with age. A dapper but countryish green suit under his black robes. Mouth tucked in an ironic pout. Eyebrows in a permanent arch; they rose slightly at Andrew's late entrance. But Andrew was not the last. One more seat sat empty. Mr Montague exchanged some banter with the boys while they waited. The banter was larded with respectful *Sir*s, seasoned with eager, show-offy anecdotes from the newly risen Sixth Formers. All this was friendly, even affectionate, Andrew noticed. (At FW, the baby boomer faculty who had chosen such a low-paying career as *teaching* were treated with suppressed contempt by the students, children of Wall Streeters, who knew that grades didn't matter, didn't help you make millions; that these teachers, then, must be little better than servants.) At last a strapping, peach-complected boy entered, hair shower-wet and tousled. *Good morning, Utley*, said Mr Montague pointedly. *Morning, sir*, Utley said with a blush. Mr Montague stood. He held up a volume of Chaucer.

'A-Levels are upon you, kiddies. And what better time to learn to read, pronounce and comment upon ... Middle English.' He smiled wolfishly as the anticipated groan went up from the class.

ANDREW REMAINED LOST and late through the morning. He ran to his next activity. The New Boys' Tour. A throng of little boys in hats pushed down the High Street. *That must be it*, he thought, and only when he approached did he realize that he would be joining a company of Shells. Eighth graders. Andrew joined their ranks. They were herded from one Harrow landmark to another. He towered over even the tallest of them, feeling like the big hairy dumb one who had been kept back five times. Cam had been right – there were no new students in the upper forms.

Finally they came to the Vaughan Library, oppressively quiet, more a museum than a place to study, boasting stained-glass windows and Plexiglas cases protecting rare manuscripts. There the librarian – small, round and sixty, with an orange bob and the no-nonsense air of an Englishwoman on camelback – introduced herself with the Bond-villainish name of Dr Kahn, and opened with a five-minute harangue scolding them *not to eat in the Vaughan Library* before launching into her prepared remarks on school history. Andrew zoned out. The little boys fidgeted with boredom. That is, until the girl was introduced.

'Miss Vine, would you stand?' called out Dr Kahn.

There followed a shuffle of interest, and a craning of necks.

As you see, the adoption of the Harrow uniform chosen by Miss Vine for a girl's use is by chance – or simply good taste – the closest thing you will see to the original boys' uniform, continued the librarian. *No tie. An open collar. White shirt – the original would have been linen, of course. You see before you a reasonable facsimile of how a Harrow boy would have appeared before, say, 1850.*

Names and dates and school history are no way to get a twelve-year-old boy's attention. Miss Vine, however, was. Little boys – a hundred and sixty of them, delicate, with pale, sticky fingers and peering, earnest faces – stood up, jumped into the aisles, and, in the back, even climbed on the benches to get a glimpse.

'I didn't know Harrow had any girls,' Andrew whispered to his nearest benchmate, keeping his eyes on the girl.

'Persephone Vine. Transferred here for her A-Level year,' hissed the boy.

Andrew gaped, along with the others.

This girl was worth the extra attention. She was five foot seven, with fair skin, a dusting of freckles across her nose, a wide, heavy mouth, and something exotic in the eyes: an elongated Cleopatra quality, green and carnivorously lazy, blinking patiently as she stood with hands behind her back before the assembly, as if she were a crocodile on display before a flock of pigeons. Her hair curled in corkscrews, auburn, chaotic, piling up and spilling down to her collarbone. Her bones were fine. Long fingers, feminine nails. She chewed her lip, trying to conceal their fleshiness. But it was her chest that had the boys clambering for a view. Her breasts strained, tight and smooth, against the white shirt that Dr Kahn was so proud of. A hundred pairs of X-ray vision laboured to make out a nipple. As Miss Vine endured the sudden commotion, she blushed slightly. At that the librarian realized what she had done, and with an apologetic *That will do, dear*, gestured Miss Vine back to her seat.

Andrew whispered. 'Girls are allowed to transfer?'

The boy shrugged. 'Housemaster's daughter. Special favour. So she can say she took her A-Levels at Harrow.' He stood on tiptoe, then lowered himself with a sulk: 'She sat down.'

Andrew felt his heart rate accelerate, but persuaded himself it was pointless. He did the mental maths. A girl like that would have a boyfriend. And even if she didn't, how many boys at Harrow were there, Sixth Form boys, stumbling over each other to get to her? It was too obvious anyway – the one girl at a boys' school? She would no doubt make every effort to show she was here to study, not to date.

*

WHILE SLUMPED IN chapel some time later, Andrew looked up and saw *the girl*, Persephone Vine, staring at him. He at first dismissed it. He recalled his earlier logic. But she continued peering at him with undisguised curiosity, as if he were a coveted antique she had spotted in a flea market.

And then afterwards she waited for him. He saw her in the sea of bluers, holding the door for the younger boys and waving them through with an amused smile, playing crossing guard. The kids fawned like puppies. She mussed their hair. As Andrew came closer, he saw her eyes pick him out of the chapel gloom.

'You there. Young man.'

You thehhh. Andrew knew enough to recognize the accent as upper-crust; if he hadn't, he could have just noted the imperious tone.

'Hi,' he said.

'I wanted to speak to you. Hang on – say that again,' she commanded.

'All I did was say hello.'

'Oh *God*, you're American!' She shrieked this, as if he had stabbed her.

'What?' he stammered. More Shells jostled past. The chapel was almost empty.

'It will never work.' She regarded him coldly. 'Pity. And you look like him, too.'

'L-look like who – whom?' he corrected himself. (*It's England*, some part of him was saying; *they notice how you use their language.*)

'Lord Byron, that's *whom*,' she said sarcastically.

'Lord . . .'

'I know you're American, but you *have* heard of Lord Byron?'

But he did not have time to answer. She began tugging at the chapel doors to close them. They were heavy, and this required effort, but when he rushed to her side she snapped again: *I've got it.*

'Yeah, I've heard of Lord Byron,' he said.

She started towards the gate. 'What?'

'I said I've heard of Lord Byron,' he half shouted.

'You must be very proud,' she said, drily.

'Well, you asked.' Andrew felt put out. Girls were supposed to be nicer than boys. Girls were especially supposed to be nicer than boys *to him*. By this time, if they were back home, she would have been brimming with curiosity, her voice just beginning to warm . . .

'You look like him,' she conceded.

'Like Lord Byron?'

'Yes. Why do you think I was staring at you? You thought I was scoping you out? God, you Harrow boys are so full of yourselves, aren't you?'

'I'm new,' he stammered. 'Not really a Harrow . . . boy . . . yet.'

'I'm sure you're just like the rest,' she said in a fatigued voice.

'Why are you looking for . . .'

'Someone who looks like Byron? We're casting a play. Well, we *cast* a play. In the spring. About Lord Byron. But our lead failed his exams. Very handsome. Totally stupid. Not even that handsome, if you ask me. How sexy can you be in a bloody straw hat?' Andrew blushed. She continued. 'The Rattigan Society play. An original, this time. Not the usual Shakespeare. A play about Lord Byron . . . you *do* know Lord Byron went to Harrow?' Andrew nodded. 'Written by a Harrow master. Piers Fawkes.'

'Piers Fawkes?'

'You know him?' For the first time her voice rose with interest.

'He's my housemaster.'

'You know his work?'

'You mean . . .'

'He's a poet,' she finished for him. 'He's completely brilliant. I thought maybe you'd read him. But Harrovians are not known for keeping up with contemporary poetry, are you? I'm in it.'

'Oh, you act?'

'Yes, I act. You're a bit thick, aren't you, even for an American?'

Finding his voice at last, Andrew observed: 'There's really not a good way of answering that question.'

A hiccup of laughter escaped her, as if against her will. She stopped walking.

Andrew had been following her. They had plunged down the High Street until it dipped downhill and grew leafier, the shops yielding to hedges. Now they stood at the mouth of a driveway that veered down to a stone house – another dormitory – with yellow brick chimneys and a shaggy half-acre garden.

'If you're in Piers Fawkes's house, you're going the wrong way,' she said, more gently. 'This is Headland.'

'Oh?'

'The Lot is that way.' She jabbed her finger back the way they'd come.

'Oh, OK. Thanks.'

'Have you done any acting?'

'A little. I played the bad guy in a play called *The Foreigner* . . .'

'*Liddle*,' she mocked. '*Bad guy*. You're *so* American. If you were Scottish, maybe. Byron had a bit of a brogue. But *Yank*. The governors would have a fit. They commissioned the play, you know. Of course, they want it to be all grand and heroic but all Byron did was fuck. Boys and girls. I play Augusta, Byron's sister – or half sister – and he fucks me, too. We'll see how much gets past the censors. Sorry, am I shocking you?'

'No,' Andrew answered untruthfully.

He wasn't shocked by her language – as he had a feeling he was intended to be – but by a gorgeous girl saying the words *fuck me* so casually. It was like a form of heresy. *Don't disparage what I would hold so dear*. He saw in her eyes, observed in her edgy manner, a desire to push away, alienate.

'Well, can I try out? I've come this far,' he said, forcing a laugh to show he was making a joke, about coming down the hill ... She didn't laugh.

'What, for the Byron play?'

'Yeah.'

She shrugged. 'I can't stop you.'

'So how would I do that?'

'Ask Piers.'

'Mr Fawkes?'

'Yes, *Misterr Fawkes*,' she mocked in Americanese.

'I'm Andrew. Taylor.' He extended his hand. She ignored it. Instead she appraised him again.

'I'll take you to him,' she declared at last. 'I want credit for bagging and mounting a Byron doppelganger. I'm speaking metaphorically, of course.'

Andrew's pulse raced. 'Of course.'

She finally extended her hand and pumped Andrew's in a mock-businesslike way. Then she turned on her heel and strode down the gravel drive.

'*Kalispera, Andrea*,' she called in a language he did not recognize.

Housemaster's daughter. She must live here, with her parents. Andrew considered this as he waited, staring at Headland House.

As Persephone reached the door, a head heaved into one of the window frames and peered up the drive suspiciously. It scowled at him. Bald crown. Wire-frame glasses worn on the nose tip. Ferocious, flared nostrils. *That must be Mr Vine*. Andrew backed away as instinctively as if he'd heard a dog's warning bark.

NOT ONE OF *his*, was Sir Alan Vine's assessment of Andrew as the housemaster watched the boy from his living room. No meat on the shoulders or back. Long hair. Arts type. An extreme specimen, even. No, not one of his, but hanging about nonetheless. Sir Alan understood why, when he spotted his daughter three-quarters of the way down the drive. *She had been speaking to the long-haired character at the top of the drive*. He grew alarmed and approached the window for a closer look. The boy's appearance – that hair, that slouch – affected a counter-cultural pose. Just the kind he knew his daughter would sniff out. Sir Alan's shoulders tightened in annoyance.

The front door banged shut and her greeting rang in the hall.

'Who *is* that boy up there?' he called out.

He walked into the hall to pursue her but she had clattered upstairs too quickly. A second door slam; her bedroom. Was she ignoring the question? Or had she just not heard it?

He returned to the window to stare at the top of the drive where the shaggy Harrovian had stood. The spot was empty now; just hedges and trees.

He frowned. *He would have to keep an eye out for that one.*

ANDREW TURNED AND trudged uphill. He found himself exhausted and excited by Persephone's many-angled verbal attacks, and he groaned inwardly at all the ways he had acted like a dork. He became so preoccupied with revisiting every word of the conversation that he did not immediately realize he was lost. One of his fellow new boys that morning had told him emphatically, when heading back to the house on the High Street, *not to take the fork that goes down the hill. That leads away from the school. You're sure to get lost*. But now, trudging *up* – ostensibly the right direction – the road looked distinctly wrong. There were no houses or shops. He found himself on a steep slope, with the school buildings he'd toured that morning below him, on his right. To his left was a brick wall. Ahead stood a gazebo-like wooden gateway leading to an old stone church and a graveyard. Carved into the wood on the left side of the gateway arch were the words BLESSED ARE THE DEAD. On the right, as if it were a condition in fine print, was added WHICH DIE IN THE LORD.

Andrew hesitated. Someone had told him that Harrow-on-the-Hill was the highest point between London and the Ural Mountains. Here, at the crest of the hill, he believed it. The sky, which had grown white with low-hanging clouds, felt close enough to touch. No one stirred in the churchyard. After travelling in a pack all morning, he found himself drawn in by the isolation of the place. He followed its twisting stone path. Weather-worn headstones thrust out of the grassy churchyard like fingers. Thick trees, vines and bracken encircled the place. Soon he had passed behind the church and saw a footpath down the far side of the hill. Again he paused. The path, also shadowed by heavy boughs and vines, had the silent, airless quality of a nook for bad behaviour. But he did not smell the urine or see the garbage or the broken crack pipes he expected, and the path seemed to lead down and to the left, where he needed to go; so he pushed forward.

A sound cut the air. A growling, a barking. Andrew froze and searched around him for the origin of that noise.

Then he found it. Twenty paces down the path, a man straddled another man. The one on the bottom lay almost flat. The man on top was the source of the noise. He was wearing a long black frock coat with tails, which hung on him baggily and bunched at the shoulders. With both hands he thrust his weight upon the other man, smothering him. He snarled from the effort. The attacker's face horrified Andrew. The eye sockets were sunken; the eyes protruded, a vivid blue; his flesh was a morbid grey. Long blond hair – almost white, albino-looking – hung over his eyes. Once he was forced to break from his labour to cough – and Andrew recognized the noise that had drawn him. The cough combined the bark of a sick animal with a wet, slapping sound. The skeletal man drew his hand across his mouth. Then he looked up. He locked eyes with Andrew.

Those eyes seemed to stab him across the space separating them. They belonged to a young man. His figure was scrawny, diseased: he reeked of death.

Andrew felt sick to his stomach. He staggered back a step, turned and began to run, escape. But something stopped him after a few paces.

The victim. The figure on the ground.

There was something familiar in the grey trousers and black shoes that he could see protruding from under the attacker.

They looked like Harrow clothes.

Andrew stopped and forced himself to turn back.

He advanced. The scene came back into view. The victim lay there, supine, in silence. No attacker. Nothing moved. Just heavy tree branches enclosing the space. Vines entwining the fence rings. Andrew moved forward, taking in more information with every step.

Black wingtips.

Grey trousers.

White shirt.

Arms crooked, one flung over the body, protectively.

A smear of blood stained the right cheek.

Then another kind of alarm came over Andrew, and he ran towards the reclining figure.

Even before he saw the cracked Harrow hat, he knew it was a student. But he stared at the face in shock. It had lost all dignity: gravel and sandy grit stuck to the eyebrows and mouth. The eyes were turned upward. The mouth hung open, a swimmer gulping for air. With the skin a translucent white – all of that sunshine leached away, already – Andrew could scarcely recognize his friend. He knelt, he grasped the hand – then quickly let it go. It was cold. The nails had gone purply grey. Not knowing what else to do, he placed his hands all over the corpse and searched him – neck, wrist, chest – feeling for pulse, or breath, or any sign, as if Theo Ryder's life were a set of keys he could find by patting him down.

3

The Death of a Boy at School

A STEADY, LAZY rain fell. An ambulance backed up to the spot. Its reverse-gear warning beeped several times; its lights twirled. Two white police BMWs, with sirens and orange stripes, blocked the entrance to Church Hill Road. The area had been taped off, and the forensic team was doing its job. One detective, a man, stood waiting: for the forensic team to finish, for his partner to get the statement from the witness. The witness was a teenager, so his partner, a woman, was doing the interview. He was one of these schoolkids, the ones in the straw hats who looked like they belonged in a different century. This one had long, shaggy black hair, and he was tall, too adult to be wearing those school clothes. He looked like he should be playing in AC/DC, the detective smiled to himself. The kid sat in the back seat of their car, his legs turned out of the open door, facing the female detective, who stood on the pavement; the kid's body language indicated shock. He fingered the hat he held in his hands, never raised his eyes, mumbled, shook his head. The detective saw his partner gesture back to where the body had been found – she was trying to get a reaction, prodding the kid to give up more. The detective watched closely. The boy raised his eyes. They flicked back to the spot where the body was being zippered up, and the face recoiled, as if the boy were afraid the body might heave upright and begin walking like a zombie. Soon the partner gave it up and ambled back.

'Anything?' the detective asked his partner.

'Not really. The constable found him here, shouting for help.' She checked her notes. 'Andrew Taylor. They were mates. Next-door neighbours in the little dormitories here. Houses, whatever they call them. Mr Taylor came walking up here and found the body.'

'Anything about the victim? What was he doing back here? Drugs?'

'There was nothing on the body. This one's American.' She nodded back at Andrew. 'Arrived yesterday. First day at school.'

'Bad luck. Did he notice anything?'

'He said the body already seemed stiff. Saw the blood on the face.'

'Did he move him?'

'Checked for a pulse.' She hesitated, then turned back to look at Andrew.

'What?'

'He's awfully jittery,' she said. 'Like he saw something. Seems afraid.'

'He didn't look too responsive from where I stood.'

'No,' she agreed. 'Want to have a go?'

'Not really.'

'What else have you got to do? Get rained on?'

The detective ambled over to Andrew, still seated in the back of the detectives' car, his legs resting on the pavement. The detective squatted and faced him.

'I'm Detective Sergeant Bryant. I think you just met my partner.'

'Hi,' Andrew murmured.

'Rather a bad shock,' Detective Sergeant Bryant offered, with a grimace of sympathy.

Andrew did not react.

Bryant decided to take a random shot. 'You saw what happened, didn't you?'

Andrew raised his eyes quickly.

Bryant felt a thrill. He took another shot. 'Not what. Who. You saw who killed him. Am I right?'

Now the boy's eyes went wide. Terrified.

'Who was it?' Bryant kept bluffing. 'One of the locals? Someone from school?'

Andrew searched the detective's face. For an instant Andrew thought the policeman knew something; knew, somehow, what he had seen; but no one familiar with the gaunt, white-haired figure could have assumed the detective's flat, factual expression. The detective was groping in the dark. Andrew went back to staring at his hands.

'The other detective told me he died this morning,' said Andrew. 'So how could I have seen it happen? I didn't find him until noon.'

The detective silently cursed his partner.

'Then what?' Bryant demanded, a little too urgently, sensing his moment was passing. 'You're frightened, I can tell. What of? I won't tell anyone,' he added in a flourish of disingenuousness.

But the boy's eyes had focused on something else. The detective turned to follow his gaze. A heavyset woman in a black raincoat had arrived at the crime scene perimeter. She was breathlessly asking for help from the policeman standing guard there, then bickering with him as the answers he gave were evidently unsatisfactory. Eventually the policeman looked over at Andrew and pointed. Matron fastened her eyes on the boy and advanced.

'Last chance,' said Bryant.

'I didn't see anybody,' said Andrew.

'Don't lie to me,' snarled the detective.

Their eyes met in a stand-off.

Moments later, Matron reached them. 'There you are!' she panted. 'No one would give me any information,' she scolded

Detective Sergeant Bryant. 'Can someone tell me what is going on here?'

'Now you're in trouble,' mumbled Andrew.

Bryant rose from his haunches, obliged to answer the woman's many questions and to listen to her moans of sorrow. He was forced to watch in silence – cowed by her busy, blowsy manner – as she wrapped an arm around Andrew and marched him down the hill.

'I'm still interviewing him,' he called after them, helplessly.

'He's underage and the school's responsibility,' Matron snapped over her shoulder.

The road stretched empty and slick for thirty yards. Andrew and Matron descended together, leaving the bustle of police activity behind them. Ahead they faced a throng that had gathered below, in silence, blockaded behind another police car: countless bluers growing dark in the rain. A sea of Harrow hats. The black robes of beaks. The police let Andrew and Matron pass. They were immediately pressed by the boys' damp bodies and awed faces.

What happened?

Is it true someone died?

Is it someone from school?

Did you see anything?

Andrew pushed past them. They crowded him, asking, demanding, some grabbing. The rain intensified, pelted his face, trickled down his cheeks. A beak took his elbow, *Let him through, please, boys. Come now, please,* and ushered him, with Matron, through the crowd. The beak asked him if he was all right, what house was he in, and Andrew lied, *Yes,* and Matron answered *The Lot.* But Andrew he did not see his fellow students or recognize any of their features; he perceived only the ashen face, the sunken eyes; the flaps of the frock coat and the echo of that horror-filled cough.

*

'NEVER BEFORE,' MATRON muttered, half grief, half grumble.

She removed his wet things with all the care of a farmer shucking an ear of corn. She told him to lie quiet. She put a blanket over him. She did all this while maintaining a stream of talk, mainly to herself.

'In fifteen years.' She shook her head. 'And, oh, what will the poor parents say? Imagine getting that phone call. You'd wish you were dead. I hope they have other children. Oh, but they do – Theo had brothers and a sister. Won't break their hearts any less but it's good to have others.' Then, almost angry, already converting the fresh news to gossip and rumour: 'God knows what happened to him. He was too young for a heart attack, or an aneurysm. Healthy boys just don't up and die.'

Andrew sat up in bed. He wanted to explain to her, help her understand. 'Matron, I saw . . .'

She met his gaze and waited for him to finish.

I saw a murder! he wanted to shout. *I saw someone dressed in an outsize, costume-like overcoat suffocating Theo.*

Yes . . . and then what?

This is the question he had been asking himself since he scrambled down the hill, shouting for help, and then returned to wait with the body. He had been alone there some five minutes before he realized that the attacker had disappeared. Not run away, with a fading footfall or a scramble down the path. He had simply vanished. With the high fence on either side, there would have been no means of escape. Andrew would have seen the gaunt figure run off. But Andrew had been so shocked – shocked? or was it something else: a kind of swoon, a surrender to an oppression that lingered on that spot? – that he had not even noticed the attacker's disappearance. In such a gloom, it was almost *natural* that the snarling, uncanny figure had snapped out of existence so suddenly.

And then he disappeared, Matron.

Andrew's mouth hung open.

If you say those words, he assured himself, *she will think you are crazy. She will tell others. Then every kind of attention you don't want, you will get. Think what St. John Tooley and Cam would do with information like that. They'd rip you to shreds. Brand you a psycho, a freak.*

Fortunately for Andrew, Matron took that moment to indulge a rare moment of sympathy, and leapt in to finish his thought.

'I know. Your friend, like that. Poor Theo. Of all . . . people.' Then Matron's eyes screwed down on Andrew – it was the nasty American she was talking to, she seemed to remember – and he understood quite clearly in that moment that Matron would have rather seen *him* a cadaver on the Church Hill path than sunny, charming Theo. 'You're in shock,' she announced, standing. 'Lie back and rest. I can't sit here with you all day. The housemaster and the head of house need to be told. And the head man. And the parents. But that's not my job, thank goodness.'

Then, without a glance back, she rushed off to get Mr Fawkes, leaving Andrew alone.

HE LEANED ON one elbow and peered out of the window. The rain, ignorant of the tragedy now beginning to stir the school, patiently tapped each leaf of the plane tree outside his window as it fell.

Andrew flopped back on to the bed. He was at last warm, dry and alone, but as though suffering a delayed reaction, he felt a shudder rack him from shoulders to toes. He pulled the blanket tighter. He began a kind of wandering debate with himself.

You're sleep-deprived, he reasoned. *You're wigging because you're starting a new school.*

But the body had been real. He had felt it, cold and stiff and heavy. It had rolled a little when he had touched it.

It. Him.

Theo is really dead.

Andrew's mind recalled the few images it had gathered of

Theo over twenty-four hours. He felt sick to his stomach.

He thought of the gaunt figure. If it killed Theo, could it kill others? Andrew had locked eyes with it. Something had passed between them, a kind of recognition. *Could the figure find him somehow? Would Andrew be the next victim?*

He sat up. He must tell the police, let them know that the pale figure had strangled Theo. Whatever it was, it was dangerous.

No. They will think you're insane. They will call your parents.

And his parents would pull him out of school. Then he really would be fucked.

With trembling hands he sought his mobile phone in his desk drawer. Out of power. There was a charger somewhere. He found it and plugged it in. Pressed D. Saw names appear.

DAD
DANIEL

He let the cursor land on DAD. The 203 area code popped up. His thumb went to the green button. He ached to hear a familiar voice. Even his father's. An American accent. He wanted to tell his father the whole story. Not pieces of it, not the parts he thought his father could handle, but everything, just to hear him out, just to hear somebody nod their heads, say *Yeah, that's pretty weird.*

The thumb rose off the button. He knew his father could not do that.

Even if the three thousand miles had not been separating them (he knew this put his father on edge, made him his most controlling), Andrew could never draw out the kind of reaction he wanted now from his father. He might have once. At the dawn of Andrew's puberty, his father had bought a canoe and had begun taking Andrew out on the Housatonic. He pointed out birds in the marshes and told stories – of his days at Penn, or his generally paranoid theories about surviving the corporate life-struggle, and asked Andrew about the soap operas unfolding among his school friends. Sometimes they even forgot to row and just drifted, talking and listening to each other's voices and watching the ospreys carry off their prey; not forced to face each other; pointed in the same direction. But the arguments waited for them, a year later, back at the house. At first about ordinary things like grades and curfews. Then they grew bitter. His father's frustrations mounted (Andrew's choice of friends, his haircuts, his getting caught smoking cigarettes at fourteen; with a bag of pot in his sock drawer at fifteen). His father's own ingrained rage seeped into all their dealings (the unfairness of his treatment at American Express; his inferiority complex about his lineage – all those Taylors in daguerreotypes, and he, a middle manager in suburbia, still wanting but failing to live like a southern aristocrat, heaping debt upon himself to keep up the vacations in Aspen or Biarritz, then suffering brutally with the burden, the humiliating day a fat man with a lip full of tobacco arrived to repossess the Audi). And after the first nine or ten screaming fights – recriminations, slammed doors, false accusations, top-of-his-lungs frustrated screamed red-faced *fuck-you*s – all that remained between them was a sprawling lake of bile. One vacation Andrew came home and noticed that the canoe was gone from the garage. His mother told him casually that his father had sold it.

I'm pulling you out of there

He could hear his father's voice say it.

Controlling. Angry. Taking away from him. Grabbing. His son made passive, brutalized by the storm of temper if he moved or rebelled.

Pulling you out? said a voice inside him. *Isn't that what you want? You'll be safe from*

The hands pressing on Theo's face.

We're through with you, his father had told him. *You make this right or we're through with you.*

DAD
DANIEL

He lifted his thumb from the phone.

No, he could never tell his father. Because of *the incident* at FW. It had destroyed what little was left of their trust.

This was not Andrew's first time in the acrid presence of death. It had brushed him once before. He had peered into its fog and shuddered. That time it had been a disaster. That time it had ruined everything.

You cannot tell about the white-haired boy.

He climbed back on to the bed. He curled into a ball. He stared at the blue wallpaper striped with brown.

HE IS IN another dormitory room in country Connecticut, where the roads spin and dip and each village boasts its own white-washed Puritan church. Where Frederick Williams Academy keeps you safe with its black iron gates and attenuated brick dormitories and groomed grounds and acres of trees and playing fields. Andrew is sitting on the floor, his legs splayed. There is a small glassine bag beside him with a ridged top. The word FLATLINE is stencilled on it, a kind of perverse brand name. Across from him is Daniel Schwartz. Daniel sags. Andrew struggles with himself, trying to stir, *wait*, he is saying, *wait*, then shaking his friend, because this doesn't look right, but his friend is no longer there, his friend is turning blue, his mind has been kidnapped, carried off on a gypsy adventure on sunlit hills while Andrew is fighting struggles of his own against the drug *fuck how much did I do this must be lots more potent than the last bag we tried* because Daniel seems to be left alone there on the ground while he, Andrew, rises aloft, he is standing in the giant wicker sun-warmed basket of a hot air balloon, and up here, God is talking to him in great silent lightning flashes, showing him he has wasted everything, showing him that his life is an empty lunchbox. Andrew vomits, vomits from the self-disgust and the loss, from the dead serious fear *Daniel looks really fucking BLUE* and he takes his mobile phone from his jeans pocket. Andrew punches the three numbers and then SEND and lies back gazing at Daniel and idly wondering what the paramedics will think when they see him with an overdosed teenager at his feet and vomit on his legs.

WHEN HE HEARD months later, he was comparatively calm. He was in his room, at home, in Killingworth. There was a lawn mower buzzing near by. And it was just a phone call. No one implicated him. He was just . . . informed. He was able to hang up the phone quite calmly, roll over in bed and begin, in private, the long, slow process of feeling his own guts corrode.

'ARE YOU ALL right, man?'

Andrew turned his head, Roddy recoiled. He was standing in the doorway, holding a long black umbrella.

'You gave me the shivers. You look like a dead thing lying there. You coming?'

'Coming where?'

'To dinner! God, you don't look well.' Roddy shook his head. 'Come on. I'll wait for you.'

ANDREW RECOVERED SUFFICIENTLY to pad behind Roddy to the dining hall and he stood in a half stupor in line. As he made his way through the tables, he caught the first wave of sidelong glances, the whispers behind hands. Boys' faces lifted and stared. The younger ones openly curious; the middle forms furtive; the Sixth Formers awkward, as if Andrew were the bereaved. Andrew attached himself, with Roddy, to the least objectionable group, the house squares, Henry and Oliver and Rhys. Conversation stopped when he sat down at the table. Henry defensively admitted, 'We were talking about *Theo*.' When dinner was over

Andrew trailed behind them to the house, passive, listening with detachment as they tried, alternately, to process the death and distract themselves with their ordinary chatter.

FOR THE DAYS following, the rain continued, dull, pounding, remorseless as a headache. The Hill came to resemble not so much a proud crest, the highest point west of the Urals, but a set of shoulders hunched against the downpour and the winds. Black umbrellas appeared in profusion; skinny-legged boys clutched them earnestly while balancing books and trying to keep hats on their heads; laughter vanished from the High Street, replaced by coughing. Temperatures dropped; chills invaded. As if in sympathy with their dead friend, boys became ill, dry-coughed or wet-coughed through the night, sprouted fevers. Older boys grumbled as rugger practices were cancelled. *It's like there's nothing to do but sit and think of Theo*, griped Roddy, voicing the sentiments of many: *forced bloody mourning*. On the day of the memorial service for Theo – presided over by the Reverend Peter in the chapel, and thronged with Lottites – it was the blackest day of all, cloud cover like a steel ceiling and gushing, pouring rain, an absurdly tragic scene; alleviated, momentarily, by the bright rhetoric and charm of the many speakers, but ruined again by the wet sobs of the smaller boys, the vindictive downpour awaiting them outside, their need to puddle-hop, without dignity, to the dining hall after. And in the Lot, even the boy with the plummiest accent, a Fifth Former named Clegg-Bowra (who, it was known, personally owned a share in a Formula One team and took nothing, not lessons, not sport, seriously), began holding court in the snooker room and gossiping like a charwoman. *There's a curse on the school*, he drawled nasally. *It's never rained like this in the history of Harrow. At this rate it will still be raining by Speech Day, and we'll all be here with our parents, sneezing. People are getting ill. Theo Ryder was just the first victim. I think they should close the school, personally,* he continued. *And where's the communication? No one's saying what killed Theo. For all we know it was a murder and some psychopath up in the church graveyard is lying in wait to throttle more Harrovians. They hate us, you know, the Kevins,* he said, using the school lingo – an Irish slur – for local, townie. Due to the chill, the heat was turned on, unseasonally; the pipes clanked and hissed. No one could get the damp out of their shoes. The felt on the snooker tables buckled.

No explanations were forthcoming about Theo's death. Only a terse note, posted on the bulletin board in the Lot and signed by the assistant housemaster, Macrae, requesting that everyone soldier on with their work while the coroner did his, and that anyone who desired to speak to a counsellor should avail themselves of Mr Macrae or Matron or the Reverend Peter. Piers Fawkes was conspicuously missing from the list, and from sight; Matron suggested to some that he was busy with arrangements with the family, who were in South Africa, and with the police and coroner. Macrae seemed to be enjoying the spotlight, and Andrew suspected that Macrae was using Fawkes's absence as an opportunity to ingratiate himself with the boys, especially the older, more influential ones – St. John and Cam and their fawning crew – with teas and bull sessions, visible through the window in Macrae's kitchen, just to the side of the Lot in the assistant housemaster's residence. Once Andrew passed under this window on his way to Mr Montague's lesson, and all the faces turned to him. Cam, St. John and Macrae in a tall-backed chair, with a smug but guilty look, like a duke caught trying out the king's throne. There was a moment of mutual apprehension. Andrew suspected they were talking about him. He moved on, ducking his head against the rain.

Andrew avoided these gatherings; he avoided the common room, the dining hall; anywhere the whispers might arise, *there's the American, the one who found Theo*, or the questions might resume, *did you see what killed him? was there any blood?* He went straight to his room after lessons, even skipping meals, getting by on a handful of the biscuits Matron left for the boys in a wicker basket in the snooker room. He would sit cross-legged on his bed, spilling crumbs on the scratchy wool blanket. He knew that he should tell someone what he had seen, crazy as it was. Maybe information about a vanishing, skeletal, strangling figure could help the detectives. Or the family. Or someone. But he also knew the most likely outcome was that he would be branded mentally ill, or fatally damaged by the shock. So rather than speak out and add to the chaos and fear, he isolated himself. He did not call his parents. He did not check his email. He plunged into his lessons, abandoning TV and hallway chatter. His class on Roman Britain became, for him, an addictive serial; he wrote a five-sided essay on *Camulodunum, Fortress of the War God*. He read Chaucer for Mr Montague and whiled away hours training himself to read the lilting, alliterative-inflected Middle English. From his window he watched the rain beat down on the Hill.

ONE NIGHT AT dinner he found himself sitting across from Cam. The table seemed tensed, poised.

'Hello,' said Cam pointedly.

'Hey,' he replied.

Forks clinked on plates, but all eyes were on Andrew. Flickering between him and Cam. It seemed that the house had something to say to Andrew and had appointed Cam its unofficial spokesman.

'Everything all right?' asked Cam, almost chummy, a little too loud.

'Not really,' said Andrew.

'It's a tragedy,' agreed Cam.

'Yeah, it is. Theo was an awesome guy.'

'People are saying he died of drugs,' said Cam. 'That he got from you.'

Andrew's stomach dropped. He forced himself to swallow.

The table fell quiet. 'Why would anyone say that?' he asked.

'You were caught with drugs at your old school. They wouldn't let you into university in America, so you came here.'

'What?' objected Andrew, weakly.

Cam's eyes narrowed. 'I know Theo would never take drugs.'

'Not in a million years,' piped in St. John.

'So either it's a lie,' continued Cam, 'or you pushed them on him.'

The food in Andrew's mouth turned to cardboard. He glanced around the table. All the faces – Oliver, Henry, Roddy, Rhys, Nick, Leland, names he had struggled to learn – turned to him, watching for his reaction.

'I don't do drugs any more,' he said. 'I was never that into it. Just a couple of times. I don't see how you know this anyway.'

Cam regarded him coolly, confidently. He definitely *knew* something. Andrew recalled that tableau: Cam. Macrae. The others. Macrae would probably know the background of how Andrew got to Harrow. Andrew grew angry.

'If it wasn't drugs,' sneered Cam, 'then what happened up there, with Theo? Why isn't anyone saying?'

'If he died from drugs he got from me, you think I would still be sitting here?' Andrew countered, finding his voice.

Cam, undaunted, shrugged. 'What is it, then? You were there.'

The boys leaned in, watching Andrew.

He opened his mouth. The image of the pale face rushed at him. That baying gurgle. Andrew blanched. He pushed away from the table, infuriated and humiliated by Cam's ignorant, implacable fat face, those black eyes that stayed locked on him – amused. Andrew stood. He walked away from the Sixth Form table, shaking.

Psycho he heard someone mutter.

Nothing like this happened till he came.

Don't mind us we'll clean up after you called Cam, shoving aside Andrew's plate in a gesture of disgust.

*

THE SIXTH FORM table at the Lot was not the only place where the absence of facts, and the ominous rain, led to speculation. It was a murder. A drug overdose. A murder by a drug gang. A mysterious illness.

These rumours led to calls home. Calls home produced parents' calls to the school. These calls fed indignation – boys' and masters' – about the unexplained situation, leading to talk of little else. In Ancient History: *Sir, was it drugs?* In Maths: *Sir, is the school hiding something?* In French: *Sir, were Kevins – sorry, the local townspeople – involved?* The masters bumbled. They hadn't been briefed. The request to *let the family grieve privately* . . . to *honour the dead by keeping up the mission of the school* . . . just wasn't working. Somebody must have told the headmaster it was getting absurd – nothing was getting done.

On the third day, a school meeting was called, in Speech Room.

SPEECH ROOM WERE words spoken with special emphasis at Harrow. They conveyed gravitas and pride. Speech Room, tucked into the hillside, was the heart of the school. The site of the main school plays, school meetings; in the summer it would be host to Speech Day, an annual event where Sixth Formers, about to leave school, addressed students, parents and important guests with prepared speeches, poetry, and soliloquies – a kind of valedictory-address-as-entertainment; a display of their maturity through oratory.

The day of the meeting, clumps of students pushed their way into Speech Room. Andrew entered alone. As he shuffled his way to a seat, he felt that silence descend again. Cold, inquisitive eyes bore into him. He wished he had waited for Roddy.

Speech Room was not a room, in fact, but an amphitheatre, seating five hundred in tightly packed, high-backed chairs. Stairs climbed to the back walls and their stained-glass windows;

slender columns rose to an ornate panelled ceiling. At the front rose a stage, and on it stood a podium. On this day, a day with a darkening sky, at eleven in the morning, the headmaster, Colin Jute, took the podium, draped in his black robes. A fireplug of determination: shorter than average, maybe five-nine, but wide in the chest, square-jawed, freckled, with red curls, and meaty hands gripping his notes. His jaw flexed. Next to him slumped Piers Fawkes, legs crossed, with several long nights written on his face. Next to Fawkes sat a thin man, just forty, with wavy brown hair and tortoiseshell glasses. He was the only person onstage not in beak's robes, and the only one in the room not dressed in dark colours: he wore a seasonal light green sports jacket and casual trousers. He held a thick folder. Not a detective. Too skinny and professional. A doctor? The man pivoted his head, birdlike, not masking his curiosity at the sight before him: several hundred boys, washed and unwashed, beefy, pre-pubescent, peach-skinned, brown, the full diversity of schoolboys despite their identical dress and narrow range of social class, fidgeting in unaccustomed silence. The great semicircular room – which usually bounced with joshing and chatter – sounded only with coughs and whispers and creaking chairs. The headmaster stepped forward to speak. The whispers faded instantly. Andrew sank into his seat. He felt sick. He closed his eyes and waited for the words. *Theo Ryder was strangled on the morning of September 9th . . . If only someone had spotted his assailant, we might be safe today, and his killer brought to justice . . .*

The headmaster confirmed the key facts: that Theodore Ryder, a Sixth Former in the Lot, died on the morning of September 9. Ryder appeared to have been ill, and he appeared to have died of that illness. The pathologist (the headmaster gestured to the man in the sports jacket) had graciously agreed to join the meeting; Dr Sloane . . . (even in mourning, the five hundred boys could not resist a ripple of amusement: *Oh, WELL, Dr Sloane, Mrrrowww*; Dr Sloane peered at the crowd, puzzled and curious why his name would cause a stir, not realizing that to a pack of toffs, having a name shared with London's toney Sloane Square, but not *being of* Sloane Square, was pretentiousness itself) . . . Dr Sloane would speak shortly and allow the boys to hear the details first-hand, to ask questions, and to satisfy themselves with the answers. This would be the first time and, the headmaster sincerely hoped, the last, that he would be forced to report the death of a boy at school.

Theodore Ryder . . . the pathologist was speaking now. He gazed from his glasses – thick ones – as if staring into blinding stage lights. He spoke nasally, clinically. A computer nerd of medicine.

Theodore Ryder died of a pulmonary sarcoidosis, a disease which, when left untreated, attacks the function of the lungs. What was at first puzzling to us was the apparent speed of the onset of the disease, pushing glasses up the nose, *since according to the family Theodore exhibited none of the traditional symptoms associated with the onset of sarcoid, such as fatigue. Even up to the night before* – here the pathologist checked his notes – *Theodore Ryder's next-door neighbour reported him apparently in perfect health.* Andrew reddened, flush with a combination of relief – it wasn't drugs! it wasn't a murder! – and mortification. He would have given anything not to be mentioned today. *Just leave me out of it,* he pleaded.

'Suh?'

A hand shot up. Electric bolts shot up Andrew's back. *What would this boy ask? Would it be about him?* The pathologist looked around, disoriented.

The headmaster rose in a billow of gown. 'The boys are encouraged to ask questions,' he reminded Dr Sloane. 'Thank you, Mr Cave-Calthorpe. Please.'

The boy rose. 'Sir, what was Theo doing on Church Hill?'

Piers Fawkes stood quickly to explain the place-name in the doctor's ear. *The place where he was found. Up on the hill.*

'I am a pathologist and not a psychiatrist,' replied Dr Sloane with a smile, unctuously; 'therefore I cannot explain any *motivation* Theodore Ryder would have had for walking to a certain spot. But from a medical perspective . . . perhaps we *can* find a motivation.

'Time of death I place between seven and nine in the morning. Let us assume therefore Theodore died while walking to breakfast. His lung volume would have been greatly reduced by the presence of granulomas and swollen lymph tissue. They would be hardened, unable to stretch. He would have experienced shortness of breath. Then difficulty breathing. He would have experienced acute distress. As this difficulty became urgent, then life-threatening, panic would have set in. If such an event transpired at the hospital, we would at this point take emergency measures such as inserting an endotracheal tube to force the patient to breathe . . . but of course Theodore was not in hospital. So he did, I would suspect, what is natural – again, conjecture,' another incongruous and wholly inappropriate smile, '– which is to seek high ground, associating an open environment with open air. More oxygen. Which he would have badly needed since he was, in effect, suffocating.'

Colin Jute had grown intensely uncomfortable throughout this long-winded and depressing answer. He had invited the pathologist to provide clinical reassurance, not to frighten the boys and add his own colourful terms. Another hand shot up. Jute leapt to his feet and pointed, hoping the question was not a medical one.

'So there were no drugs involved?' barked a black-haired boy.

'We tested for drugs and found nothing,' responded the pathologist nasally. 'But that might be a question better answered by the police . . .'

The headmaster had had enough of the pathologist. He took back the podium. The police, he thundered, had investigated thoroughly and found absolutely no sign of drugs, or crime of any kind. Theodore Ryder had died of natural causes. He delivered these words in a scolding voice implying *And just let me hear any more nonsense to the contrary*. This was not turning out to be the outpouring of emotion he had planned, and he was willing to force the discourse back into line if necessary.

'More questions,' the headmaster commanded.

There were several. Was the infection contagious? The pathologist redeemed himself here. *Not in the slightest ... sarcoidosis is actually a fairly mysterious disease whose causes and development are poorly understood by science; but one thing we do know is that it is not communicable* ... and so on. The headmaster sniffed. *Not communicable* was better: authoritative, reassuring. Something the boys could pass on to their parents.

Was the body to be buried in the grounds, in a special memorial?

No, the parents had arranged transport back to Johannesburg ...

Would any further school days be cancelled?

Their goal was not to disrupt the boys' lives any more than necessary ...

The headmaster relaxed. Much better. They were on the home stretch. He counted the minutes until he could wrap up. He pointed to boys' raised hands with the aplomb of a talk-show host, almost enjoying himself. Until he pointed at the skinny fellow at the back.

'It sounds like tuberculosis,' the boy shouted.

It wasn't a question; it was a hand grenade. The room froze. The headmaster puffed up like a bullfrog. *It ... you ...* he stammered.

Now it was the pathologist's turn to come to the headmaster's aid. Tuberculosis, he drawled, had an extremely low rate of incidence in England. At Clementine Churchill Hospital, they saw zero cases per year ... virtually unknown ...

'But Theo was from Africa. There are millions of cases in Africa,' belted the boy. 'I was there last summer. There were public warnings about spitting.'

A nervous rumble from the crowd. *Theodore Ryder did not have tuberculosis. You just heard from the pathologist. Thank you, Mr Ross-Collins, that is the end of that line of questioning*, stormed the headmaster. He nearly hip-checked the pathologist back to his seat. Shifted to housekeeping. The school would send the family a wreath and make a contribution to a charity in the boy's name. Classes would resume tomorrow. Mr Moreton would take a group tomorrow to *Hairspray*, playing in the West End; sign up in the Classics Schools. Thank you all. *Dismissed.*

WHEN THEY EMERGED, the morning sky cast its first fat drops of the day like stones, whacking the boys' hat brims as they spilled on to the Speech Room promenade. The throng buzzed about the strange meeting and the provocative final exchange. And before the first boys had walked fifty yards, the drops came fast and hard and heavy, drumming the Hill in all-out artillery fire. The boys scattered, holding their boaters and their notebooks over their heads and darting for their houses. Andrew hung back, taking refuge in a basement-level doorway. But the rain did not relent. It came down in sheets. At last he bolted out into it, alone, isolated in the spray and the torrent, and finally arrived at the Lot sopping wet. The Lot lobby was packed. Boys gathered in clusters, steaming in the warmth, vigorously debating the events of the school meeting. Voices rose and chattered; eyes cast around uncertainly, as if expecting someone to pop through the door with more news. Though they could not articulate it, they all felt it: *No one, not even the top man, had seen the pathologist's explanation coming. Lung volume? Suffocating?* They shivered and wiped the rain from their faces.

Seeing Andrew enter, Cam fell silent, and the others around him took his cue. Andrew stopped, feeling the pierce of Cam's black eyes. Andrew should have felt triumph. *See? I told you it wasn't drugs! I told you it wasn't me!* But it didn't matter, he now realized. In Cam's eyes he was a scumbag. A stooped, shifty drug dealer. Andrew's past had come out, and it now defined him. He did not belong at Harrow, those eyes told him. He was an undesirable. An interloper.

Then Cam's glance shifted, leading the room's with it. Something behind Andrew attracted their attention.

Andrew turned and saw what they saw: Piers Fawkes, in a raincoat, damp and unhappy-looking. He led two oversized adults into the foyer. A bear-like man with a creased, over-tanned face in a black raincoat. A woman with sun-bleached hair, carefully curlered but dampened by the weather. Something in the woman's face was hauntingly familiar. An avian nose and deep-set eyes. Theo's eyes.

The two groups stared at one another for a moment. One by one, the students picked up the clues:

Both adults wore black – black raincoats, black suit, black dress.

The woman looked expensive but wore no jewellery.

Sorrow fogged over their faces. Their eyes were watery. Their frowns deep. Watching them, you had the sense that the funniest joke, the wildest adventure, could not rouse in them a speck of joy, not if you tried for weeks.

And there was something else. It pulsed from the two grown-ups as they stood staring at the boys.

Bitterness. Envy. Resentment at the living. They clearly had not expected to see such a crowd, and the sentiment just slipped out of them. Hot blood coursed through all these boys' veins . . . while their son Theo lay refrigerating in some London funeral home.

The crowd of damp boys hung back. Fawkes motioned for the couple to move towards the stairwell. They were on their way to Theo's room to retrieve his belongings. But the stand-off continued. Mr and Mrs Ryder were transfixed by the vision of all these uniformed copies of their son.

Rhys Davies broke the spell. He strode across the foyer and

extended his hand to Mr Ryder, then to Mrs Ryder.

'Theo was the best of us,' he said.

One by one, and then in small groups, all the boys, the Sixth Formers and the smallest Shell, followed Rhys, crossing to the grieving couple and shaking their hands. They expressed their condolences or just smiled briefly and sympathetically and moved on. Fawkes watched, surprised but gratified. The parents smiled to the extent that they could. They shook hands; they murmured politely and nodded. The father was a great sunburned ape, with feathery blond hair and heavy lips, and to their surprise it was he, not the mother, who began to blubber. He was too overwhelmed and too polite to pause and find a handkerchief, so he kept on shaking hands and nodding and thanking the boys while tears slicked his face.

MATRON OPENED ANDREW'S door some time later, huffing as usual.

'I've been looking for you,' she said. 'This came for you. From Sir Alan Vine's daughter.'

Her vinegary tone left no doubt that she questioned what business Andrew had communicating with Sir Alan Vine's daughter. She held out a small purple envelope.

Andrew Taylor, the envelope announced in girlishly looping blue ink. Matron retreated. He ripped it open.

Andrew,
Pick me up at Headland after supper tomorrow and we'll surprise Piers with his new Byron.

Persephone

PS If possible please learn to act before then.
PPS Sorry about your friend.

He smiled his lopsided smile in spite of himself. Just what he needed, he thought. More drama.

4

A Play About a Caterpillar

THAT FUCKING JUTE.

Piers Fawkes burst through his own door, sweeping with him wind, rain, oak leaves in a whirl, hands shaking with anger and alcoholic craving.

Enduring his crap, that's what it was – *enduring*. It had been Fawkes, after all, who had driven in the ambulance to the morgue, with the gurney holding the body bag jostling his knees on the turns. It was *he* who had accompanied the body to the dungeons of the hospital (and who had then burst from its doors and hiked a half mile to some random suburban hotel – with, mercifully, a pub – to down two pints and suck countless cigarettes in an attempt to wash away that image of the stainless steel tables – like oversized kitchen sinks, he could not help observing; designed to drain fluids). After the post-mortem, *he* had signed the death certificate. All the requirements of a housemaster, a lone man *in loco parentis*, suddenly transformed from the caretaker of sixty boys to the Factotum of Death for one. God, what a nightmare.

And after all this, because of that ridiculous school meeting, the headmaster had the gall to chew him out. Badly. For an hour. Taking it out on him.

Had it really been Fawkes's idea to invite the pathologist? He didn't even remember, frankly. (*Let them hear it for themselves.* Had he said that, or Jute?) But Jute pinned it on him. The boys respect *authority*, Jute had stormed, pacing, they respect *firmness*. (*And how should I respect you*, Fawkes had thought, darkly, *heaping shit on me when you know I need this job, know I can't respond. What kind of leadership does that take?*) They want, Jute had continued (now the expert on what the students wanted), to push their childish games so far, *but they need someone to know where the line is. You* (he had actually pointed) *are distant. Not engaged. You're not respected. You're the wrong man for a crisis, and God knows* – Jute finally coming to it, at last the dagger thrust – *whether a better man could have prevented it in the first place*. Fawkes had clenched his fists at this point and growled *I think this conversation is over* before charging from the room and into the swirling, nasty weather, snarling and snapping to himself like a wounded dog until he found himself at the dimly glowing lanterns of the Lot.

Fawkes tore off his wrinkled black robes and flung them on to a chair. He fumbled around his desk for a cigarette. He would walk out, that's what he would do. See if they could fill his spot at such short notice. He would make sure his resignation received publicity. He wasn't so far gone as a poet that some journalist wouldn't care. WHITESTONE WINNER QUITS. He liked that. He lit the cigarette and dragged deeply. The nicotine revived his brain and brought with it several sobering and probably quite accurate notions: that this daydreaming was childish; and that quitting was exactly what Jute wanted him to do.

Fawkes knew he had not been the school's first choice as housemaster of the Lot. At first he'd only been offered the position of English master. But then the commission for the Byron play followed, lending Fawkes a whiff of prestige. Then the school's top candidate withdrew (the man's wife got breast cancer); an outside candidate was lost to a competing offer; two other assistant housemasters were deemed too young; and summer was waning. Someone suggested Fawkes. He was the right age; he was looking for a nearby flat anyway; he had some charisma. Fawkes never pictured himself as a caretaker; but his living expenses would be covered; he was assured Matron and the assistant housemaster, Arnold Macrae, would do the heavy lifting; he would still have time to write. He found himself flattered, stroked, coaxed – and frankly it had been a while since he'd had that kind of attention. No one, in the whirl of mutual flattery that accompanies any hiring process – especially a last-minute, desperate one – stopped to recognize that Fawkes had never been responsible for anything more than writing a hundred lines of poetry per day. He'd never held a proper job; never even had a salary. He'd divorced early, it was said, so he'd never cared for children; and he was a heavy drinker.

Fawkes had tried to fit himself to the role. But a dull panic seized him when he was faced with the tedious and, he soon realized, incessant demands of the job. Emails – hundreds of them – flooded his school account daily. Parents enquiring about a poor mark; about sniffles in a young one; about the timeline for the refurbishment of the squash court so their son could practise; about a knee injury in football; about bullying, and name-calling, and so on, around the clock. The boys, it turned out, were all amateur arsonists, hackers, pornographers; he was forced to walk the halls at midnight, shutting down computers and breaking up pranks. His 5 a.m. writing schedule went to hell. He started delegating more and more to Macrae. He used his commission as an excuse to write more, housemaster less. Still, it had pained him when he discovered – through a younger colleague, who in confiding his own anxieties, naïvely blurted it all out to Fawkes – that he was unpopular. Hated by Matron. Despised by Macrae. Viewed as a drunk and a wastrel by the other housemasters, who took their duties seriously, their dislike stoked by their (false) supposition that Fawkes was unfirable due to his commission from the school governors (those shadowy, super-rich aristocrats who managed the school's investments and affairs) to write the play. Never mind that Fawkes wanted to commit the whole draft to the fire, and that he had been avoiding sharing the current manuscript with anyone even though it was months late. As far as the great Harrow School was concerned, Fawkes was vain, sloppy, unqualified and detached. A hiring mistake – now exposed by a boy's death.

Bad luck? Or bad housemastering? The facts, Fawkes suspected, would not matter. He would take the fall for it. Maybe not sacked publicly – Jute was too shrewd for that; that would be admitting that the school had been at fault – but vilified, scorned. Blamed.

Fawkes angrily stubbed out his cigarette. He *would* leave. He would take the tube to London. He would call his old friends – the film-makers and painters and editors and writers he'd come to London to be with and to be. He would get loaded – pints, smokes, pubs, clubs – and dine out on stories about the Hill, a Jurassic Park of British aristocracy. Just walk away, put it all on a credit card for a while, deal with the consequences later. Yes. He breathed deeply, happily. It was the right decision. He felt a sense of elation, as if he'd been trapped in a stuffy room and someone had just thrown open the windows. Oxygen at last. He jumped up to fetch his coat. Snatched his keys. Felt his trouser pocket – wallet, a few notes. All systems ready. He was seconds away from freedom.

And that was when the doorbell rang.

TWO PALE FACES. The porch light cut their features; they seemed to peer, half materialized, from another dimension. Fawkes was prepared to slam the door on them. But it was Persephone Vine, under bedraggled heaps of auburn hair, and another Harrovian: Sixth Form, judging from height.

'What do you want?' he grunted.

'That's not much of a welcome,' said Persephone.

'It isn't. Because you aren't.'

'I told you I was dropping in. Are you really going to send us back out into this?'

Fawkes had a soft spot for the girl. Not only because she was beautiful and exotic and delightful to look at – no, that was another liability he was conscious of and, thankfully, able to manage (the notion of sexual frisson between them was ludicrous; Fawkes had a saggy behind and love handles and a tragicomic view of his own former sexual conquests) – but also because she was fun. All these teenagers were desperate for attention. They looked at you with faces like empty plates, wide, open, eager, wanting you, willing you to tell them who they were; Persephone was as bad as the others. But she had a saving grace: she pretended that she and Fawkes were equals. Pals. It was presumptuous, impertinent and – given that it sometimes involved inappropriate drinking and smoking together – also a great relief. They had met the previous spring when she was cast in the Byron play. She would come to Fawkes's apartment to talk about The Play – or as she put it more often (and more annoyingly), *our play* – and he would give her smokes. Soon their project would be long forgotten, and she would ramble about her interpretation of *Antony and Cleopatra* or yet another chapter in her parents' epic dysfunction, and he would catch himself: he had been listening. Actually enjoying himself.

'I'm going out for smokes, P,' he lied. 'Can't we do this later?'

'No, we can't.'

Persephone, clearly and inconveniently at her most insistent, wedged herself and her guest into the hall. Fawkes felt his moment of decisiveness slipping away. She and this stupid boy were blocking his escape. He was about to tell her so.

And then Fawkes saw the face.

He had passed over it at first, distracted by his thoughts. But he doubled back now.

The boy looked at him, strands of hair dripping down over his eyes, not understanding yet that he was being stared at. He had long hair, which only added to the effect, and Fawkes found himself gripping the door jamb, instinctively touching cold, present reality.

Persephone grinned, watching him.

'You see it, then. Ha! Got you, Fawkesy.'

Fawkes didn't respond. He just gaped. The pale crescent moon of the boy's face. The mouth – red, round, a brazenly erotic droop in the lower lip, like a rose petal about to drop. And then the eyes. Grey as a wolf's. These eyes, he noticed – coming back to reality, awakening to the fact that he was beholding an individual, alive and breathing, not a portrait or an apparition – these eyes were sulky, fearful. Something unsettled in them. The usual teenage need, accompanied by a warning.

'Who are you?' Fawkes managed. 'I'm Piers Fawkes.'

'I know. You're my housemaster.'

'You're American.' It was a statement. 'Wait. The American! Oh God. You're the one who found Theo.'

The boy tensed. 'Yeah,' he said warily.

'I've been meaning to stop by. Check on you. I feel terrible. It's been an awful week. Especially for you.'

'Awful,' echoed Persephone impatiently, 'but we're here for an *audition*.'

'Audition?'

'For the play. *Our* play?' prompted Persephone. 'You see the resemblance to Byron, don't you?'

'Extraordinary.'

'And you got my note? I knew not to bother with email.'

Fawkes cast a guilty glance at the magazines, newspapers and unopened letters heaped on the dining table.

'For goodness' sake,' she fumed.

'Listen, chaps. Whatever you're here for, it's been a long day. If you're going to stay, how about a drink?'

ANDREW HELD A cold, fragrant martini in his hand, wondering what the protocol was for drinking gin in the apartment of your housemaster when you were underage and had narrowly escaped lynching for being a teenage drug lord. Was this ... allowed? Apparently it was. Persephone tucked her bare feet under her legs on the sofa and nibbled the lemon twist (which Fawkes had peeled with professional skill as he chatted with them from the kitchen) while Andrew took in the apartment. Nicely proportioned, with a dining room giving on to a patio through French doors, and a small kitchen in black-and-white tile. But so messy it bordered on foul; a squatter's place. Newspaper littered across the sofa cushions. A modern white desk held letters, papers, folders, a laptop, books with faces down and spines broken; a cordless phone (no cradle), two coffee cups, a full ashtray, a bottle of Advil, a dirty plate with a dirty fork and a bunched-up napkin on top. Andrew sized up Fawkes. His appearance confirmed Andrew's suspicions in Speech Room: Piers Fawkes had been sleeping poorly. Brown circles stained the skin around his eyes. His eyes were bloodshot, his clothes wrinkled, his hands shook. There did not seem to be much stowed beneath the surface. Piers Fawkes was a wreck all over.

'So you want to play Lord Byron?' Fawkes asked.

Andrew mumbled, 'Yeah, I guess.'

'Is he always so enthusiastic?' Fawkes asked Persephone.

'He's American,' she answered. 'They're laconic.'

'I thought they were bubbly and naïve.'

'I do want the part,' Andrew put in, spurred to speak for himself. 'Do I really look like him?'

'See for yourself.'

Fawkes snatched up one of the broken-spined hardcovers from the desk and thrust it into Andrew's hands, flipping pages for him until he reached the illustration plates. They contained multiple portraits of a dark-haired young man in Regency dress – linen collars and cloaks. The images seemed varnished and remote.

'Are you convinced?'

'Do I really look like this?'

'Are you complaining about looking like one of the most beautiful men of all time?' Persephone was indignant.

'Close enough,' drawled Fawkes. 'Can you act?'

'I've done a little acting,' Andrew said.

'How little?'

'He played the *bad guy* in a play called *The Foreigner*,' piped up Persephone. 'I looked it up. Owen Musser, the racist sheriff. Am I right?' Andrew nodded, impressed. She continued: 'The role has quite a few lines, actually. The play won two Obies.'

'Not our production,' Andrew added hastily.

'My condolences,' said Fawkes.

'So,' said Persephone, bursting with impatience, 'he looks like Byron. He can act, or at least, he *has* acted. Now tell him about our play.'

'Our play,' repeated Fawkes. 'Our play was commissioned by the governors of Harrow School. They provided me with a rather large sum of money – to a poet anyway – to play the poet's time-honoured role for institutions. Paid flatterer. Immortalizer of invented virtues. Byron was rich, pugnacious and a sex fiend. But he attended *Harrow*. So let's put some Vaseline on the lens, add some soft lighting, and make him into a play-in-verse. Longer lasting than a brochure. And the children can play the parts.'

'You're rather biting this evening,' said Persephone.

'The plot,' Fawkes continued, 'is simplicity itself. Byron, dying of a fever in Greece, finally reveals who of all his many, many sexual partners was the love of his life. Sort of a literary Rosebud. Not half bad, actually. The least of my worries.'

'What are your worries?' asked Andrew.

'Yes, what worries?' asked Persephone, growing anxious at Fawkes's tone; she caught the odour of anger and abandon in everything he said; the sarcasm of a man who moments ago had been ready to run. 'What are you on about, Fawkesy?'

'I have only three concerns,' he answered. 'The beginning, the middle and the end.' He tossed back his drink.

'So who was it?' Andrew asked. 'The love of his life, I mean?'

'I . . .' Fawkes broke off in a bitter laugh. 'I haven't decided yet.'

'You never told me that,' Persephone said, hurt. 'I thought it was Augusta, his flesh and blood, his Sieglinde.'

'How could you not know how it's going to end?' Andrew blurted.

'It's just that nothing makes sense,' Fawkes exclaimed, rising, warming to the subject. 'Does anyone want another drink?' They didn't. He went to the kitchen. They heard an ice tray snap. Andrew watched Persephone. Her brow furrowed: she had not been expecting this. Andrew felt a kind of relief. *Not everyone here is perfect*, he thought.

'Thing is,' Fawkes resumed from the kitchen, 'Byron at twenty was not a bad poet. His poems weren't unpleasant to read. But they were conventional. *O wilt thou weep when I am low.* Buh *bah*, buh *bah*, buh *bah*, buh *bah*. Iambic quadrameter, and he makes it *so* dreary. Love. Ladies. Plenty of puerile keenness. He had *one* poem from his first collection that stood out. But he cut it. He was *conventional*.'

'What was the poem?' Andrew asked.

'"To Mary". It was about a whore. Apparently he fell in love with her. He had a bad habit of doing that. A weakness for saving strumpets. What's the line? *And smile to think how oft were done, What prudes declare a sin to act is.*' He sipped his drink. '*A sin to act is*. A mix of metrical anticlimax and a dirty joke. *That* is the author of *Don Juan*. Laughing at himself for loving. That's mature. Sorry, chaps, but it is. And he cut it.' Fawkes wrinkled his nose. 'If he'd died at twenty, no one would know Lord Byron from a hundred other minor nobodies.'

'So what happened? How did he improve?' prompted Andrew. He was sipping his drink freely now. In a haze of Fawkes's cigarette smoke, mind buzzing with the alcohol, Andrew started to feel at ease for the first time since he had arrived. If he had paused to think about it, he would have realized he was feeling more at home than he had at home. But for now, he was merely aware of an excitement welling in his chest.

'Good question,' said Fawkes, jabbing in Andrew's direction with his cigarette. 'People search for the mystery of Shakespeare – how a middle-class nobody from Stratford could write great plays. Byron's story is much more unlikely. At age twenty, he's writing namby-pamby verses. Then, for some reason . . . he flees England. No one knows precisely why. *I will never live in England if I can avoid it. Why – must remain a secret.* He takes a long sea voyage. Then a few months later – on Halloween night, in Epirus, Greece – he starts a poem. In Spenserian stanza of all things. Which is suddenly . . . a masterpiece. Epic. Rich. Mature. It invents, whole cloth, *the Byronic.* The young man, brooding and fated, bearing a burden of unspeakable sins. He's famous, overnight. A genius,' Fawkes said, dubiously, 'overnight.'

Andrew and Persephone exchanged a glance. 'Is that a bad thing?' asked Andrew.

'It's not bad. But it's impossible!' Fawkes ranted. 'You're either a prodigy with talent, or you earn that talent with long hard work. You don't grow wings in a few months. Poets,' he declared, 'aren't caterpillars.'

Having spent himself, and finished his cigarette, Fawkes rose and fetched a fresh packet, tapping it into his palm. Persephone slumped, looking bereft. The burden of the conversation was now on Andrew. He seized it eagerly. He felt like he hadn't spoken for days. 'Were *you* a prodigy?' he asked.

'I?' said Fawkes, taken aback.

'Yeah.'

'Piers won the Whitestone Prize at age twenty-nine,' offered Persephone. 'He was the *enfant terrible* of English poetry.'

'Notice the past tense.'

'Are you still famous?'

'If you have to ask,' said Fawkes sourly, 'then there's your answer.'

'So what's slowing you down?'

Fawkes cocked an eye at Andrew. 'I can't write about who Byron loved, or what he cared about, when I don't even know who he is. I can't write a play about a caterpillar.' Fawkes ripped off the cigarettes' cellophane wrapper with a vengeance.

'Sorry. I offended you,' said Andrew.

'And what do you know about Byron?' Fawkes demanded.

'Me? Ah, nothing.'

'Ever read any?'

'Nope.'

'I suppose you read nothing but Walt Whitman, in America?' said Persephone.

'Robert Frost in anthologies,' countered Andrew.

Fawkes scrabbled around in the desk for another hardcover. He flipped through it quickly, cigarette jabbing from his lips and threatening to ignite the page, then thrust the volume at Andrew.

'Read that,' Fawkes said. He pointed at a poem. 'Out loud.'

Andrew was taken aback. 'What, now?'

For an answer, Fawkes flopped onto the sofa alongside Persephone, watching Andrew expectantly.

'Of course now. You came here to audition, didn't you?'

'Yeah, but it seems like you're mad.'

'Mad, in the American sense. Mad, as in angry. Yes, I am angry. I have been angry since I was fourteen. It's been my trademark. I write many poems about it. But I am not mad at *you*. I want to hear you read this poem. It may well be the highlight of a truly abominable day. And you're the one, by the by, who needs to be mad. Mad, bad and dangerous to know!' Fawkes and Persephone said the last part together, and laughed. Then they sat and waited.

'Um,' Andrew began.

He attempted to read sitting on the sofa, but Persephone forced him to stand. Then she moved him to the centre of the room, and he stood there, holding the volume like a first grader about to recite a poem at assembly. Andrew felt ridiculous.

The book – *Selected Poetry of Lord Byron* – had a green cover and a second-hand-bin smell. He scanned the lines. This was not romantic stuff, trees and mountains and wispy epiphanies. It was something else. He looked up. The same two faces: Fawkes pulling alternately on his Silk Cut and his martini, Persephone's jaded expression gone, a kind of openness in its place.

So he began.

'I had a dream,' he pronounced.

The two audience members sniggered. Andrew reddened.

'Just read normally,' Fawkes said. 'In your normal voice.'

Andrew swallowed. 'I had a dream,' he resumed, 'which was not all a dream . . .'

The poem began, sonorous, authoritative, vivid, like the words of a correspondent from a war zone.

> *. . . The bright sun was extinguished, and the stars*
> *Did wander darkling in eternal space,*
> *Rayless and pathless, and the icy Earth*
> *Swung blind and blackening in the moonless air.*

The poem – the first he had read of its kind: a horror poem, he decided – built, line by line, into an evolving and meaningless tragedy where regular people were stripped of their humanity and were reduced to their animal selves. It was a description, seemingly first-hand, of the world's demise; a devolution from a grassy, fruitful habitat to a stark, stony rock; a shocking and sudden reversal, from life as history and biography to life as astronomy – volcanoes and darkness and grubbing for food and survival. *No Love was left*, he read. And by the time he came to the end – *the waves were dead* – he felt himself swaying, hypnotized by the rhythm – *the winds were withered in the stagnant air* – dizzy from never taking a breath and stricken by the violence of the poem. He raised his eyes, surprised, almost, to see the dimly lit apartment, and not the wasteland of the poem. *Darkness had no need of them*, it concluded, and he pronounced the final words, without quite meaning to, while gazing into Persephone's eyes:

'. . . *She was the Universe.*'

Persephone's face had gone flaccid. Fawkes smoked, an ash stem hanging from his cigarette. Had he bombed? Gone too fast? Been unintelligible? He had slurred once or twice – he was used to beer in cans, not straight liquor – and cursed himself for accepting the drink. Anger and embarrassment choked him.

FAWKES KNEW HE would stew later over being called a has-been by a brat. The anger coming not so much from the boy's impertinence (which in principle Fawkes valued) but from the fact that he himself was so transparent. That a teenager could, literally, walk in off the street, and after hearing a few unguarded comments, dissect him with ease. Mediocre. Stuck. All true. And not writing – or writing well – plagued him worse than failing at his job. *Fuck Jute*, he thought for the eleventh time that day, but differently this time, a dismissive *fuck off*, not an angry one – Jute was nothing compared to writer's block. Producing thin stuff and knowing it's thin stuff and not being able to will yourself to quality. Poetry for Fawkes had always been his private treasure room, the secret hoard at the centre of the castle, where you sought and sought and finally found the bullion, the pure metal of indivisible value: the ringing, absolute, true-pitched capture of some shred of experience, so right, so dead-on – a bit of dialogue, a comparison, an image – that it almost reminded you of death, the way a sentimental snapshot does: freezing time, to make you notice how relentlessly it passes. But the Byron play – flailing. Until now. Until seeing Andrew. It was almost cheating. Somebody loading the DVD of the Byron documentary, allowing Fawkes to watch the real man (boy) being followed around Harrow by a shaky videocam. Fawkes listened – *their feeble breath blew for a little life and made a flame* – and felt himself treading the steps of the castle – cold, uncertain, but holding his breath. He was sure now, with this curious sulky American before him, that he saw that golden glow under a door; he was certain he'd found the treasure room.

A MOMENT PASSED, a long one. Andrew stood there, blushing.

Fawkes returned to the moment. He had not been paying much attention. But it was a good sign, probably, that the boy's reading had sent him down that lane of – what? daydreaming? *What the hell; why not*, he thought.

'Can you limp?' he asked. The two students looked at him, puzzled. 'Byron had a club foot,' he explained. 'If you can limp, you've got the part.'

They laughed. Andrew hammed a stage gimp around the room.

'All right, all right. You're not playing a pirate. You've got the part of George Gordon Byron, the sixth Lord Byron, author of *Childe Harold*, *Don Juan* and many broken marriages. Who surely, at some time, somewhere, fell in love with someone that he never forgot.'

5

The Claw-Footed Tub

'DO YOU KNOW what's wrong with this place?'

'No, Roddy, tell us.'

Andrew had the feeling that this was a practised routine. Gather in a room when the homework had become overbearing. Snack. Waste valuable hours getting Roddy wound up. Then snicker at him.

Rhys, the head of house, reclined on his bed, a biology diagram untended on his lap. Roddy had stopped by to borrow some jam. Henry had poked his head in. Andrew had wandered by. Oliver had heard their voices. Before Rhys could stop them, they had arrayed themselves on his furniture, a party in white shirts and black ties.

'Where do you begin . . . that it exists at all?' said Henry.

Andrew forced a smile. Henry's humour seemed stuck in sixth grade. He had watery, uncertain eyes and the twitchy manner of a mouse in a snake house.

'Nobody laughs,' Roddy declared. 'When I was younger, we used to laugh, really laugh. My friends and I, we used to *piss* ourselves laughing.'

He guffawed just with the memory of it. Rhys, Oliver and Henry passed around their accustomed glances. Rhys grinned. *Here he goes.*

'Over the stupidest things,' Roddy continued. 'Over nothing!

My mates and I used to make up songs. Completely wet. We made fun of the staff. You think our Matron is fat. *This* Matron was.' He made a balloon face. His audience chuckled. 'I mean, a fucking planet, man. And the women who cleaned were foreign and they *reeked*. How can you *clean* and smell like that? I mean, they smelled worse than the toilets they were cleaning! You find the bathroom dirty and you leave it stinking? I don't know what they were, those cleaning women. Romanian? Filthy gypsies. The immigration in this country . . .'

'Fo-cus,' called Rhys.

'You were saying how you used to laugh,' Andrew prompted.

'Right. Right,' said Roddy. 'We used to piss ourselves laughing. And then I came here. That was one of the first things I noticed about this place.'

'The scholarly seriousness of it,' offered Oliver.

'The academic gravitas,' Rhys expounded.

'Oh yeah, this place is really serious,' echoed Henry limply.

'*Nobody laughs*,' Roddy blustered. 'Not like that. Not like we did. Just laughing to laugh. Weeping with laughter. I came here and I just stopped.' Roddy paused. He disappeared into memory. The other boys watched him. Suddenly Andrew pictured a shorter, rotund Roddy, forlorn and picked on savagely by older kids, misguidedly looking to this crew for sanctuary – Rhys, Henry, Oliver; a grab bag; a strange lot. 'This place,' Roddy intoned at last, 'took my laughter from me.'

They paused; then dissolved in derision.

'Get out.'

'What a loser.'

'Git.' Someone threw a pencil at him.

'That's it, everybody out. I have work to do,' announced Rhys.

They spilled out of the room and into the hall.

'Andrew, I'd like a word,' Roddy said.

Roddy's room displayed his few but serious passions: a black gym bag for racquets (an obscure sport Andrew had never heard of – something between tennis and squash, he guessed), comic books, and a hiding place for food. As Andrew hovered, Roddy produced a loaf of bread in a plastic bag.

'Pay attention,' he commanded. He put his lips to the bag – *vwwwwp* – and sucked the air out, then set the bag spinning and choked the neck closed with a twist. He looked at Andrew in triumph. 'My technique. Keeps the bread fresh for five days.'

'That's . . . that's what you wanted to talk about?'

'I heard you're in the play with Fawkes.'

There was something accusatory in his tone. 'Yeah.'

'Don't line yourself up with Fawkes, man. You've already got a reputation.'

'As what?'

'As a drug dealer, for one. Now people are saying you've cracked. After finding Theo. I take your side, though. I say, "Andrew is odd. No doubt about that. I mean, he is *fuck-ing* weird,"' Roddy guffawed, '"but he's no druggie. And he's no more cracked than I am." Well. Quite a bit more in fact . . .'

'Thanks, Roddy.'

'But if you start up with Fawkes, who is the most despised man on the Hill . . . I don't know if I can help you.'

'Wait, why is he the most despised man on the Hill?'

'Don't tell me you *like* Fawkes?' Roddy choked at the absurdity of it.

'He's smart,' Andrew said defensively. 'He's a cultured guy.'

'He's a pornographer. Have you read his so-called poetry?'

'No,' Andrew admitted.

'Neither have I. I can't stand poetry,' said Roddy, aside, before resuming his harangue. 'Fawkes does not understand the school *at all.* He gave a *skew* to Henkes, in the *lower Sixth.*' He waited for this to sink in. Andrew blinked. 'A skew? To a sixteen-year-old? It isn't done,' he continued. 'Also, I was on the long ducker team last year and we trained for weeks. *Weeks*. Every house-master was there, cheering for their house. Fawkes was nowhere to be seen. Off God knows where, drunk. It was crushing! Not to me, of course, but I thought some of the Removes were going to burst into tears. He just doesn't get it, man. He's off. Way, way off.'

'Hm.'

'I'm trying to save you, Andrew, before it's too late. I'm trying to show you how to be normal.'

Roddy was still holding his spun-and-sucked loaf of bread. Andrew smiled.

'Got it. Thanks.'

'Don't say I didn't warn you.'

ANDREW STARED AT his sloping ceiling. It was like the cosy attic room you wanted when you're a kid. Each night the orange street light filtered through the leaves of the plane tree and pressed a checkered map on the walls. Tonight the rain had momentarily relented and a breath of warm air had swept over the Hill, and the Lot boys were throwing a ball in the yard in an improvised game under the floodlights and lanterns. They roared lustily, cheered for points, and hollered *Oi* at fouls. The corridors below echoed with hallway chatter; TV noise; fag calls (decades after fagging had been nominally eliminated, the practice remained; Cam standing outside the common room booming *Boy boy boy!*, sending some tiny Shell on a mission to fetch him crisps and a beer from his cupboard). Andrew lay on his back. He thought about Persephone Vine.

A high-pitched shriek cut through the other noise. Andrew sat up and listened. There were plenty of people between him and whatever poor Remove was being tormented on a lower floor. But the scream came again. He rose from his bed. The ball game in the yard had been abandoned. The TV noise had stopped. He felt a sudden anxiety, and with it a suspicion that his reality had been jolted in an unpleasant way.

No, he was just being jumpy. He'd been traumatized. He

would ignore the cry. Let someone else deal with it.

The cry came again. Desperate.

Andrew went into the hallway and called out, 'Guys?'

No answer. But then a boy's voice came hurtling up the stair-well.

Oh God stop it!

Andrew took a tentative step down the hall, but stopped himself: wasn't somebody, anybody, near by to help? The shriek came again – no words, just anguish – and Andrew plunged down the stairs, two at a time.

The ground floor lay quiet. Maybe everyone had already scrambled to the scene of this emergency, whatever it was?

He heard voices. They came from the basement. He descended the stone staircase to the bottom floor of the Lot.

The lights down here had been extinguished. He stood uncertainly in the corridor. When his eyes adjusted, he saw a weak glow through the opening that led to the showers. He entered the long shower room. Once inside, a shadow caught his eye. Just a flicker in the corner. Then another. A scampering, skittering noise on the tiles. *Rats.* They flitted in the shadows. A whole family, a dozen of them. Andrew raised his hand to his mouth, suppressing a retch.

'Get his trousers off,' came a commanding voice.

Andrew followed it. It came from the prefect's bath, to his right. The glow came from there, too. And as he came alongside the open entrance, he saw the source of the screaming.

There, around the tub with its claw feet and chipped paint, three older boys surrounded a younger one. Andrew did not recognize any of them. But he knew hazing when he saw it. The younger kid reclined on the metal tub's shallow dais as if he'd been thrown there, clinging to the tub's rim. His white shirt had been torn down the front, and his hair and shirt clung to him, soaked. His face and chest were red, welted, from struggle. The three larger boys, standing, wore bathrobes. They carried towels.

The light was very dim, as if some bulbs were not working.

'Get away!' screamed the younger boy. His voice was high and sharp. The voice Andrew had heard.

Two of the larger boys – not the speaker – grabbed the boy's ankles and tugged. The kid slipped, head hitting hard against the wet tile. A sickening *clonk*.

Andrew woke from the voyeuristic stupor he'd fallen into.

'What are you *doing*?' he yelled.

He charged them. One of boys whirled and moved to meet him.

'Who do you think you are?' the boy growled. Without warning he sank a fist into Andrew's gut and shoved Andrew to the ground. Andrew took the full brunt of the punch. Gasping for air like a fish on a dock, he was forced to watch the rest of the hazing ritual.

The two assailants tore off the boy's wet trousers. One of them pointed off into the corner of the room. A rat, about the size of a small, furry sneaker, had emerged sniffing from the corner.

'Come on! Pss pss pss,' hissed one of the boys, squatting down and holding out his fingers over the boy's crotch, as if offering food. 'Have a tiny little prick for your tea.'

They cackled. The smaller boy writhed.

Meanwhile the third boy dropped his robe. He wore a towel underneath, thin, white and wet, tightly wound around his buttocks. This, too, he peeled off. Now Andrew and the others could see the third boy's penis – heavy, floppy, uncircumcised, and beginning to rise in an erection.

The two companions held the smaller boy to the floor. One of them reached down, grabbed his underpants in a fist, and ripped them off in two violent tugs. The boy screamed again, and thrashed, but the older kid, standing over him now, stroked himself, his erection growing.

'Hold him down,' he commanded. Then, breathing heavily, he advanced towards the bath. 'All right, bitch.'

Andrew struggled to his feet. He couldn't let this happen. He got what traction he could on the smooth floor and put his momentum into a punch. It caught the would-be rapist in the kidney, who cried out and fell. The other two boys jumped at Andrew. One gave Andrew such a shove he went down again on the wet floor. Now he was on his back, with two assailants upon him. The second boy came at him, ready to wrestle. But Andrew had an advantage. He still had shoes on – his heavy wingtips. Andrew kicked the kid in the face and drew blood on his cheek. The boy retreated.

Only the third remained. He looked the toughest – he had spiky hair and a confident way of squatting, hands out, ready for him. They engaged. The boy came in quick. He gripped the back of Andrew's head, taking a fistful of hair. Andrew bellowed. Then he found Andrew's ankle and pulled, and Andrew flipped, falling hard on his back – *again*. He groaned. The boy straddled his chest, reared back his fist, and swung. Andrew moved his head in time so the punch caught his ear. Then the attack ebbed. Andrew quickly scooted himself backward and looked up to see the smaller kid – the victim, nearly buck naked now, the shreds of his shirt dangling from his shoulders – strangling his opponent. He was using the largest boy's abandoned robe-tie as a garrotte. The wrestler gripped at his throat and gurgled.

'Stop,' commanded Andrew. 'I'm OK. Stop it!'

The smaller boy's expression was one of fury. He did not relent.

'For fuck's sake, dude, *stop it*!'

Andrew reached forward and pried the boy's fingers from the robe-tie. The red-headed attacker fell to the floor, hacking and wheezing. The smaller boy kept coming, but Andrew pushed him back.

'Take it easy!'

The boy's face was twisted in frustration, anger, fury. But there was something else. Andrew stopped. All at once, he felt a deep, subterranean fear, like a hum or the tremble of an oncoming train.

'You're OK now,' Andrew assured him. 'It's cool.'

The boy turned to Andrew and they locked eyes. Andrew felt a thrill pass down his spine. The boy's hair had at first appeared dark because it was wet. Now strands of it had been shaken loose by fighting. It was longer and lighter than it had first appeared – almost albino white. The eyes were a vivid blue.

Andrew's mind churned, seeking some connection it could not quite make.

The boy – tattered, soaked – turned to him with an obsequious smile, as warm and inviting as his rage had been frightening.

'You saved me,' he said. His voice trembled in a rich, pre-pubescent counter-tenor.

Andrew backed away. 'Who are you?'

'I will not forget this,' he said, coming closer, his eyes never leaving Andrew's.

Andrew kept taking steps backward. *Don't let him touch you*, he told himself. *Don't take your eyes off him. Don't let him get close.*

The boy, inexplicably, began peeling off his shirt – what was left of it; his trousers were long gone. The boy's chest was smooth, his stomach curved, his pubic hair blond and scarcely visible; he glowed in the light, warm from fear and exertion.

'They wished to rape me,' he said. 'But I will let you.'

Andrew gaped. The meaning of the words struck him. An erotic charge crackled in the air. *The pure submission of it.* The boy advanced, his legs bare, smooth and feminine, his shirt hanging in shreds. The boy pulled the remnants of his shirt apart, offering himself. Andrew took another involuntary step back.

Then something caught Andrew's eye. Down and to his right. A candle, in a dull metal holder. This had been the source of that dim light all along.

Wait – a candle?

The boy moved faster towards him now. Andrew continued his retreat until his foot struck something. A tinkle of metal on tile. A *pssh* sound.

The candlestick.

The room went black.

'HELLO.'

Andrew found himself hoarse. The lights from the basement stairwell cast a highway of fluorescence between the rows of showers. All else remained in shadow.

'Are you there?'

He rose slowly. He crossed the darkened floor and found the light switch. The lights came up. Bluish, fluorescent, flickering.

Chrome shower heads. Soap dishes. The room was empty.

Andrew's mind spun. He had struggled with real people. He was slick with perspiration. His back hurt like hell. The seat of his trousers, his elbows, were all wet. But where were his defeated combatants? Where was the boy in the torn clothes? He walked stiffly back past the showers. He approached the claw-footed tub on its pedestal of tile.

Water filled the tub. It was brownish, slightly cloudy – used bathwater. It rocked back and forth in a lazy, swinging motion, as water would that had been recently disturbed.

Andrew rolled back his sleeve. He reached down and stroked the surface with his fingertips. The bathwater remained steamily, pleasantly warm.

6

Mrs Byron's Short Skirt

ANDREW GROPED HIS way in a dark passage. Was he in the right place? Was it the right hour, even the right night? Andrew scarcely knew any more which door led to which place. What set of rules governed him. Who he was.

He pushed open the door. Colour, people, steamy warmth enveloped him.

'Lord . . . Byron,' announced a heraldic voice.

His eyes adjusted. Speech Room lay before him.

'You're fifteen minutes late,' snapped the same voice. 'For the first rehearsal. My God, what an ego. Go on, take a seat. You're not the last, for what that's worth. No one, not even title roles, are to be late for rehearsal, is that understood? Those are my ground rules. We'll have enough trouble pulling together this production without prima donnas. To start, it would be nice to have a script.'

Andrew stood there. Speech Room was warmer, cosier at night. You noticed the deep rust hue of the paint, the touches of gilt, the pillars rising like slender trees. A dozen students sat scattered across the first rows of chairs, down the front; there was something strange about this scene, but Andrew couldn't put his finger on it. On the stage stood a small man of about forty-five with fashion-forward wire-rimmed glasses and gelled hair. He had square-featured good looks and wore a snarl and a collared sweater of bunched white wool that gave him the air of being a really pissed-off lamb.

Then it struck Andrew what was strange about the students lounging in the seats.

Some of them were girls.

Of course. He had heard about this from Hugh at lunch. *Fawkes sees himself as an iconoclast*, Hugh had told him in the affectedly knowing and bitchy style of theatre folk. *Fawkes recruited girls from the Middlesex School for Girls to play the female parts in the Byron play. People say he does it to annoy the headmaster, because boys are supposed to play the female roles. That's the tradition at Harrow*, Hugh had continued, haughtily. *If it was good enough for Shakespeare, it should be good enough for Piers Fawkes.* There were three, four, Andrew counted . . . with Persephone, five girls; they were dressed to withstand the attention a boys' school would bring – meticulously, but not ostentatiously – with two exceptions. One wore an attention-grabbing short brown dress and black stockings on curvy legs and possessed rich, brushed, chocolate-coloured locks, with stylish bangs. The seat next to her – front row – was open. Up in the back sat Persephone. Andrew had to smile. She wore full Harrow dress – grey skirt, white shirt and black tie Annie Hall-style – because she was the only girl who could. She had wedged herself between the pale Hugh and a strapping red-headed Sixth Former in whom she seemed to have acquired great interest. Her body turned towards the redhead and away from Andrew, while Andrew felt all the other eyes on him, heard all the murmurs: the whispered names of *Byron* and *the American*, and, quieter, with a hiss, *Theo Ryder*. He willed her to turn, but she wouldn't. His smile faded. A vengeful hand guided him towards the seat next to the girl with the black stockings and short skirt.

He sat down and waited for a moment, then leaned over to her.

'Who *is* that guy?' he growled resentfully in her ear, with a nod at the man on the stage.

Strands of perfumed, chocolate hair brushed Andrew's cheek. *Female contact*. His skin sizzled. He wondered if Persephone was watching, or whether she was so preoccupied by the redhead that she would not see him.

'The director? That's James Honey,' answered Short Skirt in a whisper. 'He went to Harrow years ago. He did Royal Shakespeare. Then eight seasons of *Morning, Minister* as the chief of staff.' She paused. 'He teaches here now. Didn't you know?'

He didn't. 'What are we waiting for?'

'Piers Fawkes. He's the real ego,' she said.

'Is he?' Andrew prompted. His evening with Fawkes suggested that the man knew a great deal about poetry and maybe he did have a healthy professional ego. But Andrew had noticed something else, too: a lack of formality; a sincerity about his work. Andrew had liked it. Yet Fawkes seemed to inspire sour reactions in people. Andrew wondered why.

'Well, he *is* a Whitestone winner,' she sniffed.

Maybe that was it, Andrew mused.

But he won for a collection he wrote sixteen years ago, she added. (This was the other part, Andrew decided; Fawkes once was mighty, and now that he was fallen people felt entitled to take their shot.) After casting for the Byron play was announced, all the actors had read it. *She* didn't think much of it. Nothing but smut.

'Really?' said Andrew. He allowed himself a glance back at Persephone. She was still speaking, gesturing to the redhead; but her eyes had wandered to him. A bolt of adrenalin passed down Andrew's spine. She turned away quickly.

'Scenes from his sex life,' Short Skirt was saying. 'Travelling across America. Are American girls really like that?'

'Like what?'

'You know, getting soaped in the bath by twins.'

Andrew's eyes went wide in answer.

'One's called *Thirteen Ways of Buggering a Black Bird.*'

'Wow,' Andrew said, imagining a younger Piers Fawkes leering like a satyr. It wasn't hard to picture.

'He beats the bird joke to death. The girls have birds' names. *Robin, Jewess, large white teeth / footsied; cocked her til she queefed.*' She blushed. 'Revolting. And racist.'

'Yet you seem to have read it closely.'

'Well.' She tossed her head. 'He did write the play.'

'Who are you?' Andrew asked.

She swung her head back around and met his eye. 'I'm your wife.'

Andrew blinked; then he recovered. 'I mean in real life.'

'What's the difference?' She met his eye dramatically, then laughed and tossed her head again. She was flirting. It was working. Andrew crossed his legs. He hoped he wouldn't have to stand up and read any time soon. Now he felt Persephone's presence keenly, beating at the back of his head like a hot sun.

'Rebecca.' She extended a slim, warm hand.

He took it. 'Andrew.'

The door from Speech Room passage banged open. Piers Fawkes propped the door halfway, pushing it with his backside, then paused; he was carrying an armload of photocopied and stapled scripts, and he was reading through the top pages, proofing them as he walked. Honey cleared his throat. Fawkes looked up, did a stagey double take, earned a laugh from the cast. Then he charged into the centre of the group at the level of the chairs, black robes flying behind him, leaving James Honey alone onstage. Honey waited for anybody to notice that he remained there, then, grumbling, he descended to Fawkes's side. The cast clambered to Fawkes, hands extended for their copies, and sat back to bury their noses in the pages.

'Save one for me, Piers,' boomed Honey. 'I'm only the director.'

Rebecca fought her way to the stage and brought back two scripts: one for her, one for Andrew. Andrew watched Persephone pass without giving him a glance.

Rebecca observed this. 'Do you know Persephone Vine?' she asked privately.

'Uh, yeah.'

'Hm,' Rebecca opined primly. 'She *does* know a lot of *boys*.'

A part of Andrew withered, as it was no doubt intended to. He watched Persephone chatter with the redhead, who had accompanied her to the front.

'I know her father teaches here,' Rebecca continued. 'But it does seem ironic. *Her*, of all people, attending an *all boys' school*.' These words were pronounced more loudly than was necessary. Persephone stood eight feet away; her antennae went up. Rebecca addressed the rest of her speech directly into Andrew's ear. Her whisper tickled his nerves and he tried not to squirm and cringe with pleasure. 'She's slept with half of London,' she hissed. 'Her nickname is Thumper. Like the rabbit.' Rebecca withdrew and screwed up her face in disapproval. 'You understand?'

Andrew merely panted from the sensory assault. But he had no time to enquire further. Fawkes stood waiting for the students to settle.

'Tonight,' announced Fawkes, 'is my night. After tonight there will be movement ... emotion ... brutality ... and violence – all James's department.' (They laughed. Honey mugged.) 'But tonight, it's words, words, words. We'll read through the first act. You have it in your hand. By the way, we finally have a title. No longer 'the play about Byron.' Now, officially *The Fever of Messolonghi*. Until I change it.' He turned to the first page of the script. 'We join Byron at the end of his life – a mere thirty-six; still young, eh, James? – dying of a fever in Messolonghi, Greece, after joining the cause of Greek independence from the Turk. His one friend, a munitions officer, persuades him to tell his life story.' Fawkes paused for effect. '*To find out who was Byron's one true love*. There are many, *many* to choose from,' said Fawkes with a grin. 'Byron was, shall we say, a highly motivated lover. Let me introduce them. I'm having them come to Byron like the ghosts come to Scrooge. In order of appearance, then.' He gestured to one of the students in front of him, a skinny girl with short red hair and a nervous manner.

'Lady Caroline Lamb,' he announced with a flourish. The girl stood. 'Byron spends two years abroad, in what he would call self-imposed exile. What others would call a holiday.' This got a chuckle. 'He publishes the first two cantos of *Childe Harold*, and – in his own phrase – he wakes up one morning to find himself famous. He's invited to fancy London dinner parties, suddenly a sensation, ostensibly to scout out a wife. But he finds instead the married *Caro* – his nickname for her. She is potty about Byron. It later becomes clear, potty full stop. She chases Byron relentlessly, once gaining entrance to his rooms by disguising herself as a pageboy, another time stealing into his study and scrawling *Remember me!* across the pages of a book. Byron responds with a poem.' Fawkes lifted a green book that Andrew recognized as the one he auditioned from.

> *'Remember thee! Aye, doubt it not.*
> *Thy husband too shall think of thee:*
> *By neither shalt thou be forgot,*
> *Thou false to him, thou fiend to me!'*

The red-headed actress gave a mocking demonic cackle, and earned a laugh.

'Next. Miss Rebecca?' Fawkes gestured to the girl in the short skirt. Rebecca stood up next to Andrew in a cloud of perfume, her black stockings so tantalizingly close, Andrew thought he could feel their static electricity. 'Annabella Milbanke. History has not made up its mind. Victim or victimizer? Either way, Byron makes a classically bad decision to marry her. He thinks she's rich. She's not. He thinks he can push her around. He can't. He later satirizes their marriage, in *Don Juan*.' Fawkes read:

> *Don Jóse and the Donna Inez led*
> *For some time an unhappy sort of life,*
> *Wishing each other, not divorced, but dead.*

'It was a spectacularly unhappy marriage. And with good reason. All the while Lord Byron was having a sexual relationship with his own sister. Or half-sister, Augusta Leigh.' He gestured to the back of the room, where Persephone had retaken her seat next to the redhead. 'Miss Vine, if you please?'

Persephone rose.

'He brings his half-sister along on his honeymoon, and perpetuates one of the most miserable and sadistic *ménages à trois* in literary history; the seeds of Brontë's Heathcliff. Needless to say, I have a lot of fun with it. Byron is rather more sincere: *For thee, my own sweet sister, in thy heart / I know myself secure, as thou in mine*. He fathers a child by this sweet sister ...'

Rebecca, in character, groaned.

Fawkes grinned. 'And now that Byron has created a national scandal, he goes into proper exile, in Switzerland and Italy, and after much *sampling*, finds himself in love with the Countess Guiccioli. Stand up, Amanda?' A heavyset girl a few rows behind Andrew stood and blushed.

'Teresa Guiccioli is the closest Byron came to a nurturing, supportive, adult relationship in his life. No storms, no temper, no madness. Yet like Byron's poetry, his late love turns from brooding to comic, and this one is a drawing-room farce. First – typical – she's married. And Byron somehow gets himself invited to *live* with the Count and Countess Guiccioli at their villa near Ravenna, and, a grown man, scampers around the place like a teenager trying to find places to snog without being caught. You can understand why he would choose political martyrdom, after that. He's run away to Greece to fight for freedom. It's there we find him. Lying on a pallet mortally ill. Where's our munitions man? Hugh!' Hugh stood. 'The prologue, if you please.'

Hugh cleared his throat and started in a clear, ringing voice, setting the stage with confidence and an affected cockney. Silence fell on the group.

Expert in my own craft, demolitions,
My tools in trade dynamite, nitroglycerine,
I never thought to find myself co-habitant with greatness.
Yet here lies the person of Lord Byron, whom even I, unlettered,
    know.
My dear mum, when I wrote and told her, chided me to stay
    away.
(Then asked me many details – is he as handsome as they say?
Is his foot clubbed or cloven? Is he poxy with corruption?
Or does he shine with the surface perfection of the Enemy of God?)
    She does not ask about his poetry.
I do not tell her we share a chamber pot.
Byron stoops to make himself my companion.
Tells me tales of the Levant and the crimes of Lord Elgin.
Drinks late, till poetic madness takes him (and then quotes himself
    at some length),
Warns against donne Italiane *and even here, watches his weight.*
Or did. Now he's sick. And a poor place to be so this is:
Bound in a bunker, surrounded by bogs, mosquitoes, Turks;
I mop his brow for him. We wait upon a surgeon.
We wait for everything. Powder. Bullets. Dry food, clean water.
To while the time – when he's conscious – he's taken to confessing.
Heaving over his living secrets, to make a lighter deathly crossing.
My mother writes me not to listen, or I may myself learn lore
Unsuited to my station: how to love like a baron,
Prowl palace and gutter for conquests; how to cuckold at scale.
Yet even the corrupt and very rich deserve friends, at death's brink.

I will hear for myself, in this tiny theatre —
A rectangle of cold plaster, with dampness creeping in the corners—
The deeds of a hero, of sorts, from his own lips.
Why should he spare me any humiliating truth?
His looks grow waxy. His time is short. He speaks!

And suddenly Fawkes – with his sad, popping eyes – rounded on Andrew and pointed. All faces turned to him. He went hot. He gripped the pages of the script until they buckled, damp in his sweating fingers, and began to read.

THE GROUP TUMBLED out through the narrow Speech Room corridor together, excited. The play was rollicking, more fun than they'd expected. The actors liked their roles, each secretly believing his or hers was best, from the nervous, thin and spotty Lady Caroline Lamb to the tall, very sincere athlete who'd been recruited to play Hobhouse, Byron's best friend. Andrew had fared pretty well. Though James Honey had embarrassed him by informing him, in front of everyone, *twice*, that he would need to work on both elocution *and* accent training – *Lord Byron can't be from Connecticut*, he had said – Hugh had stopped Andrew afterwards and told him he'd been *not bad at all, really*. After the read-through, he felt himself jostling right along with the others. But then he stopped in the Speech Room passage, waiting there in the dark. He heard the wind roaring outside; he saw yellow leaves dancing on the spindly boughs and heard the rain patter against the brick. At last Persephone emerged. She stopped short in the entrance when she saw him. She stood in the light, he in the dark. She pushed past him into the rain.

He followed her. Drops smacked his face. He caught up with her on the stairs that led down to the street.

'Why are you upset?' he called after her.

She turned, looking up at him, her face grim and set. She was clutching her books, shielding them from the rain. But she was growing wet herself, the white Harrow shirt staining grey.

'I thought we could be friends, that's all,' she said. 'But I see you'd rather be with them.'

'Who's . . .'

'I heard you and *Rebecca* in there. I'm not deaf, you know.'

'Rebecca?' Andrew sputtered, blushing.

'You know exactly what I'm talking about.'

She set off again, across the road, buffeted by wind and rain and chill. She cut between two buildings on the High Street to a steep stairwell that led down to the rolling park behind the school.

Andrew followed her. The high walls of the chapel and library on either side protected them from the wind, but raindrops smacked the roofs and walls and managed to spatter them. Andrew shivered.

'I didn't say anything to Rebecca,' he called to her back.

'Stop pretending,' Persephone said, still clutching her books to her chest. 'I went to school with those witches for four years. I know what they think of me. I just thought that by coming here, I'd have a clean slate. Which was totally stupid.' She stopped and turned to him. 'You're new. Be their friend. They'll make you popular. They'll be your personal PR agency. They seem to be mine.' She started moving again and Andrew saw that they had come to the verge of Harrow Park.

'I don't want Rebecca as a friend,' he said while trying to keep up. 'I want *us* to be friends.'

'That seems unlikely.'

'I'm sorry,' he said.

Then he hesitated. He had only a moment or two to keep her attention. He would tell her, then, even though he had promised himself he would tell no one. Persephone surely was different. He took a deep breath and blurted: 'Something weird has been happening since Theo died.'

Her nose wrinkled. 'Theo? Don't use that as an excuse.'

He almost choked the next words out. 'I haven't told anyone about this. I've been scared to.'

'Then why tell me?'

'I want you to see I'm not like the others. And I trust you because . . . you're not, either. You just said so.'

She searched his face. 'All right, then. Come on,' she finally said, testily. 'I'm freezing to death.'

SHE LED HIM around the foundations of the chapel to the Classics Schools and opened a door on the first floor. It was a rectangular classroom, and in the near dark Andrew made out a long oval table in the centre and a corduroy-upholstered armchair in the corner. A line of Latin was scribbled on the blackboard, pockmarked with scansion.

CONUBIIS SUMMOQUE ULULARUNT UERTICE NYMPHAE

'It's never locked,' explained Persephone. 'Mr Toombs's classroom. One of my refuges from Sir Alan.'

Since night was falling on the rain-soaked park outside, the overhead lights would have set the room aglow and made them visible for a mile. So, in tacit agreement, they stood in the patchwork glimmer filtering from the lanterns in the nearby headmaster's garden. Persephone squeezed the rain out of her hair and shuddered. Andrew lunged for her bluer, which she had been carrying, and started to wrap it around her shoulders. She jerked it away from him.

'I've got it.' She moved a few paces away. 'So what's your story?'

'I . . .'

'Better hurry,' she snapped. 'I swore to myself I would never speak to you again.'

'Yeah, OK . . . so something has been happening. Only . . . I was wrong, just now. It hasn't been *since* Theo died. It was *when* he died.' He crossed his arms, shivering himself. 'I saw something.'

'You found him. I know. I am sorry.'

'I saw him.' He held her eyes. He wished he could tell her without being forced to put it in words. 'I saw him being killed,' Andrew said, whispering now, even though there was no one to overhear them. 'He was suffocated to death.'

'*What?*' Her eyes searched him fiercely. But she saw sincerity there. 'By whom?'

'This . . . guy.'

'Did you tell the police?'

'No.'

'Why ever not, Andrew?'

'Because.' He rolled his eyes at himself, laughing a nervous and despairing laugh. 'Because the killer disappeared.'

'Disappeared.'

'He was there one minute, and then he wasn't.'

They both hesitated.

'Are you having me on, Andrew?'

'I wish.'

'So you're seeing things.' Her voice was crisp, distant. 'Have you seen Dr Rogers about this?'

He snorted. 'Why? Because I must be ill?'

'I only . . .'

'Well, what if there *are* things to see?' he went on hotly. 'Am I still crazy? Never mind. I thought you would understand. I was obviously wrong.'

Persephone became conscious of the fact that just moments ago she had been flinging accusations at *him* for being conventional, for believing what others told him. This was supposed to be her turf. She drew a deep, preparatory breath.

'I'm trying to be helpful,' she countered. 'I won't judge. Go on.'

'You mean it?'

'I swear.'

Andrew crossed to the corduroy chair. He needed to sit.

'I saw the guy again,' he said.

'Again? Here at school? Who is he?'

'In the Lot,' he said. He raised his eyes to her. 'He was being picked on. He was a student here. A long time ago, maybe.'

'How many years ago?'

'A long, long time ago.'

Persephone's eyes opened a little wider as she started to understand what he was getting at.

'Hang on . . . you think he's a ghost?'

'Something happened to him,' Andrew went on. 'He was normal. Or looked normal, when I saw him in the Lot. But before, with Theo . . .' Andrew scowled. 'He was emaciated, like a . . . cadaver.'

Andrew's eyes glowed at her: grey, arctic, pleading for help. Insane or not, this boy is completely alone, she realized. He has no one, he is miles away from anyone he knows, *and you were browbeating him*, she scolded herself. She took two steps and knelt beside him. She placed a tentative hand on his shoulder to comfort him. The rainwater, gathered in the fibres of his wool jacket, was cold.

7

The Wolf May Prey the Better

THAT NIGHT ANDREW shivered under his covers. The rain seemed to have leached through his clothes and on to his skin and clung there. From the moment he'd confessed to Persephone, he'd felt a cold grip on him. As if this chill were some kind of punishment, a warning. He dismissed this thought. It was paranoid, unhealthy. But his dreams, when he was able to fall asleep, were feverish. And when he woke up later, to a black and silent dormitory, he was full of a dull dread.

The dormitory was silent. It was not yet dawn.

Andrew listened. He heard nothing. But at once – had it been there the whole time? – he noticed the glow. A peach-coloured line underneath his door. He stared at that glow for a long time. His pulse beat. He could not interpret what he was seeing. The glow was the wrong colour – too warm – to be the corridor light. Could it be a fire? At last he rationalized: the sooner he found out what it was, the sooner he could go back to sleep. Despite the warning sounding in his head, he rose. The cold linoleum stung his feet and he opened his door.

In front of his room had been placed a candle, burning in a holder. Soft, orange, the source of the peachy light. *Like an offering. An invitation.*

He looked both ways in the corridor. No scampering footsteps.

No giggling prankster. He bent down to lift the candle and in doing so stepped through the doorway.

Andrew reeled.

Outside his threshold sprawled a wide dormitory, packed with cots. Beds with rumpled bedclothes, dozens of them, in cockeyed rows. The beds contained bodies. The beds and bodies splayed over a large room, some thirty feet long. Andrew feared he had stumbled into some dreadful death scene, but then the sounds came to him. The intake of breath, the stirring cries, the snores of dozens of people.

He turned quickly. The door to his room was no longer there. A row of windows with ragged curtains had replaced it.

He turned back. At the far end of the room he saw a flicker.

Another candle, disappearing through a doorway at the far end of the room.

The odours hit him now. He flinched. God, what a stench. Urine in abundance, soiled clothes, mildewing mattresses, the stink of ash and smoke. Another odour topped them all off. It was hard to place: savoury, hay-like and acrid all at once. What was it? A now-familiar *cheeping* from the corners gave him his answer. *Rat shit.* He spotted their shadows. Dozens of rats, sniffing, shuffling along the walls in hairy clumps, their claws making tiny *tick tick tick*s on the floorboards.

He had no way back. He did not wish to stand in this chilly, rat-infested place in his underwear. He gripped the candleholder, put his hand around the flame to shield it, and began making his way across the room, in pursuit of the other candle glow. Whoever it was – and he could guess – he was no doubt intended to follow him.

Andrew hurried to the opening at the other end of the dormitory. This led to a staircase constructed of thick walnut banisters and shallow steps that creaked. The other figure must have descended here. He followed. After several plunging flights he came to a door. Inauspicious, with a brass knob battered with dents. He swung the door open. Stone-carved steps, slick with damp, descended before him. He took a step forward. The temperature plummeted.

He took the stairs carefully and found himself in a round chamber that had been carved from solid rock. The walls stood rough and jagged. Water oozed over them from a dozen holes that had been punched in them. The water then collected in a slanting floor that tilted toward the centre. There lay a kind of deep basin or reservoir. Its black mouth gaped, jagged at the rim like chapped, cracked lips, sucking in all the water: a cistern. Andrew stared at it. *You could fall right in*. It was some ten feet deep. A tin pail on a string sat near by to haul up fresh water. He was so transfixed by the sight of the cistern that he did not at once notice the glow of the other candle.

'Terrify babes, my lord, with painted devils,' a voice rang out. 'I am past such needless palsy.'

Andrew saw him, standing on the far right side of the cistern mouth. The small-framed boy of the showers, his white-blond hair (now dry and recognizable) tucked behind his ears. He wore a nightshirt. He spoke in a voice that was unnatural, tremulous and irresistible, a boy's masquerading as a woman's, charged with crystalline ferocity and with a towering regal contempt.

'For your names of whore and murderess, they proceed from you – as if a man should spit against the wind: the filth returns in his face.'

Then a deeper, scratchier, less certain voice emerged.

'Did you forget your bit again?' he whispered. '*Your champion's gone*. That's the cue. Then I say, *The wolf may prey the better*. I love that. I have no idea what it means. But it sounds *wicked*.'

The what? Andrew asked himself. *The wolf may prey the better?* Was even language garbled and confusing in this place? Bewildered, and without thinking, he took the last step down into the cold chamber.

The boy picked his way around the treacherous cistern. He

came to Andrew and placed his hands on Andrew's chest – a grown-up gesture; more play-acting, only this time the white-haired boy was playing at being a mistress, or a wife collapsing on the chest of a beloved husband, long separated. Andrew stood still, helpless in the face of these shifting personas.

'Do you always forget?' the white-haired boy continued. '*The wolf may prey the better.* Her champion's Bracchiano. I suppose the cardinals are meant to be the wolves. But I fancy she's the wolf. A *she*-wolf.'

Cardinals? Wolves? Confused and alarmed, Andrew pulled away.

'You,' he managed. 'You killed Theo.'

Now the eyes flickered fiercely – the mask was torn away. The boy's face contorted and snarled.

'*Who was it?*' the boy screamed. '*Tell me!*'

Andrew recoiled. Fell back; tripped against the staircase. The boy followed and flung himself on Andrew. But not in attack. Something else. Another shape-shift. Back to the cringing mistress.

'You came, you came,' he gushed, and pressed his cheek to Andrew's chest. Andrew, to his own surprise, felt himself momentarily surrender to the gesture; he realized how little he had been touched at school. No one *hugged* him; there was barely any handshaking; nothing. His body, without consulting him, responded to the white-haired boy; devoured the press of another body against it. He felt languorous, tended to, connected.

Now the boy hovered over Andrew and gazed into his face, intoxicated by their closeness. The boy's mouth fell open. His breathing came heavy. Andrew struggled to move. His legs were paralysed, his arms pinned down. His eyes bulged. *Let me up!* he wanted to yell, but found he could not. The boy closed his eyes and let his two thin, open lips descend on to Andrew's. Then he moved his hands out of sight and squirmed, and Andrew felt his zip being tugged and a wriggling at their joined hips. The boy pulled out a handkerchief. Excitement and fear and revulsion jolted through Andrew. With a grimace of both concentration and lithe effort, the boy straddled Andrew and squeezed. Andrew's eyes popped open *whoa what was happening* and the boy's hands wrapped the handkerchief around Andrew's neck and tightened it. Andrew lay pinned against the stone stair while the boy, still with his determined grimace, rapidly rubbed up and down, and Andrew's eyes and face and skull felt tight with the pressure of blood and trapped air in his neck, and then despite himself the pleasure built and Andrew almost felt he was falling. The boy was watching Andrew now, hovering over him with those black eyes blazing, delighted, curious and observing, the hand still gripping the handkerchief, and Andrew thought he would lose control – and he did, with a groan. An astounding gratitude spilled over, with shame less than a second behind. Then the handkerchief tightened and his world went black.

HE AWOKE IN a narrow corridor with a thin red carpet.

It was daytime.

He needed to be somewhere urgently. He heaved, breathing hard. He had been running. He was still running. *He had to catch up with him.*

Around him crashed a booming sound so loud he thought he would lose his mind. It pounded like a surf.

He staggered forward. He reached a stairwell. He took the stairs – spindly, painted, wooden – and nearly broke the railing off in his hand, ascending like a mountaineer.

Through monumental effort, despite the pain, he reached the top stair. He stood in another corridor. Andrew leaned against the wall to catch his breath, but was assaulted again by the horrible noise, which beat his brain like hammers.

And there he was, standing ahead of Andrew.

His quarry.

Grey, bent over in the shadows, unlocking a door with a key from around his neck.

The moment had arrived.

Andrew stepped toward the figure. The noise thrummed. It rose. Grinding, unbearable.

ANDREW AWOKE SCREAMING in his room. He could feel it, a monstrous apprehension of what was about to happen. An understanding that he wanted to push away but could not.

He knew the violence would be ghastly.

Rhys appeared in a pair of pale-green boxer shorts. *What's going on?* He flicked on the lights. Then Roddy charged in, gripping Andrew's shoulders and pressing him to his bed, telling him to *Calm down, for fuck's sake, you'll wake the whole house.* But Andrew couldn't calm down, because it had arrived, the moment something horrible was going to happen. He had not seen it, but he had felt it coming, and the only way to get it out of him – his body knew, even if he didn't – was to scream, scream over and over, as loud as his lungs allowed. Roddy backed off and laughed nervously, putting his fingers in his ears, grinning helplessly at Rhys. *Screaming bloody murder!*

8

The White Devil

FAWKES CROSSED THE gravel drive, biting a nail, worrying about gin and sleep. When would he get any?

His hands trembled. He yawned. He could scarcely remain conscious during his lessons. The boys called him out on it, in that insouciant, arrogant yet unerringly perceptive way: *Sir, are we boring you?* (Any disrespectful slur, he noted, could be made acceptable with the amendment of a *sir.*) He needed to finish the play, and he would never be able to, at this rate. Words didn't come when he couldn't sleep. He would sit there, the windows black in the predawn, staring at the page with nothing in his mind – no music, no driving rhythm – merely the twitchings of a brain laid bare. He had been lying awake for hours, thinking about Theodore Ryder once again.

If he could have done more. If he had stopped in the boy's room. If he had lingered after that first house meeting, instead of scuttling off like a cockroach, and had seen a tinge of pallor in the boy's face and said, *Ryder, I think you should go to the sickbay* . . .

Instead he recalled the family's utter misery. The crushed expressions. The hopelessness. The great blond paterfamilias who was gracious enough to tell him *of course it is not your fault*. That 'of course' made it a wounding blow. If only Tommy Ryder had known what ruin his choice of words had visited upon Fawkes.

And so, time and again, he had reached for the gin: after writing in the morning, to gain equilibrium; at three, to keep the momentum for his four o'clock class; at five-thirty and beyond, to anaesthetize, and to sleep.

But it never worked. He did not sleep.

Walking now, he bit the nail off too close to the root, and it bled.

He needed to finish the play.

The day before he had called his editor, giving her his best impression of health and confidence. He had even grinned as he spoke, hoping she could hear him smile.

Tomasina, it's Piers Fawkes.

Piers Fawkes! He could hear her multitasking; sense her drawing her attention away from email to the phone; mentally opening his file as she did so. Her Italian accent rang as she grasped for some idiomatic English to greet him. *This is a blast from the past!*

(*Cunt.* It hadn't been *that* long.)

He had pitched her the whole Byron project, the play, his own story about teaching at Harrow – how it had brought him extraordinary insight into the material. *And a play,* he said, unsuccessfully trying to wring the desperation out of his voice. *I think it would be a thrilling publishing project.*

(*You're overdoing it,* he warned himself. *Since when do you call poems 'projects' . . . or call anything but cold, dry gin 'thrilling.'*)

A play, you know: something different, he continued. *A bit of a comeback. Like Auden and Isherwood. Only no Isherwood.*

I didn't know Auden ever needed a comeback, she said matter-of-factly.

(*Double-cunt,* he cursed her.)

They had hung up with her avoiding any commitment to publish the play or even to read it. She had done it in the way of publishing people, making her refusal sound nice, even sensible. And it *was* sensible. For her. Tomasina – a long-legged, olive-skinned Oxonian, always in some simple dress that showed leg and cost five hundred pounds, sitting behind her piled-up desk; she had a rich husband, some private banker type who spent his hoard supporting green causes and Tomasina's pay-nothing editorial career – had been a lifeline for him in the past. She'd published his last two collections, treated him like he mattered, after everyone else lost interest. But now ... she had casually listened to him flounder. Fawkes suppressed panic. He would drink. He would think of something. He would finish the play and *show* Tomasina how good it was. Or find another publisher. What did she know about poetry anyway. *Trifler.*

'Hi.'

He jumped. A boy stood on his porch.

'Hello, Andrew,' he said, forcing cheer. 'Waiting for me?'

'Yes, sir,' he muttered.

'Spare me the "sir" today,' Fawkes sighed.

'Sorry, sir. I mean, sorry.'

The American stood, gripping his schoolbooks tightly. His usual surliness had been replaced by a nervous edge.

'Everything all right?' asked Fawkes. 'You look how I feel.'

'I'd rather talk inside, if that's OK.'

St. John Tooley bounded through the front gate from the High Street, leading a crowd of rowdy boys. They fell silent when they spotted Andrew and Fawkes together.

'All right, sir?' hailed St. John with a note of mockery.

'Yes, thanks, St. John,' grumbled Fawkes. He unlocked the door while Andrew and the cluster of Lottites traded glares.

FAWKES HAD FORGOTTEN to tidy up that morning. Smoke still hung in the air, heaviness that stirred when he opened the door. He pulled open the blinds and windows. He dumped a full ashtray in the rubbish and dunked two cocktail glasses in the soapy water still sitting in the sink.

'What's on your mind, Andrew?' Fawkes said, glancing sidelong at his visitor. The boy continued to clutch his schoolbooks; he took a seat but sat up straight, like someone facing an examiner. Nervous. 'Are you coming for advice about the role? About Byron?' Fawkes, not finding a kitchen towel, wiped his hands on his trousers. 'Difficult, playing a legend, isn't it?' he said, re-entering the living room. 'Difficult writing about one. You must force yourself to remember: Byron was an individual human being, who went to this school, lived in this house, just like you. You have as much perspective on him as anyone. More.' Fawkes lit a cigarette and sat down in a chair across from Andrew. He pontificated. 'What motivated him? Perhaps he did not even know himself . . .'

'Mr Fawkes,' Andrew interrupted. 'I have something to talk to you about.'

Fawkes liked *Mr Fawkes* even less than *sir*. 'Why don't you call me Piers,' he suggested frostily.

'I wasn't sure whether I should come see you.' Andrew was talking to his lap.

'You're here now. Out with it.'

'Do you believe in ghosts?' Andrew asked.

'Sorry? Do I . . .?'

'That's a weird question, isn't it?'

'That depends,' said Fawkes. 'Why are you asking?'

'I, er . . .' He stopped. Regrouped. 'If I tell you something, can we keep it between us? Or maybe, like . . . talk about it hypothetically? Sort of, just, a situation? And you can give me advice on it?'

Fawkes lit another cigarette.

'It would be the sensitive and kind-hearted thing to say, to say yes, and let you burble on until you were satisfied that I could be trusted. But I'm really not smart enough to talk in code, Andrew.

You'll leave, and I'll still be working it out next week. So why don't you just tell me in plain English. What's going on?'

ANDREW SLUMPED IN his chair, trying to hide from himself. In the short time he had been at the school, he had observed the many dozen epithets for 'homosexual', the abuse heaped on those boys unlucky enough to already show it (Hugh, or that chubby one in Rendalls, a member of the Guild for his piano scholarship). The abuse was public; there was no check on it; the *mrrrowwws* and mocking were hurled at them right there in Speech Room, in full view of the masters, like stones in a public square. These boys just simply *were gay*, had developed the feminine mannerisms, the sibilant voices, that host of signals of gesture and voice that indicated *I am speaking a different language to you.* Andrew, searching himself, did not feel he was one of them. Yet he felt no special pride, or sense of belonging, to the alternative tribe – the square-shouldered rugger stars in their Philathletic gear, or those boys distinguished by their lack of sensitivity, the St. Johns and the Cams, who were, therefore, presumably, the definitions of straight. And, caught in between, he felt a gnawing anxiety.

And then Andrew's mind started skidding around a closed track. *Maybe this fear I feel is the natural fear* anyone *feels when confronted by the truth about themselves. Maybe this is denial.* If he could only charge through, he would emerge the other side . . . the person he was meant to be!

But this, quite simply, did not feel right. Andrew's body had been touched by the fierce and lithe boy, but it was his spirit that was wounded. *I am a person who lets other people do things to him.* He was merely a receiver (the physical details of the white-haired boy's tactics notwithstanding); a vessel; he had no tribe.

And then there was the stark fear of being outright odd. Of being the kid who *saw things*. Mentally ill. Or so traumatized as to be damaged goods.

All of this passed through Andrew's mind as Fawkes stared at him, squinting against the smoke of his own cigarette.

'I've been having these, sort of, nightmares.' Andrew's mouth felt dry.

Fawkes grunted. 'I've been having trouble sleeping myself. Not sure what it is, really. The play, the beginning of term. Same for you?'

'Ah . . .' Andrew's faced writhed. As if half his face were trying to force the words out, and the other half to rein them in.

'Is it Theo?'

Andrew's face opened wide.

'Yes, I thought so.'

'You went with the body, didn't you? To the morgue?' countered Andrew.

'We were talking about you.'

'Yeah, OK,' Andrew sighed. 'After last night,' he said, 'I need to tell someone.'

'What happened last night?'

'I had this dream.'

'Ah. One of these sort-of nightmares. Can you be more specific?'

'I've been seeing things. *Like* in a dream? But some of it seems . . . too real. More than real.'

Fawkes frowned sceptically. 'And last night?' he prompted.

'I saw . . . that's not true,' Andrew corrected himself. 'I *felt* . . . a, a murder. Felt it was going to happen. I woke up, screaming. Rhys and Roddy came. I felt . . . it was . . .' He gestured. *It was right there.*

'Imminent?'

Andrew nodded.

'That's . . . alarming,' Fawkes said, not knowing what to make of this story. 'A murder, in the Lot?'

Andrew explained: he had wandered around a place he felt certain was the Lot – but in the past.

He had seen a white-haired boy in a strange basement room.

He had been transported to a scene where, he was certain, a murder was going to take place. It was as if the white-haired boy was showing him the murder.

'And this white-haired boy is ... what? Some kind of ghost?' Fawkes asked.

Andrew shrugged and nodded.

Fawkes chewed on this, far from satisfied. 'Showing you something from his life, I suppose,' he went on. 'The white-haired boy ... was he the murder*ee* or the murder*er*?'

'Murderer,' Andrew answered quickly. Then he involuntarily shivered.

Fawkes watched him carefully. 'You seem very certain of that.'

'Yes, sir.'

'Why?'

Andrew's eyes pleaded for understanding.

'You've seen him before?' Fawkes guessed.

Andrew nodded.

'You're scaring me a little, Andrew. Saw him when? In dreams, or reality?'

'Reality.'

'This same boy?'

'Yes,' he answered hoarsely.

'And he seemed ... the violent type?'

'I saw him kill Theo,' Andrew said at last.

Fawkes froze, mouth open. 'I'm sorry. You saw ...'

'On the hill. That morning. When I found him,' Andrew explained, in a torrent. 'The white-haired boy was there. I saw him, suffocating Theo. But he was different there. His face was all ... sunken. I saw him and then he was gone. I couldn't tell the police. But now ...'

'Go ahead.'

'I'm afraid something else will happen, if I *don't* tell someone.'

'Something else? Like what?'

'Another murder.'

The ash on Fawkes's cigarette had grown very long. He crushed it in the dirty ashtray on the coffee table. The housemaster suddenly felt very, very thirsty. His mind filled with the taste of the clear liquid in the cabinet in the kitchen. When iced it acquired a marvellous sluggish quality, and when you put it to your lips, the cold seemed to kiss you back . . .

To shake off these images, Fawkes rose, then paced.

'The most obvious explanation is that you're traumatized by Theo's death. Your mind can't handle the anxiety, so your subconscious invents this figure – this boy with white hair. *He* becomes the focal point for your anxiety.'

'But I didn't know Theo was dead yet, when I saw him,' Andrew argued.

'Hm.' Fawkes raised his hands in surrender. 'All right. I'm crap at this sort of thing. We should call your parents.'

Andrew started. 'Don't do that.'

'Why not?'

'They'll pull me out of school.'

'Ah. The proverbial over-protective American mom and dad. You don't think they'd understand an old-fashioned English haunting?'

'They wouldn't try to understand. They'd blame me and take me home.'

'Why?'

'I wasn't exactly a model student at my old school.'

'No? You seem pretty on top of it.'

'I made a few errors of judgement.'

'At seventeen?' said Fawkes. 'Hard to imagine.'

'If I screw up one more time, they're going to throw me out of the house.'

'Parental rhetoric?'

'Not this time.'

'What did you *do*?' asked Fawkes.

'I had some problems with controlled substances,' Andrew admitted.

'Right. So they catch you with a few joints, and they put you in this posh detox clinic masquerading as a school. And they say, "One more mistake and we wash our hands." No proud visit at Speech Day. No graduation trip to France. Nothing but tough love.'

Andrew slumped unhappily. 'Something like that.'

'It seems you *are* my problem.' Fawkes sighed. 'I think I'll have a drink.'

He rose and went back to the kitchen, poured gin on to ice, sipped. He gave it a moment to reach his bloodstream. There was something fundamentally wrong about this, he recognized; drinking gin with students at two in the afternoon while they admitted to having a drug problem; but even as he thought this, the first fumes reached his brain and he lit up like an uncharged device getting its first blast of voltage. *Ahh.* He could make it. He could hang on. *Now then.* He returned to the living room.

'Do you believe me?' Andrew stared at him balefully, awaiting judgement.

Fawkes took another sip and smacked his lips. He pondered for a moment. 'I believe you believe what you're saying.'

'But you're not sure.'

'How could I be?'

'I couldn't invent what I just told you,' Andrew protested.

'Yes, but it's hardly proof.'

'My ghost quotes poetry.'

'What, Edgar Allan Poe?'

'No ... more old-fashioned. Maybe that's proof. He quoted poetry I've never heard before.'

Fawkes lit yet another cigarette. 'All right, you have my interest – setting aside the fact that I'll have to take your word for it you've never heard the poetry before. This is my area of expertise. I should be in position to expose those who would take advantage of the credulous.' He paused. 'Would it be too much to hope that you remember any of this poetry?'

Andrew sat quietly for a moment. '*The wolf . . . the wolf may prey the better.* He liked that line.' He searched his memory. 'And something about a whore. And spit.'

'When was this? Your ghost was quoting poetry during the murder?'

'No, before that. In the basement. In that cistern room.'

'*The wolf may prey the better.* And you'd never heard that before? Could be, you know, auto-suggestion, or something.' Andrew shook his head. Fawkes considered the line. '*The wolf may prey the better.* No, neither have I. Or maybe. Once upon a time.' He leapt to his feet. 'Technology to the rescue.' He went to the laptop at his desk and booted it up with a chime. Fawkes started his browser and began typing. 'The wolf may prey the better,' he murmured. He stared at the screen for a moment. He punched a few more keys.

Then he paused again, reading.

He shot Andrew a significant look and turned the laptop away so Andrew couldn't see the screen.

'I am going to ask you a few questions, Mr Taylor,' said Fawkes. 'And let me warn you. I am a poet and I have a high regard for Truth. I am Apollo's representative on earth. Do you understand?'

'Yes, sir. I mean, yes . . . Piers.'

'Who is John Webster?'

'Ah . . .' Andrew blanked. 'I don't know. Is he at Harrow?'

Fawkes scoffed. 'Let's try again. Did you study Shakespeare in the States?'

'Sure.'

'Which plays?'

'Um, *Julius Caesar . . . Macbeth*.'

'Anything else?'

'I saw *Midsummer Night's Dream* a couple of times.'

'Ever read any of Shakespeare's contemporaries? Thomas Kyd? Christopher Marlowe?'

'I've heard of Marlowe.'

'Try a bit later. Anything in the Jacobean period?'

Andrew frowned.

'John Webster?' Fawkes prompted again.

Andrew shook his head.

Fawkes spun the screen around for Andrew to read. Andrew drew close and peered at the white screen: a page from Google Books. The page showed a scholarly edition of a play. The words in the centre of the screen were highlighted yellow, from Fawkes's search:

Vittoria *The wolf may prey the better.*

There were more lines, attributed to other characters with Italian-sounding names. 'That's it!' Andrew cried. 'That's what he said!'

'This,' declared Fawkes, turning the screen back towards himself, 'is *The White Devil*, by John Webster. Jacobean tragedy. I saw this performed once at the Barbican, come to think of it. Nineteen twenties costume, flappers and white tie. You're sure you've never read this play? Seen it performed?'

'Positive,' said Andrew, excited now. 'What is *The White Devil*? Who is Webster?'

'John Webster is sort of a seventeenth-century Goth. Jacobean, referring to James the First, Queen Elizabeth's successor. Just after Shakespeare's time. Webster wrote bloody plays about nasty people. *The White Devil*, if I have it right, is about a duchess who cheats on her husband and then becomes the scapegoat for a bunch of very nasty cardinals. Your average cardinal, in a Webster play, is about as morally wholesome as a *mafioso*. She dies in the end. Strangled, I think. Haven't read it since Oxford.'

'He mentioned cardinals.'

'Who? Your ghost?' Fawkes asked.

'What does it mean?'

'The play?'

'The ghost quoting it.'

'I haven't a clue,' replied Fawkes, at a loss.

Andrew turned the laptop towards him, scanning the page again. 'These lines here ... *Bestow'st upon they master* ... all that ... that's not what the blond boy said. He was reciting something, but,' he continued, crestfallen, 'the rest of this doesn't fit.'

'You said something about *spitting whores*?'

'Spit and whores, separately.'

'Let's try *spit*. Whores are as common as dirt in Jacobean tragedy. But spit ...'

Andrew waited while Fawkes clicked through the pages.

'Wait, what's that?' Andrew said, catching something.

Fawkes paused.

'There, that's it!' Andrew pointed at the text on the screen. '*Murderess ... whore* ... those are the lines! Right there!' Fawkes murmured the lines to himself.

> *'For your names of "whore" and "murderess",*
> *They proceed from you – as if a man should spit*
> *against the wind: the filth returns in 's face.'*

'I'm not crazy!' Andrew said, excited again. 'Right? I mean, the play is real. Those words are real!'

'The question is ...' Fawkes muttered, staring at the screen. 'Well, I have a lot of questions.'

Andrew continued poring over the text. 'I wonder why he skipped this part here,' he said, pointing to a section on the screen.

Fawkes considered this for a moment. Then pointed himself, in turn. 'Your ghost said these lines? *Terrify babes* and *The wolf may prey the better*? But not these in between?'

'That's right.'

'You're certain?'

'Yeah. Why?'

'Those lines are spoken by Vittoria.'

'Who's she?'

'She's the slutty duchess I just told you about.' Fawkes felt something pass through him. He turned to Andrew. 'You understand, don't you? You of all people should.'

Andrew shook his head.

'Your ghost was rehearsing.'

'He was an actor?'

'An actor . . . and if he was a young boy, in the Lot, then he was also a student here.'

Andrew nodded.

'So he must have been rehearsing for a school play.' Fawkes sat back in his chair, chewing his nails again. 'Just like you.'

RAIN PATTERED ON the paving stones leading to the Vaughan Library. Its slitted windows, like the high windows of a cathedral, glowed in the mist. Andrew held his hat to his head against the rain and wind. It was darkening, after supper. At Fawkes's urging, Andrew had come here *to meet someone helpful*. Fawkes had added: *Don't let her scare you*. Andrew had not set foot in the Vaughan since that first day. But so many memories of that first day had been blotted out by finding Theo cold and stiff on the hillside. It was one of those old Harrow buildings intended principally, he felt, for postcards and promotional photographs.

He pushed open the heavy carved doors, with their giant brass rings, and entered the long, high-ceilinged room. A Fifth Former manned an information desk, sorting books.

Andrew approached him. 'I'm looking for Judith Kahn,' he said. 'Um. Dr Kahn?'

The boy's eyes widened, and without a word he raised a finger and pointed past Andrew.

Andrew turned.

She had come up behind him. The same Dr Kahn of the New Boys' Tour. Her bush of orange hair streaked with grey, her black suit hanging like armour. Scowling.

'You're late,' she announced. Then without warning she charged past him, across the wide stone tiles in the library – coloured deep red, blue and ivory; great slabs like squares on a giant chessboard. Andrew trotted to catch up.

'Mr Fawkes,' he protested, 'didn't tell me he'd set a time.'

'I cannot be accountable for what Mr Fawkes did or didn't tell you. We keep hours here. We don't march to the vagaries of poetic inspiration.' She barked this so that it echoed against the beamed roof and the rose windows; and even though he knew it was *her* library, Andrew found himself cringing at the noise.

'I don't think he realized . . .'

'Don't defend him. Piers Fawkes is childish the way all artists are childish. They become enthusiastic over nothing, and invent their own little nothings when there's not enough nothing at hand. Not the temperament required in an historian, academic or for that matter any adult human wishing to accomplish things related to real life. And that is my study: real life. I am an archivist. A research librarian. Not a book retriever. When Fawkes goes playing literary historical sleuth, he has all the self-important silliness of a boy playing dress-up in his father's shoes and hat, or better yet, a Sherlock Holmes hat and pipe. He has no idea that what he's asking is very difficult to get to. And I've laboured far too long over this collection to go flipping pages at a moment's notice when Mr Fawkes gets a twinkle of inspiration. I'm not Google bloody Books,' she boomed, and a half-dozen students lifted their heads to watch Andrew and Dr Kahn barrel past – then, seeing the speaker, put their heads down again. 'That's where he found his *clue*, isn't it?'

Andrew didn't answer. They came to a carved and studded door at the end of the main reading room. Dr Kahn pulled a keyring from her pocket and unlocked it. It opened on a dark stairway, headed down. The odour of dust, glue and stillness wafted up.

'What time is it?' she demanded.

'Uh, seven-thirty,' Andrew answered, surprised.

She reached into the darkness. 'Thirty minutes.' He heard the snick of a time-set light being set, followed by the ticking away of seconds. 'Light fades the books,' she explained. 'We only use what we need. *Rupert*,' she bellowed back at the Fifth Former at the information desk. 'I'll be in the catacombs.'

Rupert turned to them and raised his fingers to his brow in acknowledgement; but it seemed more of a salute.

Andrew followed Dr Kahn down the stairs – surprisingly modern metal steps that rang slightly as their feet struck them – and found himself in a long room with a low ceiling and yellow lamps hung at intervals. The space was honeycombed by shelves holding books and document boxes that had been mummified in plastic and laid on their backs.

'These on the left are letters. OH's,' Dr Kahn observed as they passed one shelf. *Old Harrovians*, Andrew translated to himself. 'A good section just here. Winston Churchill's letters to his housemaster. Just after Gallipoli. Completely sentimental. Churchill had a miserable time at Harrow.' She tapped another box. 'There's a manuscript of an early play by Rattigan. Alternative ending.' She grunted. 'The vagaries of great men. Their schools know who they really are. We see the sausage being made. Anyway, what you're looking for is back here.'

She resumed her charge to the back of the room, to a shelf that held a row of leather-bound volumes, as big as tombstones. Andrew peered at the titles apprehensively. They were all the same:

HARROW REGISTER.

'Can I look?'

'You may.'

Andrew eased one of the books on to a shallow table and opened it gingerly to the first page.

Head Master
REV. JOSEPH DRURY, D.D.
LIST OF HARROW SCHOOL, OCTOBER 1800
(From a list in the possession of Miss Oxenham)

'Mr Fawkes tells me you're interested in the performance of a play,' said Dr Kahn.

'That's right.'

Andrew flipped the pages. They were full of entries, all names, accompanied by *son of*, accomplishments at the school (Monitor, Head Boy), university attended, and inevitably *Died*, with a corresponding year. Some long lives, some short, all receiving the same terse obituaries in telegram style. He could not resist a sense of wonder – to touch such an old book containing names of the dead – and feel awe at the history and consistency of the place. The eccentric names he had snickered at before arriving at Harrow – *Shells, Removes* – were here, and in use, as far back as 1800. The house names too. *Headmaster's. Headland. The Lot.*

Tower, Charles (The Lot). Son of C. Tower Esq (OH), Weald Hall, Brentwood. Left 1802. Univ. Coll. Oxf, BA, 1805. Author of various religious works and a Tamil grammar. Died Sept. 25, 1825.

'Are you going to tell me which play?' Dr Kahn interrupted his snooping.

'Sure,' he said. '*The White Devil*, by Webster.'

'Are you going to tell me why you're looking for *The White Devil*, by Webster?'

'I . . .'

'Yes?' Dr Kahn watched him intently.

'Research,' he said, feebly.

'Of course. And for your re*search*,' she pronounced it the English way, with the emphasis on the second syllable, as if to correct him, 'were you planning on reading every page of each one of those volumes?'

'I . . .'

'You'll need more than thirty minutes.'

Andrew turned back around and assessed the long row of volumes. They stretched out for a century.

'Did Mr Fawkes make you aware of my title here?' she demanded.

'Title?' Andrew struggled. 'Um, are you a dame or something?'

She fixed him with an angry glare. Then her lips tugged, fighting a smile.

'That,' she said, 'is perhaps the most ignorant thing anyone has ever asked me in this place. And the competition has been stiff. No, I am not a dame. I am *Doctor* Judith Kahn.'

Andrew debated whether it would be better to speak or stay silent.

'I am known as Dr Kahn,' she continued, 'because I am a doctor of philosophy. I received a D.Phil. in history. At Cambridge, if that matters.'

Andrew opened his mouth.

She held up a hand. 'Don't say anything else. I'm not sure I could bear it,' she said. 'Let me help you.' She waited, then repeated: 'I said, *Let me help you*.'

'Oh,' he said quickly. 'Got it. Could you . . . help me? Find it? I'm looking for *The White Devil* . . .'

'By John Webster, yes yes,' she said; '1804.'

'It was performed in 1804?'

'Its only performance, that I'm aware of, on the school stage.'

'You just . . . know that?'

'I looked it up. That's what I do,' she said. 'And you were not just interested in the play, according to Mr Fawkes?'

'No. I'm looking for someone who may have acted in it.'

'That, I have not had time to research, despite the urgency of the message from your housemaster. Male or female role?'

'Female,' stammered Andrew. 'How did you know to ask?'

'Most plays have male and female roles. That takes no guessing. But if we're going to look for your student, we must know his year of entry to the school, give or take. And to know his year of entry, we must know how old he was in 1804. And if he played a female role . . .'

'He would have been younger,' finished Andrew. 'Before his voice broke.'

'Very good.'

'1803?' suggested Andrew.

'Let's try it.' And then, to Andrew's surprise, she smiled.

They stood side by side, flipping through the *Harrow Register*, scanning the pages for names. Each leaf they turned sent up tendrils of dust and the whiff of centuries-old paper, thick and brittle as vellum. They carried on for a while. Then, at last, Dr Kahn pointed.

'There's our boy.'

HARNESS, JOHN (The Lot). Free Scholar. Northolt, Harrow. Drama: The White Devil, Beggar's Opera. Left 1807. Died July, 1809.

'How do we know it's him?' said Andrew.

'The register would only mention a play if the boy had a prominent role. Fawkes told me your boy played the lead.'

Andrew gazed at the entry. 'John Harness,' he murmured, staring at the words. 'Now I know your name.'

'And much more besides,' interjected Dr Kahn.

'Like what?'

'You tell me.' She hung back, watching Andrew.

Andrew scanned the entry again. 'Uh . . . Northolt, Harrow. He was from around here.'

'Good.'

'He died two years after leaving school.' Andrew thought of the white skin and the sunken eyes. Could that have been the face of a twenty-year-old?

'You've missed the two most important words. And you've also missed two important words that aren't here.'

Andrew looked at her, puzzled.

'The two most important words: *free scholar*. They go to the origin of the school. Harrow was founded as a charity to educate the local poor. Until the masters discovered they could grow wealthy by taking on boarding students. They could overcharge for room and board, let the boys live in squalor, and pocket the proceeds.'

'Teachers did that?'

'Shocking, isn't it.'

'Squalor,' repeated Andrew. 'Like with rats running around the dorms.'

'Vivid – and yes, that's the idea. The boarders, because they came from outside the immediate vicinity, were called *foreigners*. They were from all over England. Often titled. Always rich. They subsidized the whole operation. You can imagine how they treated the free scholars.'

'How?' ventured Andrew.

Dr Kahn lowered her eyes to the page and lightly touched the spot where *Harness, John* was printed. 'Like bloody garbage. They called them *town louts*. The abuse grew to be so severe . . .'

'They called them bitches and raped them,' uttered Andrew without thinking.

Silence fell then.

'Not far off the mark,' said Dr Kahn, her eyes boring into him curiously. 'I was going to say, the abuse grew to be so severe that in the end, the scholarship funds remained unused. No one wanted them. To enter Harrow as a free scholar was all but a death sentence. John Harness would have been one of the last for some time.'

Andrew recalled the scene he'd witnessed in the prefect's bath.

'What are the two words that are missing?' he asked after a long pause.

'Look at the other entries,' she prompted.

Andrew scoured them, then called out: '*Son of!*'

'I will think better of American education after this. Quite right. *Son of* is missing. When you're the son of a local tradesman – or worse: the lamplighter, or the dung carter gathering manure for fertilizer – no one gives a damn who your father is. Class differences were less like England today – where one person shops at Harrods, another at Oxfam – and more like the third world. The rich in comfortable homes, plenty of fuel and food. The poor crowded in tiny houses, family members sleeping in the same bed along with the bedbugs and the vermin. Living on bread and cabbage, everything adulterated to make it last longer, your bread leavened with alum. Pigs in the backyard. Few baths. Clothes patched. Windows sealed shut to keep in the heat – but also keeping in the stench and the soot. Which leads us to another clue on this page: 1809.' She eyed Andrew. 'Your Mr Harness met his demise early. With those conditions, disease killed the lower classes like flies.'

'You can tell a lot from a few words, Dr Kahn.'

'My father was the Jew assistant financial manager at Harrow his entire career. *Assistant* to none; he was the only financial manager. But he assisted the governors, and he was humble; thus the title.' The words stung, and held both bitterness and pride. 'He kept the school on track financially. Honest and straightforward. I am doing the same, in my way. Accuracy is everything.'

'I can tell.'

He had gone too far in presuming informality. Dr Kahn recovered her acid air to put him in his place. 'I can only help you so much without context, without a research thesis. You and Mr Fawkes haven't given me much thus far,' she said indignantly.

Andrew weighed his words. 'We're still developing . . . a research thesis.'

She crossed her arms, unsatisfied. 'You're involved in Fawkes's play, I'm told?'

'Yes.'

'Well,' she continued impatiently, 'is this related?'

'Why would it be?'

Her eyes popped. '*Why would it be?* The play is about Byron, is it not? You see the dates here?'

Andrew glanced at the page: '1807.'

'Byron matriculated in 1804. He would have overlapped with this boy for several years. I thought the two of you were engaged in some meaningful research. Is this all a whim?'

'No, ma'am.'

'Then what is this about? Are you *acting* in Fawkes's play?'

'Yes, ma'am.'

'Whom do you play?'

'I'm Byron,' Andrew said.

At that moment they heard a click, and were plunged into blackness. Dr Kahn stood silent for a moment, her eyes adjusting. *The timer. Not to worry*, *I can find my way blind*, she was saying. But Andrew had a different reaction. It was as if the feeling had been lodged in his breast for hours, since his visit to Fawkes, since the night before, since he had heard that terrifying drumbeat in his ears and felt the drive and fury of impending violence and had been its terrified and unwilling witness *unwilling had he been unwilling to everything the handkerchief around the throat he had submitted to it* and all it needed was this little snap to release it. He felt himself grabbing Dr Kahn's arm in the darkness. *Turn on the light, turn on the light*, he repeated, his voice a whisper of panic. *All right*, she replied. *Stay here*. He remained for a moment, clutching the tabletop to root himself; listened to her footsteps until they rang out on the metal stairs. Then he heard the click of the light and the persistent ticking of the timer. She returned.

'You're shaking,' she declared. 'What's going on?'

'Sorry.'

'*Sorry?* That's all you have to offer? You're as white as a ghost!'

At this word, Andrew's eyes snapped to her – too quickly.

She caught it. She watched him now, taking him in, calculating. Andrew cast his eyes downward. He was revealing too much. He was ashamed of himself. He needed to get control. But the adrenalin soaked his system; his legs quivered and jumped. She watched it all, her eyes growing into rounder circles, her mouth into a tighter one.

'Mr Taylor,' she began. 'Is there something I should know?'

He kept his eyes cast downward.

'There are a number of suspicious elements here – now I see. The sudden haste. The upside-down request. Instead of "Please tell me everything you can about the school in Byron's time," you ask for an obscurity, a single isolated fact: who played the female lead in *The White Devil*. And perhaps you can explain,' she continued, 'how you seem to know so much about life at Harrow two hundred years ago?'

Andrew felt his face get hot. 'Oh, just from learning about the school,' he bluffed.

'Your sources?' she demanded.

'Ah,' he stumbled. 'Just, you know, stuff I pick up around the house.' That much was true, anyway.

'Mr Taylor,' she said again. 'I wonder if you and Mr Fawkes have been completely open with me. Would you like to tell me why you had that reaction just now?'

'Not really.'

She crossed her arms. 'You came here for my help. If you want it, you must tell me the truth.' She looked at her watch. 'And the library closes in twenty-five minutes, so I suggest you get on with it.'

9

Voraciously

ANDREW CHECKED HIS watch. He was alone in his room, in his bluer and his tie, seated on a chair, leaning over his bed like a desk – his preferred way to study – holding the stapled pages of the script, muttering the words. He checked his watch again. Two minutes had passed. Time had changed for Andrew. Back at Frederick Williams, it moved in horrible jerks, sometimes dragging out cruelly; he would measure out time in bummed cigarettes and drifting conversations he would pick up and discard around the common rooms like a small-town browser going back to a shop for the hundredth time. Then it would pounce. An exam. A paper due. As if time were some wicked funhouse machine, tuned by a moustache-twirling villain. But at Harrow, his isolation – fewer classes, fewer friends – slowed time, and made it a different element. At FW it had been fire: hypnotizing, then suddenly consuming. At Harrow, it was water: heaving, dense; deliberate. Every moment – having seen the name of John Harness under his fingertips – now spent anxiously questioning his own senses. Was an overheard whisper real, or the latest signal that reality had warped? Which was worse – suspecting you had seen a ghost, or confirming with solid facts that you had?

Or perhaps it was the prospect of meeting Persephone alone that afternoon that made the minutes drift.

It tops any trick that our old man did. He spoke the words aloud in his new stage English accent.

He checked his watch again. To hell with it. He would go. He would be early. He could not stand waiting any more.

HE STOOD ON the empty High Street holding his script, waiting under the heavy grey sky. Behind him stretched the stairwell to the Classics Schools, where he and Persephone had taken refuge a few nights before. They had arranged to meet there again: a place to rehearse. A moment later, voices started to become audible, in a trickle. Then came a stampede of Harrow hats. The two o'clock lesson had let out.

Persephone, books in hand, finally crossed the street, hailing him. At FW, it might have been a mark of triumph to be seen meeting up with the prettiest girl in school. But at Harrow, to be seen meeting up with the *only* girl in school prompted jealousy and abuse. A cluster of his classmates from the Lot passed. Moroney, Mims, Hugo and Cumming, four of the sulkier Sixth Formers.

'*Mmmrow*, Andrew, making friends?'

'Going to get your hair done, girls?'

Hugo leapt forward, antically. 'Going to the *thpa*? Letth make a day of it!'

Andrew smiled and shook his head. Harrovians were artists with an insult. They could have improvised this way for an hour – and probably would, beyond his hearing.

'You're popular today,' muttered Persephone.

'It's not me, it's you,' Andrew grunted back.

'Oi, piss off,' she called at them.

'Ooh, not very ladylike,' came the rejoinder.

'You're the only lady around here, Cumming,' she called.

This met with hoots of delighted derision, and a shamed blush from Cumming.

Andrew and Persephone turned to descend the steps, when

Andrew received a bump from behind that sent his script pages flying.

'Dude, what the *fuck*.' Andrew spun around angrily.

Cam stood there, mountainous. Several mates – not St. John this time, but other boxing pals, broader in the chest and more ominous – hovered behind him.

'It was an accident,' Cam said evenly.

Not quite ready to back down, Andrew snapped: 'Yeah, right.'

Cam's black eyes took in Persephone. 'You're quite a pair, you two. The scum and the slut.'

'What did you say?' Andrew snarled.

'You heard me. Now he's all gentlemanly,' Cam chuckled, walking away. 'Don't let this one slip you anything,' Cam called back to Persephone as he heaved down the High Street, followed by his sniggering teammates. 'You'll end up in a body bag.'

DEFLATED, ANDREW AND Persephone entered the classroom. Persephone flung her books on the table with a loud thump.

'The ever-charming Harrovian.'

'Now I see why you acted that way when we first met,' said Andrew.

'Acted what way?'

'Hostile.'

She took a moment to remember. 'Because I thought you were one of them.'

'You don't, now?'

'You're different,' she acknowledged. 'And if I didn't have this play I think I'd go mad. Piers is the only island of normality in this whole place.'

'You think Fawkes is normal?'

'You don't?'

'He's smart. He's accomplished a lot. But he's kind of a train wreck.'

'At least he's not mummified.'

'But he's doing his best to be embalmed.'

She released a bark of laughter. 'Like I said, cleverer than you look.'

Andrew felt a part of him go runny. To be in the same room with her, alone, with her open-collared white shirt . . . he had been not thinking about it for a few moments, distracted by his anger, by Cam's insults . . . but now . . . 'Well, let's get on with it,' she said. 'I don't want to spend any more time brooding about fat Cameron than I need to.'

'Yeah,' he said, quickly coming to himself. 'Yeah.'

Andrew shuffled, as he always did, as if trying to find the right spot to stand. Persephone waited, standing erect, script in hand, practised.

'All right?' she asked.

'Yep,' he said. 'Yep. OK.'

She began.

AUGUSTA
Your father bagged my mother
In that other English hunt
Not by blue-bloods, but for them . . .

Andrew attempted to keep up with her. Her voice practically sang: rich, round and from the diaphragm. His felt cloddish, nasal, buzzing with head tones. She inhabited the emotion of the scene (flirty, sexy, but also full of the wonder of mutual discovery – *like the two Dromeos in* Comedy of Errors, Honey had said, unhelpfully). He struggled to remember the blocking.

TOGETHER
You must be, like me
Mad Jack's progeny
Let's engage
In adultery

BYRON

But why stop there

AUGUSTA
That's hardly sisterly

TOGETHER
Incest adds a little spice
And fulfils our destiny

AUGUSTA
Knocked up by a brother?

BYRON
Let's be candid.

TOGETHER
It tops any trick that our old man did.

They circled each other – two fighters sizing each other up in the ring – then came together and gripped hands. The scene ended. Persephone dropped Andrew's hand and stepped back.

'Right,' she said, pleased.

'It, uh . . .' Andrew's brain went numb, as if he were even now onstage, staring into the lights. He fumbled for his script and pretended to read it even though the final stage directions in this scene were the only words he had truly memorized. They'd been imprinted on him the moment he got the script. 'It says, *They come together, attracted . . . pull apart in revulsion . . . then surrender to temptation and kiss voraciously*. So pull apart in revulsion. That shouldn't be hard,' he joked, desperately self-deprecating.

'Sort of a fascinated approach,' Persephone remarked thoughtfully.

She gripped his hand, striking their former position, then took two slow steps towards him, eyes locking with his, about to kiss him . . . but no, it was acting. *How does she do that?* Andrew wondered, crestfallen. He gamely mirrored her.

'Now the revulsion,' he said.

She spun away from him, looking over her shoulder with regret and fear, as if he were a looming figure she had encountered suddenly in the street.

'That was good,' he said.

'Thanks,' she said.

'No, really, you're a phenomenal actress.'

'Compared to what?' She laughed.

'So, should we . . .'

'You want to kiss voraciously?'

He was rendered speechless by this question.

'It will be hard to explain if someone passes.' She nodded to the windows.

'No one's coming.' His voice hit a high note. God, he was almost begging.

She came at him, theatrically. She tilted her head. She pressed her face to his.

Andrew met her kiss, eyes open. He could hear her breathe through her nose. It was all too sudden, too mechanical, and yet was true torment. It was what he desired, but it had no flavour, no meaning. She was merely acting, and he was somehow still terrified. (He'd had some half-dozen girls, he reminded himself; stripped them like mannequins and smelled their earthy sex and ground his way to drunken satisfaction in empty bedrooms at my-parents-are-away keg parties. But this bravado was poor currency here; a weak dollar.) He tried to calm a trembling right leg. What was the matter with him? He had been thinking about this, about her, too much. And to win his prize, get the kiss . . . and have it be *this*? A dry, lip-protected, scripted face-lock? Shame and resentment brewed in him, as if she were taunting him.

They pulled apart.

'I wonder,' he managed to say, in the awkward silence, 'whether that was voracious enough.'

'We'll work on it. We could grip each other. Could actually be funny.'

'Funny?' His heart crumpled.

'Yes, sort of a comic . . .'

He cut her off, voice bitter. 'I'm actually disappointed.'

'Disappointed? Why?'

'By the kiss.' He shrugged.

'What do you mean?'

'I mean . . . *you* . . .'

'Me, what?'

'You're supposed to be good at this.'

'Oh, am I?' She turned scarlet. 'According to whom?'

'According to . . .' Anyone with a modicum of brains and experience would have shut up and reversed course at this point; Andrew knew this, but now he felt locked into a dialectical track and did not know how to get off it. 'Well, you heard Cam.'

'You're calling me a slut?' She blinked, stunned. 'And what about you? Why is Cam calling you scum? He's the authority, suddenly?'

Andrew felt his mouth turn dry. They were in a real fight. How had he brought them here so quickly? 'Because people accused me of giving Theo drugs,' he muttered. 'There was a rumour he died of an overdose.'

'Yes, I heard that. Absolute nonsense. Theo was *sheltered*.' She used the word pejoratively, as if Sheltered were a subcaste of Harrovian. 'But why would they accuse you, unless maybe you *are* some kind of drug-dealing scum?'

'I don't do drugs. Any more,' he added.

Andrew regretted this turn in the conversation. He was lucky she hadn't stalked out. He desperately resolved to make up for his stupid remarks by revealing how much worse off than her he was.

'My father paid for me to come here,' he began.

'Doesn't everyone pay?' she said, still angry.

'He paid, as in made a gift. A big one. There was no other way to get me in. I did do drugs. I got expelled from my school, in the States, about three weeks before graduation.' He hesitated. 'For heroin.'

'*Heroin?*' she said.

'My friend Daniel and I did it. Twice.' Andrew sighed. 'He knew a dealer in Bridgeport. I was chicken. I did the tiniest amount the first time. But it was ... awesome. I mean it *felt* awesome. So we were going to do it again. It was a Saturday. We had the whole day free. What I didn't know was that Daniel had only done it a couple of times. He made it seem like it was ... his thing. So we're snorting from these bags in my dorm room, and I'm just doing *some* ... but he's, like, almost finished the bag by himself. And I look over after a while, and he's kind of ... waxy. He was barely breathing.'

'What did you do?'

'I got out my phone and I called 911. That's the emergency line,' he explained. 'I told them I was on the third floor of Noel House at Frederick Williams Academy and that my friend was dying of a heroin overdose. Then I sat there trying to get him to stay awake until the sirens came. But by the time they arrived, I'm ... I'm way into the junkie zone.' Andrew rubbed his forehead.

'What happened?' Persephone's voice was quieter now.

'They saved him.'

'To you.'

'Um. We were both expelled,' he said matter-of-factly. 'Daniel went to rehab. I did community service. I had to take a urine test every couple of weeks. My offers to college got rescinded. So ... I needed to do something totally different. According to my dad,' he added. 'Get away. My dad had a whole pitch: I got in with the wrong crowd ... I had never done drugs before ... I had ninetieth-percentile SATs. But Harrow has zero tolerance for drugs. It ended up requiring a cash donation. I even signed a document swearing I would never even *think* about doing drugs. And here I am.'

He picked at the lint on his trousers, disgusted with himself – for being at Harrow for such a lame reason; for telling such a crummy story; for having the story to tell in the first place.

'That took courage,' Persephone said, her tone changing. 'To call for help for your friend.'

Andrew scoffed. 'He died anyway.'

'*What*? Your friend, Daniel?'

'Yeah.' Andrew's voice fell. 'Over the summer. He OD'd.'

'Oh God, Andrew,' said Persephone, flush with pity and disgust. 'I thought you said he went to rehabilitation.'

'He did. He started using again.'

'Well, you couldn't control that.'

Andrew did not respond.

'Andrew?' she insisted. 'That isn't your fault.'

'No, I know.' He was distant, non-committal.

'And,' she continued, 'you were brave.'

He turned to Persephone in surprise. 'No one's said *that* to me before.'

'Well, now they have. You saw your friend dying and you took control. You risked your school career to do the right thing.'

Andrew grunted, eager to change the subject. 'What about you?'

'Me?' she said. 'Oh, I'm just a slut.'

He wanted to rewind not just the last fifteen minutes, but the last five years of her life, find those times where she had offered herself to the wrong people for the wrong reasons and coil them up like some hopeful, chivalric Fate; respooling Persephone's time; undoing and anointing all that self-inflicted damage. He wanted, with a sudden, painful urgency, to make her see herself as he did: precocious, brilliant, agonizingly beautiful. But what came out were just a few words, spoken with all the warmth he possessed:

'No, you're not.'

'Yes, I am,' she said.

They stared at each other a moment.

'For instance,' she said, 'if you kissed me now, I would do nothing to stop you.'

Andrew's heart thumped. Persephone clutched the table behind her, as if miming someone clinging to the ledge of a building, about to fall. But he sensed that these were not theatrics. He crossed to her in two steps, hesitated, then kissed her gingerly. With his left hand he found her curls; with his right he wrapped his fingers in hers, and he pressed against her. This time he got it all, the perfume and warmth of her body and the swell of her belly and breasts; their loneliness came crackling down between them. They were starved. They kissed harder. Their tongues met; their teeth parted and knocked together. For some ten minutes they devoured each other, then finally pulled apart, lips numb, and gasping.

10

Sledgehammers

FAWKES SAT UNDER an overhang on the porch, Moleskine notebook in his lap, ballpoint in hand. Raindrops slapped the iron table the former housemaster had left there (which Fawkes had bought off him, knowing he would be too lazy or preoccupied to buy his own porch furniture) and the spray dotted his notebook. The paper curdled; the ink made tiny blue pools. But Fawkes would not move. This nook was his refuge, rain be damned. No windows looked on to it. Here Fawkes could pump himself full of coffee, smoke and scribble. Here old instincts took over, thirty years of habit. He reverted to a primitive state; heard the rhythms of all his life's reading like the clanging of a great, shared workshop; rows of poets pounding hot stressed and unstressed syllables into forms. The second act of the play was flowing, faster than he could write. His fingers shook from excitement – not, he told himself, from the gin racking his system. He reread it. It had the music. It would need shaping; there was flab there. But that was rewriting, mere sifting. The important thing was, he had found a vein of gold.

He snapped his notebook shut and strode to the centre of the porch, and let the drops soak him, holding up his face and letting it get wet, soaking his grey sweatshirt, his mind still echoing with rhythmic thunder.

'Sir?'

Fawkes leapt. 'Good Christ! What are you doing here? What time is it, Andrew?'

'A couple of minutes to eight.' Andrew stood in the French doors, in bluer and tie. 'Sorry. I buzzed but there was no answer.'

'That means no one's home!'

'But you are home.'

'No, I'm not!'

'I found the name,' said Andrew, eagerly. 'Of . . . you know . . .'

'Ah,' said Fawkes, now trying to be casual, keeping his place in the centre of the porch, pretending the rain didn't bother him. 'Judy helped you out? Jolly good. The mighty Kahn knows her archives, eh?'

'Should I . . . come out there?'

'Ah. No.' Fawkes pushed past Andrew and grabbed a towel off a chair-back in the kitchen to mop himself up.

'What were you doing?' asked Andrew.

'I was communing with the gods.'

'How are they?'

'They're back.' Fawkes led them to the living room, plumped himself onto the sofa, and lit a cigarette. 'In no small part due to you, Andrew.'

'Really?'

'Mm. I'm beginning to understand: playwrights draw energy from their cast. Having an actual Byron . . . and you're a very, very close copy – you know that, don't you? Well, it's damned inspiring.'

Fawkes grinned. Andrew perceived that Fawkes was trying very hard to make out that he was kidding, which made him believe Fawkes was actually telling the truth.

'Well,' Andrew said, 'that's good.'

'So, what have you got from Lady Judith, eh? Will I need a drink to withstand the news?' Fawkes rose and went to the kitchen, where he began fondling a half-consumed blue bottle of gin like a bowler caressing the ball on his way back to his mark.

'Piers,' Andrew said, 'it's not even nine.'

Fawkes made a face. 'I was joking, of course.' It took him a long moment to peel his hand off the bottle.

Andrew checked the paper where he'd jotted his notes. 'So the guy,' he said, 'was the only one who was in the Lot *and* in a performance of *The White Devil*. His name is John Harness. He left school in 1807. So the play must have been performed . . .'

Fawkes started. His hand, still near the bottle, jerked, causing it to flip and crash on to the tiled floor.

Fawkes cursed. He dropped to one knee and began picking up the shards. There was a scramble while Andrew leapt to his feet and supplied a soiled kitchen towel to mop up the spirit.

'Did you just say John Harness?' Fawkes exclaimed, cupping the shattered bottle-bottom, like a boozy crown. '*John Harness*?'

'Yes. Do you know who he is?' Andrew replied.

'You're sure about this name? Judy confirmed it?' The heap of glass was flung into the rubbish with a clatter.

'Yeah, she helped me find it.'

'Does she *know* about him?' Fawkes was standing over Andrew now, watching the boy clean up the rest.

'Know . . . ?' Andrew looked up at Fawkes. He had gone a little pale. 'She – she said he was a free scholar.' He rose and shook the glass from his hand into the bin. 'Free scholars were poor financial aid students from the town. Picked on . . .'

'Picked on, yes. But this one was defended by an older boy, with a famously rotten temper. *If any fellow bully you tell me and I'll thrash him if I can.*'

Andrew hesitated. 'She didn't tell me that. But she did say Harness might have known Byron. They overlapped.'

'*Overlapped?*' Fawkes scoffed. Then he stared out of the kitchen window into the emerging white-grey morning.

'Uh . . . Mr Fawkes? Piers?'

Fawkes felt the gooseflesh crawling from his lower spine and over his back like an army of furry spiders. 'Whether this proves the existence of your ghost or not, I can't say, Andrew,' he stammered. 'But it is awfully strange.' Fawkes resumed staring out of the window.

'Is something the matter?' Andrew asked.

Fawkes stirred. 'Follow me.' He led Andrew back to the living room. He started flinging open desk drawers, not finding what he wanted, and slamming them shut with a curse. 'Come on.'

Andrew trailed Fawkes up his narrow staircase. He was not especially eager to see Fawkes's private living area, given the state of the rooms he showed to guests. The upper regions of the house were dim and stuffy. A towel lay on the floor of the open bathroom. The sink had a hairy look to it, and an uncapped toothpaste tube lay on the porcelain like a wounded soldier left behind. They passed the bedroom (bed unmade; a pair of dingy underpants visible on the bedspread) and charged into Fawkes's study, a boxy room with shutter blinds, largely unfurnished and seemingly unused. In the corner lay a pile of some dozen manila folders of varying thicknesses. Fawkes squatted over these for a moment. Then he stood, holding a thin one out to Andrew. He watched the boy's expression carefully.

'What's that?' Andrew asked.

'That's the John Harness file,' Fawkes declared. Andrew's eyes widened. 'I made files on each of Byron's major lovers.'

'His lovers?' Andrew demanded, puzzled, taking the folder. It contained photocopies of poems.

'Not *all* of them. Only the biggies. He had hundreds.' Fawkes gazed at the heap of folders on the floor and sighed. 'It's what you do when you're blocked. Research. Facts are the long way round to Truth.'

'So why do you have a file on this John Harness? They were school friends, not lovers.'

'Ah, you naïve Americans,' said Fawkes. 'John Harness *was*

Byron's lover. At Harrow,' he amended, in response to Andrew's shocked expression. 'It was common in those days. Little love affairs among boys. Harness and Byron "took up together". That was the phrase at the time. What attracted Byron was the fact that Harness was also lame. Childhood accident. Harness's lameness healed eventually. But in the early years, Byron was his defender. The older, tougher schoolboy protecting the younger. Yet another way Byron is hard to pin down.

'The bodyguard relationship turned romantic. They wrote passionate, jealous notes to each other. Again, rather commonplace. What was uncommon – why we care – is that it grew into something else. They both went to Cambridge. And it turned into love. Real love. Scholars ignored it for a century because the gay part made it taboo. By that time most evidence had washed away.' Fawkes tapped the thin folder. 'But Harness is unmistakably still there, in the poems and letters. A face staring from the page.'

Andrew held the folder as if it were made of uranium. 'Harness is the white-haired boy,' he said.

'If John Harness is your ghost,' Fawkes went on, 'you are in a very strange position.'

Andrew didn't like the use of the word *position*. He looked up at Fawkes suspiciously, as if Fawkes knew the substance of that encounter with the boy by the cistern.

'What do you mean?' Andrew asked.

'Well . . . he's Harness. You're Byron.'

'Yeah, in the play . . . wait, sorry?'

'Persephone saw the resemblance immediately.' Fawkes leaned against the wall, crossing his arms, eyeing Andrew. 'Don't you see?'

'No,' Andrew said stubbornly.

'Maybe this ghost *thinks you're Byron*.' Fawkes's lip curled in a fascinated half smile.

'Thinks I'm his boyfriend?' Andrew said, wilfully incredulous.

Fawkes started to pace the tiny office. 'Maybe that's why he came back. He saw you. Or felt you. Or whatever. Here. He wanted to *contact* you. Do you think he could tell you things? About Byron? God, this is a weird, but fascinating, research opportunity!' Fawkes laughed with excitement. 'We could hold a séance to summon John Harness. "When Byron was writing *Manfred*, did he, you know, *say* anything about it?"'

'*I*'m not summoning him,' Andrew replied, morosely. 'I saw him kill Theo.'

Fawkes frowned. 'Right. I must say, this doesn't help me over to your view of Theo's death. John Harness, a murderer? The poor, gay, local boy with the crippled foot? Not my notion of a cold-blooded killer.'

'Why, what was Harness like?' Andrew asked.

'Harness was always been treated as something of a victim. You know: Byron toyed with him for a time and then discarded him.' Fawkes shrugged. 'No record of murder anyway. Though admittedly his life is poorly documented.'

'I thought you believed me,' Andrew said morosely.

'I believe you saw something,' Fawkes said. 'But just because you *saw* John Harness kill Theo ... doesn't mean he actually *killed Theo.* The coroner made his judgement. Sarcoidosis, or what have you. Do you want to call the police? Or maybe the head man? Tell them, "Theo Ryder was killed by a ghost! Name: John Harness. Residence: The Beyond. No, that's not in Middlesex."'

Andrew rolled his eyes. 'We can't say that.'

'Rather my point,' Fawkes replied.

Andrew brooded. As he did so, he felt a kind of heaviness come over him; a sickliness; a vivid perception of unhappiness, self-doubt, anger; so tangible, it infiltrated his senses as if it were a terrible smell; the mental equivalent of a carrion odour. He felt both sleepy and anxious. The air in the room had gone hot and stale, creating the desire to nap in its unhealthy fog. Andrew looked at Fawkes. Fawkes was staring back at him, his eyes wide.

'Do you feel something?' Andrew said. Speaking required effort. His words seemed to die in the thick atmosphere.

Fawkes nodded. 'We need to leave this room,' he declared with equal effort.

Andrew dropped the Harness folder. He stooped to replace the copies that had fallen out. They had names like *The Cornelian* and *To Thyrza*. Andrew was mesmerized by the titles. He distractedly began to read them.

'Come on.' Fawkes tugged Andrew's elbow. Andrew bundled the photocopies to his chest and allowed himself to be dragged out of the room and into the narrow corridor. They breathed somewhat easier here. Fawkes clattered down the staircase. He was at the bottom before he turned and realized Andrew remained at the top. Dreamy again, distracted.

'Andrew!' he shouted.

Andrew came to his senses and followed Fawkes. Together they stood at the bottom of the stairs and gazed up at the landing from which they had just escaped.

'That was very strange,' stated Fawkes.

They paused, as if waiting for something to follow them. But nothing did.

'I ... did not like that,' the housemaster ventured. 'Is that what you've been experiencing?'

Andrew nodded. 'Yeah.'

'You're braver than I gave you credit for. Let's go and sit down.'

They did, in the living room. Both on the sofa, just staring while their senses recovered.

'I don't think I'll be using that room for a while.' Fawkes made a face.

Andrew didn't respond. They shared another moment of baleful gazing into the middle distance. Unexpectedly, Fawkes started chanting, or reciting, in a rich baritone; a voice that knew poetry, knew how to draw out the vowels, make them into music;

a voice at odds with the sarcastic leer of his ordinary conversation:

Lest man know not
That he on dry land loveliest liveth,
List how I, care-wretched, on ice-cold sea,
Weathered the winter.

'That Byron?' asked Andrew after a pause.

'Pound,' corrected Fawkes.

'What does it mean?'

'Ah, children who want to know what poems *mean*. They don't mean. They express. They are songs. When you sympathize, you *make* them mean something, up here.' He tapped his head. 'That is a poem called *The Seafarer*. It is about going off to sea; back in the days before navigation, before radios. When that meant being completely, irrevocably, on your own.'

Andrew absorbed this. 'We're on our own?'

'On this … yes.' Fawkes smiled thinly. 'Welcome, Andrew Taylor, to the ice-cold sea.'

FAWKES CLOSED THE door behind Andrew a few minutes later. His first thoughts were of the room upstairs. The cloud seemed to have cleared from his rooms. Should he go back to the study, and check? *No, thanks!* came the quick response. Fawkes smoked and paced his living room, sending furtive glances to his staircase. How would he get back to his bedroom, at night, alone? And then, with a wave of pity and fear, a realization came to him: that feeling, that sensation, was not resident in his study. *It was attached to the boy*. To the American.

Fawkes flopped onto his sofa, thinking. God, what a nasty notion. How could he protect the poor kid?

But as he sat there, and smoked a second cigarette, and then another, the direction of his thoughts changed. He stubbed out his third cigarette. He hesitated. Then picked up his cordless phone and dialled a London number. He spoke to an assistant. He was forced to wait several minutes. Then, cheerful:

'Tomasina! Piers again. Remember my play about . . . ? Right. There's an angle I stupidly left out. I was being vain, as usual, and hoping that the poetry alone would be enough. But what if . . . what if there's a scholarly angle, too? Well, I'm finding new material on one of Byron's lovers – a gay lover – that's just emerging. So we wrap the publication of the play in sort of a literary discovery.'

Tomasina wanted to know whether the story was documented, and whether it was really new.

'Absolutely new,' he answered. 'Working on the documentation – but I'm here at the source, at Harrow School, where Byron went, of course. And the story, well . . . it appears that one of Byron's little pals at Harrow, who was also his lover, was a murderer. Never before known.'

Tomasina spoke enthusiastically, talking herself through how she would promote it. *So we would treat this as a scholarly event* and *a literary event. Make it an off-the-book-page story . . .*

Fawkes let her talk, grinning to himself. He walked to the kitchen holding the cordless phone, and while she prattled and pitched, he made himself a drink.

ANCIENT HISTORY FELT like a straitjacket. Boudicca, berms, javelin warfare, and the literary style of Tacitus . . . Sir Alan Vine sneered his way through a lesson, bathing the class in the acid of his nasal voice. Andrew sat at his desk in the Leaf Schools – so named because the small brick building nestled into the arboreal northern slope of the Hill. He daydreamed and gazed at the trees. Their leaves seemed to have passed poisoned into autumn, sickened by all the rain and gone a soggy, withery brown. He was anxiously waiting for the moment when Sir Alan would look at his watch and dismiss them. At last the bell rang. Andrew leapt. He had another Vine on his mind.

The hall filled with boys. Hats, jackets, chatter. Fifty teenage boys crammed into the small foyer, cross-currents of classes arriving and leaving.

Fifty boys, fifty bluers – and one white shirt. Andrew's heart pulsed. He forced his way through.

Oi.

In a hurry?

He reached her and grabbed her elbow.

'I've got something to tell you,' he hissed.

'Andrew.' Persephone's voice rose, a warning. 'Do you know Seb?'

Andrew saw the tall Sixth Former from rehearsal, the one with red hair. Up close he was even more handsome – square chin, athletic build, and the coolly affronted expression of someone who's just had a biscuit taken out of his hand. Rebecca-the-short-skirted-girl's words came back to him. *She seems to know a lot of boys.*

Andrew frowned. 'Hi.'

'The famous Andrew Taylor,' Seb drawled.

'Would you excuse us?' Andrew said.

'Of course. See you Thursday, Miss Persephone,' Seb said with a mocking bow, raising a hand to his hat. Persephone laughed. Her glorious eyes crinkled and shone. Seb shot a sharp look at Andrew. *I see her two times a week for English A-Levels*, the look said. *Don't think I'm done here*. Andrew watched him stride off. He was fucking *jaunty*.

'New friend?' he said sarcastically.

'Seb is the cleverest boy in my class. We were discussing "The Pardoner's Tale".'

'He seemed sorry to go.'

'Are you my chaperone now?' she returned. 'Let's see. I have boys in my lessons for English. And ... Art! And ... Biology! My God! There are boys everywhere! Andrew, it's not safe!'

He fumed. They walked side by side in silence for a few paces.

Then he charged ahead. 'It was important,' he snapped. 'But never mind.'

Andrew, she called behind him.

HE LAY ON his bed. Staring at the wallpaper.

In the back of his mind, a stampede of snorting buffalo trampled a landscape, ripped up turf and kicked stones. They thundered in a brutal, endless charge.

In the front of his mind, he was aware of the silent room.

I fucking hate this place.

Andrew heard footsteps approach. He prepared a cutting remark to Roddy. Something especially heartless. But after his usual, perfunctory knock-and-enter, Roddy spoke in a different tone. 'Oi, man, stand up, you have a girl visiting.'

'Thank you, Roddy, you're a gentleman,' a female voice stated. Roddy blushed and withdrew, savouring the compliment. Andrew remained splayed on the bed.

'Should I leave?' Persephone said when the door had closed.

'Are you even allowed to be here?'

'Ironically, so few girls visit Harrovians in their rooms, there are no rules against it.'

Andrew grunted. 'That's about the only thing.'

'Lucky for me. And you.'

The air grew charged, as if lightning were about to strike. Persephone glowed: her white shirt, her curls, the erectness of her posture; pert, mysterious, feminine, fragrant. She dignified the cruddy little space. A part of Andrew cringed over his rotten behaviour. Yet he felt compelled to keep up his angry sulk. He'd come this far.

To his surprise, Persephone sat on the bed next to him.

'You left me there,' she said.

'I found out something important,' he moped. 'The ghost. It's real. Even Fawkes believes it now. He thinks it's Byron's boyfriend from Harrow.'

'Fawkes?' She was surprised. 'He thinks that?'

'Yes, Fawkes. You still don't believe me, do you?'

'I'm not sure,' she said. 'He thinks it's Byron's boyfriend? That's odd. I thought Byron . . .'

'He went both ways. For a while, anyway.' Andrew picked up the battered manila folder. 'Poems about the boyfriend.'

She took the folder and thumbed through it. 'This whole obsession of yours is weird,' she declared.

Andrew lay back, wounded.

'Does that door lock?' she asked suddenly.

'No,' he grumbled. 'None of them . . .'

Her lips were on his. He resisted for a microsecond, then opened his lips in response. Their tongues touched. Andrew abandoned his pose and sat up.

'I thought I was *weird*.'

'A little,' she said. 'Maybe a lot.' She laughed.

'What about *Seb*?' Andrew asked bitterly.

She frowned. 'Don't spoil it.' Then she offered: 'If you were normal, I wouldn't like you.'

She kissed him again. Her hands – white, small, freckled – were twisting around her shirt, popping two, three, four buttons. Andrew's heart stopped. Then she reached inside and twisted the fastener of the pale beige bra, and her breasts suddenly appeared in the faded daylight of his room – pale and freckled and larger, more nipply than he could have dreamed of – proffered like a kind of sacrifice; as if to say, *If you don't believe I like you, here is the only token of sincerity I can offer.* If Andrew had stopped to think, he might have found this offering a little sad – why would stripping, surrendering herself, be her first and instinctive means of getting his attention? But he wasn't thinking. When he gained his breath back, he crouched down and took her breasts in both hands, tenderly – they were cool to the touch – and his powers of observation ceased. He dived for them, groped them, licked them hungrily, a starving man offered a bowl of sweets, and she held his head there until he had had enough, and then she raised him, *Come here*, and Andrew pressed himself to her, kissing her, gnawing her neck, hoping desperately this would lead to more. She pulled away. Stood. Began to fasten back up. He watched her in agony.

'Why don't you come to my house,' she said, her cats' eyes glowing, her hands working the bra and buttons. 'The next exeat weekend.'

'Your house ...' He had trouble speaking. 'Headland House?'

'My mum's. In Hampstead. She's in Athens. We'll make a weekend of it.'

Andrew felt a jolt of adrenalin, an unexpected terror. *Of sex. Of the moment of truth*. 'OK.'

He tried to fight the memory descending on him. Of the humiliating (*exciting strange*) ritual in the basement with John Harness *now he could name him* who had stirred him. More than stirred. Delivered him up.

John Harness was Byron's lover

Maybe this ghost thinks you're Byron

He felt an unexpected gloom. And a terror that Persephone could read his thoughts.

'I like you, Andrew.'

'OK.'

'Is that all you can say?'

'You've kind of left me speechless.'

She liked that. 'Good.'

Then a look of insecurity shadowed her face. Perhaps she could read his mind.

'So you'll come?' she said, standing there.

'Of course. Yes.'

She smiled again and departed with an actress's outward dignity.

*

EVENING CLASS, THE one that ended at 5.15, nearly dark, in this northern latitude: French. A kid from Druries was butchering some lines of dialogue when a boy knocked on the classroom door with a message – for Andrew. Oohs, aahs and catcalls erupted.

His housemaster needed to see him urgently.

On the walk over, every kind of doomsday scenario played in Andrew's mind. His father had run out of money. He was being withdrawn from Harrow. But as soon as Andrew entered the Lot foyer it became clear that none of these melodramas was the one unfolding.

Fawkes paced the foyer, in black robes, whirling on Andrew as soon as he entered. Andrew immediately grew wary. Fawkes's eyes were red-rimmed; he had a wobbling, slurry appearance, overlaid with an affected calm, a Mona Lisa smile, intended, no doubt, to give him an air of confidence, self-containment; but it only had the effect of making Fawkes seem as if he were listening to some other conversation, the ongoing and ever-charming party in his bloodstream.

At Fawkes's side stood two shuffling workmen, both bored (they had been kept waiting) and suspicious (the housemaster was loaded). Around these three men, several younger boys hovered, curious. Andrew could see why. The two workmen – in dusty, paint-stained jeans and sweatshirts – carried sledgehammers. The handles were three feet long, the heads as big as iron bricks.

Fawkes waved Andrew to his side. 'C'mere.' Over his shoulder, he called, 'One moment, chaps.'

He took Andrew by the shoulder – a chummy, we're-old-friends gesture, in keeping with his off-kilter management of the whole scene, almost as if he needed to prove how *in* with Andrew he was, to the labourers – and escorted him to a stairwell, where they could speak in private. The elder of the two workmen rolled his eyes. 'Whenever you're ready. Sir.'

'We have thirty minutes before the next lesson gets out and the house fills with boys,' Fawkes hissed near Andrew's ear.

'OK ...' said Andrew uncertainly. 'What's going on? Why did you pull me out of class?'

'We can find the room!' Fawkes said with a crazed grin.

'Find ...' Andrew was puzzled.

'That room,' Fawkes said impatiently. 'The room ... in the past ... where John Harness took you. It could still be here. In the house. These places are mazes. If you can find it, find that actual room ...' He gestured grandly. Andrew waited. Fawkes leaned forward and breathed gin on him. '*It would prove it.*'

'Prove what?'

'Proves the ghost exists!'

Andrew squirmed. 'I don't need any more proof.'

'But you do. I do. All of these things – *The White Devil*, Lord Byron, John Harness – could be in your mind. Weird coincidences, certainly. But not proof. No one knows exactly what Harness looked like. There are no portraits. There's no place to *check*.' Fawkes drew closer. 'Think about what we're trying to accomplish with the play. This is a one-in-a-million ... *confluence*. A *discovery*. The ghost, returning? Trying to tell us something? It could be important. Very, very important.'

Andrew regarded Fawkes. 'You mean it will make *you* feel very important.'

Fawkes drew back, stung. Was he being too obvious? He needed to lighten up. He was sounding desperate again.

'I admit. I want the play to be unique. I want it to be wonderful. I want it to be ... published.' He gave a bitter laugh. 'There's nothing wrong with that. And *you* can help.'

The American's tone was worldly and deflating: 'I'm just an *actor* in your *play*.'

Fawkes's eyes flashed. His diction might be slurry, but his mind snapped with alcoholic inspiration. He saw an angle and did not hesitate to take it. 'We're not just helping ourselves, Andrew. We're helping *Theo*.'

Andrew glanced at his housemaster sharply.

'You said it yourself. How he died. It happened. It's real. But no one will believe us,' Fawkes continued. He placed a confiding hand on Andrew's shoulder. 'Don't we owe it to Theo – you and I – to find out for certain?'

ANDREW FELT LIKE a bloodhound. A string of people followed his every move as he traipsed around the house, guided by some invisible scent. The first clue was finding the right staircase. He started in his bedroom, paced the length of the corridor, but then, seeing the new construction of the western staircase, doubled back, forcing his entourage to squeeze, grumbling, back through the tiny space. 'We're going on a guided tour of the Lot, Reg, aren't we fortunate,' cracked the elder workman, Dick, to his mate. The handles of their sledgehammers bumped and nicked the walls. Eventually the group descended the eastern staircase together, with Fawkes watching Andrew's every move with his bulgy eyes.

At the bottom, Andrew paused. He turned around slowly, once again forcing the dubious sledgehammer bearers to back away. That door, with the battered tin handle, would have been . . .

'Here,' he said.

'You're sure?' Fawkes cried.

Of course I'm not sure, he thought, snappishly. But he restrained himself. The workmen had already been making remarks. *They invented somefing called plumbing, Mr Fawkes. No need for cisterns any more*. 'Yep,' he said aloud.

They came to a stop, crammed into the tiny crossroads of basement corridors, all seven of them. Andrew, Fawkes, the two workmen, and three boys who had trailed along to see what happened next: one, the messenger from French class, and two of his pals – all Shells.

'Now what?' Dick challenged Fawkes.

Fawkes hesitated. 'Now . . . smash through.'

'Smash through? Are you joking?' The workman rubbed his meaty palm lovingly on the creamy-yellow surface. 'This is new plaster. We just fixed this up last year.'

'Dick . . .' reminded Fawkes.

'All right,' grumbled Dick. 'New paint, have to redo everyfing . . .'

Now that they had their orders – though not without some final, sceptical head shaking – Dick and Reg got to business. They paced out the area, measured how much room they had to swing. They produced plastic goggles. They spread their legs for leverage, gripped the base and neck of their hammers – and began pounding. The noise was terrific. Dents appeared. Paint and plaster cracked and flew in white chips, chunks and finally whole honeycombed slabs. Metal rods were exposed. The men's clothes grew dusty. More students appeared, hovering in the stairwell, whispering, asking for explanation, receiving uncertain replies. From the original three, there were now more than seven boys watching. They kept coming, gathering in a queue up the stairwell. Fawkes ignored them, his big eyes never wavering from the action. Until Matron arrived.

'What the devil is happening?' she said, pushing down the stairs. The boys parted for her. 'My apartment's shaking like an earthquake!'

'We're doing a bit of exploring,' said Fawkes.

'Exploring?' She took in the mess. 'You're destroying the house!'

'We're not destroying it, Matron . . .'

'This fella says there's somefing behind this wall,' said Dick, pointing at Andrew, and puffing from his efforts. 'An old cistern, he says.'

'How would he know?' Matron scowled at Andrew. Andrew wished he could crawl into his collar. Then her eyes squinted at him suspiciously. 'I hope this isn't any silly business with the Lot ghost.'

For an instant, Fawkes's nervous glance skittered across the faces of the gathered boys. They in turn stared back at him, eyes wide.

Dick grinned: *Now he's in trouble.*

'It's of historical interest,' Fawkes declared, summoning his peremptory English arrogance. 'Nothing to do with ghosts, Matron. Now please, let us get on with the work.'

'Work!' she scoffed. She retreated up the stairs, grumbling. Fawkes gestured for Dick and Reg to resume.

Despite Dick's shuffling manner, he was hell with a hammer. He and Reg moved like pistons, swaying, smashing, in orchestrated rhythm. On their tenth stroke, Reg's hammerhead vanished halfway into the wall. Dick stopped swinging. For a moment they just stared. Fawkes lit up. *Is that it? Is that it, Dick?* he called out.

Now the hammers reared and slammed quickly. They beat a large, rhomboidal crack in the plaster. Reg gave it a terrific kick with his thick-soled yellow boot. The wall curled in. A hole stood about four feet high and two wide. Dick pulled his goggles on to the top of his forehead. He got down on one knee before the dark gap and peered through. His head disappeared. When it reappeared, his expression was begrudging.

'Looks like you got yourself a new basement, Mr Fawkes.'

A LADDER APPEARED, and a large flashlight with an orange grip. The ladder was shoved through the gap and secured. Andrew stripped off his jacket and tie. *Why is he going down?* the gathered boys asked. Reg descended with the flashlight. He called up that the ladder was secure.

Andrew stepped backward, through the hole. Eager boys,

peering after him, crowded the opening. The last face he saw as he descended was Dick's, scowling and dubious.

Inside, the temperature dropped. All went black. The bobbing wisp of the flashlight below him illuminated the rungs.

'I got yer,' came Reg's voice, echoing.

'You holding the ladder?'

'Yeah.'

'Is it secure, with the water?' Andrew asked nervously. He clung to the braces and made deliberate steps until he felt Reg's strong grip on his triceps easing him to the floor.

'How did you know it was wet?' Reg asked.

Andrew followed the light. The floor had been littered with distinctly twentieth-century evidence of their demolition: plaster, dust, nails, wire.

'How did you know it was wet?' repeated Reg.

'Wet?'

Andrew followed the beam of the flashlight. He saw the sloping floor. The holes punched in the stone wall. The slick of dribbling water. And the cistern mouth, some seven feet wide, with its jagged stone lips.

'Look there,' grunted Reg, casting the light into the gloom of the hole. 'Fall righ' in there. Break your neck. Eh? Careful!'

Andrew circled the hole, staring into its depths, mesmerized. On the far side he stopped. Reg was saying something. Telling the group assembled above what they'd found. Fawkes's face appeared in the opening. He was calling Andrew. *What is it?* Curious and anxious. *What's down there, Andrew?* But Andrew was not listening. There, on the floor, straight and stiff, as if someone had been tugging hard on both ends, lay a clean white handkerchief.

PART II

What are a thousand living loves
To that which cannot quit the dead?

11

Suffocation

DR JUDITH KAHN entered her home. It was a modest two-bedroom on Covey Lane, a ten-minute walk from school. It had been her father's home (her mother had died when Judith was young), and she had redecorated it completely in a desire to make the place her own, to avoid that feeling that she was still living in her parents' house. New paint, new furnishings. But that had been thirty years ago. Now the place looked battered in its own right. Scuffing on the walls, papers on the desk, too many picture frames on bookshelves and windowsills, her old comfortable caftan flung over the back of her favourite chair. She was proud she had avoided becoming old-lady-cosy; she could live with being bohemian-shabby. Her father had taught her how to manage money. She owned the houses on either side and rented them, as well as one of the nearby shops at the corner of Dudley Gardens and Lower Road. If the swaggering aristos of Harrow knew how much their school archivist had put by, they would have a shock.

The message light blinked on her phone. She saw it winking orange from where she stood by the front door. She punched the code into the burglar alarm (a concession to living alone), then crossed the room in the dark, illuminating a lamp along the way, to hear the message. It was Fawkes. He sounded both drunk and excited. She smiled. Everyone needed a Fawkes. A fountain spilling over with ideas. Or was that an overbrimming bath, threatening to flood the house: lately she had sensed, in addition to his usual narcissism, a careening, out-of-control quality, and it worried her. His message tonight was more garbled than usual. *Could you help us once again?* Fawkes asked. They had found a hidden room in the Lot; did she know anything about it? He thought it all linked back to Byron's time, and suspected an element of the bizarre. Those were his words: *element of the bizarre.* Dr Kahn frowned. Fawkes's voice cracked when he said the words. As if he was trying to be comical, to cover up for something that upset him, and the strain was too much for his voice. Dr Kahn picked up the phone to return his call.

Her finger never touched the buttons. Her senses tingled and she became aware of another person in the house. Whether it was through some small, scarcely detectable sound or true instinct she could not say, but she knew it instantly. She went to the hearth, attempting to remain calm, not to startle anyone. She wrapped her fingers around the heavy poker, then turned, and carried it in front of her like a bayonet. Her strategy lacked finesse – what would she do when she'd cornered the intruder? – but she was scared, and curious, and outraged. How did they get past the alarm? And what on earth would anyone want to steal? Books? Dr Kahn edged into the corridor.

'Hello?' she called. Her voice was weak. *You can do better than that*, she told herself.

But she didn't. Her senses more than tingled now. Something had changed in the house: she felt an oppressive cloud on her, a thickness in the atmosphere. It made breathing difficult. Her movements dragged, as if a weight lay upon her limbs. Even her thoughts came sluggishly.

She stepped forward into the first-floor corridor. She had only turned on one lamp in the living room, so the far end of the hall was bathed in shadows. The door to her bedroom stood halfway open. She had not left it that way, she was certain. It was as if someone had pulled the door closed, just enough to conceal themselves as they stood behind it.

Dr Kahn felt a presence.

A body, *some*body, waited there behind that door. Then she heard it. An irregular wheezing; a gurgle. Gooseflesh rose on her arms and neck. She stood frozen, unnerved at last. Was it an animal? Had she cornered some beast? She heard a sharp intake of breath – human breath, shaped by lips, but ghastly, ragged, popping – that struck a note she knew. The deep inhalation before somebody started a nasty task – say, beating to death the old lady they were robbing. She saw four white orbs appear on the rim of the door. What were they? Her heart thrummed a beat before she realized. Fingertips. She felt something at her feet. She looked down. Now she screamed.

Rats had gathered at her feet, greasy, swarming. Dozens of them, there in the corridor, her corridor. One stood up on its hind legs, staring at her with eyes glowing orange in the reflected light. Then she felt a rush of motion behind her. She realized her mistake.

She had turned her back on the bedroom door.

SHE DID NOT know how long she lay there, but she came to, to the sound of the telephone ringing. It rang and rang. She took stock. Felt her head – no injuries. The hall was free of rats. Free of anyone. Her bedroom door was open wide, the way she'd left it that morning. The poker stood by the hearth. But the greatest shock came in the words she heard, projected from her answering machine:

Judy, it's Piers. Listen, we've made something of a discovery in the Lot. A room, like a cistern, that had been blocked up. Could you help us once again? To learn more? It's all related. Tied up with Byron, I think. There is an element . . . of the bizarre about it. More when we speak.

It was Piers Fawkes, *leaving* the same message she had heard when she first came into the house.

She struggled to her feet. She felt like someone over whom a wave has crashed: battered, but with all evidence of that violence dissolving into sand and sea.

She flipped lights on in the kitchen and with shaking hands made herself tea to calm down. She thought of Fawkes's message. *Could you help us once again?* The *us* tripped her up. But the first hot sip of tea brought the answer. The American boy.

The one who had told her he had seen a ghost.

IT TOOK ONLY twenty-four hours after the expedition into the basement.

Fawkes received a note, shoved through the letterbox. No postage, hand-delivered; even *he* could not miss it. (Clearly this was the intent.) *See me after lessons tomorrow*, it said, in Colin Jute's angular script.

And here he sat, in Jute's long, polygonal, well-windowed headmaster's office, like the captain's quarters on an old ship. Sofa and chairs at one end; vast desk at the other; view of the Harrow park beyond. It lay at the centre of the school: at the crest of the High Street; Headmaster's House built all around it.

Nervous about this meeting, Fawkes had drunk too much the night before. Gin before dinner, wine during, gin again after. A horrible idea in retrospect, but he had kept pouring it down, as if his nerves were a blocked pipe he could flush out. He'd been fighting nausea all day.

Jute stood at his desk, shuffling papers, his jaws clenched behind a dangerous-looking scowl. He spoke without raising his eyes to Fawkes. 'Word has reached me about your incident in the basement.' He spat out this last word as if a basement were the moral equivalent of a strip club.

Fawkes suddenly knew exactly where this was going, and how it had happened.

The boys. It would have been the boys, the Shells, standing in the stairwell while the workers with sledgehammers bashed through the walls of their own dormitory. Not enough happened in the school in the average day – the average week – that such an incident would pass unremarked. Those boys would have emerged with reports, and distorted explanations, and spread these around – passed them from boy to boy in dining hall and classroom and High Street and tuck-shop like flu germs. And, of course, there was Matron, who would have complained to the assistant housemaster, Macrae, within the half hour.

'You seem to have lost your way, Piers,' said Jute. 'Your house needs you more than ever. And you literally go about destroying it.'

His tone was not even angry, Fawkes observed ruefully. Calm and cutting. Fawkes, it seemed, no longer merited anger, or even bluster.

'The reason I wished to see you was the story I heard. That the American had seen a ghost down there. That true, Piers? *The Lot ghost?*' Jute's nose wrinkled. 'Old wives' tales?'

Fawkes's face went red. 'The boy suspected,' he stammered, 'there was a . . . a bit of the old house . . .'

'So you took the archaeology upon yourself? With sledgehammers?'

'I didn't know what I would find. I didn't know . . .'

'Were you drinking?'

Fawkes nearly choked. 'I beg your pardon?'

'My question was clear enough.'

'The . . . it was four-thirty.'

Jute stared balefully.

'*No*,' Fawkes responded. An instinctive, self-protective lie. 'May I enquire *why* you asked me that?'

'You drink, Piers. Don't act so bloody shocked. The school, once upon a time, tolerated such behaviour. And I suppose, as a writer, you think it's part of your mystique. But those days are gone. We hold everyone to professional standards.' He sighed. 'It's written on your *face*, Piers,' he said. 'Your eyes. Nose. Blood vessels and cobwebs. People notice. I notice. *Boys* notice. In lessons, I'm told,' he added, with a note of outrage.

'Never.'

'Other times, then?' Jute asked, his voice now reclining into certitude. Fawkes realized his grave mistake in answering that last charge – to deny one instance was to acknowledge others. 'House meeting? Taking the register? You missed all your lessons on the day in question,' he said, referring to his notes.

Fawkes opened his mouth, but waited a second too long to speak.

'I've heard enough,' Jute concluded firmly, disgusted. 'You're on probation. Those boys had one of their fellows *die*, man. A Sixth Former, a popular one. They need reassurance, not excavations. Or bloody ... *ghost stories*. I don't want any more disruption to them or to the school. And I won't have a drunk in charge of sixty boys. I have asked Sir Alan Vine, as one of the more senior housemasters, to monitor your performance. In four weeks' time he will make a recommendation to me about your continued employment. That is all.'

The secretary poked her head into the office. The headmaster's scowl broke into a sunny smile. *What is it, Margaret?* Fawkes got the message – loyal servants treated kindly; bad ones punished. He did not need to be dismissed. He shouldered out past the spindly Margaret, who, sensing the headmaster's mood, sniffed at him as if he were a dog that had rolled in something.

Fawkes burned as he left Headmaster's House. He had been expecting the worst. He had been expecting consequences. But not this humiliation. Who had talked to Jute about the ghost? And that shit about drinking? Every master drank at school. Look at Blakey, soused at every holiday dinner. The beer allowances, the Sixth Form pub, the leavers' parties ... the place flowed with booze.

He shuffled down the High Street, letting the drops pelt his face. More rain. It never stopped, not since Theo died. Drowned in his own lung fluid, and then the school goes soggy for a month. No wonder Jute was edgy. The place *did* feel doomed, cursed. Fawkes would be lucky to leave. And given all his daydreaming about life after Harrow, Fawkes should have been elated. His employment agreement ran for a full academic year. He would be paid up to July if he were sacked. Ten months. He could write a magnum opus in that time. Getting fired from a job he loathed, and which he performed poorly? Getting paid for not working? Getting time to write? This was his lucky day.

A wave of self-pity crashed over him. The play. He could take all the time in the world on it, and no one would want it. It wasn't publishable without his association with the school. He felt a grasping sense of panic. And what about Andrew Taylor? What about John Harness; the cistern in his basement? Fawkes would lose his source material. For a few days, Byron's life had come into focus for him, from this weak, two-dimensional prison (diaries, letters, who gave a shit; it was like listening to recordings of people's phone calls; who cared about the everyday minutiae; give me the friction; take me inside the hour you became miserable, lost your soul, changed your life) into stark, three-dimensional reality; it rose before him like a fleshy pop-up book, in the form of the staring, sorrowful eyes of this American kid. Fawkes had been given *access*. As if – mopey as he was – Andrew Taylor were a member of an exclusive club that Fawkes, a born non-joiner, was now desperate to enter. He wanted to spend time with this boy. And not just because of the play, he reluctantly admitted to himself. He actually *liked* Andrew. Their mutual discoveries had been the most . . . *fun* . . . he had had in a long time. Between teaching, and emailing parents, and administrative duties, and writing, Fawkes had had very little fun of late.

Probation. Four weeks. He didn't know how long he wanted or needed to complete his unfinished business at Harrow. But he knew it would take longer than four weeks.

He reached the Lot and found the front door of his apartment standing open.

Fawkes stood in the rain staring at it. Not because he was afraid – of burglars, or of someone breaking in. But because he had forgotten to close his own damned door.

He'd forgotten an umbrella, too. The rain dripped down his nose.

Small things. They made him suddenly furious.

Forgotten to close his own door! If Jute needed more evidence of a man not fit to care for others … well, here it was. *Get it together*, Fawkes fumed at himself. He kicked the door wide, beheld the miserable heap of cigarette butts and mess inside. All other thoughts were crowded out by immediate, visceral disgust. Fawkes gritted his teeth in anger. At Jute. At the school. At himself.

'Get it together,' he growled, this time aloud, stamping inside and slamming the door behind him. '*Get it together!*'

DOWN IN THE cistern room, it had been worse than Andrew feared. When he first saw the handkerchief, Andrew merely felt dizzy. He did not want to show it, with Reg there, in his work boots and paint-spattered trousers. But then Andrew nearly toppled over. He caught himself against the ladder. A strange sensation flooded him, as if some narcotic had been squeezed into his veins. He tried to shake it off. He ascribed it to the descent down the ladder. To the disorientation brought on by pitch blackness. *Pretty … pretty weird down here*, he muttered nonsensically to Reg, hoping to conjure cold reality back, through conversation. Reg merely grunted. When Andrew ascended a few minutes later to the light and the conviviality of his curious housemates in the basement corridor, the feeling, instead of dissipating, grew stronger.

He nodded at their questions, faked a smile at Fawkes, and climbed the stairs to his room. Each step brought him closer to unconsciousness: a warm, welcoming, drowsy feeling, like the sleep arctic explorers reportedly feel as they slip into a freezing death. And now he did not have the strength to deny what he did feel down below: the lustrous atmosphere of physical desire, so overwhelming as to be sickening. An overdose of furtive pleasure in that cistern room.

BACK IN HIS room, undressing, he swam in unbidden associations.

If any fellow bully you I'll thrash him if I can

Andrew saw the prefect's bath.

It is steamy here.

A white-haired boy rises from the water: pale, perfect, fragile, his pectorals shapely but soft. His skin slick. He rises, coming for him . . .

Andrew staggered and lay down. He needed to go to bed. Didn't feel well. He drowsed in the fading light, forgetting supper, only distantly aware of the crunching gravel and chatter below his window, the sound of boys heading to dining hall.

And at last it came when the sun faded. The breathing. Undoubtedly real now. The moisture and motion of lips, inches from his ear. Panting, desirous, ragged. Andrew wrestled with his senses for a few seconds, resisting – *I am alone in the room*, he recited, *there is nobody here* – but he could not stop it. He could not move his limbs. He could not escape, and did not have the will to, anyway. He lay there, in his boxers, as passive and full of dread as a drugged prisoner awaiting captors.

You came for me

A hand gripped his chest, icy cold. Andrew convulsed, gasped, his back arching *am I being attacked or caressed is this fear or some kind of* he could not say it, some kind of thrill, an involuntary moan. The cold spread from his chest, penetrating his thorax. It swelled inside him. He let go.

He heard it first.

The thundering noise he had heard – when? In that dream. Weeks ago.

Hrr hrr hrr hrr hrr hrr

The one where he had woken screaming.

The sound changed.

Krch . . . krch . . .

Hrr hrr hrr hrr hrr hrr

He had at first thought it was some external noise, a crashing or a booming, as if he was being overtaken by a thunderstorm. Now he realized it was something else. Something smaller, more ordinary, only tremendously amplified:

The breathing he heard on the Hill

The baying gurgle of the gaunt white-haired boy.

Only closer. No, not just closer. *Inside.*

Hrr hrr hrr hrr hrr hrr . . . *inhale*

Krch . . . krch . . . *exhale*

And then the vision came.

He is back in the stairwell.

The thin red carpet is the same. The spindly railing, the candles.

He rounds the corners of the stairwell. He is climbing, vigorously. The noise continues. The light is dim.

He is hot, angry. Lubricated with sweat. He is ready to do something terrible but so exciting he trembles. No time to stop. He turns the last corner.

The figure.

There he is.

Like last time. Standing at the end of the corridor.

There are many doors here, at regular intervals. The figure leans forward, towards one of the last ones, at the end. It is an odd gesture.

There must be a key tied around his neck, Andrew concludes. *He is unlocking a door.*

The figure straightens, opens the door, and enters.

Andrew's chest tightens as he sees the figure disappear through the door. Andrew lunges forward to follow.

Is it the right door?

He knocks. The noise grows louder.

To his delight, the door pushes open under his hand. It had not been relocked.

Andrew steps inside. He looks around the room – a bedroom, with a small writing desk and a washbasin in the corner. It is hazy in the premature twilight, shaded by heavy drapes.

The figure is there. Turns, surprised.

Oo 'er you?

Andrew freezes. For a split second the notion comes to him: *he cannot kill another person*. Then the notion is gone. In two steps he's on him. Andrew reaches for his throat. A quick cry of protest. Andrew's fingers clutch the larynx and squeeze. His own lips bare his teeth. He surrenders to a primitive, animal pleasure – *fighting winning* – until the real battle begins. A person does not give up life so easily. He scarcely notices the face: boyish, fine-featured, pretty, made ugly by the struggle.

The boy thrashes. A swat close to the boy's eye draws blood. A new strategy: the boy flings himself backward. A table goes over.

Someone will hear!

Andrew casts about for a way to end it faster. He sees the answer: a pillow on the bed. He snatches it. Puts his weight on the figure

How light and small he is

and shoves the pillow over his face. Now comes the kicking. Flailing. Knees and fingernails. Andrew grits his teeth. His fingers and arms are numb. The vigour is draining from him. He cannot hold on much longer. He puts all his weight on the pillow.

Slowly, the thrashing yields to twitching. Andrew leans in and presses.

Cannot give up

Then the twitching ceases.

Finally – stillness.

He rolls off the body, spent. Sweat slicks his face, neck. His gasps threaten to split his chest. That terrible thunder comes louder than ever. He coughs. It racks his ribs and tears at his throat. But the struggle is over. *The face*. He must see it. He staggers to the window, pulls the curtains back. The room swells with a white glow. He grips the corner of the grey, worn linen pillow. He tugs.

ANDREW SAT UP, clamping both his hands over his mouth, suppressing a scream.

He could not let them hear him again. They would think – they would know – he'd gone crazy.

I am seeing it again.

It was as if Andrew was growing closer and closer to the real event.

My God this time I saw the whole thing.

Not just saw it. Did it.

He was that much closer to what had really happened. A strangulation. Or, technically, suffocation. Just like he had seen with Theo, on the hill.

It was as if the white-haired boy, John Harness, had dragged him halfway to the Lot of another time. Andrew's existence in twenty-first-century Harrow suddenly seemed tremulous. It was as if – the walls to the cistern room opened – it had become so much easier for Harness to drag him all the way down, down into that cold dank room

that's what he wants

and maybe not just the cistern room, maybe farther below,

maybe into that hole and into whatever black hell produces faces like the one he saw on the hill

gaunt sunk-eyed

full of rage, full of a regretful horror at its own actions

it's why he is showing me, he can't even stomach it himself.

Andrew's shirt was sweat-soaked. A chill seized him. He wrapped himself in his damp sheets, and he shook.

PIERS FAWKES ANSWERED his door in jeans, a white T-shirt and bright-green, elbow-length rubber gloves on both hands.

'I'm not sure I've come to the right house,' said Dr Kahn after a stunned pause.

'Judy, come in.'

Night had fallen. Orange street lights had engulfed the hill. The scent of cooking oil and beer were borne by a crisp autumn breeze sweeping the Hill. A nice night to be out. No rain.

Dr Kahn unwrapped her scarf and entered Fawkes's apartment. Then she turned around in place, unbelieving. The floor had been mopped. The ashtrays had been emptied – and washed. The magazines and newspapers had been stacked. The dirty plates were no more to be seen, and beyond, in the kitchen, stood rows of dishes in a drying rack, and a bucket and mop. The stereo thumped a song by the Police, high-pitched and driven.

'Now I'm certain this is the wrong house,' she repeated. 'What's got into you? Is someone coming for a visit?'

'Sir Alan Vine.' He held her gaze. 'I'm on probation.'

'You're joking.'

He shook his head.

'They're not blaming you for the boy dying?'

'Not directly, of course. But if I had been more vigilant . . .'

'That's horribly unfair!'

Fawkes shrugged, turned down the music, and went to the kitchen to put on a kettle. Dr Kahn flung her coat on the sofa and followed him.

'Who did it – Jute?'

'Who else.'

'Why did he wait so bloody long, then?' she said, indignantly. 'It's been weeks.'

'There were other contributing factors of more recent vintage.'

'Such as?' she asked.

'Let's see … the fact that I smashed down the walls of my own house, and frightened the boys.'

'Yes, I received your message.'

'Were you able to find out anything?' he asked. He went to retrieve a box of tea bags from the cabinet. Dr Kahn watched as his hands shook violently.

'Piers, are you ill?' she interrupted. 'Shall I come back another time?'

He looked at her in surprise. 'No, not ill. Please, stay.' His expression turned plaintive.

'All right. Well. I did some cursory reading,' she said. 'The Lot is actually constructed around the core of the old house. On the same spot. It was done a hundred and fifty years ago, to save money on demolition and reconstruction, I suppose. What you found is no doubt part of that original house.'

'So this is not a discovery,' he said, disappointed.

'Still, it's fascinating. I'd like to see it.'

'Jute thinks I'm spreading hysteria.'

'Hm,' she said, taking another look at Fawkes and his spotless kitchen, which had scrubbing powders and paper towels and rubbish bags flung about. 'I'm still trying to understand all this cleaning, Piers. You're not yourself.'

Fawkes flung open one of his cabinets and stood aside to show his guest that the white wood box stood empty. 'Notice anything?'

'I notice nothing.'

'Exactly. This cabinet used to contain gin, vodka, eau de vie, whisky, bitters … Calvados … Filfar …' He took in Dr Kahn's questioning look. 'My sobriety was called into question,' he explained.

She pursed her lips. 'I see.'

'I know, I know. You've been warning me.'

'Jute said this.'

'He said the boys were noticing.'

'Did he suggest some sort of programme?'

Fawkes snorted. 'Jute is not the programme type.'

'No.'

'He said we must uphold professional standards. He wants me out, obviously.' Fawkes slammed the cabinet door shut. 'So I'm stopping.'

'Stopping drinking!' she declared. 'You?'

'Don't make fun, Judy. I'm about to fucking fall apart as it is.' He put a hand to his forehead and used the other to lean against the counter. 'I feel like a badly made toy. Like I'm about to *sproing* all over, my gears falling out . . . like I'm held together by tape.'

'Your metaphors are suffering as well,' she observed wryly, but he gave her such a mournful glance that she broke into a pitiful laugh. 'Oh, Piers, I'm only teasing. I'm relieved. You were drinking far too much. You would have been dead by sixty.'

He grunted. 'I can't write.'

'You'll readjust.'

'I can't sleep.'

Dr Kahn chewed her lip. 'Piers,' she said at last, in a gentle tone of voice.

'Hm?'

'Your kettle's boiling.'

'Ah!' Steam had been billowing and frothing from the spout. Fawkes grabbed the kettle and promptly burned his hand. He leapt back, sucking the wound, then thrust it under cold water in the tap. Dr Kahn calmly turned off the gas and watched her friend in pity.

*

THEY SAT AT Fawkes's kitchen table with two steaming mugs of tea in front of them. Fawkes spooned four teaspoons of sugar into his. Then, after a moment, a fifth. He smoked. He hugged himself with his arms. His foot tapped the floor. He offered Dr Kahn milk for the third time.

'The fact is, I couldn't write before, either,' he said suddenly.

Dr Kahn waited.

'I was frozen on the bloody play for nine months. Not until the American showed up did I have the slightest whisper of inspiration.'

'Why him?'

'He's the picture of Byron! Well, Byron at that age. Angry, needy. Also, there's something ... *skittish* about him. Have you noticed? Like if you don't feed him the exact morsel of attention he needs, he'll fall apart. Do you know what I mean?'

She nodded. 'At the library, two nights ago, he became quite unhinged.'

'He's got me back on track, somehow. Like giving me a sitter, to paint. *Emotionally Starved Orphan*. Oil on canvas.'

'Why do you think that is?'

'Hm?'

'Why do you think meeting Andrew inspired you?'

'The ghost story, for one thing. He told you?'

'He did.'

'What did you think?'

'Credible,' she said after a pause.

Fawkes gave her a look of surprise.

'I felt something strange when I came home the other night,' she said, explaining herself. 'When you called. It was extremely unpleasant.'

'You, too?' Fawkes described what he and Andrew had experienced in his study. 'I wondered if it was just me. Just us.'

'Us meaning ... ?'

'Andrew and me.'

‘Hm,’ she grunted. Then ventured: ‘I think there’s another reason why Andrew Taylor is inspiring you.’

‘What’s that?’

‘I think he’s a reflection of you. Because you’re the one who’s emotionally starved.’

‘Are you going to psychoanalyse me?’

‘Why did you start drinking so much?’ she countered.

‘Because I’m thirsty,’ he said. ‘Not because I’m starved.’

‘Be serious.’

‘Because a bloody teenager died in my house!’ Fawkes burst out. ‘Because every family within a hundred miles is emailing me, wanting answers, wanting explanations. Because the head man, and Theo Ryder’s parents, are blaming me! They say, *Oh, sure, it’s an undetectable disease*,’ he said, flatly, ‘*and you’re not a doctor*. But underneath, you can tell. It’s the way they look at you. *Somehow, if you were doing your job right, it wouldn’t have happened.* But of course! How could I have forgotten my Handy Housemaster Undetectable Disease Kit! I could have saved the day!’

‘Quite right,’ said Dr Kahn, coolly.

‘You’re humouring me. I did everything I could for him, Judy,’ he said. ‘I took him to the bloody morgue.’

‘I know.’

‘And still I get the blame! What am I doing wrong?’

‘You’re being,’ Dr Kahn said, in answer, ‘a selfish, narcissistic prick.’

He sat up straight, stung.

‘Really.’

‘Yes, really.’

‘Would you be so kind as to explain?’

‘A boy died, Piers.’

‘I’m aware of that.’

‘What do we do when other people die?’

‘We drink ourselves silly.’

‘Yes. And we make it all about us, and we make it a big drama involving the headmaster, and we spend a lot of time whinging about how it's going to affect our poetry,' she said acidly.

'Ouch,' said Fawkes.

'What do *other* people do when their loved ones die?' She repeated the question rhetorically.

'I haven't the foggiest. Weep. Ululate. Tear their hair out.'

'No one close to you has died?'

'My dad, some years ago.'

'And?'

'I went on a bender. I drank and fucked everything in sight for six weeks. I gained ten pounds. I got herpes,' he added. 'So I'm maturing.'

She wrinkled her nose in disgust. 'The word I'm searching for is *mourning*, Piers.'

'*I'll be that light, unmeaning thing*,' he intoned, '*that smiles with all, and weeps with none.*'

'Quotations. You're a bag of them. But you're all ashes and straw inside.'

'Ashes and straw. I'm going to use that.'

'To mourn is a transitive verb. You should appreciate that, at least. You mourn *someone*. Have you mourned Theo Ryder?'

'I barely knew him,' he grunted.

'He was a boy in *your house*.' Dr Kahn watched him. Fawkes's face hung slack. Puffy, pale, spotty. He did look ill, and miserable. 'You cared for him. In every sense.'

'Did I?'

'You did,' she said emphatically. 'You did a fine job.'

'Thank you, Judy.'

'But we're still talking about you, aren't we?'

'I barely knew him!' He threw up his hands.

She changed tack. 'When Jute put you on probation, why did you decide to stop drinking? Why not just go on another bender?'

'I need to finish the play,' he mumbled.

'Because you're better than Jute thinks. You said it yourself.

You did everything you could for Theo, and if you quit now, you're the housemaster who *let* a boy die in his house, who couldn't cope. And that's not you. And you've got boys relying on you now, who need you. Andrew Taylor. What did you call him? A beggar? An urchin?'

'Orphan.'

'He's Oliver Twist, holding out his bowl, begging. You're not the kind to walk away. You think you are. But you're not, really.'

'Andrew Taylor is merely a means for me to understand Byron better,' Fawkes said coldly, stubbing out his umpteenth cigarette of the day. 'I want this ghost business to pan out. I want to use it for the play. If not in the actual plot, then to get the play published. Andrew is the lynchpin.'

'Surely even you are not that mercenary?' Dr Kahn eyed him searchingly. 'Are you?' He did not answer. 'Tell me you're joking, Piers. That's a despicable way to treat someone.'

He avoided her gaze. 'Of course I'm joking.'

'Are you helping him?'

'I'm helping him with his research,' he said.

She shook her head. 'You need to do more. He's suffering. He's your next Theo, Piers. But this one, you *can* save.'

'Me? Save someone else?'

'I know. It sounds improbable.'

Fawkes slurped the sugar sludge from the bottom of his teacup and set the cup down with a shaking hand.

'How long has it been since you've had a drink?' she asked, with sympathy.

'Forty-six hours.' He glanced at the clock. 'And forty-one minutes.'

'You made that decision on your own, Piers. You knew you had to change. That means you're doing it already. I have faith in you.'

'I feel a hundred years old.'

'You look awful,' she acknowledged.

'Thanks,' he drawled sarcastically. Then added: 'Cunt.'

She smiled. 'Give me one of those.' She reached over and lit herself a cigarette.

'What if I'm not cut out for it?' he said at last.

'Cut out for what?'

'For being . . . you know. *Caring*. Being *a human being*.'

'Of course you are. We all are.'

'You're not,' he said accusingly.

'What an awful thing to say!'

'You and your archives,' he continued. 'Barking at your assistants, frightening the boys to death. Guarding your library like an ogre.'

'You're calling me an ogre now!'

'Maybe some people are just not cut out to be with other people,' he concluded.

They both reached for their cups.

'Well,' she said, after a silence, 'I'm here now, aren't I?'

Their gazes met, and held. Fawkes's frown melted into a reluctant smile.

12

Essay Club

'TAYLOR.'

The voice was a commanding tenor, nasal, even though it came from the great round ribcage of Sir Alan Vine. The other boys cast sidelong glances at Andrew, as they might at a traffic accident, before they filed out of the Leaf Schools classroom with their hats cocked and their green-and-white Harrow-issue notebooks in hand. Andrew watched them enviously.

'Sit.' Sir Alan held out a hand towards an empty desk.

Andrew squeezed into it. The desks were designed for your average fourteen-year-old. Sir Alan remained standing. He leaned against the podium on the shallow dais from which he taught. He wore a grey suit under his black beak's robes.

'I don't know you well, Taylor,' he began. 'But I'd like to have a talk.' He crossed to the classroom door and closed it. 'Just the two of us, for a moment.'

Andrew gulped. Persephone. Sir Alan had found out about their plans for Saturday, he was sure of it.

The night before Andrew had received a series of texts:

My mum's house in Hampstead will be empty this weekend.
Care to join me? Discretion, discretion. Sir A need not know.
Her name so you don't cock it up is Fidias. Don't call her fiddy-ass in your American accent. Fee THEE ES.

He had read the texts voraciously, reading each one as if it were a novel. Begun an obsessive imagining, of seeing Persephone boldly naked, of wrapping up in sheets with her like man and wife, of exercising independence in ways such as: watching a DVD; ordering takeout; not having seventy-nine boys tussling around you, sharing your table, crapping in your toilet, leaving scum on the bathroom floor for you to rub your toes in as you shower. He knew she would be better alone, not furtively ducking in and out of classrooms and dorm rooms but romping around in a whole house. Letting her great eyes blink at him the way they did, letting that strange womanly quality pour over him . . . Anyway. Fuck. Now it was ruined. They were busted.

'Sure, what's up?' Andrew asked, trying to sound braver than he felt.

Sir Alan winced at the familiarity of his tone, but shrugged it off. 'I'm concerned,' he said. 'About you.'

'Why?'

'It's an adjustment coming to a new school, a new country. And you've come to it in most unusual circumstances. It's not every day a Sixth Former dies at Harrow.'

Andrew looked down.

'I knew Theo Ryder,' Sir Alan continued, pensively. 'I taught him for his O-Levels. Not the best scholar. But a good temperament. He would have done well. Despite what we project to our students here, being proficient in lessons is not always the greatest indicator of success. Sport is better. Means you're competitive, you like to win, you can handle being bruised and buffeted. It means you can be a leader. There are others here, and not just the students, who fail that same test.'

Andrew waited. 'Is that what you wanted to talk to me about? That I should get more involved in sports?'

Sir Alan's eyebrows rose. Andrew's tone was even, but there was something insolent about his question. 'Not sport. I want to talk to you about your housemaster. Piers Fawkes.'

Andrew looked up in surprise.

'Mr Fawkes is a poet.' Sir Alan let that hang there, his pause casting a shadow over the word. 'Which is all very well. I was a solicitor before I became a teacher. We each have our crosses to bear.' He grinned a wide, yellow smile. Andrew tried to smile in return but instead found himself noticing the tiny grey hairs growing along the bridge of Sir Alan's nose, and the thicker ones tufting in his ears. 'I am evaluating his performance as a housemaster.'

'Mr Fawkes's performance?'

'After Theo's death, we have to enquire. Too much at stake, with eighty boys in a house. One chief concern, frankly, is his stability. It's hard, when one of your boys suffers a tragedy like that. I have a daughter. As you know. And the thought of anything happening to her ... well, it can undo even the strongest. I see that. But ...' His tone rose higher, as if to disguise the significance of what came next: 'I understand there is some business between you two, and ... something about the Lot ghost. Can you explain that to me?'

Andrew stalled for time. 'Business?'

But Sir Alan was too practised a solicitor to fall for that. He clamped his mouth shut and stared fiercely back at Andrew, waiting for him to answer the original question.

'People in the house told me about the Lot ghost ...' stammered Andrew.

'People?'

'Matron.'

'Go on.'

'So that's how ... that's how I know about it.'

'Everyone knows about it,' persisted Sir Alan. 'I want to know what you have to do with it. In particular.'

Andrew felt his face flush. 'On my first day,' he said, 'Matron gave me a tour of the Lot, and I thought I felt something in the basement.'

'Something like?'

'Just . . . a shiver. Gave me the creeps, that's all.'

'Did you see a ghost?'

'I was jet-lagged,' Andrew said quickly. 'I guess I got kind of scared.'

'How did Fawkes get involved?' he asked.

'I told him. He was concerned.'

'You told him about the ghost?' Sir Alan grew animated. 'Did he believe you?'

'Sir?'

'You said he was concerned. Is that why? Because he believed you had seen a ghost?'

'He thought I was stressed from . . . you know . . . from Theo dying.' Andrew added: 'He was concerned about me.'

'He thought you saw the ghost . . . because you were stressed from Theo dying.'

'That's correct, sir.' It was a darned good version of things. Andrew was proud of himself for packaging it up this way.

'But the first day,' Sir Alan continued, 'Theo was not dead yet.'

Andrew opened his mouth.

'So you did not see the ghost due to stress.'

Andrew hesitated. 'Well, I told Mr Fawkes later. After Theo died.'

'You had continued to see a ghost all that time, then?'

'No,' Andrew mumbled. 'Just . . . you know.'

'No, I don't know.'

Andrew said nothing. Sir Alan chose a new approach.

'Explain to me how you both came to smash the walls of the basement in the Lot. Before you answer, you should know I have accounts from six different boys in the Lot that you and Fawkes were chasing a ghost.'

'Chasing a ghost? What does that mean?'

'You tell me.'

'*You* said it.'

Sir Alan smelled blood now and did not back down. 'The two of you ordered workmen to smash down a wall. Why?'

'I had heard there were some old underground rooms in the Lot.'

'*You* had? And then you told Fawkes?'

Andrew desperately tried to think of all the angles – why he should or shouldn't answer this. But there wasn't time. 'Yes,' he said, his face growing hotter.

'And this wall smashing was linked to the ghost.'

'No.'

'You heard there were old rooms in the Lot. Heard from whom?'

'M-Matron,' Andrew invented.

'Do you think if I asked Matron to confirm what you've just said, she would do so?'

Andrew swallowed. 'I don't know.'

Sir Alan fell silent. 'You're lying, Taylor,' he said after a moment. 'My daughter tells me you have a dodgy reputation in the school already, and now I see your character for myself.'

Andrew's world was rocked. Persephone had told her father, about him? Told him bad things?

'You're a practised liar, the worst to catch out. Not because the facts are so very hard to track down, but because of your demeanour. You more than half believe what you say, because you feel you need to to survive. And you'll cling to the lies until the last moment. I've seen it many times. A sign of a character that's already compromised. I've heard about you. About the drugs.' He paused. 'Seen the record. You know we have a zero tolerance policy. You know that if you were to touch drugs here, you would go *straight home*.' Sir Alan leaned over Andrew now, his face close enough for Andrew to smell his coffee breath. 'It's unfortunate that you feel you need to lie to me. But that's how it is sometimes. Boys don't respect a master's authority. After all, we're just the staff to them. One might, as a master, feel inclined to phone home, to parents, to procure the extra backing required. But even that is a slippery slope. Boys can be so spoiled, you see, the parents so deluded as to their character, that the power balance can go the other way. Then it's two against one.'

Andrew had a hard time imagining his father taking sides against Sir Alan; Sir Alan seemed like his father's kind of guy.

'I've made that mistake, and I won't again,' Sir Alan was saying. 'I prefer a different approach. Serve a letter of warning first. That the boy in question is a proven *liar*, and as such, that boy faces expulsion from the school. Then wait for the parents to become engaged. A blot on their dear boy's record! Oh, they get to the heart of the matter very quickly, and I either have a problem student to worry about, or I don't.' Sir Alan sneered at Andrew triumphantly. 'I will send that letter to your parents, Andrew. I will have you thrown out of this school.'

'For what?' Andrew replied, frustration and anger growing.

'For lying,' he thundered. 'For destroying school property. For ruining morale. For frightening the youngest boys. This isn't America, where students sue their schools. I have maximum discretion.'

Andrew saw himself getting off the plane at JFK.

You make this good or we're through with you

'But it needn't come to that, Andrew,' sighed Sir Alan. He moved to Andrew's side and squeezed his thick frame into one of the little desks next to him. 'It needn't. I become passionate defending my school because I feel a need to preserve it, improve it. We need the best people possible taking care of the boys. Fawkes,' he added, 'is just wrong for the role. That's all. I don't want to ruin his career. He's already more successful than I'll ever be, as a poet,' he said, sounding disingenuous. 'But a house-master? I think not.' Sir Alan put a hand on Andrew's arm. Andrew stared at it. 'All you have to do' – *squeeze, squeeze*; Sir Alan had a mighty grip – 'is tell me the accurate truth of what happened in the Lot with the ghost.' Three more squeezes. Then he leaned over and tilted his head so he could look Andrew straight in the eye.

'Is Mr Fawkes in trouble, sir?'

'Possibly. I must find out the truth.'

'He's a good housemaster,' said Andrew, not quite believing it. 'For people like me, anyway.'

'What kind of people is that?'

'I don't know. Artistic.'

'Wasn't Theo Ryder artistic enough, then?' Sir Alan said heavily.

Andrew suddenly had had enough.

'I've got to go, sir.' He extricated himself from the desk. 'I'll try and remember more. I really will. What's the best way to be in touch with you? Just come by Headland? I'll be sure to. Thank you, sir.'

Andrew fled the Leaf Schools before Sir Alan could stop him, and trudged up the Hill in a blindness of worry and isolation.

'ARE THE WEALTH-CREATING powers of a truly global economy now proven?' The upper-class English accent, rich and arrogant, plucked the words like the strings of a lugubrious harp. 'Or do we merely live in a borderless world that allows contagion of all varieties to spread further, faster? The meltdown of the global banking system. Civil war and cross-border conflict. Pandemics such as AIDS, SARS, bird flu, swine flu. Or the more serious threats to civilization.' The voice paused for effect: '*Pop Idol* and its many spin-offs.'

An appreciative chuckle passed around the room.

They sat around the oval table. Twelve boys, men and women. The boys – Sixth Formers – wore their tailcoats; the men and women wore suits. In the centre of the table – an old one, its wood softened by decades of use – stood two candelabra. The flames stood tall. The faces around the table glowed a pinkish orange in that light, and their dark clothing seemed to thicken to a chiaroscuro black, as if the group had been gathered, not for a group photo, but for a group etching – and they quivered there together under a sketching hand and the flickering light. Before each member sat a silver goblet that had been filled with Madeira. At the head of the table, a boy with long limbs and fingers and deliberate movements that gave him the air of being a giant praying mantis with a forelock read from a typed essay, flipping pages as he went.

Andrew found the candles mesmerizing. It was the same room he and Persephone had wandered into several nights before. But the room had been transformed, filled now with purpose, as if these figures sitting here were part of a brotherhood, a cabal, lined up against the darkness that lay below them in the wild green of Harrow Park, and they were the tenders of the light. A Madeira bottle, crusty and green, had been set on a silver tray to the side. Even the quotation on the board had changed:

NOCTES ATQUE DIES PATET ATRI IANUA DITIS

Essay Club is by invitation only, Fawkes had explained, as they had walked together from the Lot, Fawkes in a suit, Andrew in his tailcoat; *for the more serious scholars. Members write essays, one hour in length, thoroughly researched. Judy's the staff adviser*, Fawkes added. *She told me to invite you. You must have impressed her when you came to see her at the library.* Andrew recognized the students from his classes: Scroop Wallace from Ancient History (with spiky hair and an eccentric's hunch); Domenick Beekin from English (skinny-necked and tiny-headed, a human heron); Nick Antoniades, also from English (swarthy, compact and confident); and Rupert Askew, the boy currently reading his essay in a plummy accent.

The adults included Sir Alan Vine, leaning his elbows on the table with his bald head held low, with his spectacles and his flared nostrils, like a rugby player preparing to charge. Piers

Fawkes sat two spots from Andrew. He had seemed jumpy on the walk over; his face was pale, his upper lip damp. He had waved off the Madeira when they first sat down, but doing so seemed to have deprived Fawkes of the benefit of the force of gravity. He clutched the table as if he might be sucked unexpectedly into the sky; he kept noisily unwrapping butterscotch sweets and rolling them against his teeth. Sir Alan stared at him ferociously for this. *Do you mind, Piers?* he had snapped, at last. Mr Toombs, the Classics beak – thin, kindly, nervous, sibilant – in whose schoolroom they all were, sat smiling, listening to Rupert Askew talk about mutating avian flu viruses. And next to the speaker sat Dr Kahn. With Mr Toombs, she was the host of Essay Club. She too had been attentive to Askew for a time. But now Andrew noticed her staring at him, peering as if she saw something she did not like.

MR TOOMBS PULLED the heavy door closed, chattering amiably. *Electrifying essay tonight, don't you think, Piers? All those horrible symptoms. And the section on the Plague – something for you, Judy. Bit of history.* Mr Toombs kept up his patter until he realized the three of them were hanging back and waiting for him to leave; so he said his goodbyes and they stood facing each other in the gloom as he walked away. Mr Toombs's classroom sat at the bottom of a long stair to the High Street, its back to the silent, wooded park.

'What did you think, Andrew?' Dr Kahn asked him.

'I loved it,' he said, with unaccustomed enthusiasm.

'Did you?' She smiled. 'Good. I love it too.'

'I think we should start serving Sprite at Essay Club,' grumbled Fawkes, looking drained.

'It would corrode the goblets,' she answered coolly. 'Follow me, please.'

She led them into the shadow between the chapel's grey flanks and the Classics Schools. 'No one will overhear us here,' she said, her voice lowered. 'There's something I wanted to say to you both.'

They waited.

'I believe you,' she announced.

'About what?' Andrew said.

'Fawkes has been telling me about your ghost. About how you think it's Byron's friend John Harness. I have been curious, of course. But neither convinced or unconvinced. Then two things happened. First, I had an odd experience in my own home. I thought I *felt* someone. A threatening someone. Not an actual person, mind you, but a presence. The feeling came just at the moment Piers asked me to help investigate the underground room in the Lot. Curious timing, don't you think? It was almost as if this ... someone ... *knew* you were asking me to help research John Harness, and then came after me. Made a show of strength. I call that intimidation,' she said. 'And then the second was tonight, at Essay Club.'

'I didn't notice anything,' said Andrew, puzzled.

'But I did. You,' she said. 'You are the very portrait of Byron.'

'You're the last to notice,' said Fawkes.

'Sitting there, in the candlelight. In your tailcoat. We could have been transported in time. And it dawned on me. This may be precisely what is happening to your spirit. He sees you. Then thinks he's somewhere else. Or some-*when* else, if you like – with Byron. It all points to John Harness as your ghost.'

'You've had the epiphany,' said Fawkes.

'I have. But I don't like it. The presence I felt was menacing.'

Andrew felt a rush of hope. 'Then maybe you can help me,' he said. He turned to Fawkes. 'Remember that ... vision ... that I told you about? Where I'm in a dormitory, like the Lot, but with sconces, and carpets, and I'm chasing this figure?'

'Yes, of course.'

'When I first had it, it felt like something terrible *was going* to happen. But I had the dream again. Two days ago, after we found the cistern. And something terrible *did* happen, in the dream. I saw a murder.'

'Then, or now?' demanded Fawkes, anxiously.

'Then,' Andrew reassured him. 'Except. Um. I was the one committing the murder. I suffocated someone.'

'*You* suffocated someone?' said Dr Kahn, surprised.

'*Harness* did. I saw it from his point of view, if that makes sense. Like he was ... showing me his home movies. I kind of wish we hadn't opened up that room,' Andrew said to Fawkes. 'It's like we encouraged him.'

'He's trying to tell you something,' mused Kahn.

'What?'

Fawkes crossed his arms. 'If he's showing you a murder ... that's a fairly clear message. He committed a murder. Guilty conscience.'

'I suspect it's rather more than that. Our ghost may be dangerous in the present,' said Dr Kahn.

'*May* be? Didn't Andrew tell you? He saw the ghost smothering Theo Ryder on Church Hill.'

Dr Kahn looked at Andrew intently. 'No. I missed that part somehow.' She frowned. 'And here is Andrew, all costumed as Lord Byron, dangling as bait, for a murderer? It's time to get Andrew out of danger. Taken out of school, perhaps. Call his parents.'

'That would be the same as getting me thrown out,' Andrew objected.

'Good. I'd rather see you sent down than strangled.'

'If we're wrong,' Fawkes said, 'we would have ruined Andrew's school career for nothing. For a will-o'-the-wisp.'

'Then why don't you suggest something,' she said sharply.

'It's a ghost. How do you get rid of a ghost?'

'Hold an exorcism,' offered Andrew.

'What is it they do, with the mediums?' Dr Kahn jumped

in. 'You know, holding hands around the table with the velvet tablecloth and the candles?'

'Séance?' Andrew said.

'Precisely.' Dr Kahn nodded. 'Summon the spirit, and talk with him. Ask him what he wants.'

'That's obvious,' said Fawkes. 'He wants Andrew.'

'Then what about the murder?' Andrew countered.

'There's no record of John Harness committing murder,' Fawkes said.

'But I know he did.'

'All right. Why don't we find out for certain?' Fawkes suggested.

'You mean do more research on Harness,' clarified Dr Kahn.

'Everything's research to you,' groused Fawkes. 'No, I mean a bloody *tribunal*. Look, what is a ghost? A dead person that's still meddling with the living. Why? They can't let something go. In John Harness's case, there was a murder. He can't get over it, he can't get over Byron. So, we find out everything there is to know about the murder, and about Harness's relationship with Byron.'

'I still call that research,' she quipped.

'*Then* we have a séance. We summon Harness, and we shove it in his face. We say, we know who you killed, and why; but it's over. The ghost realizes he's hanging around the wrong century, and off he goes into the light. End of story.'

'Find out who Harness killed, and why,' said Dr Kahn. 'Not bad, Piers.'

He made a mocking curtsey. 'May I have a cigarette now?' He fired up his lighter vengefully; his edge had increased since forgoing the Madeira.

'An especially good plan, since we have a resident Byron expert.'

'Who?'

'Who? You.'

'Oh no. I'm being monitored,' Fawkes said quickly. 'I nearly got sacked over knocking down the walls in the basement. I can't go about with an ectometer, scanning for murder scenes and Lord Byron's lost socks. I won't last a day.'

'I can research it for Essay Club,' proposed Andrew.

They both turned to him.

'That's clever,' said Dr Kahn. 'You can disguise the fact that we're researching the ghost by calling it an essay; or even background for your role in the play. You're at the centre of this, Andrew. You're the closest to it. It's right for you to lead the charge. I will assist you. When you feel you've gathered enough information, we'll hold the séance. Or better yet – we'll hold Essay Club. We have the candles, the dark room and the circle of people already.'

'Do we have to hold hands?' sneered Fawkes.

'We'll confront the ghost with who he is, and what he's done,' said Dr Kahn. 'And then we'll send him on his way.'

'An airtight plan,' said Fawkes.

'Is it?' she said, still thinking. 'I just wonder if we'll be fast enough. It seems like the ghost is becoming stronger. What was the word you used, Andrew?'

'*Encouraged*.'

Fawkes added: 'Maybe he senses he has our attention.'

'Getting the attention of a murderer. Not advisable,' said Dr Kahn. She pondered for a moment, then perked up. 'We can do both. The séance *and* the exorcism. How does one perform an exorcism?'

'I rather think you need a priest,' Fawkes replied.

'Go to Reverend Peter, then.'

'Me? I just said I was on probation for corrupting the young.'

'Well, Andrew and I can't invite a priest into the Lot for a bloody exorcism.'

'Whereas housemasters do it all the time.'

'If anyone can, you can.'

'We're talking about getting sacked on the spot!'

'We're *talking* about Andrew's safety.'

Fawkes churned. He needed more information about Harness to make his play publishable. If a priest were able to put a stop to the ghostly activity immediately ... then he would be left with no evidence, no story. He was about to object again. Then he caught Andrew's grey eyes on him again, waiting for an answer.

'All right,' Fawkes said, petulantly. He hungrily sucked on his cigarette. 'I picked the wrong week to stop drinking.'

'*What are you three doing in the dark?*' A voice lashed at them like a whip. 'Conspiring?'

They stood squinting in the gloom between the chapel and Classics Schools. Below them, on the gravel where they had emerged from Essay Club, stood a figure in silhouette.

'Is that Sir Alan?' Dr Kahn called, tugging Fawkes's sleeve.

'It is indeed. Who's there, smoking? Ah, it's you, Piers Fawkes, in the flesh. I was going to hand out a skew, Piers. I think I might after all.' He snickered. 'Are we still on for tomorrow morning? Nine sharp? Not too early for you?'

'I'm up at five every day, writing,' puffed Fawkes.

'Are you? How virtuous. Inspired by Dionysus?'

'Apollo,' Fawkes returned.

Sir Alan charged into their midst, rather too close in the dark, trying to peer into their faces. He turned his sharp nose and glasses, reflecting the faraway light, on Dr Kahn. 'What did you think of the essay, Judy? Up to snuff?'

'A bit vague in its thesis, I suppose, but overall well done,' she said.

'They used to be an hour,' Sir Alan snorted. His accent rendered it *an ahhh*. 'Askew eked out thirty-five minutes. Thirty-five minutes! I timed it on my watch. Maybe nineteen sides? Twenty? Hmph. So much for the giants of old.' He turned to Fawkes and did not conceal a sniff in his direction. 'You didn't drink tonight, Fawkes,' he observed. 'Gone cold turkey?'

'I have, as a matter of fact,' Fawkes muttered in reply.

Sir Alan's eyebrows rose in surprise. 'We'll make a man of you yet.' He then turned his attention to the American. 'So you're in Essay Club now, eh?'

'Yes,' Andrew said coldly.

'Your doing?' Sir Alan demanded of Dr Kahn. She nodded. He looked Andrew up and down disapprovingly. 'Think you'll manage to write anything, Mr Taylor?'

'We were just discussing that,' said Dr Kahn.

'Really? Topic?'

'Still developing,' she said hastily, before Andrew could open his mouth.

'Then I'll wait with the other commoners, shall I? All right, then, I'll leave you to your topic development. Don't know why you're doing it here. If you haven't noticed, it's night-time,' he said, pointing at the sky. 'I think I'll go home and have a whisky. How about that, Piers?' He grinned. 'Nine sharp?'

'Nine sharp,' Fawkes repeated.

Sir Alan bustled up the remaining stairs, robes billowing, and disappeared around the corner.

'Do you think he was listening?' Dr Kahn asked.

'I meant to tell you,' hissed Andrew. 'He kept me after class yesterday and started grilling me about you, Piers. He threatened to call my parents if I didn't rat you out.'

'What did you say?' asked Fawkes in alarm.

'Nothing.'

'Nothing?'

'I walked out on him.'

Fawkes laughed, delighted. 'Did you really? Good man!'

'I'm no sell-out,' said Andrew with a grin.

Fawkes felt his stomach sink. *Selling out. That's exactly what you're doing to the boy. Making him 'bait', to use Judy's word.* He stared into that handsome face, glowing in the dark, the grey eyes glinting; the expression cockeyed; the smile only half there; the other half held back, protectively, in that fragile, adolescent way. He had seen Andrew Taylor smile maybe a half-dozen times, in all their meetings and rehearsals; and here was one, bestowed on him, and not just a smile, but a kind of supplication. *We're friends, aren't we? You approve of me, don't you?* That puppy-dog neediness. The orphan's longing. *And you're using him*, he scolded himself. *God, you're a shit, Fawkes.*

WHEN THEY REACHED the Lot, Andrew said goodbye to Fawkes and waited for him to enter his apartment.

I still call that research.

When you feel you've gathered enough evidence, we'll hold the séance.

He stood in the drive, thinking.

The handkerchief.

The handkerchief had been a piece of solid evidence. Maybe even a clue. And he'd left it down in the cistern room, mainly out of the shock of seeing it. What had happened to it? Had Reg thrown it away? Or could it have been brushed into the hole?

Minutes later Andrew was in his room, pulling on khakis and a pair of sneakers.

'Roddy,' he called through the wall. 'Hey, Roddy!'

A moment later, roused, his stocky neighbour poked his head in. Roddy wore a bulky black terry cloth robe and flip-flops.

'Hey yourself. Some of us are doing work here, you know. Some of us have A-Levels.'

'Oh, bullshit. I'll bet you five quid you were eating toast and reading comics.'

Roddy guffawed. 'All right, you got me there. But I was eating biscuits. I'll give you two-fifty.'

'Can I borrow your torch?'

'What? Why?' said Roddy.

'I want to see what's down there.'

'Where?'

'In that cistern, in the basement.'

'That cistern you found, with our inebriated housemaster? No thank you. My dad found one of those, in a terraced house he renovated in London. He said it was an accident waiting to happen. A complete liability. He had the whole thing filled with cement.'

'Well,' Andrew said, tying his sneaker. 'You can come and protect me if you want.'

THEY CLATTERED DOWN the stairs, Roddy still in his robe (but with a tracksuit bottom underneath), Andrew leading the way with Roddy's torch (just one sample of the varied equipment Roddy kept in his cupboard – extra toilet paper, bread knife, heating coils, salt and pepper, first aid kit, and, acquired from some London military paraphernalia shop, a gas mask). Andrew clicked the overhead lights on when they reached the basement. Roddy hastily turned them off again.

'Matron will be on us in no time,' he hissed. 'She can see the stairwells from her apartment. Let's hope you haven't woken her.'

Andrew checked his watch. It was just after ten.

They approached the still-unpatched hole in semi-darkness, their way illuminated only by the glowing red EXIT sign. The yellow caution tape left by the workers sagged.

'You're not going down there,' Roddy said in disbelief.

Andrew checked to make sure the ladder was still there, and hesitated. 'I saw the ghost here. I *felt* it here. From the very beginning.'

Roddy gaped. 'You mean that's true? You believe all that? About the Lot ghost?'

Andrew stared back at him.

'My God, you *are* mad. And here I've been defending you! Telling everyone you're misunderstood.'

'I think it wants me to find something.'

'It? You mean the ghost? You're communicating with it now, are you?'

'Stay here, then. I don't give a shit. I'm going down there anyway.'

Roddy grew nervous. He had few opportunities for fellowship and adventure, and seemed loath to miss out on this one.

'Now hold on. You've got my torch.' He retied the belt of his robe. 'All right. I'll come. But only because you need someone sensible with you. If they fished you out of there dead, what would I tell Matron?'

ANDREW DESCENDED WHILE Roddy held the light. With considerable cursing, Roddy followed, then swung the torch around them. 'God, it is grotesque down here.'

Reg had cleared out the boards and plaster. It had become the cramped cistern room of Andrew's dream again: a tiny, circular bunker lined with hewn stones and filled with a nose-chilling damp and the drip of trickling water.

Drawn by the same instinct, they both moved towards the cistern mouth. Andrew got on his knees and peered over. He took the torch from Roddy and pointed it down. The stone cistern walls were caked brown with decades of cobwebs, fungus, dirt and rust. They fell some ten feet. The bottom shimmered. A layer of water.

'Gutter water gathers there,' observed Roddy. 'Just like the one my dad found. Still has a seal. They don't do construction like this any more, I can tell you.'

Andrew leaned over the edge.

'Careful.'

He leaned farther. His waist now balanced on the lip of the cistern.

'For God's sake!' Roddy put a balancing hand on Andrew's hamstring. 'Do you have a death wish?'

'See that?' Andrew pointed with the torch.

'I'm keeping you from falling in; of course I can't see.'

Andrew scrambled back. He handed the torch to Roddy. 'Right-hand side.'

Roddy leaned over to take a look.

'Is that a handkerchief?' said Andrew.

'Handkerchief?' scoffed Roddy. 'What are you on about? That's metal.'

Andrew squinted and saw that Roddy was right.

'I'm going to get it,' he said.

AFTER THE EXPECTED bickering and protests, Roddy the mechanic, gear collector and petty-problem solver became intrigued by the puzzle and began to help. How to get a hundred-and-sixty-pound male down a ten-foot hole and back again in one piece, without rousting Matron. They found a nylon rope tied to the ladder (for pulling up tools) and estimated it could hold Andrew's weight, then discovered that when holding the rope – hands wrapped with his T-shirt against rope burn – Andrew could tie the cord around his waist and under his buttocks in a makeshift saddle and rappel down the cistern without injury. *Worst case, you'll hand the ladder down and I'll get up that way*, Andrew reasoned. So he rolled up his khakis and started down. Roddy, the heavier one, braced himself against the stone cistern lip and lowered the cord for Andrew. With some grunting, Andrew inched his way down.

'How deep is the water?' said Roddy, aiming the light down.

'Should I step in it and see?' Andrew called up.

'Shhh,' said Roddy in a stage whisper. 'Don't shout. Matron.'

'Are you kidding? We're practically underground. No one can hear us now.'

'Watch for nails. My dad stuck his foot through, once. Spent a night in hospital.'

Andrew gave a sudden squeak.

'What is it?' called Roddy.

'Cold!'

'Go *on* – squealing like a girl!'

'I'm going to step in.'

A few moments later: 'It's shallow. Less than a foot. Holy shit, is that cold.'

'Careful.'

'Oooooh.' The line stretched. Then: 'Got it.'

'Any nails?'

'It's a tin box. I can't climb with it. Pull it up first, then I'll come next.'

RODDY PEERED OVER and aimed the light while Andrew tied the rope around the box. Roddy pulled it up. For a moment, Roddy, at the top, beamed the torch on the box as he untied it and examined it. During those two minutes, Andrew stood at the bottom of the cistern, alone, in near total darkness, shirtless and shivering, standing in eight inches of freezing water. His feet went numb and he quietly fought a growing panic. What if Roddy, for whatever reason, left him? Or had an accident up there?

'Roddy?' he called, anxiously.

'It's an antique. This must have been there for bloody ever. I mean a *long time*.'

'Roddy.'

'What do you think is in it?'

'*Roddy, throw down the rope!*'

'All right, all right. There you go again, totally spastic.'

*

TEN MINUTES LATER, wrists and biceps exhausted, Andrew stood on the stone floor again, puffing and shivering next to Roddy.

'Look at the craftsmanship,' Roddy said, turning over the tin in his hand and admiring it while Andrew held the light. The box curved like a violin. 'No rust. Must have been submerged all this time.'

The lid bore a painting of a coach and horses trotting down a country road, with two men in tails and a dog looking on, woods in the background. The sides bore bright stripes – burgundy and gold – and a decorative pattern.

'Anything inside?'

Roddy shook it. 'Not gold anyway.' A light bump came from within. Roddy wedged his fingers under the edge. 'Hinges still work!' he marvelled. 'Made in England. That's what it is. Nowadays it'd be made in bloody China, out of toxic waste. Melt in your hands just before it melted you.' He pulled the lid off and retrieved a narrow bundle.

He put it under the torch beam.

'Paper,' he declared.

Andrew wiped the grit from his hands. 'Let me see.'

Roddy handed over a small rectangle of a thick-edged paper, tied with ribbon.

'There's writing on it,' Andrew said. He tilted his head. The writing went in two directions – crossways, and up and down. The lines were bunched closely together. But they made little sense. The handwriting stretched and curled in childish script, and one line did not seem to lead to the next.

'Is this what you were looking for?' asked Roddy.

Andrew stared at the bundle in his hand. Scanned the lines at the top of the page.

When you quit me you think forever but this is not so – I follow you two cups of blood at least caught in my hand

He tried to make sense of them, and some others, but gave

up. He shook his head. 'I'm not sure.' He tugged at the corners. The paper had become gluey with age, and the leaves stuck together.

'Don't rip it, man,' scolded Roddy. 'You'll need an expert to pull those apart. Someone who knows about old documents. Know anyone like that?'

13

Awesome Aunty

REVEREND PETER WATCHED Piers Fawkes with pity. Most of the beaks and administrators at the school had at first been in awe of Fawkes, and the chaplain had been no exception. Fawkes had been a household name in England for a time. He had been interviewed on television. His image appeared in magazines. Reverend Peter remembered a particular cover photo, in fact: a black-and-white portrait of Fawkes perched on a stool in a sweater, holding a burning fag between dirty fingernails, looking greasy and very debauched with his heavy-lidded eyes. But that was years ago. Increasingly, people at the school (those who chattered about such things) wondered what Fawkes was doing there. He was not quite the career housemaster type. Not quite a visiting dignitary or poet-at-large. *Rather confused* is how someone had described Fawkes to the Reverend Peter. Now that confusion seemed to have spilled over into something terribly wrong. Perhaps it was the boy dying, Reverend Peter mused; yes, that must be it. Poor man – he got more than he bargained for, in this job. Fawkes was now squirming on the Reverend Peter's sofa as if something were eating him from within. His skin was pale. He was sweating – there were big rings under each armpit, coming *through* his jacket, and dampness rimmed his hairline. But with English and clerical reserve, Reverend Peter chose to ignore all this; let the man bring it up, if he liked.

'How about a sherry, Piers?' he said brightly.

At this, Fawkes started a fit of violent and prolonged coughing.

'Are you all right?' asked Reverend Peter.

Fawkes waved him off. 'Fine, fine,' he croaked. 'I'll be fine.'

Reverend Peter's smile was rather thinner than before. 'Then how can I help you?'

'I, uh ...' began Fawkes. 'Do you know how to, uh ...' He resumed coughing.

'Water?' offered Reverend Peter. He stood and poured him a glass. Fawkes sucked it down.

'Something in my throat.'

'Yes.'

Reverend Peter waited. At last Fawkes was able to blurt it out. 'Do you know how to get rid of a ghost?'

The priest's smile collapsed. 'I'm sorry. Did you say get rid of a ghost?'

'Yes,' Fawkes said, as casually as he could. 'Is there a prayer? Some kind of ceremony?'

'Do you mind sharing with me why you're asking, Piers?'

Fawkes gave a rambling and vague answer ... about the Lot ghost, a legend in the house, a tradition ... but with Theo Ryder's death, he said, there was a resurgence of interest ... something to blame; you know; explain the unexplainable.

'You're saying,' Reverend Peter said, carefully, 'the boys are blaming the ghost for Theo Ryder's death?'

'Some boys,' clarified Fawkes.

'And you thought having a prayer, or exorcism, would calm them down?'

Fawkes nodded. 'I must ask you to keep this is in priestly confidence,' he quickly added. 'The head man thinks I'm a bit crazy on this point.'

'Hm,' said Reverend Peter, regarding his sweaty guest. 'Yes. Well, that's extraordinary. I've heard about the Lot ghost, of course. But I wouldn't want to be seen to lend credence to a ...

a superstition. Do you understand?' He paused. 'And you, Piers? You think there's something to it?'

At last Fawkes stopped writhing. 'I think,' he said slowly, 'I need to take every precaution. And I think my duty is to the boys.'

Reverend Peter hesitated. 'Have you ... *seen* something?' Perhaps this would explain the poet's strange demeanour. Perhaps he was in terror.

'Seen something? Not personally,' Fawkes said, dabbing his forehead. 'But some boys in the house have. One boy in particular, I should say.'

'And you believe him?'

'I do.'

'Hm. Extraordinary.' Reverend Peter chewed his lip. He was piecing together what Fawkes had told him so far. 'I'm sorry. Forgive me if I seem a bit thick about this.' He hesitated. 'But if the boys believe the ghost is responsible for what's been happening, for Theo Ryder dying ... and you *believe* them ... then *you* believe a ghost is responsible for Theo Ryder dying.' He watched Fawkes carefully. 'Do I have that right?'

'Now,' said Fawkes with a small smile, 'if I were to say yes to that, I would have to be mad, wouldn't I?'

'Quite,' Reverend Peter replied, but his tone was even, and he used the word the way only the British can: to mean *maybe* or *I'm withholding judgement*. He locked eyes with Fawkes, feeling they had reached the crux of their interview.

'And if I were mad, while in charge of the safety of sixty ... fifty-nine boys, I would be in the wrong spot, wouldn't I? The headmaster would be correct to relieve me of my duties.'

Reverend Peter said nothing.

'Yet at the same time,' Fawkes continued, 'if I truly believed that something supernatural, and harmful, were afoot, *and I did nothing*,' he said, measuring his words, 'then I would be responsible for whatever happened.' The two men regarded each other. 'Am I making myself clear?'

'Very much so.' Reverend Peter was pensive. 'If I were to say a prayer in the Lot,' he said, 'just as a precaution – as a way of providing support for the boys in a troubling time – that might do the trick?'

'That's precisely what we need,' Fawkes said.

Reverend Peter beamed, clear at last.

Fawkes had always liked the Reverend Peter. Youthful, thin, a runner; cheerful and social, but never one of those simpering clerics who sought to climb the status ladder. He would think better of the priesthood and their spells if this all worked out.

'One more thing,' said Fawkes.

'Oh dear. Go ahead.'

'Rather tricky. Ah,' Fawkes mumbled. 'Can you wait a bit?'

'Sorry?'

'Can you wait? Say, a week or two?'

'It will take me at least that long to prepare. This is what I would call specialist work. The Church of England *does* do it, but not without some enquiry. Rather like getting an estimate from a contractor.' Reverend Peter smiled, trying to be disarming. 'To make sure you're getting the right solution to the right problem. Do you feel the ghost is dangerous, then?'

'Very much so.'

'Then I'll look into it immediately.'

'A week or two would be marvellous,' said Fawkes. 'I'm grateful for your discretion.'

'Not at all,' said Reverend Peter.

He saw his guest out. As he opened the door onto the High Street, he paused. The two of them stood facing each other with the chilly breeze blowing between them.

'If you think it's dangerous,' the priest said, with suddenly clarity, 'why do you want me to wait a week or two? That seems rather a contradiction.'

'I want to study it first,' said Fawkes. The priest's eyes widened. 'I think the ghost has to do with Lord Byron. If you get rid of it too quickly, I won't get any original material for my play.'

'Surely you're joking.'

Fawkes said nothing. Reverend Peter regarded him coldly.

'Your priorities are all wrong, Piers.'

'I know.' The poet shrank into his jacket, against the breeze. 'I'm used to it.'

DR KAHN TOOK the bundle from him suspiciously, as though Andrew had just handed her a paper bag full of pound notes.

'I wrapped the letters, so the oil from my fingers wouldn't get on them,' he said.

'Well done,' she said evenly. 'And you found these where?'

'In that cistern. Underwater, in a tin box.'

'May I see the box?'

He produced it from his backpack. 'Is this a special box for letters or something?' he asked.

Dr Kahn's office was a brightly lit rectangular box set behind the elongated eastern windows of the library, with a close-up view of the stones of the chapel. A cross between an administrator's command centre, a researcher's lair and a storeroom, the office was lined from floor to ceiling with hanging shelves, each neatly sectioned and labelled, carrying books, files or folders. She presided from a desk – a wooden monstrosity, some six feet wide, sipping tea from a gnarled home-made clay mug painted with the words AWESOME AUNTY.

'Letters?' She turned over the tin box in her hands, smiling. 'It's for biscuits. Lucky for us. It's airtight for the contents to keep. It can hardly have been the preferred solution. Your letter-writer must have been in a hurry. Or perhaps I should say, your letter receiver.'

'Why do you say that?'

'You tell me,' she commanded, in that iron-firm way of hers.

She snipped open the twine around the letters with a pair of scissors. Andrew winced. He had been treating every part of the discovered letters gingerly, including the twine.

'Because . . . the person receiving the letters would be the one to have them, and therefore the one to store them.'

'Just so,' she murmured, and reached into her drawer for a small box. From this she retrieved two wads of white material and pulled them over her hands – latex gloves. She cleared a wide patch on her desk.

'Why does the writing go like that?' he asked. 'Crossways? And in bunched-up lines?'

'Writing paper in the nineteenth century was harder to come by than today. Letter writers would write horizontally, as we do; then when they ran out of paper, they would write vertically, over top.' She traced the writing going left to right with her finger, then the lines of script going from the bottom of the page to the top. 'This writer had a lot to say, but little paper; and seems to have added a second set of horizontal lines. I've never seen this before.' She frowned. 'Maddening to read.'

'Is there a signature?'

She flipped. 'No.'

'Are they from Byron?'

'Unlikely. Barons tend not to skimp on stationery, especially when they're also poets.'

'Are they from Harness?'

'Why would you think that?'

'Why else would he lead me to that room?' Andrew asked.

'I do not like John Harness,' grunted Dr Kahn. 'And I do not trust him.'

'I know. But it's a clue.'

'A clue to a murder, from a murderer,' she said. 'Why would he show us? Is he trying to reveal himself? Trying to come clean?'

'Maybe he wants us to solve it.'

'If John Harness committed the murder, it is unlikely that he requires it to be solved,' she observed tartly. Andrew shrugged. '*Two cups of blood at least caught in my hand*,' she read from the parchment through her reading glasses. 'I will box these up and send them to a friend. Miss Lena Rasmussen. A friend of my niece's; an archivist. An archivist because of me, in fact.'

'You make it look cool.'

Dr Kahn made a face. 'She's at the Wren Library, a library for rare manuscripts of great distinction, at Trinity College, Cambridge. Byron's alma mater. They occasionally take a break from worshipping Sir Isaac Newton, long enough to pay attention to Byron. I think she'll know what to make of this.'

'Thanks,' said Andrew, as enthusiastically as he could muster. He felt anxiety allowing these letters to go to someone else. 'Will she . . . will she be able to get to them in time?'

'If I ask her, Lena will do it right away.'

'How long will it take to get them to her?'

'I will send them overnight. All right, Andrew?'

'Yes, thanks.'

'Now, I have something for you,' she said. She nodded to a stack of battered and age-worn hardcovers at the corner of her desk. 'They are the best sources I can find on Byron. I was going to allow you take them to the Lot, as a special favour – since we do not lend.' Andrew smiled at the imperious plural Dr Kahn employed whenever the subject was the Vaughan Library. 'But upon reflection I would like you to read them here.'

Andrew slumped. 'Why? You don't trust me?'

She peered at him. 'The atmosphere of the Vaughan seems to be healthier than that of the Lot, just now,' she said. 'I would rather keep you with me. And away from *him*.'

ANDREW RETURNED TO the Vaughan every evening he did not have a rehearsal. On the first night, he found that Dr Kahn had cleared a carrel for him in the corner of her voluminous office, with his books stacked neatly on its shelf. On the second night she handed him a large, white I HEART LONDON mug, steaming and practically sizzling with sugar, along with a bundle of biscuits in a napkin. *You look pale*, Dr Kahn explained. *I cannot cook, but I can brew.* On the third night, there were more books waiting for him, and he had the office to himself (Dr Kahn was attending an event in London). He flipped pages but was distracted by his mobile phone vibrating incessantly.

Have permissn frm housemaster aka Dad to go London Sat.

Andrew texted back.

I have rehearsal! Can we go at 1?

A long pause. Andrew examined the yellowed gluey pages. He suspected Persephone did not like his last message and was either intentionally stringing him along or was giving up on the idea of their getaway entirely. He became panicky.

I can try and get out of it

he offered, at last.

Which of your girlfiends, she typed – he wondered if the typo was intentional – *is it with?*

Not sure. Rebecca?

The phone then went silent for twenty minutes. Andrew strained to concentrate.

Maybe you'll want to go to London with her

No no! I've been waiting . . .

To what?

He grabbed the volume of Byron poetry on the shelf above his head and flipped to find a page he'd marked.

. . . for your nameless grace which waves in every raven tress

he typed.

He waited a few seconds.

That's all right then,

came the response.

He smiled.

Then another:

Quote Byron to me and I will definitely fuck you.

Whoa. That was *out there*. He started to laugh. But he quickly stopped, as something caught his attention. It was as if Dr Kahn's office were slowly filling with an invisible gas, starting from the floor and rising quickly, until it reached the ceiling. A presence, thick and repressive, stole the thrill from Andrew's throat. Those subtle, tiny noises that arise from a human being when they stand near by – the rustle of clothing, the creak of a floorboard – came whispering through the thickened atmosphere. And yet it made no move to reveal itself. Just throbbed with a desire to watch. Predatory. Silent. Then, bit by bit, came the breathing. It started softly, as if being hidden by an arm over the mouth, or a handkerchief. But it came. And finally it emerged fully into Andrew's hearing. As if, once observed, the watcher stopped bothering to hide itself.

Andrew gripped the phone in his hand until his knuckles went white. He whirled around with a gasp. The phone flew from his hand and hit the floor with a clatter.

An empty office stared back at him. Dr Kahn's papers throbbed under the fluorescent lights as if they had been supercharged with a light of their own. Then they subsided, that sickly, oppressive gas draining from the room like it was being sucked away through a straw.

Andrew cautiously picked up the phone. Four texts pulsed there, waiting for him.

U still there?

I frightened u off didn't i.
Oh damn it. I was only joking.
Thanks thanks awfully

He thumbed clumsily into the phone.

I'm here, he explained. *Someone came in, that's all.*

THAT THURSDAY, HE found Dr Kahn waiting for him behind her desk. Her eyes were small, round and black-brown, peering at him over her reading glasses as though they could bore through steel plate.

'I've brought you the best background books in the collection,' she declared, not waiting for him to settle in. 'Now tell me what you've made of them.'

Andrew felt a nervous tremor. He placed his hand on one of the books – the shaggy blue one, *Byron at Harrow*, by Patrick Burke, published in 1908 – as if it might transmit the knowledge by electric circuit.

Byron and Harness were two years apart at Harrow, Andrew began.

Byron cut an angry and exotic figure at Harrow. His club foot disfigured him; the metal contraption doctors gave him to correct it embarrassed him; and his eagerness to prove himself through fist fights and show-offy displays in class drew attention to him. He had a chip on his shoulder because, despite his title and his wealth, Byron had come into his inheritance unexpectedly, at age ten, and had had a troubled childhood. His father was a scoundrel, philanderer and drunk – he had earned the nickname *Mad Jack* – and had abandoned Byron and his mother not long after marrying her for her money. Mrs Gordon, his mother, was obese and – at least by her son's account – something of a maniac, given to tantrums and harangues. So while being *George Gordon, Baron Byron* made Byron one of the loftier students at Harrow from a social perspective, his clanging foot and uncertain upbringing gave him a lot to prove.

'Not bad, as far as it goes,' said Dr Kahn. 'Nothing new, of course. Go on.'

Andrew proceeded.

Byron was also something of a sexual prodigy. His physical beauty was widely commented upon. There were hints that he had been sexually molested by one of their housemaids when he was as young as eleven, and that an aristocratic male neighbour, a Lord Grey, had fallen in love with him at thirteen.

'Mostly conjecture,' noted Dr Kahn sourly. 'Though not necessarily false.'

Harness, on the other hand, was more difficult to describe. The facts that survive came through in Byron's own letters about him. At Harrow, Harness was small, sickly, pale, a member of the local poor but with a beautiful singing voice and a love of plays and play-acting. Harness first came to Byron's notice because, like Byron, he had a limp. (A shelf had fallen on him, the accident taking place in his childhood home in Northolt.) Byron felt compelled by sympathy, and, according to the letters, declared *If any fellow bully you, tell me, and I'll thrash him if I can*. That was the beginning. The injury healed. They *took up* with one another. The details are sketchy here ... Andrew hesitated.

'Yes?' prompted Dr Kahn.

'Am I allowed to fill in with my own speculation?' Andrew asked nervously.

Her mouth tugged, fighting a smile. 'That's rather the idea, Andrew.'

Andrew pressed on: the Lot was overcrowded and run-down. The two boys were in love. Harness would be constantly abused for being a *town lout*. So they went to the only place in the house – the cistern room – where they would rehearse, or ...

'Yes?' Dr Kahn prompted again.

'You know. Fool around.'

'What all teenagers need. A place to experiment sexually.'

'Right. And that's why Harness goes back there. As a ghost. It's their secret place.'

Dr Kahn became stern again: 'But there were many schoolboys who had schoolboy affairs. Not all, surely, are coming back to haunt the Hill. We'd never make it down the street for the crowd. What made this one special?'

Andrew was stumped. 'I'm not sure.'

'I have a rule,' she said. 'It's silly. But it helps me a great deal in my research. Would you like to hear it?' He said he would. 'First find the heart. Then find the start.' She blinked at him. 'Don't confine yourself to chronological order. Find the most powerful part of their story and build out from there. Where did they feel the greatest love?'

'In the cistern room.'

'But that was only at Harrow.'

Silence.

'For goodness' sake, Andrew, you mean you've only been reading the Harrow books? Did you see the marks I made in Byron's letters?'

'Those are from later,' he protested. 'Like, 1807.'

'You're not paying attention,' she said testily. And to Andrew's surprise, she crossed the room, leaned over him, and began spreading open the volumes and pounding their spines flat like an overzealous baker.

'Easy on the books!' he said, withdrawing to safety.

'These are still in print,' she declared. 'Mere information.'

Andrew, she sniffed, was confining himself too much to the Harrow period. The answer, she said, waited for them in Cambridge (*Trin. Coll. Cam.*, Andrew recalled from the *Harrow Record*), where Byron had matriculated, and where Harness had followed.

'There,' she said, stabbing a page with her index finger. Andrew read:

TO ELISABETH PIGOTT, 1806 [A childhood friend who would not judge, Dr Kahn editorialized]

He certainly is perhaps more attached to me than even I am in return. During the whole of my residence at Cambridge, Harness and I have met every day, summer and winter, without passing one tiresome moment, and separate each time with increasing reluctance. I hope you will one day see us together. He is the only being I esteem, though I like many. He has, just in this week past, presented me with a ring, a cornelian, the expense of which he bore himself completely. He offered it fearfully, as if I might refuse it. Far from doing so, I said my only dread was that I might lose so precious a token.

'What does that tell you?' she demanded.

'He esteems Harness.'

'Oh, bollocks,' exploded Dr Kahn. 'Harness gave him a ring! A second-rate stone, but it cost him more than he could afford, which was nothing, and he nearly fainted with anxiety doing it. Now, when do men give people rings, Andrew?'

'When they want to get married,' he answered meekly.

She flipped pages furiously, this time in the poetry volume, and read aloud: '*There is a Voice whose tones inspire such softened feelings in my breast, I would not hear a Seraph Choir* . . . . Harness was an actor, remember? With a beautiful singing voice? That's how he earned his place at Harrow, and at Cambridge: in the choir. All right, let's keep going.' She turned the page. 'Here we are. *There are two Hearts whose movements thrill, in unison so closely sweet, that Pulse to Pulse responsive still they Both must heave, or cease to beat*. Pulse to pulse is flesh to flesh, don't you agree? This is not unconsummated.'

There are two Souls, whose equal flow
In gentle stream so calmly run,
That when they part – they part? – ah no!
They cannot part – those Souls are One.

Dr Kahn regarded the page. 'They cannot part,' she muttered. 'See the date?' She flipped the book and held it for him to see.

'1807,' he said quietly.

'Yes. Boring old 1807.'

She pulled up a chair beside Andrew, then crossed her arms over the books and spoke to him, earnestly, energetically, as she might to a colleague or a peer. Byron, she said, began dreaming of a *life* with Harness. One that mimicked heterosexual marriage. And he was utterly deluded. How deluded, she promised to reveal shortly. 'But first,' she said, 'let us examine the fantasy he spun of their life together.' She placed another letter to Pigott in front of Andrew.

Harness departs for a mercantile house in town in October, and we shall probably not meet till the expiration of my minority . . .

'Coming into his *majority*,' she interpreted. 'This means that Byron is licking his chops at all the money he thinks he will inherit with his estate at Newstead. Have you seen Newstead Abbey? It's worthy of drooling. Big, grey, medieval. Peacocks all about. One feels smug merely pulling into the car park.'

BUT BYRON WAS always overextended, spending lavishly on fancy coaches, liquor, clothes. He was eventually forced to sell Newstead Abbey, which had been in the family since the 1500s. Like a hip-hop star who goes quickly bankrupt from mansions, cars and bling, she explained.

Andrew snorted at the unexpected reference. 'Where did that come from?' he drawled.

'I have nieces,' she replied tartly. 'Read.'

Andrew read.

Harness departs for a mercantile house in town in October, and we shall probably not meet till the expiration of my minority when I shall leave to his decision either entering the firm as a partner through my interest . . .

Meaning, Dr Kahn elaborated, that Byron, like a sugar daddy, intended to fund his boyfriend's career. The equivalent of getting the trophy wife her estate agency or interior decorator's business.

. . . or residing with me altogether.

Alternatively, she added, Byron would make Harness a housewife.

He shall have his choice. I certainly love him more than any human being, and neither time nor distance have had the least effect on my (in general) changeable disposition.

Andrew stopped her. 'So I mean, it was a little ahead of his time, I get it. But . . . English people are tolerant of gays, right? Look at Mr Baldridge,' he said, referring to one of the school's science masters, who lived with a companion.

'I shouldn't have to tell you the world has changed, Andrew,' she said. 'Homosexuality was against the law then. They could never cohabitate in that manner. Never. Not only was it illegal, it was a capital crime. Part of England's Bloody Code, punishable by instant death.'

Andrew looked at the book, feeling stung.

'That's a comedown, isn't it, after reading these beautiful poems and letters?' She passed her hands over the open page. 'No doubt Byron and Harness felt the same way.

'I can forgive Byron his delusion, however,' she went on, in a musing tone. 'Cambridge is a magical place, not bustling and over-discovered like Oxford; Cambridge is *built* for secrets. You'll see it, I hope. Walls separate the colleges from the town. From England. Shutting out *all that*. Enclosing the rest. It's a glorious place to fall in love,' she said, now drifting away. 'In the Backs, in June. The leaves and lawns all green and gold in the sunshine. And no one ever stops drinking. Pimm's, wine, parties every day. Punting on the Cam, under the cover of trees. The boys, slim-waisted and beautiful – they don't deserve it with all that drinking, but that's life at twenty. What's better than a stolen kiss, your cheeks sunburned from a day outdoors, under a summer twilight?'

She fell silent.

'You want to know if I am speaking from personal experience,' she said wryly, observing Andrew's gaping at her. 'Well, of course I am. I wasn't always . . . my present age.'

He waited; she smiled mysteriously; but that was all there was.

'I'm having trouble reconciling this with what I saw of Harness,' Andrew said at last. 'His face was just . . . pure fury. Nothing nice. Nothing like what you're describing.'

'Then we're missing a piece of the puzzle. You need to go to the Wren Library and read what's in those letters you found. I'll email my friend. So you see, Andrew, you may set eyes on Trinity after all. But beware. Now you know what happened there. How Byron and Harness fell in love. True love.' She tapped the book of letters. 'The more precious the treasure, the fiercer the dragon.'

14

London Snog

'STOP!'

James Honey had tucked himself into one of the little wooden Speech Room chairs in the front row, with a quilt thrown over his knees and the script in his lap. He followed the lines with the point of a pencil, and was staring at Andrew over his reading glasses. 'I can't understand a word, Andrew,' he moaned, his pencil point pressed to the paper. 'Not a word.'

The stage manager whispered in Honey's ear.

'One moment, please,' the director barked.

Rebecca sidled up to Andrew onstage. 'Have you done your kissing scene with Persephone yet?' She wore yet another short skirt, glossy pink lipstick, and a kind of velvety top that made her resemble a slutty and very fetching member of Robin Hood's Merry Men. Her voice was insinuating, full of venom.

'You mean, in the play?'

'Oh, are you doing other kissing scenes?'

Andrew opened his mouth, but nothing came out. He blushed scarlet.

Rebecca smiled. 'All I can say is, be careful. If Sir Alan finds out, it'll be murder. You know he keeps a Roman sword hanging over his mantel?'

'No, I didn't.'

'Funny,' she continued. 'I thought she was still going with Simon.'

Andrew turned to her – too quickly. He saw another smile creep across Rebecca's face.

'She was with him such a long time,' she persisted.

'Yeah?' he said, forcing himself to sound casual.

'Oh, yeah. She's *obsessed* with him.'

Andrew's heart shrivelled.

'But they went through a lot. Maybe that finally broke them up.'

He could no longer stand it. 'What do you mean, *went through* . . .'

'*All right*, here we go,' Honey bayed. 'From the beginning.'

'Don't let what I said distract you,' whispered Rebecca.

'Just tell me what you mean by—'

'*When you've quite finished*,' Honey snapped at them.

Andrew yammered his lines without feeling. Honey kept stopping the scenes to correct him, hopping up onstage and mocking his slumping posture. Rebecca batted her eyes at him. She made pouty, *poor-baby* smiles. At the end she hugged him. *Be better next time*, she said, and wrapped him in her perfume, a cloud of cloying late-summer blooms.

BY THE TIME Andrew reached the tube station a little later, he was as soiled and exhausted by his mental journey through Jealousy as any traveller in the bush. Persephone had deceived him. She had maintained a relationship all along with some slick, rich, tall, upright, world-travelling English aristocrat; blond, no doubt, with a huge chin; sporty; with a *car*. Andrew had been kept in the dark. Some side arrangement while Simon – Simon, Simon, of course it was a Simon – did whatever Simons did. Went to Egypt for a dig. Or studied finance in Singapore. Andrew retrieved the mental snapshots of his every encounter with Persephone and ripped them down the middle. All the preparation for the weekend – the chit from Fawkes; Andrew's roundabout explanation about a 'group get-together' with members of the cast (he did not want Fawkes to know), and his lie that Sir Alan had approved the trip; and the non-stop daydreaming – had been for nothing. Less than nothing – they had added to his insult.

WHEN SHE ARRIVED – striding down the Hill in a dress that dropped only to mid-thigh, a pattern aswirl with Matisse colours, blood red and jungle green, her legs bare, her hair a snake swarm of curls, sunglasses balanced over her brow – his heart skipped three beats. He forced himself to remain cold. He realized what a clod he looked like alongside her, with his khakis and his checked Oxford shirt and his sneakers. He was glad. Let her be disappointed. Let her see what a poor match they were, now that they were stripped of the school uniform. She was stylish, European, upper crust; he was an American middle-class nothing. Let her regret it, as much as he did.

'Hello,' she said brightly. Then she took in his scowl. 'Everything all right?'

'Yup,' he replied coldly. 'Let's go.'

'Why are you acting strange?'

'How am I acting strange?'

'You're all funny.' She bit her lip. 'I sent you a crass text and now you think I'm a whore. Is that it?'

'Nope. You're late.'

'I was getting ready,' she said, striking a pose. 'And now you're supposed to say it was worth the wait.'

'Come on.' He turned and mounted the filthy stairs of the tube station and shoved his credit card into the ticket machine.

THEY RODE IN silence on the squishy, purple-flecked cushions of the Metropolitan line, through every flavour of suburb. Persephone dropped her sunglasses to her nose and scowled. Andrew kept his face turned to the window, watching pass the wide, green fields of some minor college, dotted with flocks of pigeons – or were they seagulls? – then the housing estates, slabs of that grey-brown brick unique to English terraced houses; then finally the industrial yards: rusting train cars, a depot for old postal vehicles. At the Finchley Road stop, Persephone rose and without a word bolted out into a red-brick station and pounded up the stairs. Andrew followed, and continued to follow her up a steep hill. A bustling commercial street gave way to curling drives where muscular, mansion-like homes perched on landscaped plots, hedged in by brick walls and rhododendrons. Persephone maintained her furious pace forward, sunglasses down, forcing him to follow at a sheepish distance. At last they reached a plateau, where a few shops and a pub popped into view. Persephone finally stopped outside the pub.

'If we're not going to speak, we may as well get drunk,' she announced.

Beaten copper lined the bar. Cigarette smoke and the smell of cooking beef and potatoes swirled inside. Andrew was starving but felt the single five-pound note and the two pound coins in his pocket, and saw the chalked menu above the bar – nothing below nine pounds – and instead calculated the number of pints he could buy. Beer. *A sandwich in a can*, his friends at home called it.

They ordered lagers. They were not challenged. They did not clink glasses. They drank.

'So this is where you grew up,' Andrew observed.

She ignored this. They were in a fight. Somehow, without any prelude. So she was in no mood to share reminiscences. 'How was rehearsal?' she asked in response, an edge in her voice.

Andrew stared at her. Should he say it? Should he ask her? He knew he would never get over it if he didn't. And he wanted to get over it. Her dress scarcely covered her, wrapping her no better than the skin of a summer nut when it bulges ripe from its casing.

'Who's Simon?' he asked.

She sat stunned for a moment. Then her face twisted. '*Rebecca*,' she said. 'I knew it.'

'What about her?' Andrew back-pedalled quickly.

'I lied to my father to set up this weekend, you know. I lied to my mother to get permission to use the house. I told her I was having Kathy and Lizzie and Louise over, all my old friends from Middlesex, because we haven't *seen* each other, and it was going to be so much *fun*, couldn't we *please*. And she knew it was crap. She kept saying, *You were not such good friends with those girls*. And she's right. I wasn't. ' She looked at him. 'I take a risk. Only to have *you*' – she spat out the word, disgusted – 'take *their side* – again. You fling it in my face. Why didn't you say something before we got on the bloody tube?' she snapped. 'I would have left you there.'

Andrew said nothing. He knew he was ruining it. Spoiling their weekend – and all that was supposed to go with it. But he didn't know what else to do.

'Well, if you want to ask me a question, ask it.' Persephone was nearly shaking in anger.

'I just did. Who's Simon?'

'Simon was my boyfriend,' she said. 'There.'

'Was?'

Andrew watched, bemused, as Persephone glugged half a pint of beer. She didn't answer. Should he leave it at that? But no; it was not enough.

'Rebecca,' he said, 'seemed to think you were still together.'

'Well, Rebecca is a cunt!'

Heads turned: half amused, half surprised. A few murmurs of commentary.

'Did you and Simon go out for a long time?'

'Stop it, Andrew!'

'How do you think I feel?' he countered. 'I thought we were . . . I don't know . . . going out . . .' She snorted. 'Then I hear this . . .'

'Slander? Hearsay? Gossip? Malevolent crap from some stupid bitch?' Now people at nearby tables were turning to stare, conversation dying around them. 'And you drag me all the way here to throw it in my face? When I'm taking you home with me?'

'All I wanted to know was whether . . .'

'Whether I'm a slut,' she finished. 'It never goes away, with you. And I had a nice surprise for you. A surprise that – I'd planned out. Did you know that? But I'm clearly wasting my time.'

She slugged back the remainder of her beer, banged the empty glass on the table, and marched out.

Andrew slumped in his chair.

His neighbours eyed him. He tried to decide whether to stay in London drinking up his five pounds, or do the prudent thing and go straight back to school.

He finished his beer.

He walked outside. There were some picnic tables there, in an enclosure, with beer-logo'd umbrellas over each table.

Persephone sat at one, her back to him.

He hesitated. Almost walked off. But that would be cold. She was there. She was waiting. It was a peace offering. *Take it.* Cautiously, he approached. He waited, a step behind her, in her peripheral vision. She said nothing. So he sat down on the bench next to her. Still nothing. He lit a cigarette. He handed it over to her. He held it there for a moment. Then, as if stirring from deep thought, her white, slender hand reached for it. She took it. Puffed. She shook her magnificent hair back, out of her face. Her sunglasses shielded her eyes.

'There's something very satisfying,' she observed, 'about the word *cunt*.'

'It's a great Anglo-Saxon word,' Andrew agreed.

'It really is,' she replied. Then, after a moment: 'Aren't you going to offer me another drink?'

He practically leapt from the seat. Reconciliation. Hope. He returned with two more pints and a receipt for a credit card charge to his father's account. *Dad be damned.* The sun winked through a thin spot in the woolly sky.

'What do you want to know about Simon?' Persephone asked when he sat down. 'Let's get it over with.'

Andrew's throat tightened. 'Are you still in love with him?'

'I hate him.'

'Why?'

'Honestly, I don't like to talk about it. I could kill Rebecca.' She added: 'You have nothing to worry about.'

'How long has it been since you've, you know . . .'

'Seen him?' she finished. 'Months and months.'

They went through a lot together, Rebecca had said.

Don't ask it, you idiot! She's talking to you again. You got your answer.

He decided he would try starting the date over.

'You know,' he said, 'that's a lovely dress.'

She smiled, a growing rosy grin on those enormous, puffy lips. She understood. She raised her sunglasses.

'Why, thank you, Andrew. And how nice of you to meet me today.'

'What's my surprise?'

'You'll see.'

Then Andrew asked her about herself. (That was what you were supposed to do on a date, wasn't it?) Persephone, charged with adrenalin and an edgy tone of self-mockery, let it all hang out. Where did her father get his title? Was he a knight? A lord?

Sort of, Persephone answered. *Baronet. It's a shit title, really. Some seventeenth-century Vine bought it off the king, who used the money to kill Irish. That's what my mother says. Drives my dad crazy.*

And what was the deal with her parents? Were they divorced?

Her mother lived half the year in Greece. They were old-fashioned. Stayed married but hated each other. *They fight over me. It's like a contest,* she said. *I'm the sole judge in this endless Olympics, and they're the U.S. and the Chinese, bribing me, sucking up, showing off, cutting down the other one. They haven't had sex in twenty years. And where do you think it all goes? All the* lust*? They must have it. They are* of the species . . .

Andrew felt buzzed from the beers – the thin remnants of their second pints at the bottom of their glasses, and they still had had nothing to eat – and he didn't really know if there was an answer to this question. But then it came.

It all goes to me, she finished – she was drunk now, slurring her words, telling him this almost aggressively, as if saying, Hey, you want to hear my shit? You want to see how worthless and scabby I am? – and he half wished he was not hearing it, because he could tell these things were painful to her, but he was also fascinated (maybe his baggage was not so heavy in comparison; he felt pedestrian, in fact, compared to this pan-European erotic dysfunction). *Phone calls and dinners and presents, like I'm dating them both, trying to keep each one at bay so the other doesn't go mad with jealousy. Monitoring how much attention the other gets. If it gets to be too much, threatening to take me to Athens or to Harrow altogether. That's when I started sneaking out. Just running away from all of it. That's when I started going with Simon. The bad years. I was fifteen. The last time they lived together.* ('Going with' . . . was that a euphemism? At *fifteen*? Andrew marvelled. He remembered himself at fifteen with his learner's permit and a brand-new Adam's apple gawking around green Connecticut, just having shed his interest in manga.) *She'd call me* boulaiki, Persephone continued. Boulaikimou. *My little bird. Very sweet, of course. It also means, my little pussy.*

Andrew coughed.

I'm getting pissed, said Persephone. *Do you think I'm horrible yet?*

Of course not, he said. *You're shocked*, she countered. No, he said, even though he was; but he said it, because to him, here, in the heavy light, under the London sky, plastered, tragic, coming out of her dress and her pretences, she was the dirtiest and most lovable girl he had ever met. *Why don't we go*, he said.

THEY KISSED IN the hall. The alcohol on an empty stomach made him dizzy when he closed his eyes. They went to the living room. The house was a beachy combination of pink furniture, silver gewgaws, white walls and seashell-themed everything. They kissed on the couch and moved down to the floor. Andrew untied her sash, stripped her dress off her, then her bra. He licked her breasts, tugged at her panties. They had been waiting for this. For weeks. It had all been building up. *Now let's do it*, a voice inside him urged. Beer sloshed inside him. He went through the motions. Get her clothes off, check. Stimulate sex organs ...

'Ouch,' she said. 'Wait.'

She readjusted and helped him pull her panties off. Her legs were white and smooth and tapered; *amazing* his brain registered *and there it is*, the *boulaiki*, brown and casual there in the daylight. He felt nervous, suddenly. It was like meeting a famous person, a personal hero, with only a minute's notice. *Hey wait I'm not ready, not worthy*. He felt sweat at the base of his back. *Fear*. That wasn't good. Not good at all. He touched her. She was OK. Almost wet enough. He rubbed. But it all seemed to be taking too long. The voice nagged him. *Get it done*. He tried to enter her. But it wasn't happening. She reached for him, to take him in her hand, but that was worse – now she would see he wasn't hard. The sweat in his lower back became sweat all over him. He felt hot, oppressed. He pulled away.

'You OK, Andrew?'

'Not really. I drank too much.'

They leaned against the sofa together, their bare bottoms on the carpet. Suddenly they were very accustomed to each other naked. Too much so. She had belly rolls. He had ingrown thigh hairs. It was as if they had caromed past the exit on the motorway where all the build-up and the Victorian anticipation happened, and veered straight into – what? A sort of jaded nullity. Just two naked bodies already bored with each other. Andrew had never been inside this house before and within twenty minutes he was in the living room, naked, and in despair. He laid his head back on the sofa and groaned.

'Want me to go down on you?' she asked.

'I just want some water.'

'I scared you off, didn't I? With all that about . . .'

'No, no,' he objected. 'Can I get some water?'

'If it makes you feel any better,' she said, making no move to fetch him water, 'I can't have an orgasm.'

'Can't?'

'Can't. Don't.' She watched his expression closely. She wanted to make sure she hadn't gone too far. Scared him away completely.

'Seriously?'

She shrugged.

'Well,' he said, at last. 'We're quite a pair.'

TO CHEER HIM up, Persephone dragged Andrew on a long trek to a cooler neighbourhood thronged with leather-jacketed hipsters, and to a boutique where she bought him – on Sir Alan's credit card this time – jeans that actually fitted, a vintage shirt and a jacket; then pulled him into a hair salon. *Why do I need a haircut?* he protested. The stylist, a woman named Charlie, had platinum hair and multiple earrings.

'Time to get rid of the Led Zeppelin,' Persephone told Charlie.

Thirty minutes later Andrew looked in the mirror.

'Now I'm a choirboy,' he declared.

To his surprise, Persephone jumped into the chair next to him.

'I want to look exactly the same.' He watched her curls mingle with his on the salon floor before a dreadlocked assistant came and swept them away.

'TIME FOR YOUR surprise,' Persephone said as they left the salon.

'Is that what you were texting about?' he said. Persephone had been furiously thumbing her phone during his makeover.

'Maybe,' she said.

She led him on a long, twisting walk through a darkening London to a mid-scale commercial neighbourhood that hosted a string of Middle Eastern restaurants with fluorescent lights, and hookahs in the windows, with men seated in pairs, puffing at them. Persephone led the way inside one of these, sidled up to the seats at the bar, with a direct view of the kitchen, and instructed Andrew to watch the best chicken butcher in London. They watched him slice apart several dozen birds, whacking their wings off with single glances of his cleaver, his hands shiny and larded with guts. They ordered platters. Andrew shovelled the food into his mouth. Thick hot sauce, pasty tahini, warm pita – it felt like his first meal in months. His head rang and his nose ran from the heat.

A voice came over their shoulders. 'Persephone?'

A voluptuous redhead, freckled, and in a black cocktail dress, hugged Persephone, who introduced her as Agatha. Agatha hugged Andrew and kissed both his cheeks, then looked at him and at Persephone and made a face and hooted, *You're not boyfriend-girlfriend, you're twins!* Persephone beamed. Agatha's date was behind her, a tall, sharp-featured Indian in a dark suit, Vivek. He carried a plastic bag. Agatha, Persephone explained, was in her first year at Cambridge, and was her best friend growing up. They spent summers in Greece together. (By now these casual references to a life of exotic privilege rolled off Andrew; they merely added incrementally to his intoxication with Persephone and her world.) The newcomers drew up stools, Vivek immediately noticing and marvelling at the butchery, Agatha eyeballing Andrew and sending knowing glances to Persephone, clearly the *best-friend-who-has-heard-about-him-and-is-dying-of-curiosity*. (Andrew was glad he had changed into his new clothes; his khakis lay folded in a shopping bag at his feet.) Normally Andrew would feel threatened by an unfamiliar couple materializing on a date, but he was flush with nutrition and with the swirl of London, and he embraced it.

Vivek asked the burly man at the bar for some plastic cups. 'I'll be flogged if they catch me,' he said to Andrew, privately. 'Eighty lashes. They're Muslims here. If you hadn't noticed.' Vivek reached into his plastic bag and gripped the neck of a frosty champagne bottle. The cork popped softly, expertly.

Vivek poured golden, bubbling champagne into the clear plastic cups and they toasted. The burly man taking orders glanced at them angrily but allowed them to drink.

'So,' said Vivek. 'The girls tell me you're seeing the Lot ghost.'

Andrew turned to Persephone. Her cat's-eyes glistened, amused and proud that she had kept her surprise a secret until now. But Andrew grew grim at the reminder of what was waiting for him back at school.

'You went to Harrow?' Andrew asked.

Vivek nodded. 'I was in the Lot. I saw it, too.'

'Are you serious?' Andrew sat up straight.

'In my second year my parents divorced,' Vivek explained. 'My brother and I were not getting along – he was in Fifth Form. I was picked on very badly. I was miserable and lonely and all those horrible things that get worse because they are happening to you at school, and you have nobody.' He said all this with a kind of matter-of-fact ease. Andrew noticed that Vivek wore a pocket square, and that the weave of his jacket was silky and many-threaded, and he wondered what breed of international gentleman this could be, whose life was so multifarious and rich that minor family tragedies were reduced to mere anecdotes, lyrically told, while pouring champagne in a North African chicken bar. 'My escape was the bath. Aha! I see from your face I'm on the right track.'

Agatha and Persephone looked back and forth between the two young men, delighted by this mystery. Vivek refilled their glasses and continued.

'I was even skinnier than I am now, but I had to play on the house rugger team. One time I left the game early after being completely crushed, and I went back very angry. You know, to hell with these English people and their game. So I was going to transgress. I was going to take a hot bath in the *prefect's* bath.' He smiled and raised his eyebrows to emphasize what a taboo this was. 'So I filled the tub. Steam was rising. I couldn't wait to steep my aching limbs. But when I took off my towel, I saw a face in the water.'

The girls made a show of shivering and oohing.

'I sprang back like I had got an electric shock!' said Vivek with a laugh. 'It was just *there*. Not like it was actually in the water, but like the surface of the bath was a window, and he was looking through it right at me. I ran to my room, completely naked. I was terrified.'

'What did the face look like?' Andrew asked.

Vivek started to answer. 'No, you should tell me,' he said, instead. 'And you know what, before you answer,' said Vivek, 'give me a piece of paper.' Persephone handed him their bill, a long strip of cash-register receipt, and a pen. Vivek began doodling, hiding his work with his hand. Then he theatrically folded the bill and placed it in his pocket. 'I just drew a picture of what *I* saw. Now: tell me what *you* saw.'

'He has white hair,' Andrew began, finding his voice suddenly small. 'Sunken cheeks. And blue eyes. He has a speckling across his face. Like a rash.'

Vivek frowned.

'That's creepy, man.' He nodded gravely. 'Same guy. I don't remember the rash or the cheeks. But the white hair – definitely.' He took the bill and placed it on the counter.

They crowded around to gaze at the figure he had drawn. It was a long face with a mop of blank white for hair, and Vivek had carved in the eyes deeply with repeated pen strokes, as if the memory of those in particular had not left him.

Andrew swallowed. He heard the girls commenting, but his eyes were glued to the scribbled figure.

'You all right, man?' Vivek said to him quietly.

'Yeah,' he managed.

Vivek patted him on the shoulder with a grimace of commiseration.

Before long their group bundled out into the street. Agatha and Vivek had a party to go to.

'Don't worry,' called Vivek over his shoulder as Persephone pulled Andrew down the block towards a taxi. 'The ghost never harmed anyone. That I know of!' He grinned and waved.

PERSEPHONE LED HIM upstairs. The house was warm, stale, sterile; her bedroom was anonymous, serving now as a guest room. They stood before the dressing mirror. They saw their reflections together, symmetrical images of the two sexes, long white necks, dark curls.

Andrew placed his fingers on her neck. Persephone sighed. She still wore her wrap dress. Andrew peeled it off. Her skin was moist, sticky, vulnerable. They fell to the bed. She eased backward and guided him into her. The only sound in the silent, sealed house was their shallow panting. Only later, half asleep, did he remember, and sit up and whisper, *Did you . . . ?* Even though he knew, or at least suspected, the answer. Persephone found his hand in the dark and held it to her chest in a tight, possessive grip.

15

Sputum

ANDREW CLIMBED THE Hill, proud as a conqueror, deliciously guilty and greasy in his jeans. Yet every step recalled the clamp of school rules. He passed students in Sunday dress – the tailcoat, the striped trousers. Chapel and lunch had evidently just concluded. He increased his pace. Crossing the street, he was nearly run over by a screaming ambulance gunning up the Hill. He leapt to the far kerb and bumped into Rupert Askew, the praying-mantis-like reader from Essay Club.

'You're a sight, Taylor. Just returning now? You'll be crucified, walking back like that.'

Andrew crested the hill, trying to look inconspicuous. It took him several moments to realize that the ambulance that just passed him was now backing into the Lot.

He began to run.

When he rounded the gate the ambulance had pulled to a stop by the front entrance. One paramedic was rushing inside. A second followed, carrying equipment.

Andrew finally reached the foyer. No lights on because of the sunny day; a strange sense of calm. Then: raised voices, up the stairwell. He followed them. They became clearer with each step.

Can you hear me, Roddy? Have you been ill?

Roddy, listen to me, have you been taking any medication?

Check his dresser there, bedside – see any pills?

Roddy, can you hear me? Do you know where you are?

Andrew reached the top landing and saw Rhys standing outside Roddy's door. The head of house was biting his lip anxiously and staring inside the room. He stood in his white shirtsleeves and his black silk vest. Roddy's door was being held open by a paramedic in coveralls and some object that looked like a combination surfboard-papoose.

All right, we're going to have to move him. You have the bag? Here we go. Give me a hand. The paramedic called for Rhys.

Rhys moved into the room. Andrew rushed to the doorway. Two paramedics were digging their forearms under Roddy – also in white shirtsleeves and striped trousers; post-chapel casual – to prop him on to the papoose. Roddy's face was half covered by a black latex mask and a paramedic's hand gripping it. The mask was attached to what looked like a black boxer's punching bag, inflating and deflating. Rhys grabbed one end of the stretcher.

Clear the way, clear the way, the paramedic barked at Andrew.

Andrew backed up against the corridor wall. Rhys and the paramedic grunted as they carried Roddy, strapped to the stretcher. The second paramedic came alongside, holding the mask to Roddy's face. Andrew caught a glimpse of Roddy as they passed. His skin was waxy. When he saw Andrew, his eyes, at first drooping, opened wide. He tried to speak. He reached a hand out to Andrew. *Steady there*, cautioned the paramedic, who hustled him past.

'Wait!' Andrew called. He clambered down after them as they bumped down the stairwell, into the foyer, into the sunlight.

FAWKES – IN A blazer and tie – nearly rammed into the group of them, Andrew right behind. Fawkes had seen the ambulance and was charging into the Lot.

'Who is that? Good God, what happened. Rhys?'

Sweat trickled down Rhys's cheek. He gave a shove to help

launch the stretcher into the ambulance, then wiped his forehead and turned to Fawkes.

'I was in my room,' he puffed. 'I heard a thump. A big one. I went into Roddy's room. He was gasping. I got him upright. He hadn't swallowed anything – nothing blocking his throat. I was going to go for Matron. But it got worse. His coughing.' Rhys's face twisted. 'It was almost a . . . a barking noise.'

'*Barking?*' asked Fawkes.

'And there was something else.'

The expression on reliable, plain-spoken Rhys Davies's face revealed that the *something else* had made him very uncomfortable.

'There was something . . . *going on* in there. It wasn't good.'

'What was it?' Fawkes demanded. He and Andrew exchanged glances.

'Any of you coming?' shouted the driver, swinging his one door shut.

'I'll go.' Fawkes clambered into the back of the ambulance. 'Rhys, get Mr Macrae. Tell him I'll phone him.'

The second paramedic closed the back doors and the ambulance lights swirled again. The vehicle beeped as it reversed. Boys, still returning from lunch, now scattered before it. A small group also gathered around Rhys as he explained again what had happened: Roddy had fallen ill; they had had to call an ambulance. The boys' faces fell.

'Is it the same thing that got Theo?'

'Is this an epidemic, Rhys?'

'Should we evacuate?'

The younger ones chattered anxiously, almost panicked. Rhys told them to *calm down, there was nothing to worry about, Roddy would be fine* – then he escaped by charging off towards the small side building where the assistant housemaster lived. Andrew followed.

'What the *hell*,' exclaimed Andrew when they were out of

earshot; he didn't want to show fear in front of the young ones. 'What exactly did you see?'

'I walked in there and felt like I was on drugs,' Rhys said, keeping up a trot. 'It felt terrible. Like a cloud. A fog.' He scowled. 'Then a minute later it was back to normal. Except for Roddy wriggling on the floor. I don't know . . . maybe I lost it for a minute there.' They reached Macrae's door. 'You'd better go back,' he said to Andrew.

'Why?'

'You'll only make it worse, dressed like a pimp.'

Rhys turned his back on Andrew and thumped Macrae's door.

Andrew hastily returned to his room to change into school garb. Now there were only two rooms occupied on his narrow corridor. His, and Rhys's. Roddy's and Theo's lay empty.

THE STUDENTS MILLED about, waiting for news. The common rooms sat empty. No one could watch television; no one could study. The snooker room, by contrast, was packed. St. John and Cameron held the cues. The smaller boys hung around the periphery. The basket of biscuits had been devoured.

'What did you do to this one, Andrew?' Cam challenged him as he entered and took a seat.

St. John sneered from the shadows. 'Thought you'd keep Roddy alive. He's the only one who'll talk to you.'

'Fuck you,' Andrew growled.

'Are those the only words in your vocabulary?'

'I also say, "Suck my dick."'

'This is an uplifting conversation,' pronounced Cam, sinking the yellow ball with a *thunk*.

A rustling noise came down the darkened corridor. A hush fell over the group. The silhouette of the headmaster soon filled the doorway. It took them a moment to recognize him, it was so out of context to see him, here in the snooker room.

'Boys,' said Colin Jute.

Headmaster, they all murmured, subdued. Not so much because it was him, but because his presence, so unexpected, portended terrible news. *Roddy is dead*, they all thought silently to themselves.

'Mr Taylor,' he said. 'I need to see you a moment.'

Andrew rose.

'Davies here? Rhys Davies?' said the headmaster.

'No, he's with Mr Macrae,' said Andrew. The headmaster eyed him. 'Sir,' Andrew added.

'Right. Someone find Davies for me. You.' The headmaster designated a Remove by the door. 'Tell him to meet us by the gate.' The Remove dashed off. The headmaster crooked his finger. Andrew followed, wondering along with everyone else in the room – especially St. John, whose eyes were dancing delightedly – whether the headmaster had heard Andrew say *Suck my dick*.

THEY WAITED UNDER the plane tree. The headmaster said nothing. Whatever this visit portended, its matter was worse than a reprimand for bad language.

At last Rhys strode across the drive, all purpose and energy, a head of house ready to take action in his full Sunday regalia of tailcoat and waistcoat and striped trousers. Jute didn't offer a greeting. Merely turned and waved them up the High Street. He walked deliberately. In his casual clothes (grey slacks, green jumper) he had the air of someone whose Sunday with the newspaper had been interrupted by bad news. Andrew skulked along like a prisoner. He could only assume that Roddy was critically ill, or that he was being expelled for going AWOL, and that Rhys was in trouble, too, for covering for him.

In Jute's office a woman waited for them. Tiny-framed, fiftyish, she was Indian with an enormous mantle of black hair, and dressed in a stylish cotton dress.

'Boys, this is Miss Palek.'

They introduced themselves.

'I am from the Health Protection Agency,' she said. She had a soothing alto and massive soft brown eyes.

'Is this about Roddy?' Andrew asked in disbelief.

She pursed her lips. 'There has been an incident of infectious disease, and we think you were exposed.'

Andrew's stomach dropped.

I'm a nurse, she explained. She worked for one of the Health Protection Units for the London area, North-west, which covered Harrow and Harrow-on-the-Hill. One of their responsibilities, which they took very seriously, was response to epidemiological emergencies such as possible outbreaks.

Andrew's heart jolted again.

A few weeks ago, one of their classmates, a young man, died of a pulmonary infection here at the school.

Rhys and Andrew nodded. 'Theo Ryder.'

'But he died of sarcoidosis,' added Andrew.

Miss Palek nodded sagely. Yes, because the death was sudden and the cause of death unknown, the medical authorities at Clementine Churchill Hospital – which they were very lucky is top-notch – performed an inquest, and in doing so revealed a pattern of tissue damage. This was at first diagnosed as sarcoid, but for completeness, a culture for mycobacterium tuberculosis was also performed. Those tests returned positive. Yesterday.

Rhys, whose studies allowed him to follow this jargon faster than Andrew, broke in, indignant. 'Wait . . . you're saying Theo died of tuberculosis? *Here?*'

'It is probable that the student, since he was from Africa, brought the infection with him,' Miss Palek said.

'Very few cases from England,' sniffed Jute.

'Most of our patients are AIDS patients or from sub-Saharan Africa,' confirmed Miss Palek, but her eyes flashed; the snobbery in the headmaster's remark was not lost on her. She continued.

The hospital notified the HPA when the results returned

positive, and the first action they took was to put a watch on the databases for the medical facilities surrounding the school. So when their classmate, just a few hours ago, was *also* brought to Clementine Churchill, with symptoms consistent with TB, he was immediately moved to another, even better-equipped hospital in London; and Miss Palek's team was notified. It was their duty to review the circumstances around the incident – or index event – to determine the extent of the outbreak.

'So . . .' stammered Andrew, catching up. 'Theo had TB.'

'That's correct.'

'And Roddy has TB.'

Miss Palek hesitated. Obviously she was not supposed confirm the name of any kid who had fallen ill. 'Anyone with symptoms consistent with active tuberculosis will be isolated in a special ward. We need to take precautions with those who have been living in close proximity to the victims, to find out whether they have been infected.'

'You mean us,' said Rhys.

'Isolated?' barked Andrew. 'You mean *quarantined*?'

'Please do not be alarmed. As I said, only those with active TB – fevers, coughing, lung tissue damage – need to be isolated. It is all for your protection. The gentleman accompanying the victim to Clementine Churchill – '

'Fawkes,' interjected Jute with distaste.

'A very quick thinker. He immediately understood the risks, and he provided your names.'

'Never mind the risk of a panic at the school,' mumbled Jute resentfully.

'Panic is not good for anyone,' she intoned, sympathetically. 'Right now I would advise only telling the parents of those affected. What we call the inner circle.'

'That means you boys will keep absolute mum, or we'll have a real crisis,' Jute said.

'Mum about what?' Andrew asked, his voice rising with his confusion.

Miss Palek smiled tightly. 'We recommend you submit to a test.'

And there it was.

'A test,' Andrew repeated.

'When?' said Rhys. 'Now? Here?'

In answer to his question, she produced two clipboards from a bag at her side and told them, no, it was suggested they accompany her to London, not far, the Royal Tredway Hospital ... *one of the best in Europe for this sort of thing*, interjected Jute, *certainly the best in London* ... They would need to review and sign these forms ... this was for their own benefit ... The remainder of her words vanished into a haze. They were actors in a play that had been carefully staged by Miss Palek and (grudgingly) Jute. Andrew and Rhys signed the papers. They found themselves being ushered to the street, where a car waited for them. The driver, seeing them, placed a white surgical mask over his face. He started the engine. Miss Palek sat in front. She too placed a mask over her face. She handed the boys their own surgical masks. They were made of spongy, fibrous cotton, folded over in a rippling pattern. Miss Palek looked at them expectantly. Rhys and Andrew pulled the masks over their faces, stretching the pink bands behind their heads. The masks smelled of rubber. Andrew's made him painfully conscious of his breathing. He involuntarily started counting his breaths as they descended the Hill, passing the Old Schools ... *one, two* ... passing the drive to Headland House ... *six, seven* ... then down to the roundabout, where, for the first time in weeks, sun shone on the red warning street sign.

Andrew pulled out his mobile phone. He had Fawkes's mobile number programmed in it. He lifted his mask to speak and turned to the window so he would not be overheard. *They're taking us to some hospital because they think we all have TB. TB as in tuberculosis. Can you come find us?* Rhys glared at Andrew, nodding his head at Miss Palek in the front in warning. *You're the only person who understands what's really going on. Rhys said he felt something when it happened. Harness!* he hissed. *If you don't come get us, I'm not sure what's going to happen. If we don't make it out alive*, he added, *write me a good epitaph.*

He now counted like a child praying, as if, when he stopped counting, his breathing might somehow stop ... *Eleven, twelve* ... The car swept down the Hill and into the flow of traffic. Andrew realized that, from the moment the headmaster had appeared at the Lot to fetch them, no one had physically touched either him or Rhys. They were pariahs.

THE HOSPITAL WAS located in an upmarket corner of London, near sweeping blocks of multi-storeyed and prosperous-looking town houses. Constructed of ruddy pre-war brick, it sat high over a busy thoroughfare with only a modest sign and a shallow loading ramp to distinguish it. They parked, and Rhys and Andrew were forced to walk back several yards, masks over their faces, feeling a sense of shame that only deepened when they passed a family of Scandinavian tourists, who spotted them and pulled their children closer to them protectively as the pair walked by.

Miss Palek removed her mask and led them through the main lobby, down a long, straight corridor to a bank of lifts. The narrow halls bustled with doctors in white coats, orderlies and administrators with name tags.

They took a battered lift four flights. Where they emerged was quieter.

'This is our Chest Centre,' Miss Palek announced with a hint of pride.

Rhys and Andrew were checked in by a nurse in scrubs. They were told they could remove the masks. They provided their information. They were led to a treatment room with two beds and curtains that drew around them. They were asked to change into gowns. They did. Andrew resented the semi-nakedness, the flimsy gown. It transformed you from citizen with full rights, to inmate – suspect – in a few moments. The nurse re-entered, asked them to place their clothes in plastic bags, and after storing these under a cabinet, immediately wrung her hands under the hand-sanitizing foam dispenser.

Another nurse, older, grey-haired, with a wattle and an air of authority, entered with a clipboard and gestured for Andrew to follow her. He coughed. She looked alarmed.

'That's quite a cough.'

'Ah, I was smoking too much last night.'

'Have you had that cough long?'

'As long as I've been smoking.'

'So, for a month?'

'Sure.'

Her face drew up like the mouth of a cinched duffel bag.

'Please replace your mask,' she commanded.

'Oh, come on . . .' he protested. 'It's a smoker's cough!'

Her face went flat and implacable. He complied.

'Follow me,' she told Andrew.

'Have fun,' advised Rhys, who slumped on his bed, his hairy legs protruding from his gown.

She led him to a small, bare room whose only feature was a flat examination table and a bulky camera encased in metal that swung from a flexible mechanical arm bolted to the wall. They were going to take an X-ray, she told him, of his chest.

'My chest,' he repeated.

'That's right.'

She laid him on the table. She stepped out of the room. She re-entered and adjusted him several times, taking different X-rays from different angles. The vinyl of the examining table was cold on his back where the gown didn't cover him. She came back in a final time and lifted the camera up and away. Then she led him to an examination room.

He waited there in his draughty robe. A long time later, a doctor arrived. He was in his mid-forties with a solid build, a shaved head and extraordinarily thick eyelashes. He introduced himself as Dr Minos. Another nurse appeared – petite, with a choppy haircut and double earrings. She wore a face mask and busied herself with equipment in the corner. She ripped the plastic off some packaged implements. Andrew watched her warily. Then the doctor came to him, pulling on a mask of his own. All Andrew could see was his scalp and those lush, almost mascara'd-looking eyes.

'I'm going to perform some tests,' the doctor said. 'We're going to be more aggressive than normal. You have symptoms.'

'What?' said Andrew. 'Wait, you mean my cough? I told the nurse, it's a smoker's cough.'

Thinking about it so much, he got a tickle, and coughed right there.

'You have phlegm,' confirmed the doctor.

'Come on,' said Andrew, angrily. 'What are the odds that I have TB?'

'You mean exposed to TB? Nearly one hundred per cent.'

Andrew's eyes widened.

The doctor chuckled grimly. 'I know what you're thinking. *In England? At Harrow School?* Oh yes, my young friend. Millions of people carry TB. It's all around us. In the air. In enclosed spaces. The tube. Restaurants. It's communicated through coughing – sputum. Carried through the air, by coughs like yours, breathed into the lungs. In most cases the immune system fights it off. But not always.' He tried a softer tone, seeing Andrew's discomfort. 'You spent a lot of time with the index patient. Tell me about your relationship with him.'

'So it *is* Roddy?'

Dr Minos blinked. 'Let's assume.'

'Will he be OK?'

'Possibly. He's very advanced. Did you know that?'

'Advanced?'

'Fever. Weakening. Coughing. He's frightened. As he should be.'

'Jesus.' Andrew shook his head. 'He wasn't even sick before.' The doctor's face showed surprise at these words but Andrew missed it. 'Where is he?'

'I thought I was asking the questions,' said the doctor.

'Is he here?'

'I'll tell you, because I want you to answer my questions honestly. If you don't tell me the truth – the more you hide from me – the greater the chance you could end up like him.' He paused, his eyes flashing a warning. 'Your friend is in an isolation ward. A room with an antechamber, a special ventilation system and ultraviolet lights on the ceiling to kill the mycobacteria. And he'll be ingesting a nice bag of snacks every day: INH. Rifampicin. PZA and ethambutol. That's unless the strain turns out to be drug-resistant. Given that I hear we have Africa in the picture. Yes? The original fatality?' Andrew thought of Theo and his family burned pink by the African sun. He nodded. The doctor continued. 'Then your friend Roddy will get injections. Some unpleasant side effects. Renal damage. Even hearing loss. So I want you to be forthright. Do I make myself clear?'

Andrew nodded again. He felt alone, cold in his gown, and towered over by the doctor.

'What's your relationship to Roddy?'

'We're next-door neighbours.'

'In a dormitory?'

'A house, yeah.'

'Roddy and the other bloke, the South African – were they close?'

'No, not especially.'

'Close at all?'

'I guess. I mean, they were in the same house for years.'

'I'll lay it out for you, Andrew,' said the doctor. 'Schools like Harrow have a certain reputation.'

'OK . . .'

'You know the word *buggery* in America?'

Andrew snorted. 'You're kidding, right?' Dr Minos's dark-rimmed eyes assured him he was not. 'Ah, *yes*, I know that word,' Andrew said sarcastically.

'See any of that at Harrow?'

'*No*.'

But Andrew's face burned. *No*, except for the buggery that happens in a small, cold, stone room, that either was or wasn't real; *no*, except for the boys with giant uncircumcised penises performing rape in the showers; *no*, except for the slippery white-haired boy with the twisted grunting face holding a kerchief to his neck . . .

'Ever hear of any? Say, between Roddy and the African bloke?'

'*No*. Why are you asking me this?'

'Did Roddy have HIV?'

'Are you *kidding*?'

Suddenly Dr Minos came very close to him, mask to mask, finally losing his composure. 'Do I look like I'm fucking kidding, mate?'

The nurse glanced up from her work.

'He's seventeen years old,' Andrew objected. 'He's straight. Healthy. *No*. I mean, not that I know of.'

'Drug user? Did he shoot up?'

Andrew held his breath for a second. 'Definitely not.'

'The other one?'

'Theo? No.'

'What about you? Do you engage in anal sex or intravenous drug use?'

'No,' he said, going scarlet. John Harness could not count, he told himself: he was not a living person. And the heroin – well, that had been months ago, and he had always snorted it. 'Why are you asking me this?'

Dr Minos stood back. 'You said it yourself. Not ill one day. Ill the next. That's very aggressive. Know how long it takes a normal TB patient to show the kinds of symptoms your mate is showing?'

'No.'

'Two months. According to you – according to everyone – he made these advances in twenty-four hours. Same with the index event.'

'Theo.'

'The only explanation is that your friend Roddy, and Theo, have HIV.'

Andrew shook his head. 'I really don't think so.'

The doctor gave him a sad, sidelong smile. 'How well do you know your friends?'

Andrew did not answer, but Dr Minos did not seem to notice.

'You should have seen this place around, say, oh, 1986,' said the doctor. 'Out of nowhere – over the course of a summer – we had ten, twenty, then scores of patients in here with tuberculosis. Not your typical African or Asian immigrants arriving here looking for work, too ill to walk. Nice English stock. Lots of men. Place full of them. We had to clear out beds, bring in additional equipment, doctors. The place was flooded. Everyone working eighteen-, twenty-hour shifts. We thought it was an epidemic. I went home at night and couldn't sleep, lying awake wondering how I was going to help save London from a new plague. We didn't realize susceptibility to TB was part of the HIV pattern. The immune system that protects you and me from those floating mycobacteria wasn't working for those patients then.' He paused. 'And that's the only explanation now.'

'But what if they don't have HIV? Does that mean it's a . . . virulent strain?'

'No. No TB strain on its own is that potent. If they don't have

HIV . . .' The doctor turned to Andrew and shrugged. 'Then I don't know.'

'But what about Theo. At first they told us he had' – Andrew groped for the word – 'sarcoidosis.'

'Sarcoid? Did they?' The doctor nodded. 'That makes sense. One has necrotizing granulomas, the other non-necrotizing granulomas.'

'Huh?'

'They look the same on the post-mortem table. Honest mistake. Both cause caseosis in the lungs. That's when your lungs turn to cheese. The culture from the post-mortem no doubt corrected the error.'

Andrew imagined a grey chunk of Theo's lung growing mould in a Petri dish. Nausea rose in his gorge.

Then, unbidden, came the image of John Harness. The sunken cheeks and putty-coloured skin. The wild, desperate eyes.

'So this would be a mystery,' Andrew prompted, suddenly eager. 'Something you couldn't explain.'

'That's correct.'

'Can – what are they called, mycobacteria – can they survive in a building? Like, the dorm?'

'For how long?'

'Two hundred years?'

The doctor gave a curious half smile and shook his head. 'No chance.'

'What do you look like with TB? When, say, you don't get treatment, or you get, like, antiquated treatment?'

'Antiquated treatment. I've seen plenty of that in Africa. Bone-skinny. You're starved because the lesions on your throat prevent you from eating. If you get far enough along you'll be coughing blood. But at that point . . .'

'Your breathing . . . does it gurgle?'

'It can.'

'What does it sound like?'

Dr Minos raised his eyes to the ceiling, thinking. 'Like a hookah,' he said. 'Necrotic fluid. Pasty dead cells, liquid, from the infection.' He eyed Andrew. 'Why are you asking me this? Have you seen these symptoms?'

Andrew ignored his questions. 'And are people – living people who have these symptoms – infectious?'

'Extremely. Even dead people are infectious. We're lucky the pathologist who examined your first dead friend wasn't infected.' He looked at Andrew again, suspiciously. 'Anything you want to tell me, mate?'

'No.' Andrew shook his head.

'Sure?' Dr Minos continued staring.

'Just curious what happens.'

We'll do our best to keep you from reaching that stage. Now, Dr Minos continued, *consistent with the high level of care you are to receive at the hospital, you will participate in a four-part screen. The chest X-ray was the first* . . . But Andrew wasn't listening. His pulse raced. He recalled the figure, bent over Theo. The groan that was part gurgle. *Rachel here will administer the first test*, the doctor was saying, leaning in close. He and the nurse muttered back and forth. *More oblique angle. There you are.* 'Feel that?' he said to Andrew. Andrew winced at a stab in his arm. 'You now have a small injection of tuberculin in your skin, which we will watch for a reaction. A good standard screen. But it will only tell us if you've been infected, not whether your infection is active or latent. Rachel will now draw blood for test three.'

Andrew looked away while the nurse wrapped a tourniquet around his elbow, poked for a vein, found one, pricked him, and drew two small vials of blood.

'Now for number four. Rachel, all ready to go?' the doctor said.

'Is this the fun one?' joked Andrew.

'It's the one that makes getting poked with a needle *look* fun,' the doctor replied. 'A last warning. Do what you're told. Stay quiet about the test. Don't alarm people. If you get ill, and you mess about, we'll get a court order and bring you back to the isolation ward – involuntarily. Do you understand me, mate?' Dr Minos looked serious. 'Locked up. That's right. If we don't get full cooperation. A school is the *worst* place for an outbreak. I've seen it, and it's chaos.' He snapped his gloves off, tossed his mask in the lidded waste bin, squeezed a healthy dose of sanitizer into his hands, and disappeared out the door.

'JUST ONE MORE to go, huh?' said Andrew, feigning cheer. 'How bad could this be, after the blood?'

Nurse Rachel held the door open for him. 'We're going somewhere else for this.'

He followed her down the corridor. The halls were wide and square and strangely empty-feeling down here. They eventually came to a large sign, in capitals: SPUTUM INDUCTION ROOM. Rachel knocked and pushed open a door into a small, rectangular room with two transparent plastic cubes, like mini phone booths, on the right. A waiting technician rose and started murmuring over equipment with Rachel.

'All right,' said the technician, a small-framed black woman. 'You're going to sit in the chamber, and breathe in air through the tube.' She indicated an accordion tube draped inside one of the phone booths. 'And then you'll fill the cup with sputum. Not spit. The thick stuff. All right?'

'Very much not all right,' Andrew replied. 'What am I breathing?' He was paranoid now. Were they pumping him full of tuberculin, or whatever?

'Air with vaporized salt water. To stimulate coughing. We need the sample for a culture.'

Andrew realized he didn't have much of a choice and sat in the booth. It was cramped. The seat was low. He heard motors whizzing overhead and felt a current move around him. Some kind of fan was sucking the air out of the chamber – *to keep it clean for the next guy*. He put the tube to his mouth and inhaled. And winced – it stung. But it made him cough all right. He hacked, and dribbled a globule into the cup. The technician nodded encouragingly and said something. But he could not hear her over the fans. He took another toke on the plastic tube. Hacked again. Spat. His throat burned. Rachel stood in the corner, watching. He stared out at them from his whirring chamber. He was entombed, looking out at the living, the well, the free. Suddenly Andrew felt a sense of connection to John Harness. The loneliness of being ill. Having everyone stare at you in this detached, disgusted way, asking themselves, not, *Poor person, how can I help?* But: *How do I keep from getting what he has?* He sucked on the tube. The gag reflex began somewhere around his fifth attempt. At his ninth, he opened his mouth and retched.

16

The Caregiver Would Like a Drink Now

FAWKES RODE A prolonged and horrible wave of adrenalin in the ambulance, lasting from the suburbs all along the A104 into London. Panic sluiced into his veins whenever he looked at Roddy struggling to breathe. The boy's grey face registered not only acute discomfort, but a kind of dreadful, wide-eyed surprise, as if each time the boy pulled for breath his body was telling him *something is wrong, something is scary, I'm not getting enough*. And every few seconds he had to do it again. *Fill the lungs*. And then: *terror*. Fawkes kept up a reassuring patter for a time. *It's going to be all right, Roddy*. But he kept having visions of Theo's body bag. The aluminium sinks. He was afraid that if he said anything more, these images would somehow leap from his mind into Roddy's. So he shut up. Merely placed a hand on the boy's shoulder. *What the fuck am I doing here, doing this?* Fawkes wondered. *Why me? I'm the last person anyone wants as a nursemaid, a caregiver.* He kept waiting for the ambulance to stop; for the doors to swing open and for some mature, responsible individual to launch himself into the back of the ambulance with the vigour and confidence of an expert, and say *All right, thanks for bringing him this far, Piers; you're all done; you can hit the pub*. This person would wear a joking, knowing smile; this person would know all about him, that he was a drunk, a poet, not the man for this job. But nobody did. So far, they appeared to take him seriously.

They appeared to believe he was in the right place. The ambulance bumped along. Fawkes kept his hand on Roddy's shoulder. This was like wartime, he observed. When people were drafted to do things they were not prepared to do, and then did them anyway.

At the hospital, they were separated. The paramedics rolled Roddy into triage, then into the jammed staging area. Fawkes was instructed to sit on the benches in the corridor. He waited. A doctor eventually came out through the door. He was a bald man with an intense manner. They were wheeling Roddy upstairs, he said. Did Fawkes need to notify the parents? Of course – but where were they taking him? To the Chest Centre. Where he would receive a cocktail of unpronounceable drugs. The doctor actually cited survival rates. Then, before Fawkes could recover, the doctor vanished and the Health Protection representative, a smiling man with a moustache and an earring, appeared. Fawkes just murmured, told Mr Earring what he wanted to know, filled out a sheet on a clipboard. At last he was left alone again.

He felt trembly, pale, weak. These were things he did not understand. Things he could not control. He remembered precisely the half-dozen wine bars they had passed on their way to the hospital. He could nose the booze from a block away, like a shark sniffing blood. God, if he could, he would have taken one of those black rubber blotters on the bar – the ones with the little rubber cilia to hold up the glasses, but leave room for the spill – and would have lifted it to his lips, and drunk the tepid soapy water, just to taste the diluted white wine and ale mixed in. He closed his eyes to regain control. He wanted a drink, he needed a drink. No one knew where he was. Roddy did not need him, not for some time anyway. *He was going to have a drink*. A couple of pints, to stabilize him, warm him up. Or a gin. He knew he shouldn't. He stood anyway. It would only take thirty minutes. Maybe forty-five.

At that moment he felt the reminder-buzz of the mobile phone in his jacket pocket. He flipped it open, hands trembling. *Voicemail.*

His hands shook harder. He stood staring at the phone in his palm.

It was enough to stop the momentum.

He would not *have that drink.*

The frenzy of desire passed him by.

Saved.

Whatever message this was, he said to himself in a kind of prayer, he would remember it for ever. Someone selling insurance, holidays in Majorca, whatever it was. He pressed a button to listen to it. He heard a voice he knew – who was it, that accent? – and listened to Andrew's message.

If you don't come get us, I'm not sure what's going to happen.

An unaccustomed flood of feeling overcame him. He had avoided close relationships for so long that the closest thing he had to a friend, in that moment, was a seventeen-year-old American whom he hadn't even met a few months prior. He viewed the selfish, snarky, cold-blooded creature he had become, and felt the acid sting of regret.

Piers Fawkes sank back on to the bench without listening to the whole message. He pressed his hands to his face and, abruptly, began to weep. His shoulders shook. His hands grew wet. People continued passing him in the hallway. This was not so unusual a sight in a hospital. The staff knew to let grief run its course.

ANDREW SETTLED ON to yet another examining table expecting another round of testing, prodding, injecting. The original nurse had returned and handed him his bag of clothes. He had grown so pliant and passive, he received them like a hostage: ransomed, but still broken in spirit. She told him to complete his paperwork at the desk on his way out, and that someone from the school would come to take him and Rhys back to Harrow so they would not have to take public transport. She reminded him to avoid direct contact with others as much as possible until the tests came back, and to specifically avoid travel; to stay in contact with the hospital ... the instructions continued. He repeated 'OK' several times. Then she left. He began to dress. With each article of clothing, a layer of dignity returned. The school uniform now – to his own surprise – lent him a wily sense of adventure, as if he were disguising himself for a masked ball. The Harrow School uniform: what a cheeky rebuke to this whitewashed medical maze. Soon he stood outside the examining room door, in his greyers, bluers and black tie. Over to the right, he saw glass-windowed doors with darkness beyond. Next to them were wide windows. He stared. Something in his mind turned. *Antechamber.* Hadn't Dr Minos used that word to describe the units where tuberculosis patients – the advanced ones – were treated?

Roddy, he thought.

The halls were quiet. A nurse sat behind a glass partition, staring at a desktop computer. Footsteps passed and receded. Andrew went to the first darkened door. Felt the handle. It turned. He entered the antechamber. He heard the whir of a ventilation system. He had five feet to change his mind. He opened the second door. He saw a television set on an extending metal arm, and blinds, closed, admitting a white glow.

'H-hello?'

No answer.

He opened the door more widely. Pushed his head inside.

The bed was made. The room was empty.

He retreated back to the corridor. He had been inside only a few seconds. Nothing had changed. Andrew quickly crossed to the next antechamber door. This handle also turned. As soon as he entered, he knew this room would be occupied: the blinds, in the interior room, were cracked; and while the television remained off, there was another source of illumination: a bank of lights on the ceiling, emitting an intense aqua blue. *Ultraviolet lights to kill the mycobacteria.* Andrew pressed inside. Lumps in the sheets – a patient. No one in the visitor chairs – a patient alone.

'Hi . . . is, is that Roddy?'

The lump in the bed stirred. A clear oxygen mask turned to see the visitor. The pale, round face of his next-door neighbour gazed at him. Roddy sat up.

'What are you doing here?' came the muffled demand.

It was followed by a round of coughing. Not a smoker's cough. Not a hacking, laryngeal cough. This cough used the whole thorax, as if Roddy's chest were a bag full of wet sponges being flogged with a carpet beater. Andrew recoiled. Roddy held the oxygen mask to his face tighter, as if a better grip on it could restore him.

'The doctors think you have TB . . . because you have HIV or AIDS,' Andrew said quickly. 'That's not true, is it? You haven't . . .'

Roddy's brows furrowed angrily. 'I thought this place was a hospital. It's Sodom and Gomorrah! All they want to know is if I bugger my friends! I said, don't you have medical training? I can't breathe, you're worried that I take it in the arse? It's my lungs that need help – not my arse! I might have been a doctor if I'd known all I had to do was enquire about . . .'

His tirade gave way to another cough. This time Andrew witnessed the panic in Roddy's face as the cough extended through the length of what anyone would consider a normal cough, then continued, then continued some more. At last it subsided. Roddy wheezed. He sucked greedily on the oxygen mask. Suddenly its narrow air tube seemed woefully inadequate. Andrew hesitated, not sure whether he should stay. But he needed an answer; needed to confirm the suspicion that had struck him during his conversation with Dr Minos.

'Roddy,' he said. 'When you first got it . . . when it first came on . . . did you see anything? Did you feel anything funny? I mean, not in your breathing. But did you, well . . . see somebody? Feel something in the room?'

Roddy stared at him from behind the mask.

'Rhys said there was a heaviness in the room when he came and got you,' Andrew added.

Outside, in the corridor, Andrew heard voices. Someone was close, facing the room and holding a conversation, poised at the entrance.

Andrew gave up his oblique approach. 'Did you see a boy with white hair?' he hissed.

Roddy's eyes opened wide, frightened.

Andrew felt a thrill. 'You saw him?' he asked, eagerly.

The outer door opened.

'Tell me, please, Rod,' he begged. 'You did, didn't you?'

Roddy's expression went distant, as if he were reliving the moments back in his room. Piecing it all together. 'I don't know *what*'s going on,' he said mournfully.

'What on earth!' exploded the nurse, who had now entered. Andrew jumped. 'No one is permitted in these rooms! And in street clothes!' Her face was covered by a white face mask. Her eyes coiled in anger. 'Get out of here! Who are you? It's very dangerous!'

Roddy sank back into the bed, resigned, exhausted. The nurse turned her attention to him. Andrew bolted to the stairwell, breaking into a sweat; not from exertion, but from fear.

THEY HAD BEEN in the taxi for twenty minutes, nosing through the London traffic. The boys' faces were drawn, fatigued. Their school uniforms hung on them like wrinkled costumes, as if they were actors who had been abducted in the middle of a play. Rhys in particular brooded. Fawkes had met them and hailed them a cab on the busy thoroughfare outside the hospital – expensive, but necessary, if they were to avoid public transport. It was one of the old black London cabs. They piled into the double-sided back seat.

Fawkes recounted for the boys as much as he remembered from his quick conference with the man from the Health Protection Agency. Andrew and Rhys, Fawkes repeated, represented the *inner circle* – the people with greatest contact with Roddy and Theo. The X-rays had been inconclusive. Their blood tests would show definitive results in forty-eight hours. During that time, they could do without masks – those had been necessary when the extent of their infection was unknown – but they needed to lie low. There was only a small chance they had active TB, he told them, trying to sound authoritative. There was an even smaller chance they would pass it to the other boys. The best thing was to keep quiet about the tests. Keep quiet about Roddy's diagnosis. What they needed to avoid was a panic.

Rhys stared out of the window, gloomily. Andrew squirmed with impatience.

'Have you called my parents yet?' Rhys asked.

'I haven't,' Fawkes admitted. 'Let's call them together, when we return.'

'They're going to freak.'

'It's Harness,' Andrew burst out. He could hold it in no longer.

Fawkes glanced nervously at Rhys before turning to Andrew. '*What?*'

'Harness is getting people sick.' Andrew leaned forward. 'The doctor told me he couldn't explain the TB advancing so quickly with Roddy and Theo.'

'Unless it's AIDS,' spat Rhys bitterly.

'Did they give you AIDS tests?' asked Fawkes, surprised.

'Think so.'

Now Fawkes understood their shattered looks. To be diagnosed with one potentially fatal disease is enough for an afternoon; to hear about two in one go would send anyone into a tailspin. And no doubt the boys had been grilled. All the prejudices about boys' boarding schools – especially a prominent one like Harrow – would have risen to the surface. They'd have been accused of living in Sodom-on-the-Hill.

'It's *not* AIDS,' declared Andrew.

'No *way*,' agreed Rhys.

'It's *Harness*,' Andrew repeated.

'What are you on about? What harness?' demanded Rhys.

'Not what, who,' corrected Andrew. 'Harness is the name of the Lot ghost. He's real. He died of TB.'

Rhys rolled his eyes. 'Oh, God.'

'You said yourself, you felt something in the room with Roddy.'

'I . . .' Rhys shook his head. 'I did. But it wasn't the Lot ghost.'

'Oh, it was the Newlands ghost, visiting from next door? I *spoke* to Roddy. I think he saw it.'

'Roddy's sick. We might have TB or AIDS. We have enough to think about without bringing ghosts into it.'

'Quite right,' said Fawkes, staring hard at Andrew and wishing he would shut up until they could speak privately. Head of house or no head of house, it was clear that Rhys had reached his limit.

Andrew leaned forward again. 'The doctor said the TB came on so fast, the only way to explain it was AIDS. You know, a broken immune system. Roddy got sick fast. Theo died fast. That's why they kept harping on AIDS. But Rhys? *Roddy?*' He made a face. 'Theo? Me? *All* of us? With AIDS? Come on. But then I remembered. John Harness had TB. He died of it. It's in the history books. The *Harrow Record*.' He sat back triumphantly, watching Fawkes's expression.

'And you think . . .'

'I think Harness is infecting people!' Andrew declared. 'We have to *do* something. Roddy's really, really bad. And Harness will infect someone else next. There's only me and Rhys left on the floor!'

'But . . . do what?' Fawkes asked him.

'Remember? Find out who Harness killed and why. We have

nothing else to go on. Have you spoken to Reverend Peter?'

Fawkes's intestines squelched with guilt. 'I have. I visited him.'

'And?'

'He's getting dispensation from the Church of England to do it. Some special ritual. It's not the kind of thing he's trained on.'

'How soon can he do . . . whatever it is he needs to do?'

'Not sure,' Fawkes said, looking out of the window. *Say something. Tell him. Come clean. My God, what if he gets it and dies; you'll have it on your conscience.* 'Andrew . . .' he began.

'Piers.'

'I . . . I haven't been straight with you. I've been selfish.' Andrew just stared at him. Fawkes continued. 'I've been more interested in the outcome of our little investigation, than in your welfare. My publisher . . .' He stopped. 'Oh, for fuck's sake, can I have a fag in here?' he shouted to the driver. The driver said yes.

'*Sir*,' objected Rhys, 'we might have *TB*. That's a lung disease.'

'It's only one fag.'

'No!'

Rhys locked eyes with his housemaster. Then broke into a wide grin. Then started laughing; Andrew joined in next, and for the first time that day, all three of them broke into hysterical, grateful laughter. When it subsided, Fawkes hurried to finish his confession while he still had the cover of good humour.

'I told my publisher I could package the play with a sort of literary discovery,' he blurted. 'If I give it to her with a story about Byron's lover committing murder, she'll publish it. If I don't . . . she won't.'

'So that's great. Our research will help you.'

And I sort of told Reverend Peter to slow down.

I decided you and Rhys and Roddy dying was less important than my work.

Go on, say it.

They had reached the motorway. Fawkes stared out of the

window, watching the apartment block whir past. At last he spoke:

'So I've been more focused on the research,' he stammered, 'than on the effect all this has on you.' He was sweating. The boys were staring at him with uncloaked curiosity.

'But that's exactly what we need,' said Andrew.

'It is?'

'Of course! I need to finish my research faster.'

'What have you found so far?'

'I found some letters in the cistern room. Old letters. I gave them to Dr Kahn.'

'Oh, right,' Fawkes said, downplaying his surprise and excitement. 'And?'

'They were damaged. Dr Kahn sent them to Trinity College, Cambridge, to some research people she knows at the Wren Library.' Andrew thought for a moment. 'How long does it take to get to Cambridge?'

'About an hour on the train.' Fawkes knew why Andrew was asking. 'You really think the letters will help our cause?'

'I think Harness *wanted* me to find them.'

Fawkes chewed his nail. 'Trinity, is it?' Fawkes glanced nervously at Rhys before addressing Andrew. 'There are lessons tomorrow,' he said dubiously.

'Roddy can't wait.'

'You're supposed to be lying low. No public transport. By order of the Health Protection Agency.'

'All right, so *you* go.'

'I have a house of fifty-eight boys to look after. *And* I'm on probation. I have a daily meeting with Sir Alan. If I miss it, I'm sacked. Then I'm no good to anyone.'

Rhys looked at Fawkes in surprise. 'Are you serious, sir?'

'You can stop calling me bloody *sir*, and yes, I'm serious. I may be the worst housemaster of all time, as far as I can tell. Look at all this mess.'

'If it's only an hour,' continued Andrew, 'I can leave first thing tomorrow and be back by lunchtime. You can say I slept in, after a trying day.'

'Right,' Fawkes said, uncertainly.

'Why are you hesitating?' asked Andrew. 'You know I need to go.'

Fawkes tried to hide the raw emotion he'd been swept with earlier in the day. 'With Roddy getting ill, I feel more protective of you boys. That's all. You especially, Andrew.'

'This is my job. You and Dr Kahn assigned this part to me: do the research on Harness, and write it up for Essay Club. I can't wait any more.'

'I'm going to say no,' Fawkes said at last.

'Are you kidding?'

'I'm not. When we get back, I'll find Reverend Peter. We'll do the ritual. We'll be rid of John Harness. And then, you know,' he waved his hand vaguely. 'All this will clear up. We don't need to know what any letters say, or what some long-forgotten murder was about. All right?'

Andrew frowned. He had seen Harness's violence, his determination. He wasn't at all convinced that a simple ritual was going to make him go away.

He tried again. 'What if I went with someone? Rhys could go with me.'

Rhys made a face.

'No. I'm sorry,' said Fawkes. 'Your safety is more important.'

The words sounded pretty good. Or they would have, coming from someone else. Fawkes wrestled with himself. This was the right thing to do, wasn't it? He had made a resolution, now, to be *better*; to help Andrew, first and foremost. Keeping him at school, under his protection, was the most important thing. Yet as he watched Andrew, he saw that the boy's gaze had grown distant; anger darkened his eyes, and he had reclaimed that lonely sulk Fawkes had first observed in him. *My God*, Fawkes wondered, *is this what it's like to be a real authority figure? To chafe people? Have them resent you? Question your decisions? Maybe this is what Colin Jute feels like all the time.*

'I think you're all completely mad,' said Rhys.

17

Tears at Trinity

ANDREW MADE THE decision to sneak away to Cambridge almost immediately. But he did not intend to take Persephone. That part just happened.

He found several texts waiting for him when they arrived back at school, time-stamped several minutes apart between the time he left the hospital and the time they reached the Lot.

U were supposed to call to say u will die without hearing my voice for another hour.
U neglected to do this.
A weaker woman would be rending garments etc
I however am doing toenails.
A lot happened today, he texted back.
Really ur awfully important do tell

So he called her and told her.

'My God, Andrew, they think you have TB? That's very operatic of you. Or is it Russian? Either way . . .' Her voice grew more serious. 'You must be petrified.'

'It's caused by the ghost.'

'Be serious.'

He explained his rationale. She listened quietly.

'So what are you going to do?' she asked after a time.

'I'm going to Cambridge.'

'Cambridge? What for?'

'To get the letters I found. Someone Dr Kahn knows has them. An archivist. I need to find out what they say. They have a connection to John Harness. I just know it.'

'When are you going?'

'In the morning. Early. Before anyone sees me.'

Persephone grew quiet. 'Why don't we go tonight?' she said. 'Together?'

'*Tonight?* Where would we stay?'

'You forget, Agatha goes to Trinity. She'll lend us her rooms. She spends most nights with Vivek in any case.'

'What about Sir Alan? Would he let you go?'

'I'll sneak out,' she said, as if this were obvious.

'Won't he notice?'

'I'll make an excuse.'

'Like what?' Andrew grew anxious at the thought of involving Sir Alan.

'Oh, Andrew,' she replied. 'He's got you scared like everyone else. I know how to handle Daddy.'

Andrew gave her more reasons not to come. He thought it was Harness causing the disease; but what if he was wrong? What if he got her sick?

'No kissing, then,' she said.

And she couldn't tell Fawkes, who had forbidden him from going.

'I promise,' Persephone said sombrely.

And what about lessons?

'I told you,' she said. 'I'll manage it. All right?'

'It doesn't sound like you need my permission.'

'I'll text Agatha. She'll be so excited.'

THEY MET AT King's Cross. All the cafés and news-stands stood shuttered; the platforms were vacant of their weekday rush-hour bodies. The station echoed. *The eight forty-one train for . . .*

Cambridge ... is now boarding from Platform ... Eight. Persephone wore a soft pair of jeans and a scarf and she smelled like honeysuckle. Andrew smiled when she approached.

'You made it,' he said.

Almost before the words were out of his mouth, she wrapped her arms around him and kissed him; long, deep, intense.

'We said no kissing!' he said when he came up for air.

'Now we have the same diseases,' she grinned.

'Same haircuts. Same diseases.'

'Nothing can separate us.' She wrapped her fingers in his.

Their carriage was deserted. Persephone leaned against the window and threw her legs over Andrew. The lights in the carriage flickered out. They watched London flick past; then the small towns, small clusters of orange and yellow lights. Then the country night.

'I had an abortion.'

Andrew blinked. 'What? When?'

'Last year. It was Simon's.'

Andrew felt a squeezing in his chest.

'That's what Rebecca was oh-so-obliquely referring to. Now you know.'

Andrew sat stunned for a moment. All the questions he wanted to ask – *What is that like? Does it hurt? Do you feel relieved afterwards, or terrible, like the abortion protesters say: like you just killed something?* – seemed invasive, all wrong. And part of him yearned for answers he knew she couldn't give. Did that mean Simon would always have some special, unerasable place in her life, her history, that he might never achieve? It was a craven, childish thought. Yet it wounded him.

'OK,' he managed.

'Do you still want to be with me?'

'Yes.'

'All right, then.'

'Anything else?' he asked.

'That's all for now.'

The train plunged through an empty station without stopping. Andrew caught a glimpse of her face in the passing lights. Mournful. Maybe he already had an answer to one of his questions.

'I hope we find something in the letters,' he said, changing the subject. 'Roddy's condition is serious. And I'm responsible.'

'Why? It's not like you raised the spirit with witchcraft.'

'But what if I hadn't come to Harrow? Hadn't been in the Lot? Maybe Theo would be alive now. And Roddy wouldn't be sick.'

'But then you wouldn't have met me, would you?' she said. 'I'm cold.'

She leaned forward and nuzzled against him, and he held her.

THE COMPARATIVELY TINY Cambridge station ejected them on to a roundabout where hundreds of student bicycles stood chained to stands. They walked hand in hand, nearly running, up the long streets. Persephone knew her way, having visited Agatha before. They stopped and kissed as they went, finding nooks in the bank entrances, or outside the windows of shops that had closed for the night, their anticipation rising, Andrew wilfully giving into it, allowing himself to escape in it, vaguely aware that the streets were narrowing, giving way to stone, to Gothic windows, to tiny lanes. Persephone took his hands, placed them under her shirt.

'Oh my God, you're not wearing a bra. I'm going to lose it.'

'Not yet,' she breathed. 'Right upstairs.'

'We're here?'

Persephone produced a key, and they ran up an echoing stone stair, into a tiled corridor. Agatha's room bloomed with dusty radiator heat. Andrew took the place in with a glance: heaping duvet, snapshots of pretty smiling pals in frames, a desktop computer, bay windows overlooking Trinity Street. Then Persephone turned off the light. So much for the room. They kissed;

their clothes were tossed to the floor. Persephone pressed Andrew down on the bed. They were solicitous of each other. *Is this right? Do I need to move over?* Persephone eased on top of him with a wince. She started slowly. Andrew watched her face. Her eyes closed; her mouth tightened in concentration. She shimmered there in the light from the street, a winter nymph; slim, fair, sad. *I love you*, he said. This made her pause, but not long; she ignored him. She was intent on getting something from him with her body; solving some puzzle; capturing some prize. She leaned over him, her hair tickling his face, her movements deeper and tighter on him. She took his hands and placed them on her breasts. She ground against him. Then a shudder, a prolonged gasp. She threw herself forward, burying her face in his neck. *You OK?* She nestled deeper into him, letting her shoulders quiver. He realized she was crying. Her tears dampened his neck and ears and cheeks.

A few moments later she sat up, bare-breasted and laughing, wiping her tears. Her body was warm under his hands, with the sandy smoothness of an Attic statue.

'I did it,' she announced. Then, in a small, embarrassed voice: 'I came!' Her cat's-eyes glinted. She giggled, then hurled herself on the bed next to him. The light from the street spilled over her face. She gazed at the ceiling as if it were the night sky.

'It feels *really good*,' she informed him, a touch of surprise in her voice.

'I know,' he laughed.

She leapt up. 'I'm going to call Agatha.' She began to rummage through her bag for her mobile phone.

'Wait. Are you kidding? Now?' He propped himself up on an elbow. 'What about me?'

She flipped open the phone.

'I have to tell her,' she explained, as if she were stating the obvious. 'It *was* in her room.'

THEY SLUMBERED, ANIMALS hibernating, the wind whipping around the old-fashioned panel windows, the coil radiators spitting heat, the single bed heaped with Agatha's embroidered pillows. Andrew might have reflected with interest that rooms such as these had been occupied by Lord Byron two hundred years before, but he did not. Eight hours before he had wandered from the mouth of the Royal Tredway Hospital, battered and disgusted with himself; and now here he lay, happy, safe, replete, entwined in Persephone, in a secret spot. He shut his eyes. He slept richly; he was a submarine, plumbing a placid ocean, passing through fronds of primitive seaweeds; aware of great golden fish with shimmering scales just out of sight in the murk; of treasure chests in the mud below.

When he woke, the dark in the room swirled thick like the ocean, pricked only by a single point of light, small, hot and orange. Andrew stared at it, blearily trying to distinguish if it were part of his dream. Or was it a light coming in from the street? Only when it came closer did he feel a thrill of fear. It was a candle. Behind it, a person. In the room. Agatha? Had she forgotten something? *She would not need a candle*, his mind answered firmly.

Then Andrew saw him. He was naked again. This time white, gaunt, his fingers wrapped around the candleholder like white sticks, his stomach a frail white tent of flesh hanging from his bony ribcage. He stooped and moved slowly, inching forward. His lips were chapped and splitting and bore red stains. The eyes had sunk into the skull, and each breath was won with shuddering toil. *He must be so cold*, Andrew thought, in an instant of sympathy. Harness stared at them. These were the eyes of someone finding his lover in bed with another, but not unexpectedly. Then, slowly, the eyes dragged towards Andrew. Andrew shivered. *He was aware of him*. Andrew struggled to move but he was paralysed. Harness set the candle on the floor. Then the mattress squeaked as a weight came on it. *He can't be getting in the bed with us!* Andrew protested in his mind. Another squeak. Weaker than Andrew would have guessed: he must weigh next to nothing. Harness had crawled up on to the bed and was now straddling Persephone, his arm planted next to Andrew in the bed, the hinge of his hipbone casting a stark and emaciated shadow. He stank of urine, like a homeless man, and a kind of savoury, fleshy rot, like the pavement outside a meat market. That white head was just inches from Andrew now, and Andrew smelled the butchery breath. Harness crouched low over Persephone. His limp penis dragged on the duvet over her. Andrew writhed. Fought himself out of his paralysis, or tried to, but could do nothing, merely screamed inside his head, because he knew what Harness was doing. Harness held Persephone's sleeping face; parted those lips with his bony hands; and breathed into her mouth long, wet gusts, each one rattling inside him like wind through catacombs. Then he coughed. It was a sickening sight. The cough seemed to begin in the hips, then curl its way forward like a wave, ending with a shudder in the head. Harness turned away, placed his hand to his mouth, as if in pain. Then the wave came again, hips, stomach, chest, and finally, with a snap of his neck, Harness unleashed a sound like someone ripping wet towels, and vomited a viscous fluid into Persephone's open mouth, spilling it all over her face. In the candle glow, Andrew glimpsed the fluid's colour, a rich ruby red. Harness closed his eyes, grimacing with pain again. Then he opened them and met Andrew's eyes. His lips were coated with blood. His gaunt eyes stared at Andrew, forlorn, as if all this were *his* doing; it was *his* infidelity, and these were the sad consequences, Harness the mere deliverer. A squeak. The presence retreated from the bed. The mattress readjusted. The candlelight faded. Andrew's mind whirled in terror, and went black.

18

Stalker

ANDREW WOKE TO a sky so low and foggy it was impossible to tell the time. Persephone lay next to him, warm, her body suffusing the bed with that luscious mix of skin-smell, hair-smell, yesterday's perfume, and the smell of sleep. She was naked, entangled in the covers. He smiled. He leaned over, stroked the tangle of her hair. As he did so, he realized that one of his hands clenched something, as if it had been doing so for hours, in sleep. He opened his hand.

A tiny object – small, translucent, flimsy – lay there. A fingernail?

He prodded it with his opposite hand. It appeared to be . . . a petal. A tiny petal, shaped like a fingernail, round and white, with a black ridge. Not a flower petal. The petal of a blossom.

He racked his brain for ways a blossom petal could have ended up in his hand, in autumn.

Then the memory of last night's vision returned to him. He froze, processing. It seemed remote, far in the past. Had it been only a dream? He turned to Persephone in alarm, the mysterious petal forgotten. Was she breathing? Was she dead? Panic flushed him. He scrambled on top of the duvet. Tugged back the sheets from her face. Her cheeks were clean.

'Thank God,' he breathed.

'Is this some American agricultural ritual?' she groaned.

'Checking the livestock after you have sex with it?'

He burst out laughing, with pure joy. Last night must have been a normal dream. Not a vision of the real Harness.

'I love you,' he said.

She said nothing and snuggled up to him.

'It's customary, when one person says I love you, to say I love you back,' he said, trying to sound like he was casually teasing, but very much alert to her response.

'But how would I preserve my mystery, after I've given you so much?'

'*You've* given *me* so much?'

He yanked the duvet from her and she screamed in protest, and they wrestled over it, but eventually lay alongside each other, gazing, as if this were the first time they had seen each other – naked or otherwise – and even Persephone let the minutes tick past without speaking.

AGATHA WAITED FOR them at Trinity Gate, in her red hair and long overcoat, a lone stationary figure in a swirl of bicycles, students, parking cars and busfuls of Chinese tourists. A fog had set in over the university. She hugged Persephone and gave Andrew a double-kiss, and immediately began teasing them for being late. *Cambridge seems to agree with you two. Will there be anything left of my room when I return?* The couple grinned, embarrassed, and they squeezed hands. Agatha rolled her eyes and shepherded them through the porters' lodge. They signed in and passed under the arch to the grounds of Trinity College.

The fog gave the place a dreamlike air, but Andrew suspected that even in bright sunlight you would think you had passed into another era. The college, made up of perfectly preserved sand-coloured buildings from the seventeenth century, surrounded a lawn edged by gravelled paths. A high, ornate fountain stood in the centre. Agatha chatted away with Persephone while Andrew marvelled at the quiet the giant courtyard imposed; how perfectly time had preserved the place. They followed the path around to the building on the far side, climbed some steps, and ducked inside a door set in an ogee arch. A passage, noisy and crowded, cut through the historic building. Students jostled them, wearing scarves and army jackets. In a few paces they reached another door, then emerged into yet another foggy, stony courtyard; only this one was smaller, and completely silent. On the far side rose a multi-storey building with an arcade on the ground floor.

'That's it,' said Agatha, leading them out into this second courtyard. 'The Wren Library. What's your archivist's name again?'

'Lena Rasmussen. Do you know her?'

'I'm reading economics,' replied Agatha. 'I don't have much use for rare manuscripts.'

They passed under the arcade and started up a broad staircase. Ten-foot-high portraits of former college grandees lined the walls: scowling, berobed, monumental.

'Those are to frighten the American tourists,' quipped Agatha.

They found themselves in a long room. It rose two storeys high, with windows on the second floor admitting the chilly radiance of the sky. Whitewashed walls curled into a series of nooks formed by walnut-brown bookshelves. These were crammed with dusty, crumbling volumes, and were cordoned off with velvet ropes to protect what looked like private study areas with lamps and tiny desks. Arranged throughout, on pedestals, were whitewashed busts of literary heroes: Virgil, Cicero, Milton. At the end of the room the largest of these loomed, a colossal hunk of white marble depicting a figure holding a book and a pen. A hush reigned here; aside from a few shuffling figures at the front, there were more busts than live people in the Wren Library.

Agatha strode up to a desk where a man sat tapping listlessly at a computer. He wore a shaggy brownish sweater and had a bald crown and a surrounding fringe of floppy grey hair; he was the human equivalent of an old manuscript. Agatha asked for Lena Rasmussen. The man seemed surprised to encounter a human here; doubly surprised for that human to be a voluptuous nineteen-year-old in expensive clothes and with torrents of attention-grabbing red hair. A woman approached from the opposite nook. She was in her mid-twenties, with broad Scandinavian cheekbones. She wore a brown T-shirt and black jeans, a nose ring, and black hair drawn back in a ponytail.

'I'm a student of Judith Kahn,' said Andrew. 'She sent you some letters I found?'

The archivist appraised him. Her eyes narrowed to an expression of knowing amusement. 'That's you, is it?' she said. 'Those papers have caused a stir. You're students at Harrow?'

'That's right.'

'Looks like you've found some letters left by Lord Byron,' Lena said.

'You found letters ... written by Lord Byron?' exclaimed Agatha, who had not known the specific purpose of their visit.

'Not by,' corrected Lena. 'To. I showed your letters to Reggie Cade. He can explain.'

'Who's Reggie Cade?'

'He's a fellow of the college. He founded the Byron Institute at the University of Manchester, before Trinity stole him away. He was just here yesterday, pawing your letters.' Lena nodded down the hall at the full-sized marble statue. 'That's him, you know.'

'Reggie Cade?' questioned Andrew. It was a ten-foot-high figure with pen and paper, heroically astride a fallen Greek column.

The archivist smiled.

'Lord Byron. It was commissioned to go in Westminster Abbey. But the church wouldn't accept the statue of a known sex maniac. So they sent it to Trinity – where sex maniacs are always welcome.'

She returned to the nook where she'd been sitting and flipped through a notebook for a phone number.

'She's an odd one,' murmured Agatha. 'P . . . you all right?'

Persephone had gone pale.

'I'm all right.'

'You look frightful.'

'I'll be fine. My blood sugar just dropped.'

Andrew went to wrap an arm around her.

'So sweet,' crowed Agatha, approvingly.

'No snogging in the Wren,' drawled Lena, returning. 'Reggie's on his way. Bicycling here at full speed, no doubt. Come on.'

'Where are we going?' asked Andrew.

'To the vault,' she said.

THEY DESCENDED THE broad steps they had originally come up and found that the Wren connected to a disappointingly modern student library with carpeting, low ceilings and cramped carrels. They wormed their way to a service staircase and began a descent of several storeys.

'We're underground now,' Lena told them. They reached a heavy door. She punched a code into a security keypad and yanked it open. 'Notice it's cooler here. Needs to be between fifty-five and sixty-five Fahrenheit, and fifty-five and sixty-five per cent relative humidity. We're next to the river. The walls are reinforced concrete, to keep the damp out. Basically we're in an underground box. And here,' she said, flicking on a bank of lights and pushing open the door of a metal cage with a clank, 'are the manuscripts.'

They faced a long, thin passageway. On the left stood high shelves; not ordinary, stationary bookshelves; these were on rollers, with steel crank handles, like the doors to old bank vaults, to slide them back and forth. Lena traced her way to the shelf she wanted and began turning the handle. The shelves oozed apart, silently. She motioned to Andrew. 'Come on. I'll show you.'

He followed her into the narrow space between the shelves, which rose in darkness fifteen feet.

'I hope you trust your friends,' she murmured.

'Why?'

'Each of these shelves weigh a ton. If they turn the crank, we'll be crushed.'

'You have a strange sense of humour.'

'Passes the time.' She pulled a grey box from the shelf. 'Come on, we'll wait for Reggie in the consultation room.'

DR REGGIE CADE arrived, red in the face, still huffing from his rapid bicycle ride (Andrew caught Lena smiling to herself at his appearance – her prediction had been accurate). He cut an imposing and strange figure: over six feet, with a vast belly; a green cardigan, green tie; high rubber boots, as if he had just been working in a garden; and large oilskin jacket. He was fiftyish, with a baggy, jowly face covered with a scruff of blond beard, going white; one of his eyes wandered severely; and his hands were soft and flabby with longish nails – that look only English men seemed to acquire, after a lifetime avoiding exercise. In all he was not an attractive man. But when he spoke, he boomed in a rich bass; Orson Welles with a Manchester brogue. Andrew could imagine him as a mesmerizing lecturer. He paused in the doorway of the tiny consultation room – a ten-by-ten box with carpeting, fluorescent lights and a round table with chairs. The young people had crowded around as Lena removed the contents of the grey box: a dozen letters, stained brown, spread out like a large and fatigued hand of cards.

Dr Cade sized them all up with his one good eye. 'I see only one male, and the letters were found at Harrow School, so I presume *you* are the finder of the letters.' He directed his remarks at Andrew, without introduction. Andrew nodded. 'Make room, then.' Lena found him a chair. He entered the room and eased his bulk into it. 'Where did you find them?' he demanded of Andrew, patting his face with a handkerchief.

Andrew told the story about the cistern room and the biscuit tin.

Cade shook his head and chuckled. 'Were they Byron Brand biscuits?' At this Andrew grinned and warmed to him. 'That's a story indeed. All right, Lena, let's have a look at the specimens.'

'Hands dry, Dr Cade?'

'Don't hector me, girl. Come on.'

'Have you read the letters?' Andrew asked eagerly.

'I have,' Cade said.

'And?'

'It's a shame your biscuit box wasn't a bit drier,' Cade said, fingering the leaves. 'These fibres adhered because they were damp and tied up – squeezed together for two hundred years. Separating them shredded the fibres, and much is illegible. Not to mention the staining. Still,' he said, 'there are parts we can read. And what a read!' He peered around the table, as if threatening them to disagree. 'When Lena told me it was possible they belonged to Lord Byron . . . how did you know, by the way? Before reading them?' Cade peered at Andrew.

'I live in Byron's house. His dorm.'

'So have hundreds of boys.'

'I'm playing Byron in a school play. Byron on the brain, I guess.'

'Was this John Harness's house, too?' Cade asked. Andrew froze. He felt the others' eyes on him, puzzled. Cade chuckled. 'So you know the name, eh? John Harness, Byron's lover and classmate at Trinity. You know a lot about Lord Byron, I see. But I'm guessing there's no plaque at Harrow School to Byron *and* his young boyfriend, hm? Schools tend not to publicize such things.' Andrew shook his head. 'Just as well. The scholarship portrays Harness as an innocent. An early Byron victim. Byron himself had much to do with that.

Those eyes proclaim'd so pure a mind,
Even Passion blush'd to plead for more.

'But what I have here . . . I beg your pardon,' he said, blustering a little, embarrassed, 'what *you* have here, is evidence that innocent young John Harness was far from *pure*. In fact, he was hell on wheels.'

'How do you know it's Harness?' Andrew managed.

'How?' the doctor replied, with a proud thrust of the chin. 'I matched these letters against a detailed chronology of Byron's life I have been developing for three decades.'

'And how did they compare?'

'Perfectly,' Cade said with a smile of triumph. 'That's why I'm here.' He arranged the letters in front of him. 'The writer is not Byron. I believe it's Harness himself. These would be the first extant letters of Byron's homosexual lover.'

Andrew leaned forward eagerly. 'How do you know?'

'Three factors. The chronology; the intimacy and mutual knowledge; and the tone. Which begins quite lovey-dovey, then nosedives into jealous obsession.' Dr Cade drew out a pair of reading glasses and squinted at the pages, leaning over them – favouring his good eye, like a bird examining a worm – and chose a leaf. 'To Byron. Summer, 1808. *The tears which I shed in secret are the proofs of my sorrow. I was and am yours. I give up all here & beyond the grave for you*. Beyond the grave,' he repeated.

Andrew found himself glancing at Persephone. Her face seemed ashen in the dim light.

Dr Cade peeled off his reading glasses. 'Harness was to die a year later. He must have known already he had tuberculosis. And he would have known his odds of survival were poor. In those days, consumptives were prescribed fresh air. Trips to Spain, or sea voyages. But you had to have money. Harness had just left Trinity, in penury, to become a clerk in London. He could afford no such luxury. And there's our fourth theme in these letters.'

'What's that?' asked Andrew.

'Death,' declared Dr Cade. 'Step by step, a desperate young man dying. Here's one addressed to Albemarle Street, in March. Winter must have been getting to him.

'*If through some accident you have never received the last letters sent by me* . . . Starts with a guilt trip – where's the money to keep me well fed? Where are the funds for *my* journey abroad? He wants his rich boyfriend to give him some cash. And Byron, typically, is selfish in all the wrong moments. We're talking about a man who later left his own daughter to die in an Italian convent.' Cade scanned the pages. 'It's illegible for a while. *My coughing and* – unreadable, maybe *fever – continue . . . but while these keep me sitting up all the night kerchief clenched to my mouth, it is you and news of you which I* . . . looks like *thirst for*. He's still feeling well enough to be rhetorical. It doesn't last. Neither does his writing paper. This is where the cross-hatched writing quite overloads the page. Next letter.'

He placed one leaf down and picked up the one beside it. '*There is a core of disease in me not easy to pull out. I have ceased to attend to the firm*. Harness's position was at a London company, in shipping, very middle class at the time, which is to say poor by our standards. Can you imagine his isolation? Grown too fancy for his impoverished family. Homosexual, alone, broke, and dying? His world would have been growing smaller by the minute. *I live on the guineas put by – and even these are scarcely put to use as I cannot eat. I cannot abide food for the cankers that afflict my mouth. My few visitors chide me for my pallor and insist I eat animal meat – but I am done with both – animals and visitors – and my chest is in a nervous state such that when I draw breath spasms shake me and I cough blood. It is black & thick.*'

Dr Cade frowned at the manuscript. 'Tough way to go, TB. But he's not through yet. The one obsession that keeps him going is Byron. *I am relieved only by your love*,' Cade continued reading. '*In those words – your love – is comprised my existence here and hereafter.* But it turns sour when he finds – again, typically – that Byron has taken up with someone else. Another young man. Now the love song shows the discord of jealousy. Mind you, Byron is in and out of London *all* this time, and seems never to have visited Harness.

'*H's letter reached me* . . . I reckon H is Hobhouse, a close friend of Byron, and as such likely a mutual acquaintance with Harness . . . *you have a new "friend" espied with you often in London whose name none know but whose countenance all seem agreed is handsome and dainty and fair. Men seldom agree on anything in such unison.* Bitchy remark. Not only is he dying; he's been betrayed. Byron has new boy toy, a pretty one, and one who's well enough to run about town with him. Let's see, from here, little is legible until *pretending fair creature* . . . *black cloud* – must be "fills" – *my mind.* Ah yes, then the imperative. *Tell me who this is.* Harness seems, now, determined to take action. *I am coming to Albemarle Street, expect me.*'

'Stalking,' observed Andrew.

Dr Cade nodded approvingly. 'I like that. Very apt. Stalking,' he repeated, as if remembering it for later. 'No letters for several days,' he resumed. 'It appears Byron has given Harness the slip.'

'What did he do? Did it work?' cut in Andrew.

'Well, Harness is very persistent,' Dr Cade answered. 'Listen. *My dearest* . . . *I trust this finds you well at Brighton. You have gone there quickly I am told – the same day as my visit to your rooms.* Byron's dodging him, you see. *Mrs Leckie* . . . must be the landlady . . . *was kind enough to tell me your FRIEND accompanied you.* See the caps?' Dr Cade held the letter up for them to look at, smiling. 'Now two days later. Pursuit has failed Harness. He tries more guilt. He should have known Byron better – the man was no nursemaid. *Can you not return to London, even for an hour? When you see me & my need you will forgo all other loves. Today I was going on in good spirits quite merrily – when – in an instant – a cough seized me and I vomited two cupfuls of blood. It is my death warrant. I must die. I wish for death every day and night to deliver me from these pains, and then I wish death away, for death would destroy my only hope for joy – a single sight of you.* Very sweet, as far as it goes, but jealousy gets the better of him. *The one who enjoys such a vision in my place, I most determinedly do hate. This hate grows and blooms even as I decay and die.* Illegible, but it goes on for a time on this theme of hate because he's still on it' – Dr Cade flipped the paper – 'on the next page. *The flowering of it*, he says, *will be to destroy him.*'

'To destroy him,' Andrew repeated. 'He means he will kill his rival.' Andrew's eyes leapt to Persephone.

'As I said. Hell on wheels.'

Persephone coughed. It was a long, itchy, persistent cough, and it interrupted the discussion.

Andrew watched her, a sudden and unnamed suspicion aroused in him. She remained pale, withdrawn.

Stalking.

Andrew had said it, trying to be the clever student, to impress the teacher. But he had unwittingly supplied his own answer. With a crash of misery, he realized his vision of Harness from the night before might not have been a dream at all.

'Are you feeling OK, Persephone?'

'I'm all right.'

'Are you sure? How does your chest feel?'

'My chest?'

The group looked at Andrew, puzzled by this question.

'Your cough,' he said, defensively.

'I'm perfectly fine,' she said crossly.

'I'm worried about you. You don't look well.'

'You're being silly.'

'Shall I go on?' Dr Cade asked.

Reluctantly, Andrew nodded. But his eyes kept finding Persephone, watching her for any change, while he listened to Dr Cade's remarks.

'So here,' boomed Dr Cade, 'is the last letter of this extraordinary series, dated June 1809, just a month before Byron sets sail for Portugal. The most passionate of all. If that's the right word. *Dearest – You are going to SD*. Not certain what that is. SD? Sounds like a place-name, but I could find no meaningful reference. *HE is coming with you. I know. H wrote me and told me all. I will summon all my remaining strength. I am coming to you. There, where we once met, I will find you, destroy him, and all will be well*. You said it very well before.' Cade nodded to Andrew. 'He is a stalker. A nineteenth-century stalker. For all Byron's flaws, you can see why he avoided Harness. The young fellow's jealousy literally drove him mad. *I will find you, destroy him* . . . doesn't leave much room for metaphorical interpretation. It's a death threat.' Cade dropped his reading glasses onto the table. 'Still, one is left with many questions. Who was this other lover? And more practically, how did these letters end up all together, at Harrow School? And what is *SD*?'

Persephone murmured weakly.

'What's that?' demanded Dr Cade, loudly, without any sympathy.

Persephone coughed again.

'Water,' said Andrew. 'Is there something here for her to drink?'

'Upstairs. The fountain,' said Lena.

Andrew ran up the flights of stairs, panic pulsing in his mind. He felt, for a moment, insane. Persephone was sick. He perceived it. The disease was taking her over at this very moment. His hands trembled as he filled a paper cup of water in the bustling library. He carried it carefully downstairs, back to the consultation room. Yes, she was definitely pale. Yet all these people were sitting around calmly. *Of course they are. They didn't see what you saw, last night*, he told himself. He handed the water to Persephone. She drank the water gratefully.

'Speech Day,' she croaked at last.

'Speech Day?' Dr Cade repeated. He tossed back his head, as if to search for the words' meaning on the ceiling.

'Speech Day. At Harrow,' Andrew explained, suddenly understanding. 'It's kind of like graduation, at the end of the school year. A bunch of seniors . . . Sixth Formers . . . memorize speeches and deliver them. Byron and Harness might have met on that weekend like . . . like old friends meeting at Alumni Day.'

'*You're going to SD.*' Cade repeated the words to himself. 'To Speech Day. Yes, of course. It's in the summer, is it?'

'Early June. So they would have got together at Harrow, on Speech Day, in 1809,' Andrew said, putting the pieces together. 'That must be where they exchanged the letters.'

'That meeting would have been a real prizefight,' Cade declared, holding the letters. 'After all these.'

Lena protested. 'But these are only Harness's letters, I'm certain. One handwriting only.'

'Quite right. There was no *exchange* of letters. Byron returned all of Harness's letters,' Cade exclaimed. 'They were toxic. Who would want to keep them?' He grew more animated. 'And it explains the receptacle. He would not exactly tie these with a ribbon. And he would not want his Harrow friends to see them. So he returned the letters . . . in a biscuit box. Probably one he picked up in a local shop, or near his lodgings at Harrow. A hastily obtained container. Lucky for us – airtight!' Cade grinned, delighted. 'This is good! Very good!'

Cade opened his mouth to ask more questions. But this time he was unable to speak because Persephone coughed again, loudly. The cough perpetuated itself; hacking; scratching; on and on, as the lungs searched for, but never found, the blockage. It bent Persephone double.

Andrew's stomach fell. Here it was. He had been both right and wrong. Right that he had seen the vision, and known, instinctively, that Harness had infected Persephone. Wrong that he had not acted upon it immediately.

The faces of his companions instinctively screwed up in disgust and sympathy – then finally – finally! – Persephone's cough seemed to have found the blockage; something *caught*, at last; and she – with a grimace; and not having time to grab a handkerchief – delivered some liquid into her palm. She held up her hand and looked at it.

Agatha spoke first.

'Oh my God! Persephone!' she shrieked. 'It's blood! Andrew! Persephone just spat up blood!'

Andrew leapt to Persephone's side, both he and Agatha immediately bending over her, staring at the hand Persephone had extended. She now withdrew her hand, trying to hide it. A puddle of blood, bright red and gleaming.

'It's nothing,' she said weakly. 'Stop worrying.'

'We are worrying,' protested Agatha. 'You've been looking funny all morning. We'd better go. We'll go to my room and you can lie down. I'm sorry, Mr Cade.' They coaxed Persephone from her seat. Dr Cade remained seated, disappointed; his audience was breaking up. Lena Rasmussen whispered to him – *I need these back, sir* – and took the precious letters from him, tucked them back in the box, and disappeared into the rolling stacks again. Then the group became a chaotic scrum, circling around Persephone, moving her through the passage between the high shelves back to the narrow staircase.

'I'm taking her back to London,' Andrew said.

'London?' protested Agatha.

'She needs to go to the hospital.'

Andrew wrapped his arms around Persephone and led her up the narrow stairs, through the student library, where they drew stares, and out under the silent colonnade. Andrew and Agatha moved their friend back through the courtyard, retracing their steps towards Trinity Street. It suddenly seemed a long way to walk.

'Are you really leaving?' exclaimed Dr Cade, who had followed them out.

'I'm sorry, sir,' Agatha called over her shoulder. 'Thank you,' she added, to Lena.

Andrew heard Cade boom out after them: 'I intend to publish this, you know!' Then he added: 'How can I contact you?' They didn't answer. As they reached the portal on the far side of the courtyard, he called out again, with a desperate note: '*Do you want credit for the discovery?*'

Andrew kept his arms wrapped around Persephone. He kept leaning over to check her face, check the pallor there, check for the shallowness of her breathing, check for things that made her look like Roddy sucking air out of that black punching bag for dear life, or like Theo *don't think it* like Theo lying cold and stiff and vaguely purple with gravel on his eyebrows. Agatha peppered him with scolding counsel *there's a sickbay we can be there in ten minutes* but he ignored this. He knew what he needed to do.

HE HALF GUIDED Persephone, half carried her, through those streets they had dashed through the night before. Now the route back to the train seemed endless. A market square, crowded, but no one offering to help. *It's OK, I know where to take you*, he told her. *You're overreacting*, she murmured, then began another attack of heaving coughs that bent her double right there in the street, people giving them wide berth, disgusted, like they were some degenerate pair – *druggies, needles, HIV*! It's like people knew, could sense symptoms that lay outside the normal curve of colds and coughs. *Did you get blood again?* he asked desperately. *I don't think so*, she answered.

At last they reached the train station. He left her on a bench with Agatha – who had stopped protesting a while back, and now merely followed and hovered – as he ran in to check the timetables. The next train left at 12.55. It was now 11.57. Nearly an hour. He choked with anguish. He could not wait an hour.

He ran back outside. Persephone remained upright – thank goodness – and had resumed that self-sustaining, self-protecting posture, hands gripped together, shoulders hunched, eyes shut and focused inward. But her face had gone the same cheesy pallor

Know what caseosis is? Dr Minos had said *When your lungs turn to cheese*

that Roddy's had. Andrew fought off panic. He needed to think. He pressed his eyes shut.

When he opened them, he saw a taxi stand.

He ran up to one of them, a sleek grey economy car, and leaned into the open driver's-side window.

'I'm going to London,' he said.

The driver was a slim guy, young, with an angular, eastern European squint. He gave Andrew a dubious grimace. 'That'll cost you a hundred quid.'

'Do you take credit cards?'

He did.

Andrew ran back to the bench, gingerly eased Persephone up, across the sidewalk, and into the back seat of the taxi.

'What are you going to do?' asked Agatha.

'I'm taking her to a hospital in London. They specialize in . . .'

'In what, Andrew? Can you tell me what's going on?'

'She has tuberculosis.'

'*Tuberculosis?*' she cried. 'How . . . how do you know?'

'It's related to what we talked about with Vivek,' he said. 'Long story. I'll call you later. I promise.'

They said quick goodbyes and the taxi nosed its way out of Cambridge, Andrew willing the traffic to part. He waited the trillion years required for his mobile browser to load a thumbed search for 'Royal Tredway London'. He gave the driver the address. As the car moved into the flow and speed of the motorway, he leaned back at last, and Persephone tucked into him, wrapping her arms around his forearm. 'Thank you,' she said. 'I don't know what I would do without you.'

'You would be well, for starters,' he said.

'No,' she protested.

'I know what's happening,' he told her. 'Harness is infecting people. But not randomly.'

'Then how? Why?'

'I . . .' Andrew looked at her pale face. A blood spot still stained her lower lip. His heart crumpled in pity. 'You should rest.'

'I want to know, Andrew. You can't keep it from me.'

'Last night . . . I saw Harness. In our room.'

Persephone's face fell. 'The ghost? Here?'

'He infected you. On purpose.' Her expression flickered with doubt, then fear. Andrew continued. 'He's jealous.'

'Jealous?'

'Remember what the letter said? *I will destroy him, and all will be well*. He thinks I'm Byron. And anybody I get close to . . . he's infecting. That's how Theo died.'

Persephone sat up. 'Theo?' she asked. '*Roddy?*'

'I spent time with them,' Andrew confirmed. 'Harness is looking for male lovers. Competition. That rival he was obsessed with.'

'I'm not a man!' she said indignantly.

'I know.' Andrew managed to grin. 'But . . .' he said, suddenly realizing, 'your hair.'

She touched her short locks. Their matching haircuts. 'Oh, God.'

'Are you OK?' he asked gently. 'You seem a little . . .'

He was going to say *better*. Their conversation – so ordinary, in a way – had given him a moment of hope, or at least a moment of denial. But he should have kept his mouth shut, he scolded himself. As soon as the word *better* formed in his throat, Persephone started a wild hacking, so uncontrollable her eyes opened wide in panic, as if some foreign being were trying to fight its way out of her body; she flung her hand to her mouth to cover it, but it came up anyway, spattered through her fingers and on to Andrew, his jacket. Blood.

two cupfuls

'Oh my God!' he cried. He was sticky with it. Like being struck by a water balloon.

'What is it?' she asked, terrified, even though it was obvious; it dripped from her hand; it coated her lips.

'What's going on back there?' demanded the driver.

'Please just hurry,' urged Andrew. 'Please.'

19

All Will Be Well

CASUALTY IN ROYAL Tredway teemed with bodies today; *seasonal*, explained the triage nurse grumpily. *General practitioners get overloaded with bronchitis and walking pneumonia and send them to us – so* we *get overloaded.* Andrew swiftly introduced the code words *coughed up blood* to earn her attention. He then followed up with *Our school was visited by the Health Protection Agency, they're afraid of a TB outbreak*, in order to jolt her from her seat. She moved into the corridor behind the triage room, where she and another nurse conferred; the words *Dr Minos* were spoken, and the triage nurse came back with instructions to place a mask over Persephone's face. She took them to one of the side treatment rooms until Dr Minos arrived. The nurse eyed the bloodstains on Andrew's jacket and trousers warily, and helped Persephone change into a gown.

'I'll go and fetch the doctor. Please do not leave this room,' admonished the nurse. Then she departed.

Andrew and Persephone sat in silence for a moment. Persephone sat on the examining table, leaning against the wall.

'How are you feeling?' Andrew asked for the fiftieth time since they had left Cambridge. A part of him stupidly hoped she might leap to her feet, wink and chirp, *All better now.*

'Chest hurts.' She winced.

They sat silently again, this time for a long while. Persephone coughed. It seemed to pass at first. Then she coughed some more. More blood. This was taking on the feeling of a nightmare. It stained her white face mask. They peeled it off her, gingerly, as if the blood were a toxin. Andrew disobeyed the order to stay in the room, bursting out of the doors to call for help. The triage nurse returned, and seeing Persephone's state, moved quickly to clean her up. Andrew felt useless, miserable. His mobile phone buzzed, informing him he had voicemail. He looked at the screen. He had three, in fact. This could not be good. Despite the abundant warnings not to use mobile phones in Casualty, Andrew furtively placed the phone to his ear.

Andrew, it's Piers. I'm in your room . . . and it's empty. Ring me.

The second was the same, only Fawkes's voice was half an octave higher.

Andrew . . . where are you? It's Sunday night. Contact me. Please. As soon as you can.

The third had a graver tone:

Andrew, it's Piers. Monday. The story about Roddy is all over the school. People know it's tuberculosis. Reverend Peter is away, damn him. You're the only one who can help with the ghost and all this turmoil. I'm covering for you in the hope that you're at Trinity and finding out something good. We're nearly out of time. Come back!

Andrew pulled the phone from his ear in a daze. The nurse had eased Persephone back on to the examining table. The girl had wilted, her face totally drained of beauty or humour.

In that instant, Dr Minos entered, with his shiny pate and his heavy-lashed eyes. Andrew snapped his phone shut. The doctor approached Persephone without even a glance at Andrew, strapped his own face mask on, took hers off, and began asking questions in a low, soothing voice. He pressed his stethoscope to Persephone's chest. Dr Minos frowned. He seemed to have found what he was looking for, too quickly. He gave a long command to the nurse. She nodded and scampered off.

Dr Minos turned to Andrew.

'Almost didn't recognize you without your uniform,' he said. 'You were in here yesterday. For the TB tests.'

'Hi.'

'I suppose you saw the signs about mobile phone use,' the doctor said. 'But the rules don't seem to apply to you, do they?'

Andrew's heart sank.

'This one your girlfriend?' the doctor said.

Andrew hesitated. He had the feeling anything he said would incriminate him.

'As I remember it, you were supposed to be back at your school, not seeing anyone, not going anywhere. Yet here you are in central London with another sick friend. I told you yesterday, didn't I? About involuntary confinement?' The doctor's eyes blazed. 'I told you if you didn't listen to what I said, I would put you in isolation.' Andrew's eyes widened. 'Well, I think you've met my criteria.' The doctor's words were bitten off in suppressed anger. He nodded to Persephone. 'She's in bad shape.'

'I know.'

'You're a doctor now, are you? Let me see your arm.' Before Andrew could move, the doctor stepped close, to corner him. 'Take your jacket off.' He did. 'Roll up your sleeve.'

Dr Minos held Andrew's wrist tightly and rubbed the spot where Andrew had received the injection the day before. The doctor looked at Andrew in surprise.

'What?' Andrew demanded. 'Is it bad?'

'Nothing,' said the doctor, puzzled. 'A positive test creates a raised bump. You're smooth.' He frowned. 'Doesn't matter. We get false negatives in fifteen per cent of cases. And I've got your bloods.' He glared at Andrew. 'I'll keep you anyway. As soon as we get her settled, I'll start the paperwork. You stay right here.'

'I can't!' Andrew squeaked. 'I have to get back to school!'

'So you can spread the disease some more? Not a chance.'

'I have to write an essay!'

Saying only part of it sounded absurd. But saying everything –

I need to confront a ghost with the murder he committed, and I'm the only person who knows enough to do it – sounded outright insane.

Dr Minos shook his head in disgust. 'Now I've heard it all,' he scoffed.

The nurse returned. She dragged behind her a small wheeled trolley bearing a slender tank with a meter and a long, transparent tube. She began unwrapping the tube. Another nurse followed with a wheelchair. Dr Minos found a floppy plastic face mask hooked to the tank and popped it from its plastic casing. He affixed this to the tube. The nurse started calibrating the release of the oxygen. Dr Minos reached behind Persephone's head to affix the mask. Andrew felt a sense of violation – that something so precious as Persephone's curly auburn hair should be treated so unceremoniously.

But he came to his senses.

The doctor, the two nurses, were distracted. Their attention and first priority went to the sick patient. Andrew would be able to get away.

Yet he wavered.

He had been with Persephone, touching her, alongside her, continually, for almost twenty-four hours. His whole reality had shifted, adjusted to having her near him. The prospect of leaving her anguished him.

But if he left, he would be able to return to school. He would tell Fawkes and Dr Kahn what he had found out at Trinity. They could help him piece together the story of John Harness. They could hold their makeshift séance at Essay Club, confront the spirit, and expel him. They could save Roddy and Persephone.

But would it work?

John Harness – gaunt, morbid – now lingered over Andrew's every move. He had followed Andrew from Harrow to Cambridge. He had suffocated some mysterious youth in the past. He had killed Theo in the present. Now he was clearly intent on killing more.

Maybe I should just leave, Andrew thought. Flee. Get on a train somewhere and draw the ghost along with him. Or hail a taxi to the airport and leave everything behind. Show up in New York with nothing but the clothes he was wearing.

No, that was no good. For starters, his passport was back at school. And he would be abandoning Persephone and Roddy. He could not just leave them here, clinging to their lives so flimsily.

Their set-up complete, the nurses pushed the wheelchair and pulled the oxygen tank; Dr Minos held the door. The trio pushed Persephone into the corridor.

Andrew was momentarily forgotten.

He clutched Persephone's clothes to his chest. It was the moment of decision. He slipped through the door behind the group. Where the others turned right, he veered to the left. He headed towards the crossing of corridors thirty feet away, where the cold daylight poured in through the front doors. He tossed Persephone's clothes on to an information counter. The attendant shot him a quizzical look. Andrew sprinted. The attendant stood and called out. Andrew reached the doors and banged through them. The cold air smacked him. The noise, the rush of traffic. An open thoroughfare. Sky. *Choose a direction.* He leapt down the stairs. In a few moments he would be lost in the urban wilderness. He crossed the street and began to run. As he hurried, he pulled his phone from his pocket and clumsily texted her, his eyes filling with tears, his thumbs misspelling

I liove u
I love tiuu
I love you

He checked behind him to make sure no ambulance or anyone in a white coat was pursuing him. He had to get back to Harrow. If he wanted to stop Harness, he needed to get closer to where

SD – Speech Day – was. He needed to understand what Harness had done. Who and why he had killed, on that June day two hundred years before.

I will find you, destroy him, and all will be well.

PART III

And a spirit of the air
Hath begirt thee with a snare

20

Where Is He Now?

'WHERE IS HE now, Piers?' the headmaster demanded, in the tone of voice with which he now always addressed the housemaster of the Lot: a mix of exasperation and contempt. Fawkes, over the course of one academic year and two months, had dropped in status from the Poet/Hotshot of Harrow to the level of some unlettered charwoman, so stupid and useless that all questions needed to be vociferous and loud if they were to have any hope of getting through.

A nightmarish sense of fear and guilt shot through Fawkes. *My God, I deserve to be spoken to that way. I don't have an answer! Not only have I killed one of my boys . . . sickened another . . . Now I've misplaced a third.*

'Come again?' Fawkes said, buying time.

'Pay attention, for God's sake. Where is the boy?' Again Fawkes hesitated, his mouth hanging open. Colin Jute mistook this for incomprehension. 'Andrew Taylor!' he exploded. 'Surely you know where he is?'

FAWKES ALREADY KNEW he was the least welcome member of the hastily assembled council that now filled the headmaster's office. He stood at the back, skulking against the wall, next to the snapshots of Jute's tennisy children, trying to avoid knocking them to the floor with an elbow and earning further opprobrium from Jute. The room was packed; extra chairs had been brought in. Two consultants from the Health Protection Agency were given the seats of honour, the two Louis XIV-looking armchairs at Jute's desk. Miss Palek sat in one, erect and unflappable, with her sweeping black hair and coffee eyes. This time she was joined by an older, puffier man, with white hair and a bald crown. At first his presence lent an air of seniority, gravitas, to the government's role here, until Fawkes looked closer and noticed the man's collar was two sizes too big, and that he fidgeted in his chair like a Fifth Former. He was pure bureaucrat. When the man introduced himself as *Ronnie Pickles*, Fawkes could not stop a schoolboy grin from breaking across his face.

On the sofa sat the school's communications director, Georgina Prisk, thirty years old and blonde (and gorgeous, Fawkes noted glumly; luminous skin, heavy lips, large blue eyes), who chewed her pen in excitement – finally a drama worthy of her talents! Sir Alan was unable to join them to represent the teaching staff. (He was *coping with a family situation*, Jute had said vaguely – prompting another flinch from Fawkes, who wondered if, somehow, Andrew's disappearance and Sir Alan's were related. He hadn't been able to reach Persephone on her mobile phone, either. *It couldn't be*, he assured himself; *my luck isn't that bad. Surely.*) Instead, Owen Grieve, housemaster of Rendalls, six foot six, glum and rigid as a Frankenstein, joined Georgina on the velvet couch.

Also present were Mr Montague, the archly ironic senior master; and Dr Rogers, the squat doctor with the hairy hands who manned the sickbay. The Reverend Peter, Jute mentioned, was expected. Fawkes started hopefully at this and kept a constant ear for the door behind him.

Jute, taking command of the meeting, had propped himself on his desk, striking the pose of leadership over his hastily gathered task force.

He summarized the situation. One boy dead. One boy ill. Two

boys possibly *carrying* the disease. One of these still on school grounds.

'Your head of house's parents have come for him?' Jute shot the question at Fawkes.

'Yes. This morning.'

'Add that to the debit column, Georgina. Heads of house fleeing the scene.' Jute fired an acid glance at Fawkes.

Parents' phone calls were pouring in, he continued. Enquiries from the media . . . ? He thrust his chin at Georgina.

She had her notes at the ready: *the* Harrow Observer: *their health reporter*, she said. Times *U.K. News. They hate us anyway, one of those yellow journalists for Labour . . . Sky TV. They've threatened to send a camera van.*

'We need a response. And to help us,' he said, gesturing to Miss Palek and Mr Pickles, 'our friends have joined us from the H . . . P . . . A . . .' – Jute boomed out the initials, as if the acronym itself merited fear and trembling – 'with the goal of advising us whether, for the first time in its history, Harrow School should be shut down for health reasons.'

Owen Grieve muttered and asked Miss Prisk to repeat it for him – had he heard right? Shut the school? Montague, uncharacteristically missing the tone, took the opportunity to correct Jute's school history, but no one caught his comments about an 1840s closing due to diphtheria.

Miss Palek informed them – in velvety tones so low they were forced to be silent and strain to hear – that the HPA had no interest in closing the school. In fact, they strongly urged them to remain open.

Jute thrust out his chin in satisfaction. 'I would never have agreed to anything else,' he declared.

'It's logical,' she said. 'Closing the school would mean dispersing children to different parts of the U.K., even globally. You would spread the disease more widely. It could make you responsible for a pandemic.'

Jute visibly soured.

Ronnie Pickles leaned forward. 'The best outcome,' he said – in a demi-cockney, Fawkes noted; with the biting intonation of a human Jack Russell terrier – 'would be to allow the HPA to complete its investigation. We'll need a lockdown,' he explained. 'We'll need to extract skin tests for every student. Time zero. Then again at eight to twelve weeks. For the ones with positive results? A special regimen . . .'

'*Lockdown?*' bellowed the headmaster.

'For twelve weeks?' Montague echoed, distressed.

Pandemonium ensued. *How will it work? Will lessons continue? Everyone confined to school? What will we tell the parents?* Pickles blanched; he seemed surprised that he was not being praised for his thorough and rigorous plan.

The key, Georgina said, *will be to position this in such a way that we don't call it a lockdown, we don't* call *it anything at all. We make no external announcements . . .*

What are these skin tests? Dr Rogers shouted to be heard.

Pickles began to answer, but Jute boomed over all of them, bringing the room back to order. 'All right, all right.' He imperiously explained to Ronnie Pickles that they would not be locking down Harrow School and administering skin tests. *This is a school, not a hospital.*

Pickles drew himself up defensively. He turned to the others. 'Perhaps someone can offer an alternative?'

Miss Palek could. They had identified the inner circle for the latest confirmed infection, she said – the boys in the house known as the Lot. (She nodded at Fawkes. Jute's scowl deepened.) Best practices dictated that they limit their actions to the boys already identified. The boys in question had been tested. Now it was merely a matter of waiting for those tests to show results. The more definitive blood test was due the next day. They had twenty-four hours during which the expectations of parents, and the school, would be up in the air. This was the most anxious time, as it involved uncertainty. Sending those two boys home during this period – and only these two boys – was the best option.

However, she added, one of the boys was from America. (Fawkes nodded his confirmation.) As a result, sending him home was impractical. They would never knowingly put a suspected TB patient on a commercial flight. As a result . . . she paused, thinking . . . maybe there was another arrangement that could be made for this American, just for the next twenty-four to forty-eight hours, that would appease parents, and yet avoid such extreme steps as testing the whole school?

The room absorbed these reasonable words.

'Where is he now, Piers?' demanded Jute.

Fawkes reddened.

He had no idea where Andrew Taylor was.

THE NIGHT BEFORE, Fawkes had felt a gnawing insecurity. He was jittery after a day of hospitals and dire warnings. He wanted to see Andrew, and confirm he had not been struck down by this ravaging disease. He had made his way through the dark passage connecting the housemasters' apartments to the boys' quarters. The house lay quiet. He stamped to the third floor (wheezing, but recovered), stopped to chat with Rhys, who was packing: his parents had insisted he return home.

But Andrew's room was dark. It had an uninhabited feel. The curtains were open, though it had been dark outside for hours. He called Andrew's mobile phone. Left a message.

Hours later he checked again, with the same result. He left another message.

He slept little. In the morning – imagining every form of mishap, crime and tragedy – he returned and found the room still untouched.

He packed Rhys into his parents' Volvo at dawn (he had asked them to come at a discreet hour), then flew into panic mode. He called Dr Kahn: what the devil was her friend's name, the one at the Starling, Nightingale, Phoenix, whatever library at Trinity. (*Wren*, she told him calmly. *Lena Rasmussen.*) After several calls to the college he found her number. Got an answering machine; and not just an answering machine, one of those completely unreassuring automated messages (*The party you have reached at box five . . . zero . . . zero . . . four . . . is not available.*) He sat down, at last, to quietly freak out. He chain-smoked until he felt ill, and ran to teach a lesson on Emily bloody Dickinson.

Americans. Everywhere but where he needed them.

HE HAD LOST his train of thought.

'Come again?' he said, sounding as useless as he felt.

'Pay attention, for God's sake!' thundered the headmaster. All the faces in the room were turned to Fawkes. 'Where is the boy? Andrew Taylor! Surely you know where he is?'

'Of course. He's back at the Lot. He's been lying low. He might have missed lessons today, in fact. I asked him to stay away. You know. Just until the tests came back.'

The room was quiet. Fawkes was not sure whether anyone believed him. There was no reason they shouldn't. Except for the fact that he was making it up.

'Ideas, then?' Jute challenged them. 'About where to put him? We should get him away from school for a day or two. That's the point, isn't it? Care to put him up, anyone?'

There was an awkward silence.

'I was joking,' Jute said, in a fatigued voice.

'Put him in the Three Arrows,' offered Montague. 'It's an inn, down the hill,' he explained to Miss Palek and Ronnie Pickles. 'It's musty and rambling enough: he's sure to have his privacy. Parents stay there, for Speech Day, but I can't claim to have seen any other guests. How the place stays in business I've no idea. But that's not our problem, is it?'

'I'll come along,' announced Ronnie Pickles. 'I will assess the location. Make sure it's suitable.'

'Done. Fawkes, and, er, Mr Pickles, you move the boy to the inn.' Jute waved them on. 'Georgina, Owen, draft some talking points. Review them with me. We'll communicate first to the staff, then parents . . .'

The room began to mill. People rose. They passed Fawkes with heads down, or with the tight smile one would give to a marked man. At last Ronnie Pickles reached Fawkes; oblivious to the housemaster's plummeting school standing, he gave him an ingratiating wink.

'Ready to make your school a safer place?' he said.

'Heh,' replied Fawkes, joining him. 'So we're partners in crime, eh?'

Pickles seemed puzzled. 'Crime? You must have a guilty conscience. We're doing good!' He slapped Fawkes on the back and grinned.

THEY MADE THEIR way into the dark, damp High Street. Fawkes fidgeted, checked his phone, lit a smoke. Pickles waited patiently. Fawkes did not see what he could do to salvage the situation. The bloody HPA man was coming with him to the Lot. He would see that Andrew was gone. What then? Would Pickles raise the alarm? Begin a manhunt?

Eventually, not knowing what else to do, Fawkes began easing down the High Street towards the Lot, asking Pickles banal questions, using the time while the man babbled to rack his brains for excuses.

Oh, too bad. He must be in the library!

Where he would be exposing other boys to TB? Try again.

Oh, I forgot, he's meeting a family friend in London.

Riding the tube? Terrible idea!

They reached the Lot too soon.

'Never been inside one of these,' said Pickles, curious. 'Boys' boarding school dormitory. Home of the rich and famous, eh?'

Fawkes ascended the stairs like a man climbing the gallows.

What would they do to him? he wondered. Did a government health agency have the power to prosecute? For endangering public health? Or maybe they just had the power to recommend arrest and jail time. 'I'm sorry,' Fawkes said, with sudden heat. 'Can I offer you a cup of tea? I'm so rude to have forgotten! It didn't occur to me, and you must have had such a . . .'

'I'm all right,' said Pickles. 'Let's get this over with. After that – maybe a pint at the inn.' Another wink. Fawkes glumly imagined himself falling off the wagon with this bureaucrat.

'Long staircase,' Fawkes apologized. 'Need a rest?'

'I'll manage.'

They reached Andrew's landing. The crack under Andrew's door glowed bright yellow. Fawkes's heart leapt. 'Ah!' he said, his voice piping an octave higher. 'Here he is!'

Fawkes pushed open the door. Andrew, in school uniform, sat by his printer, picking up sheets as they came out. He had a sheaf gathered in his hands. He turned, saw his housemaster, and leapt to his feet.

'Where have you been? We've got to go to Dr Kahn, right away! Persephone's sick! I know why, it's worse than we imagined . . .'

Pickles eased into the room behind Fawkes. Andrew clammed up.

'Someone else ill, you say?' Pickles enquired.

'Ah.' Andrew was dumbstruck. Fawkes introduced the HPA man. It gave Andrew time to recover. 'Just someone . . . in the play we're doing. You know.' He stroked his throat. 'Laryngitis.'

'Andrew,' Fawkes began – his eyes boring into him, willing him to keep his mouth shut. 'You need to pack your things.'

DID PICKLES SUSPECT them? He sat in the back, quietly. Andrew took the front seat of Fawkes's cigarette-marred Citroën and stared forward. He had been able to pull Fawkes aside long enough to tell him what had happened to Persephone in hissing tones.

'Did you tell Sir Alan?' Fawkes shot back at him when he had finished.

'No! I haven't had time! I only just got back.'

'He needs to know.'

'She's conscious. She'll tell them to call.'

'Why did you go, Andrew? And why the hell did you take *her*? I told you . . .' Fawkes began, angrily. But then Pickles strolled up, regarding them quizzically, and they threw Andrew's overnight bag into the car and slammed the boot shut.

Dusk settled over the hill. They drove only a half mile at most, but in the twisty world of suburban roundabouts and intermittent street lights and extended avenues without pavements, it felt like a long way. Any distance that took them from the well-trod crown of Harrow-on-the-Hill felt like a separation, Andrew realized; despite his initial impressions of Harrow having no campus, the school undoubtedly had one. Taken as a whole, the Hill, with its neatly painted shops, the iron railings and chapel buttresses, possessed the familiarity and scope of an entire landscape. Outside it, Andrew felt jarred, expelled from a protected zone that cultivated centuries of lore. Within its borders, the past found a home. *Only a place like Harrow*, he thought darkly, as Fawkes vroomed down Green Lane, *could harbour John Harness.*

Within a few minutes Fawkes was swerving into a shallow car park alongside a dusty, exhaust-stained thoroughfare. He jerked the handbrake. 'Here we are.' Andrew looked up at the shadow of the Hill on their left and realized they had only made a wide arc around the common on its north side. The chapel's spire rose in the darkness almost directly above them.

The building abutted the street, separated from it only by a three-foot wall of brick. It seemed typical of the Harrow area: a shambling, archaic brick structure, with too many sections for its size, multiple portals, and the appearance of being glued together by layers of thick glossy paint on the moulding. A carved sign, illuminated by a halogen lamp, announced it with a historical flourish as *The Three Arrows*, but the trucks roaring past – and, inside, the pink walls and tiny breakfast room, furnished with institutional utility – made it anything but quaint.

'You can see why they chose this place,' said Pickles.

'Desolate.'

An unsmiling young woman with glasses greeted them at the front desk. She took Fawkes's credit card and Andrew's passport.

'Do you need to look round, Mr Pickles?' said Fawkes. 'You know, inspect the rooms?'

'Hm? No,' said the HPA man. He had his hands in his pockets and was eyeing the common areas like a bored tourist. He seemed to have lost interest in the whole venture. Fawkes suspected that Pickles's motivation in coming had been to make a show of heroic action in front of the head man; but once here, and having recognized no obvious threat at the hotel, he was ready for teatime. Fawkes reminded himself that Pickles was a low-level government functionary, not a counter-terrorism expert. The pint (to Fawkes's relief) was forgotten; Pickles tapped his watch and asked to be returned to his car so he could go home.

Fawkes drew Andrew aside. 'Are you OK?'

'I'm fine.'

'Did you find anything in Cambridge?'

Andrew told Fawkes about the letters, and what they revealed about Harness's murderous intent.

'Jealousy. It makes sense.' Fawkes chewed a nail. 'What are you going to do?'

'Start writing my essay. I brought the Harness folder, my notes from the Vaughan; some new stuff I printed out from Dr Cade's website. But I still don't know who Harness killed, or why he's so obsessed by it.'

'It doesn't have to be perfect. Just enough to confront Harness with the truth about himself and the murder. Must have been this new boyfriend of Byron's. Don't you think?'

'Yeah,' said Andrew, his mind turning. 'OK.'

'Good man. I'll come back as soon as I get rid of this idiot.'

'*All right then, Mr Fawkes?*' called out Pickles on cue, standing pointedly by the door.

Fawkes waved to Pickles.

'What about Reverend Peter?' Andrew said.

'Can't locate him.'

'Shit.'

'Exactly. You going to be OK?'

'Of course,' shrugged Andrew.

Fawkes handed Andrew his room key, a plastic rectangle that looked more suited to an anonymous chain hotel. *Coming, Mr Pickles*, he called, and went to collect his guest. Andrew turned towards the lifts. His stomach sank. His bravado had been entirely fake. Andrew wondered if there were any other guests here. The place was crummy, a spot for guidebook-carrying retirees on budgets. Yet John Harness had followed him to stranger places. Andrew shivered. He turned back to find Fawkes, to ask him not to leave.

He heard the tyres of the Citroën grind out of the car park. He was alone.

21

The Face Under the Pillow

ANDREW hoisted his overnight bag and stepped into the lift the girl had indicated. It was a tiny box, a mechanized coffin, room for only one. Riding up in it, he felt lonelier than ever. He had been removed from school. No one except his housemaster and some random government official even knew where he was. And he had left Persephone alone in a hospital, coughing blood. *In your love is comprised my existence here and hereafter.* But those were Byron's words, not his ... no, they were *Harness's* words. Andrew's head swam. The hum of the lift became a throb. The overhead light glared. The distance between floors could not be more than ten, fifteen feet, but Andrew felt like the ride had taken twenty minutes. He leaned against the wall and tried to breathe, but the air felt heavy, oppressive. *Oh no,* he thought. *It's that feeling*

The doors opened and he staggered forward into a darkened, hazy corridor.

Why are the lights so low? I should tell the girl at the desk

Naturally he had expected to see more of the same décor he had found in the lobby. Pink paint, fibreboard trim, fuzzy red carpet. Instead he saw

I know this place

a slender corridor with hardwood floors. Three or four wood-panelled doors along the passage, with handles of black moulded tin. Whitewashed walls.

He turned to his left – and reared back. He nearly bumped into the back of someone standing there. Someone in a black coat.

I'm sorry, I didn't see you

But the words were shoved back in his throat by some force, as if the hall were filled with water and would not admit breath or sound. In the density of the place, there seemed only room for Andrew to stand rigid, and watch.

The figure remained in place.

Is he frozen too? Andrew wondered.

But no – he sensed that this person's movements were unhindered. Yet the figure did not move, because he seemed to be resting. He leaned with one hand on the wall. The shoulders heaved, as if the figure were out of breath from having climbed

I know this place

a stairwell. Back behind him. A narrow stairwell, with a wooden railing. It had a sconce, holding a candle, at the landing.

Andrew had climbed it, in his dreams.

pulled himself up by the flimsy wooden railings like climbing a mountain

And with that realization several things happened at once.

First: the figure began to move forward, down the hall.

Second: Andrew could hear again. Sound poured into his senses. Shoes on wood. Creaking, clomping. The swish of the hand on the wall. Very faint. Then the noise he feared most. The wet, unnatural breathing of the consumptive.

Hrch . . . the exhale . . .

hrr hrr hrr hrr hrr . . . the inhale.

It accompanied Harness's footsteps like the leer of a slow and deliberate monster. Andrew felt himself follow Harness, dragged along, as if he were attached to him by a rope. He felt, along with Harness – as if they were one *not Andrew and Persephone – Andrew and Harness!*

the shooting thrill of fear and excitement as he

they

stood outside one of the doors.

Oh yes the moment has finally come I am ready

His breathing troubled him. Too much excitement.

Hrr hrr hrr . . . hrch . . .

Harness clutched his chest. *Please, not now, remain in control.* He leaned against the wall, rested his head back against its cool, whitewashed surface, raised his eyes, calmed his breathing. He must put aside all doubt, about whether he had the physical strength, or the moral strength, to snuff out a life. He could hear the boy inside the room! The figure that had obsessed him, as a creature, as a figment, as a little flame of pure hate like the candle that lit his room; *that boy* was now so close he could hear him shuffle and snivel on the other side of the wall. That alone was a miracle so singular – Harness had done it, he had found him, even in his condition – that it shrank the other obstacles to nothing. Salvation lay at hand. He would murder his enemy. Then he would recline into glory with his lover, protected, coddled, cared for, nursed back to health in the luxury he had imagined. All it required was an act of will.

Harness reached out his hand. Touched the handle. Cool, smooth metal. The door pushed . . . open! The boy had been careless. Harness had been lucky.

And there was the young man. Alone. The room lay in a haze, lit only by daylight through the curtains. He was bent over, rummaging in an open trunk, looking for something. The door touched the wall with a light *pock.* The boy stood upright. He wore a cap. He had light brown hair and a small, pointed nose. He was indeed pretty. Large eyes, heavy lashes, a mouth of curved pink. A dainty frame. The clothes fitted poorly. He was underfed, and he had rough hands with soiled, gnawed nails. Harness noted this with the eye of someone accustomed to closely judging other people's social standing to see which levers he might pull. Would he affect the Harrow-Cambridge accent to put a challenger on the defensive? Or the tradesman's simper? Or a gutter cockney, to show his street smarts, to show he would not be bullied? He had all these voices at his fingertips.

Oo 'er you? the boy demanded.

A moment of doubt. Did he answer? Did he speak to him?

A cold cleverness came over Harness. He smiled, all friendliness. He closed the door behind him. The boy merely stared, puzzled. Harness turned back to him. He took a step towards the boy.

What's this?

The boy's passivity had given him an advantage . . . he lunged.

He had surprise on his side. He wrapped his fingers around the boy's throat. The boy was weaker even than Harness had hoped for, but he was spirited, and tried to kick over tables and call for help. They grappled in what seemed an interminable struggle. At last Harness – who for a brief, elated moment was freed of his shallow, swampy breathing; transported by the lightning flashes of adrenalin – grasped a pillow, forced it over the boy's face, and pushed, and pushed, the snarl of triumph and satisfaction growing. *Yes, yes, swallow it if you can*, the words came out of his mouth (along with something else – slaver? Yes, this felt good, deliciously good) and he held on, *pushed*, teeth gritted in a grin of pleasure, even after the boy's body stopped kicking, because Harness savoured the pure domination of it.

At last, he sat back, utterly spent. He closed his eyes. He wiped the liquid from his chin.

He opened his eyes again.

He had an idea.

He would *tell* his lover what he had done. Not with words. With a message. A symbol. With one exhausted hand, he tugged the ring he had been wearing on his left ring finger since the day before. Then he lifted the pudgy and soiled hand of his rival –

still warm! – and screwed the ring on *his* ring finger. It would only go halfway down; it did not matter. It was better, in fact, if it looked unnatural. His lover would notice, and understand.

Smiling to himself, satisfied, Harness staggered to his feet. His body was slick with sweat. He began to cool. The adrenalin that had carried him (miles from London, in secret) began to drain away. The liquid from his chin annoyed him, felt sticky on his hand, between his fingers. He examined it now. Blood. His own. From a wound? No; from his own mouth. And the blood was the kind the doctors had warned him about; rich, red, sticky, wet. The rust-coloured expectorate, the kind that looked older, scabbier, was better. This was arterial blood.

His elation rapidly ebbed. He swayed. Only one thing remained: to strip the pillow from the boy's face and gaze on his dead enemy. To feel the full triumph.

He reached out for the pillow that still lay pressed over his rival's face. He gripped one corner and tugged. The face. Yes, going livid; yes, mouth askew, a death in fear and struggle. But he scarcely noticed this. Because when the pillow pulled away, it pulled with it . . . tresses of hair.

A pin had stuck to the pillow. The pin was attached to hair. And now the pin, and pillow, dragged the hair loose; unspooling it in a foot-long strand.

Harness stared, uncomprehending.

Then he understood.

Woman's hair.

The long hair had remained, up to now, successfully concealed by being tucked under the cap.

A woman. Harness had killed a woman.

He tossed aside the pillow. He gripped the corpse's shirt, angrily, with his bloody hand. Popped the buttons. He saw bandages across the chest. He tugged these and saw them: *breasts*. Nipples, folds of flesh, squeezed and hidden by the displaced bandage. Confusion engulfed him. A woman? A girl, in disguise?

Where was the boy he had heard of? Where was his rival? Who was this person he had murdered? Why was she here, now? Was this a thief? A stranger? A chambermaid? A female lover?

He stared at her and realized he had killed the wrong person. And – even more important – he knew he did not have the strength to kill again. He would die before that. He knew it now. Shock plunged into Harness's chest like a pike. The adrenalin was gone. The slime in his lungs revived. Harness fell. There, on all fours, he began to cough, the worst he had ever experienced; it began in his hips and rolled forward like a wave until it reached his teeth – *aagh*, repulsive, he choked it back – but with the second wave it broke free, a splash of bloody vomit. He crawled through it, felt it slide under his knees. His hackney was waiting. He had paid enough so that no questions would be asked – even about bloodstains. But would he make it back? He would have to crawl. Forcing himself, fighting for every inch, he raised one knee, gripped the hotel room moulding, and stood. He caught his breath and began the journey back to the street . . . Hurry . . . A chill, and a childish terror of capture, and prison, now seized him. He wiped his face carefully with a handkerchief . . .

ANDREW STOOD IN the hotel room. Silence throbbed there after the storm of violence. He was still in the vision. He was still in Harness's world. His eyes were closed. Yet he knew what he would see if he opened his eyes. The body on the floor. The face of the victim.

You're in the centre of this, Dr Kahn had told him. *It's right for you to lead the charge.*

He did not want to lead the charge.

But you have to, he told himself. You're here for a reason. If you don't find out who Harness killed, your friends – innocent people – will die.

He opened his eyes.

That watery, oppressive world of the vision poured in on him again. The screaming began deep in his chest and rose up, screams of horror.

The face on the corpse was Persephone's

It's only the vision, it's not real, keep telling yourself that she's not dead she's not dead

coils of auburn hair tracing her features

that he could smell that he loved that he could feel tickling his face

her green eyes propped open by death.

22

Sir Angry

ANDREW RAN. THE cars with their funky super-bright-white British headlights swooshed past him. The bag bounced on his back. He had almost left it behind, but it contained his passport, and some instinct for self-preservation made him remember it as he dragged himself from the hotel and to the street, into the jarring cold air. He ran in the direction he thought would take him back to school – *uphill* – until he recalled what Fawkes had told him. *He could not go back to school.* He stopped. Pulled out his phone and thumbed for the number on his list of incoming calls.

Connecting . . . advised his mobile phone.

'*Hello, Andrew?*' came a formal, and artificially loud, voice – Fawkes had recognized his number on caller ID. Andrew wondered why his housemaster was speaking this way, then he realized Fawkes probably had company. '*Is everything all right there?*'

'Are you with somebody?' Andrew asked.

'*I'm here with Matron and Mr Macrae. We were just talking about you. I'm giving them an update. How is your accommodation?*'

'I can't stay there.'

'*There.*' Fawkes caught the lack of the word *here*. His voice dropped. '*Why? Where are you?*'

'Is that place old? The Three Arrows?'

'*Is it* old?' Fawkes was taken aback. '*I don't know. You'll have to ask Judy that.*' Fawkes faked a light-hearted tone to camouflage his concern.

'I saw the murder.'

There was silence on Fawkes's end of the phone. Then his voice came back, a murmur: '*Can you explain that, please?*'

'I saw the whole thing. Down to the dead body. And it had Persephone's face! I'm freaking out, Piers! I'm . . . I'm standing on a fucking street corner. I don't know where to go!'

'*Take a deep breath.*' There was motion on Fawkes's end. He was in motion, going to the kitchen for privacy. '*Are you still at the hotel?*'

'A few blocks away.'

'*Judy's near by. Go there. I'll come, in a few minutes.*' Fawkes gave him the address. Hung up. Thought for a moment; dialled another number; spoke a few words to Dr Kahn. Then gathered himself and returned to his living room. Forced a smile.

'Everything all right?' questioned Macrae. He wore a navy cardigan and grey flannel trousers. *Did this guy own a pair of jeans?* His eyes flashed at Fawkes suspiciously.

'Not sure yet,' Fawkes said non-committally. He went to the hall cupboard and retrieved a jacket.

'Are you *leaving*?' snapped Macrae, incredulous.

'Need to sort things out. At the hotel.'

'What's the problem?'

'Nothing! Just looking in on Andrew.'

'He's lying,' accused Matron. 'We heard you in there.'

'I've got it under control,' he replied. He walked to the door.

'No you don't,' said Matron, coldly. 'You never have.'

Fawkes hung there at his own front door. *So the truth comes out at last.* A thousand half-formed put-downs scrambled to the surface of Fawkes's consciousness. *Fuck you, you fat cow, maybe none of this would have happened if you'd been more supportive . . . ?*

Helpful ... ? Nothing quite lived up to the moment. He felt fatigued, tired of fighting these people.

'Then here's my offer to you. You two take care of the fifty-six boys here. I'll look after this one.'

ANDREW HAD ARRIVED in the dark, quivering as if he'd been electrocuted. Dr Kahn had immediately diagnosed shock and placed him on her sofa, put a sherry in his hand, and told him that Fawkes was on his way.

Andrew slurped the sherry and forced himself to breathe normally.

It wasn't her.

He had left Persephone in the hospital. Safe. Not well, exactly, but safe. Harness could not have killed her.

But if he can sicken her, he can kill her.

'Need to call ...' he mumbled.

He pulled his mobile out of his pocket. His hands trembled. He found the number for the Royal Tredway. Called it. Navigated through the menus to the visitor line. At last he reached a nurse, in the chest centre, and asked to speak to the patient Persephone Vine. Was refused. (It was after hours.) He argued. *I brought her there!* he shouted. *Just connect me. There are phones in the rooms, I saw them. Just put me through.* He was refused, more firmly. *Just ... just tell me if she's OK. Please. Is she ... is she stable? Is she breathing OK?* The nurse asked who he was. *I'm her boyfriend. I brought her there.* The nurse did not warm to him but she took pity, and she put him on hold. He waited, squirming. *She's stable*, came the nurse's voice. *Now? You're sure?* he demanded. *When did they last check her?*

She's stable, came the reply. *I just talked to the doctor. All right?* Andrew muttered thanks and hung up.

Dr Kahn stared at him, her brow furrowed in concern.

'What is going on?' she said.

'Can I have another one of these?' He held out his sherry goblet.

She topped up his glass from a black, sticky bottle. He sipped. Closed his eyes. *Persephone was safe.* Then why had he seen her dead? What was Harness trying to say? That Persephone was next? That he was going to kill her? Andrew's body shuddered. He tried to erase the image of her staring, vacant eyes.

Dr Kahn was in the kitchen, putting on a kettle. Andrew, for the first time, took in her home. He was surprised. Her imperious bearing might have suggested a Mies van der Rohe cube house, with icy white spaces and a lot of glass. Or an unreformed Victorian curiosity shoppe, with grandfather clocks and porcelain figurines. Neither were on display here. Dr Kahn lived in a decidedly middle-class cottage with low ceilings, battered ex-showroom furniture, lamps with dim wattage, worn carpet, snap-shots of relatives. Not exactly the Fortress of Solitude, but a decent place to escape to, Andrew decided: it smelled of dusty blankets, steam heat and Darjeeling. Only the books, he observed, lived in luxury. Built-in, recessed shelves encircled every room, nestling and protecting the volumes: short, fat his-tories in French with gilt spines; bound atlases, as tall and black in their leather covers as a row of ship's captains; folios of naturalist drawings; and two shelves dedicated to heterogeneous Dickens, apparently a favourite – an original serialized *Bleak House* in green binding; a colourfully splashy graphic novel version of *Great Expectations*.

A few minutes after the kettle whistled, Piers Fawkes entered the house, wearing a leather jacket and a harried expression.

'Sorry I'm late. I had Matron and Macrae lurking about. They heard everything. God knows what trouble they'll make.' Fawkes took in Andrew on the sofa, looking pale. 'Speaking of trouble.' He tried to smile. But Andrew's eyes were red; he fidgeted; he wrung his hands in his lap, unconsciously.

'Persephone,' Andrew said. 'Harness wants to kill her.'

'She'll be fine.'

'I should just give myself to him,' Andrew said.

Fawkes exchanged a concerned glance with Dr Kahn.

'Give yourself . . . to whom, Andrew?' he asked.

'To Harness. Then maybe he'd leave the others alone. That's what he wants, isn't it?'

'Andrew . . .' said Fawkes. 'Even if you wanted to, how would you go about doing that?'

'I don't know.' Andrew's voice was vacant, despondent. 'Throw myself down the cistern. Or just let him know he could have me, if he gave the others back.'

Fawkes watched Andrew intently. 'When was the last time you ate, my friend?'

'I don't know.'

'Get him something,' said Fawkes. Dr Kahn went to the kitchen and started rummaging for sandwich makings. Fawkes sat down next to Andrew. 'This isn't a chess game, where you can sacrifice one piece and win. We're protecting you. If we lose you, we've lost – and Harness wins. Please don't say things like that again.'

'What about Roddy and Persephone? And Theo?' Andrew continued. 'They would have been fine, if it weren't . . .'

'If it weren't for John Harness,' finished Fawkes, firmly. 'He's the one doing this. It's not your fault. Do you understand?'

Andrew nodded reluctantly.

'Good man. Now don't say another word until you eat.'

They watched while Andrew devoured two cheese sandwiches on wholemeal bread, seasoned with pickle, a blackish, sour relish that could only exist, and be combined with cheese, in England; and he washed it all down with a mug of hot, sugary tea. He wiped his mouth with his hand.

'Biscuits?' Dr Kahn offered.

Andrew ate four, with a second mug of tea.

'Now,' commanded Fawkes. 'Talk.'

Andrew sighed. 'I saw the murder,' he said. 'The whole thing.' He started describing the vision.

'The Three Arrows is an old spot,' said Dr Kahn. 'Some variation of guest house, inn or hostel has been in that spot since the sixteen hundreds.'

'Funny, Montague said something about that when he recommended the hotel,' mused Fawkes. 'He said its only guests were people who come for Speech Day.'

'People coming for Speech Day – like Byron in 1809?' said Andrew.

'Those kinds of traditions do have a way of sticking,' said Dr Kahn.

'So the murder could have taken place at the Three Arrows,' said Fawkes. 'Maybe Byron is out visiting friends. Harness descends on Byron's new friend, alone . . .'

Now Andrew's expression clouded. 'There's one thing I left out. The person he killed was a girl.'

'*What?*'

'Her hair came spilling out from under a cap. I saw it. She was only *dressed* as a boy.'

'But who was she?' asked Fawkes.

Andrew seemed stricken. Then suddenly he shouted, in a different voice:

'*Who was it? Tell me!*'

The two others jumped and looked at him in alarm.

'Harness said that to me,' he explained. 'Back when I saw him in the cistern. *Who was it? Tell me.*' Andrew's mind churned. 'It seemed so out of place at the time. But now I think I understand it. He killed the wrong person. He knew he was too sick to kill again and get it right,' Andrew said, turning it over in his head. 'So he doesn't actually know who he killed. He must have died without finding out. That's what we need to discover. But we don't have much time.'

'What do you mean?' Fawkes asked.

'At the end, the girl's face changed to Persephone's,' Andrew said, his voice cracking with emotion. 'Like Harness was trying to tell me she's next.'

'Not if we do our job right,' said Fawkes. 'What's all that new material you have stuffed into your bag?'

Andrew pulled out a detailed timeline of Byron's life during 1808 and 1809. It came from a website created by Dr Cade: a chronology of Byron's life. The year 1809 began with the damning reviews of his first volume of poetry, *Hours of Idleness*; continued with Byron's debauchery in London as he tried to forget his disappointment, borrowing money for clothes, hackney cabs, drink, prostitutes; leading up to his return to Harrow in 1809, for Speech Day. Then – abruptly – turning to preparations for his European journey.

'Well, that's one mystery solved. The murder is what drove Byron to flee England,' Fawkes observed. 'He finds someone dead in his hotel room. He was afraid of being accused of the murder.'

Andrew mused, 'Or maybe he left because his spirit was crushed.'

'That's only if the girl they found was special to him. Was she?' Dr Kahn turned to Fawkes.

'Hm?'

'With all these *boys*,' Dr Kahn said. 'It *is* still possible to love women, you know. Any evidence that Byron was serious about a girl at this time?'

'A girl . . .'

Fawkes lit a cigarette. He held a page from the timeline in front of his nose. He had the faraway expression of someone whose mind is grinding on a problem, like a slow hard drive.

Andrew and Dr Kahn exchanged glances and left him alone.

'Byron was all dark and tragic after that, right?' Andrew said. 'He was Childe Harold, carrying the burden of a horrible secret. Maybe what crushed Byron wasn't that *he* was accused of murder.

Maybe it was that he knew *Harness* was a murderer. I mean, he was in love with Harness, right? For years. Imagine finding out the person you loved was a psychopathic killer.'

Dr Kahn smiled. 'We'll make a proper researcher of you yet.'

Andrew managed a smile.

'But we're not done,' she continued. 'Who was Harness's victim? I'm getting confused now. Was it a boy or a girl?'

'It was both!' exclaimed Fawkes.

They turned to him. He still held up the paper.

'What are you on about, Piers?' Dr Kahn demanded.

'Covent Garden.' He pointed his cigarette at a point on the page. 'There it is.'

He was interrupted by the insistent buzz of the doorbell.

'Who can that be?' Dr Kahn rose, irritated. 'I haven't had a guest for weeks, and suddenly all of Harrow is tromping through . . .'

'One moment, Judy.' Fawkes touched her arm, stopping her. 'Andrew's supposed to be at his hotel. If that's anyone from the school and they find him here, it will be trouble.'

They looked at Andrew.

'They might force me into the hospital,' he said, then added, brightly: 'I could be with Persephone.'

'Yeah, locked in the tuberculosis honeymoon suite,' Fawkes said. 'That won't help us with Harness.'

The doorbell buzzed again.

'Come on,' said Dr Kahn. She grabbed Andrew's elbow.

She dragged him up the stairs to a small reading room, consisting of a lime-green divan under a reading lamp, and more teeming bookshelves. 'Don't move until I come for you.' The doorbell rang a third time. She scuttled off.

'SIR ALAN,' SHE said. The damp evening air curled her breath into white puffs.

'Judy,' came the familiar voice. 'I apologize for the abrupt visit.

This is Ronnie Pickles, from the Health Protection Agency. We've just been to the Three Arrows inn, looking for Andrew Taylor, who's in serious trouble. We've searched for him back at his house, and were led here. Ah, hello, Piers. Now the story comes together. May we come in?'

The four of them crowded into Dr Kahn's hall, next to a row of coat pegs, and an umbrella stand.

'How can I help you?' Dr Kahn said stiffly.

'Piers can tell you,' said Sir Alan. But Fawkes stared coldly back at him. Sir Alan continued. 'Andrew Taylor may have tuberculosis, which is disturbing enough, but now he's gone missing.'

'Missing?' said Fawkes.

'Your assistant housemaster called me, saying you ran off after getting a call. Made it sound like there was trouble at the hotel; the boy wasn't staying put. I called Mr Pickles, here, from the HPA, to return to school and join me; and sure enough . . . no Andrew Taylor in room twelve.' His eyes bored into Fawkes. 'Funny, Piers, I've been at Headland for four years now, and I haven't lost a single boy. But here, in the course of a few months, you've got one missing, one in hospital, and one dead.'

Fawkes took a step forward. 'You don't know what you're talking about.'

'My daughter's in hospital because you let someone with tuberculosis run coughing through the Hill,' Sir Alan snarled, shedding his polite façade and himself stepping closer to Fawkes. They were a mere foot apart, in street-fighting pose. 'I've been at her hospital bed. I think I know what I'm talking about.' The two men glared at each other. 'You've nearly shut us down. But you're not through yet. You're hiding the boy, God knows why, and making this into a real catastrophe. Stop mucking about and put the boy under the proper care.'

'I can't do that.'

'And just why the devil not?'

'Because he doesn't know where he is,' put in Dr Kahn, quickly.

'Really.' Sir Alan's sarcasm was thick.

She continued. 'Piers told the boy to come here, but he never showed up. We've no idea where he is. He's probably back at the Lot by now.'

'We've just come from there,' said Pickles. He looked fatigued, and out of his depth.

'Well, maybe he went out for food, or to sneak a pint,' Dr Kahn replied tartly. 'He's a teenager, not a toddler. He'll turn up.'

'You seem awfully cool about the spread of tuberculosis in Greater London, Judy. I doubt the authorities would share your sangfroid. Going out and eating and breathing in public is exactly what he's *not* supposed to be doing. Easy for you to say, when you haven't got a sick daughter. What about you, Fawkes? Any theories about where the boy might have vanished to?'

'None.' Fawkes still looked like he wanted to take a bite out of Sir Alan.

'Well, I have one.' Sir Alan adopted a new voice: that of a prosecutor cross-examining a witness with a weak story. 'Andrew Taylor, an arrogant American student, decides for himself that, despite the orders of his school, the recommendation of the government health department, and the risk he poses to other people, he doesn't like staying at the Three Arrows. He'd rather go to a friend's house. That *friend*,' Sir Alan continued, with a nod at Dr Kahn, 'gives him a sandwich.' The plate still sat on the coffee table, with two crusts. 'That *friend* then hears the mean old health authorities knocking . . . so the *friend* takes him to an upper room to hide,' he pointed upward, to the second storey, 'where he won't be discovered. And the friend cleverly turns on the light while the mean old health authorities are still standing on the front step, where they can see everything. Not exactly an inspired plan. Perhaps the *friend* isn't as bright as she makes herself out to be.'

Dr Kahn blushed scarlet. 'Get out of here, *Alan*.'

'Let me see him,' he demanded.

'I said *get out*.'

'Take me upstairs, Judy. I want to see that room.' He stood his ground, puffed up and furious. It looked like he wanted to run past her and make a break for the stairs.

'Sir Alan!' she shouted. 'Remove yourself from my home or I will call the police!'

'Go ahead,' he sneered. 'Let *them* find him. I should have thought of that myself.'

Dr Kahn's eyes bugged. '*Piers*,' she appealed.

Fawkes took a step into the centre of the hall. But Sir Alan scoffed. 'You're going to have the poet rough me up? I'd rip you apart, and enjoy it.' His eyes flashed. 'But I don't need to go that far. You're sacked, Piers.'

'What?'

'Effective immediately.'

'You don't have the authority,' Fawkes challenged, disbelieving.

Sir Alan twisted out a smile. 'You're right. I don't. I already have it from the head man. When I told him what was happening, he gave the word in about five seconds.'

He turned his back and stomped outside. Pickles scampered behind. Outside, on the drive in the dark, Sir Alan stopped and faced the upstairs window.

'You've messed with the wrong family!' Dr Kahn rushed to her front door. *Sir Alan! Stop it!* But he was possessed by rage. 'You should see Persephone now!' he shouted. 'She's barely alive. Because of you. *Eh?*' The upstairs curtain did not move. 'I know what you did,' he continued shouting. 'I talked to Persephone. Yes, I know it all. You're a disgusting, *druggie shit*!'

With this final shriek, he stomped to the car that stood waiting at the end of the drive. He turned back for one last assault.

'Do his parents know where he is?' he called out to Dr Kahn and Fawkes. 'Do you have their permission? Or maybe you want a kidnapping charge added on to all your other mistakes tonight?'

With that parting shot he leapt into the car and gunned the engine, and barely waited for Pickles to climb in the passenger side before he pulled away with a screech. Down the street, a porch light came on, and a worried neighbour stepped outside to investigate.

'Come on,' muttered Dr Kahn, pulling a stunned Fawkes inside the house after her.

23

Redeeming a Whore

THE THREE OF them took turns, pacing and sitting despondently in Dr Kahn's living room, but in the end they decided there was nothing to be done about Sir Alan.

'Their main goal is to get Andrew out of the Lot. Whether he's at the Three Arrows or here – it makes little difference,' argued Fawkes. 'Jute won't make any more of a row than he already has.'

'I don't want the police calling and accusing me of kidnapping,' fumed Dr Kahn. 'Do we have to hide Andrew in the attic like Anne Frank?'

'The police won't get involved. This will seem like an internal school matter to them – if Sir Alan were even to call them, which I doubt.'

'You're awfully rational for someone who just got sacked.'

Fawkes smiled thinly. 'I saw it coming.'

'I never called my parents,' Andrew said. 'What if Sir Alan calls them first?'

Fawkes shook his head. 'He will assume I called them long ago. Which I never did.' Dr Kahn shot him a questioning look. Fawkes tried to explain. 'After our visit to the hospital, Andrew vanished, off to Cambridge – thanks to you, Judy. It didn't seem like the moment.'

'Should I call them now?' offered Andrew. 'It's just lunchtime there.'

Fawkes chewed a nail. 'No,' he said. 'We need twenty-four hours. If you get ill, we'll call them.'

'Reassuring,' said Dr Kahn. 'And what will we accomplish in twenty-four hours?'

'Andrew will complete the research about who Harness really murdered. Reverend Peter will bless the Lot. We'll get rid of John Harness. That can be done in twenty-four hours, surely?' At that Fawkes stood; it was his turn to pace the small, carpeted living room. 'But for some reason I have a nagging feeling. Like I've misplaced something.'

'What were you saying, just before Sir Alan came?' asked Dr Kahn. 'You were holding a piece of paper.' She began shuffling through Andrew's printouts, which were splayed across the table.

'Something about the victim being both a girl and a boy,' offered Andrew.

'Thank you, yes!' Fawkes cried. 'Yes, yes.' He threw himself back on to the sofa, and joined Dr Kahn in picking through the white printer paper. He scanned through the pages, muttering – *no, no* – then continued this operation one-handed as he shook a cigarette out of the packet and into his mouth. Then: 'Got it,' he said, slapping the page down on the table. 'Covent Garden!'

'That's what you said before,' Andrew noted.

Fawkes lit the cigarette, never taking his eyes from the page. '*September 1808. Continues debauchery in London. Dinner at Mrs Moroney's brothel in Covent Garden*. God bless Reggie Cade. This is it. This is it!'

'Would you mind explaining?' Dr Kahn asked, suppressing exasperation.

Fawkes flopped back into the cushions. 'After leaving Cambridge, Byron went into one of his more unsavoury periods. Maybe he was heartbroken about being forced to split with Harness. Maybe he was just being twenty, bored and rich. Or both. He lolled around Cheapside. He hung out with professional boxers, lowlifes. He borrowed money anywhere he could – Jews, his landlady – to keep himself and his entourage drunk all the time. One night … in *Covent Garden*' – Fawkes picked up the page from Andrew's pile – 'he held a little party. Four friends. Seven hookers. I always remember that. It's an elegant ratio.' Fawkes grinned. 'Anyway, at this party, he met a whore. He really, really liked this whore. So, being Byron, he bought her.'

'Like a slave?' asked Dr Khan.

'More or less. Byron relieved her of her obligations to her madam. The madam, I suppose, was Mrs Moroney,' he said, eyeing the sheet in his hand. 'The girl's name was Mary. Mary Cameron. Does that ring a bell, Andrew?'

He shook his head.

'Byron wrote a poem about her, 'To Mary' – I told you about it; it was excluded from Byron's first collection for being 'too warm'. *And smile to think how oft were done, What prudes declare a sin to act is.*'

Andrew nodded in vague recollection. 'But what does this have to do with Harness?'

'Not for the last time, Byron really fell for this tart. They lived together; cohabiting like modern lovers. Which really meant shagging her all day long. Sorry, Judy. He wrote some very dirty letters about it, and some quite tender poetry, too: all about breasts and watching her as she slept, lyrical stuff about golden hair.'

'But Harness never said anything about a whore, or even a girlfriend,' protested Andrew.

'That would make sense.' Fawkes nodded.

Dr Kahn made a face. 'Why does that make sense?'

'Byron's snobby Cambridge friends were scandalized by the relationship with Mary and tried to hush it up. They'd come to the flat and be received by this gutter wench as if she were, you know, Lady Byron. Byron *wanted* to marry her. Across class lines. Unthinkable at the time. His friends told him he was insane. So if Byron couldn't make her a legitimate spouse or consort, he had to think of another way to keep her around. Byron took her to friends' houses, to Brighton . . .'

'The Brighton trip was in Harness's letters,' broke in Andrew.

'. . . while *dressing Mary as a boy*. They pretended she was his cousin. There he was, taking tea in country drawing rooms, with this streetwalker in drag, speaking in an atrocious cockney. And poor Mary always got the set-up wrong; she kept referring to Byron as her brother. Her *bruvva*. There are letters about it. Pure farce. It's hard to dislike Byron when you hear stories like that.'

'Wait,' said Andrew. 'You're saying the rival was a female prostitute dressed as a boy . . . not a boyfriend. Harness got it wrong.'

Fawkes threw up his hands. 'Harness made a mistake!'

'What happened to Mary?' asked Dr Kahn.

'She drops out of sight. Most biographers assume Byron threw her back in the gutter. Got bored, the way he usually did.'

'Could she be the one Harness killed?'

Fawkes thought about this. 'I can't see why not.'

'It would explain the cross-dressing victim,' mused Dr Kahn.

'Yeah, but the dead girl was here, at Harrow. For Speech Day,' protested Andrew. 'Would Byron really bring a hooker to Harrow?'

'He took her everywhere else.'

'It's rather touching, if he did,' said Dr Kahn. 'Taking a lover to your old school. It's a sentimental gesture.'

'He wanted to marry her,' Fawkes reminded them.

'Yeah. But instead,' said Andrew, 'Byron comes back from getting drunk with his friends at Speech Day, and he finds her dead in the inn.'

They contemplated this grim prospect.

'How do you *know* all this, Piers?' asked Dr Kahn after a moment.

'Mary was one of my nominees to be Byron's great love, for the play. I have a folder on her, back in my study.'

'But she's not in the play at all,' Andrew pointed out.

Fawkes smiled ruefully. 'Harness is not the only one to underestimate Mary Cameron.'

'Sexism, pure and simple,' snorted Dr Kahn.

'But you shouldn't take my word for it,' said Fawkes. 'This is just . . . background. Historical-literary anecdote. Andrew is the one who saw her. Right, Andrew? What do you think? Could it be her?'

Reluctantly, Andrew conjured up the picture of the struggle he had witnessed; the circling, scratching fight for life and death.

Oo 'er you?

She had a delicate, pointed nose; a mouth shaped like a bird in flight. Her cheeks had grown blotchy in the wrestling match; her eyes had blazed with fear. Yet there was a canniness there, a familiarity with the fight for survival. And in the moment she began to lose that fight, there had been a disbelief, that her survival skills, long honed and effective until now, had failed her.

Then, the corpse. The breasts revealed so peremptorily. So disrespectfully. They were small, young. Andrew shivered. He hovered uncertainly over Mary Cameron's tangled, despoiled body, her secret unravelled with her hair. He peered; he was not able to help; he was merely a voyeur. He pulled away.

'It was her,' he said. 'Although it's a stretch to call her hair golden.'

Fawkes smiled sadly. 'Poetic licence.'

THEY HAD A plan. Fawkes would return to the Lot to retrieve his folder on Mary Cameron. Andrew would stay at Dr Kahn's and begin writing his essay immediately.

'Do I even need to write the essay?' he said. 'I feel like we know everything now.'

'If the departed spirit of a murderer shows up to Essay Club, I think you'll want to have your ideas clearly organized,' Dr Kahn advised primly.

'And how are we going to make sure Harness attends Essay Club?' Fawkes asked.

'The ghost seems to have no trouble locating our young friend,' Dr Kahn replied.

'What about tonight? Can we be sure Andrew's safe from Harness, here?'

They both looked at Andrew.

'Seems like Harness has withdrawn, for a while anyway,' Andrew said.

'If he's clever,' said Fawkes, 'he's in retreat, preparing for battle.'

'He's clever,' confirmed Dr Kahn, grimly.

'And your plan for rousting the others – the living members of Essay Club?'

'I'll send an email. Emergency session.'

Fawkes scoffed. 'The first ever emergency essay.'

'I'm the adviser. I declare when an emergency session is needed.'

Andrew remained anxious. 'Do you think it will be enough?'

'I'll mark the email high priority,' Dr Kahn replied drily.

'I mean for Harness.'

They exchanged glances.

'For Persephone's sake, it had better be,' said Fawkes. 'And where the hell is Reverend Peter?' He checked his mobile. 'Still no calls. No messages. I've been texting him every hour, practically.'

FAWKES STEPPED OUTSIDE, started down the drive and zipped up his jacket; only then did he raise his eyes to notice what had happened since they had last opened Dr Kahn's front door.

Her quiet street – a few cottages huddled into a leafy nook in Metroland – had been brushed white. Silence padded the air. Fog. It streamed over the housetops in wisps and tendrils, and punched across the lane in cloud-heads like big fists. The street lights were muffled; the sounds of traffic seemed far away, directionless, under its cloaking. The prospect of venturing into it seemed, suddenly, to be madness.

Something primitive seized Fawkes. *Turn around. Go back inside and have tea.* He stood for a moment contemplating this. Then shook himself. What would he say? That he had changed his mind, because of the weather? No, it was absurd. He began his journey, but with a slower and more cautious stride.

At the next turn, he cheered somewhat. There were more houses on Roxborough Hill: porch lights, bedrooms, flickering blue television screens. He strode up the hill with purpose.

But soon the houses suddenly looked unfamiliar. Doubt pushed its way into his mind. Was this really the right road? Had he veered off somewhere? And if he could lose himself so quickly, in a place he knew so well – could this fog be here by design? Had John Harness brought it? All the wetness and moisture of the past months. Harness – if it was Harness; *the fact that you're even assuming it could be Harness shows how much you're panicking; stop it* – it seemed, had turned all of Harrow-on-the-Hill into one of his own spongy, diseased lungs. Had wrought upon them all the dampness and disease, the claustrophobia and terror, of his own death by tuberculosis. One reads about diseases of the past, Fawkes reflected, but rarely thinks about how they get at you; what the end would really be like, with your own oxygen cut off, with your own blood dribbling out of your mouth. His eyes twitched about the road, hyper-alert. Could Harness be here now? Was he using this fog to hide? Andrew had made a comment about Roddy and Rhys seeing something, feeling something there in the room with them, when Roddy fell ill. Had it been Harness, frigid, centuries-old? As much as he wanted to help Andrew, Fawkes did not want to see such a thing. Not first-hand. The fog carried a chill into his clothes. It wrapped around his neck, causing him to shiver. He zipped his jacket to the top and sped on.

At last Fawkes reached a familiar turning. He was not lost. This was the High Street, thank goodness. Yet his mind did not turn to sunny thoughts. The street lights and upper windows here, too, took on moist haloes – muted, as if seen through a scrim. His morbid turn of mind persisted. This was the way a dead person sees our world, Fawkes imagined, and he immediately thought of Persephone. He had put on a brave face for Andrew; but now, alone, his fears came at him. Could she really be so ill? Sir Alan seemed on the verge of grief. She might be expiring in a hospital room, at this very moment. Was she dying alone? Dread of the end: it came at him with white fingers. He rushed, started to jog. He passed through the Lot gates. He was almost home.

A figure came at him in the drive. Dark, heavy, swift, under the gloom of the plane tree.

'Oh my God!' Fawkes reared back, raising a hand protectively.

'Piers? Is that you?' came a tenor voice.

Fawkes controlled himself. He had been an ass. Panicking like that. 'Who's there? You should be inside,' he snapped, thinking it was a Sixth Former.

'It's Reverend Peter,' said the shadow, stepping closer. Fawkes made out the priest's wire-frame glasses, his skinny neck and the clerical collar under a raincoat buttoned tight against the fog and chill. 'I've come straight here from the train station.'

'Where have you been? I've been calling,' Fawkes said, more testily than he intended.

The Reverend Peter's eyes went wide. 'Have you?' he said. He fumbled in his pocket and fished out a gleaming new mobile phone. Its screen lit the fog around them a bluish white. 'My wife bought me this.' The Reverend Peter squinted at the screen unhappily. 'I haven't learned to use it yet.' He gave one of the icons a poke, as if this might bring the machine into submission.

'Come in,' Fawkes said with relief, putting a hand on the priest's shoulder. 'I am very glad it's you.'

24

All-Nighter

Sir Alan Vine stood at the doorway of the hospital room. And for a moment, he turned his attention away from his daughter.

He looked at his wife.

His guts melted in gratitude. Thank God he would not have to bear this alone. Formidable: her spine, erect as always, even there in a battered hospital armchair; her gold jewellery shining, as if she were a Byzantine noblewoman, against skin toasted by mornings swimming with her friends on Ydra or one of the islands near Athens in the last warm months of the year; her profile, classically Greek, with that high bridge; her hair, only speckled with grey (while his was thinned to vanishing); and, of course, wearing a knee-length skirt and perfectly pressed sweater, even here, so that she managed to bring order and floral scents to the gloom and chaos of the hospital wing. He wanted to rush across the room to her; to embrace her, kiss her full on the mouth; and then weep with her. But he knew what would happen if he did that. She would treat him like a salesman ringing the door-bell: unwelcome, impertinent. Resentments would squeeze between them and push them apart as if they were the wrong ends of two magnets.

Alan had always desired her. Married her for her exoticism, her style. How could he have known that Greek women of her generation were so incredibly chaste; lived like continual thirteen-year-olds, with their clucking girlfriends, their family gatherings; thrived on tea and shopping; and treated husbands like boys on a playground – occasionally entertaining interlopers. But the Vines were never the kind to pursue counselling. He almost chuckled at the idea of his wife on the Couch. She didn't have the Electra complex. She *was* Electra. Tall, busty, prone to outbursts. Very little self-examination among these Greeks, he observed snidely. The two of them had merely pulled apart, and away, over time. Now, when they met, they sniped like old enemies.

'You're supposed to be wearing a mask,' he reminded her from the doorway, through his own mask.

Lady Alcina Fidias Vine turned to him defiantly. 'I'm not wearing a mask.' Her accent had grown thicker after a few months in Greece, as it always did. 'These doctors don't know what they're talking about.'

Sir Alan could only admire her. The way she cut through the puffery of authority. But he had a role to play here. The rational male responsible for making sense of it all.

'No? So what's the matter with her, then?'

'I don't know,' Alcina replied, unhappily.

Sir Alan lifted a chair and carried it across the room to sit next to his wife.

'Be careful,' she scolded.

They sat next to each other, aligned towards their daughter, watching.

'She won't drink or eat,' Alcina said.

Now Alan sat close enough to Persephone that he could not ignore the degradation that had occurred in her, just in the past few hours. His daughter's eyes were closed. Her skin had gone putty-white. Her mouth hung open, like that of a fish in a dirty tank, dumbly hoping more sustaining air would find its way in. Her chest heaved, slowly; her limbs and head remained still as her frame's energy ebbed away to nothing.

'The oxygen tubes,' said Sir Alan, standing. 'Weren't they feeding her oxygen before?' He went to Persephone's bedside and began to untangle the tubes from around a thin tank that had been propped there.

The door swung open and Dr Minos entered, with shaved head and blazing eyes.

'What are you doing?' Dr Minos demanded.

'Look at her,' Sir Alan blustered, embarrassed to be caught tampering with hospital equipment. 'She's struggling for breath. They had her on oxygen before.'

'Oxygen won't help.'

'She has *fever*,' barked Lady Vine. 'Those antibiotics you're giving her are not working.'

Dr Minos eyed her coolly. 'We're not using antibiotics; we're using antimycobacterial medications.'

'Hang on,' Sir Alan said. 'Why won't oxygen help? Aren't the drugs working?'

Dr Minos pulled Persephone's chart from the slot at the bed's footboard. He scanned it. The couple waited in silence. He replaced the chart. He turned to them and spoke in a clear, emphatic manner that left no doubt what he was really saying.

'Your daughter's case is very advanced.'

Alcina asked some questions and received short, firm replies. And eventually the doctor left. The pair sat in despondent silence. Sir Alan suppressed the desire to touch his girl, feel her pulse, feel for breath, embrace her so that he could somehow pump his own healthy blood into her veins. But he could only stand by, helpless. He found himself counting her breaths, unconsciously measuring them to make sure the time between them remained the same, not longer; and forcing himself to imagine she was breathing more briskly, even when she was not.

*

ANDREW SAT AT Dr Kahn's dining-room table. Papers were spread out around him. He stared at the computer's blinking cursor in front of him.

'What are you doing?' asked Dr Kahn.

'I'm writing this paper.' His tone was stressful, irate.

'Like that?'

'Like what? I'm sitting and writing.'

'How are you going to start, if you have not organized your thoughts?' she fired back.

'I don't have *time* to organize my thoughts,' he snapped. 'We have one night. I have to just get this done. Or Persephone's going to . . .' He did not finish the thought.

Dr Kahn took a seat next to him and folded her hands in her lap. 'So what are you going to write?' she asked, imposing calmness on the situation.

He gave an angry, rambling response. *He didn't know. Everything. What was he supposed to write? A forensic report about the murder of Mary Cameron?* Dr Kahn asked him another question. *Who is your audience?* He merely scowled and slumped. So she asked him another. *What do you want them to understand when you have finished?* Andrew struggled to respond. She seized her chance; made a suggestion, which he accepted, and within a few minutes, Dr Kahn and Andrew were busying themselves about the table with the source material – books, papers, notes about Harness's letters – and placing it in piles; creating a chronology, and from that an outline. Then they stood back, satisfied, as Andrew sized it all up.

'This is a lot of work,' he said. 'What time is it?'

'Ten thirty-six.' They exchanged a glance. 'I'll make coffee,' she said with a smile.

'Can I stay here?'

'You may,' she said. 'Of course.'

Andrew turned back to the computer, staring again at the cursor until 10.41 p.m. Then he attacked the keyboard.

Lord Byron, he tapped, *fell in love with John Harness when the latter was what we would call a Remove, at Harrow School, in 1801. It is almost certain that neither of them, at that time, could have foreseen that their friendship would end in murder.*

Dr Kahn placed a hot mug of coffee at his elbow. She paused, reading.

'Very good,' she said.

'Thanks,' he drawled. 'Only twenty pages to go. This is an all-nighter.'

'Good luck.'

He turned to her, desperately. 'You're going to bed?'

'Staying up all night is for young people.'

'I can't do this by myself!'

'You have everything you need.'

He turned balefully back to the screen. 'I *can't*,' he repeated.

Dr Kahn stood over him. She felt his wild teenage energy, which came flinging off him in waves. Gamma rays – isn't that what they called the energy Tibetan monks emit when they meditate? Then what she felt coming from Andrew must be – what? *Zeta rays?* She smiled to herself. Teenagers. Squirting glands; anger, frustration, confusion. He was a mouse furiously bashing its head against the confines of a maze, when the way out was so close at hand. *Yet he cannot see it*, she reflected.

Dr Kahn wondered: what if she could siphon off that energy? Ground him, as it were? She rarely touched her students. Oh, she had patted the heads and backs of some of the Shells, she supposed, in their more irresistible moments; but she was not the huggy type. She was conscious that the teenage male body, in a school environment, was a volatile thing, not to be played with. Volatile. Yes. *And now – that was the point. To drain away that frenetic excess energy*. Dr Kahn reached out a hand. Held it, uncertain, over Andrew's shoulder. She had a moment of doubt – look at this freckled, wrinkly thing, those stubby fingers, with their unfeminine, unpainted nails; she had never liked her hands much – and then dropped it on Andrew's shoulder. He stiffened. She held the hand there. He did not turn. He was still staring at the screen. In her mind, she recited a little spell: *You may work*, it went. *It may seem a small, unextravagant blessing. But it is a sustaining one. You may work, Andrew.* She held her hand there. It felt warmer. Pulsed. *With Zeta energy*.

She detected a shift in his body. He frowned at the screen, leaned into it. He typed. A few words. He deleted, backtracked. He started to ask her a question, then didn't. *What?* she asked. *No, nothing*, he muttered. He typed again: a long trail this time, a sentence. More; a paragraph.

Yes, she decided. She gingerly removed her hand from his shoulder; he did not notice. *It had worked.* To her surprise, she felt a pang. Had she decided to like Andrew Taylor? Yes, she had, long since. Their consultations had ceased to be merely academic. They had become friends. Selfishly, she wished to remain; to add, shape, drive the task at hand. This was work she knew. But her best act of friendship now was to recede; let him do this on his own. She smiled, a little sadly – the typing flowed in torrents now – and crept from the room.

ANDREW TYPED. HIS hand cramped. He rubbed it. He would check the page count every now and then. But this was not something just to hand in, to a teacher. This was something that needed to make sense, to an audience. His *real* audience, as Dr Kahn had pointed out: John Harness. He stopped once – stuck! – and panicked. He had lost the trail! But he reread, and in doing so remembered his logic. It was sound. Andrew felt a moment of pride. He had met himself, in the mouse maze; the self from an hour before, when he had made the decision to include this particular set of ideas; and he . . . liked himself: liked the decision made by a sensible mind. But he did not have time to dwell on it. Andrew raced through the pages, pursuing the idea that hovered, always, just a paragraph ahead of him.

At one point, late, a knock came. Andrew raised his eyes, bleary. He trotted to the door. Fawkes stood there. Andrew merely grunted and turned back to the dining room.

Fawkes followed, emitting a stream of excited talk. 'I've found him, at last. Reverend Peter,' he said, as Andrew crawled back into his chair in front of the computer. 'Do you know where he's been? Newcastle. In training, no less. There's a whole ministry, a team, that addresses the paranormal. The C of E is getting a bit hippie! Not that I'm complaining. He's just been talking me through it – what we're going to do tomorrow. It's quite elaborate. Are you listening?'

'That's good,' Andrew said, distantly. He yanked one of the books out of the stack in front of him, referred to an old map; traced a boundary line with his finger.

'Where's Judy?'

'Asleep.'

'Oh, right.' Fawkes consulted his watch. 'It is 1 a.m. Can I help?' He paced around the table, taking stock of all the paper piled around.

Andrew did not answer.

'I can see I'm disturbing you. I'll just leave this here. See you in the morning?'

'OK.'

Andrew's fingers hovered over the keyboard. Rappity-tap. Another page came, quickly. Then Andrew stopped. He needed the Mary Cameron material now. He looked around. *Shit – Piers had it. At the Lot. It would cost time, but he needed to get to it. Would Piers still be awake?*

Then he spotted the manila folder sitting on the coffee table. MARY CAMERON written in block letters in blue pen.

Oh, wait. Piers was here. He brought it.

Belatedly grateful, Andrew retrieved the manila folder. It was identical to the John Harness folder, only fuller; full of poems, and letters, and a few stapled, photocopied academic pieces about the life of a Regency-era prostitute. He flipped through one of these.

Abortions, it was thought, could be induced through several folk remedies. One was the ingestion of sulphur, which the unfortunate young woman would be forced to perform through the chewing of many hundreds of match heads.

Andrew flung himself onto the sofa and flipped through the pages, retracing the steps of the girl he had seen die on that spring night, two hundred years before. What would Harrow Hill have looked like then? Without paving? Without street lights? All woods and grass, in the full flush of June? Andrew read, absorbed, and almost did not notice when his mobile phone rang. *Piers? It's pretty late, even for him.* Then, in a flash, he thought: *Persephone! She's calling! She must be better!* He leapt for the phone. Punched the green button so quickly, in his eagerness, that the name and number of the incoming call, displayed on the screen, only registered in his mind after he had answered.

'Hi, Dad,' he said. His voice came out in a murmur.

His whole being sank as he listened to the voice. He tapped the keyboard listlessly. *L* . . . *L* . . . *L* appeared on the screen.

'*Your mother is standing with me. Where are you? The school called and said you'd left the premises!*'

'I'm at a friend's house.'

'*Where?*'

'A few blocks from school.'

'*Is it true that you might have tuberculosis?*' His father's voice rose into almost hysterical incredulity.

'Apparently we're exposed to it all the time. In the subway . . . you know. Lots of places.'

'*But that boy who died . . . it was TB, not that other problem?*'

'Sarcoidosis? No, it was TB.'

He heard his parents conferring, digesting this unwelcome news.

(*What did he say? Is it true?*

Yes – the one who died had TB.

Oh my God! Let me talk to him!

Just give me a minute.)

'*Where are you, Andrew?*'

He told his father: he was staying with the school librarian, who had become a friend, because the school was trying to dump him in a hotel to keep him away from the other kids.

'*Well, stay there. I'm coming to get you out of that place.*'

'Dad, no, wait . . .'

But his father's voice overlapped his; with its spotty connection, his mobile phone didn't capture the subtleties. And for that matter, neither did his father. '*I don't know what the hell we've got ourselves into, with that school,*' he fumed. '*This was supposed to be a place for you to buckle down. Instead it's a disaster area. I might as well have sent you to Iraq. Are you feeling sick?*'

'I'm not going to get sick.'

'*Are you sure?*' His father's voice was anxiously hopeful.

'No,' he said. 'It all depends on this essay I'm writing.'

'*What? You're not making sense. Are you feverish?*'

The conversation lurched forward in this manner for a few minutes. Finally Andrew gave his father Dr Kahn's address. By the time his father landed at Heathrow, the séance, the Reverend Peter's prayers, would all be over. His father's presence would make little difference. Andrew promised to meet him at Dr Kahn's house at about eight in the morning on Wednesday, in thirty hours' time – the soonest Mr Taylor could arrive. Then they would fly to New York together. At last Andrew pressed the red button on his phone with a trembling hand.

It was 2.17 a.m. The silent house hummed.

He was leaving Harrow.

He was going home.

Would he see Persephone again? A wash of images overcame him: late-night phone calls. Thousand-word emails. Photos sent and pored over (*who's that guy in the picture and why does he have his arm around you?*). He had seen this: the long-distance relationship. The *international* long-distance relationship. *Expensive and unsatisfying*, one of his more cosmopolitan female classmates had called it. And all this depended, of course, on Persephone surviving. One way or another he was going to lose her.

He wanted to cry, to sleep.

But he couldn't. He had work to do.

Arms numb from fatigue, eyes drooping, he reached again for the Mary Cameron folder and began writing again – one letter at a time, at first, but slowly resuming his former clatter – to peck out the remainder of his essay.

PIERS FAWKES AWAKENED with a start. Phantoms and wolves fell away, back into his dreams. Crucifixes, and dark canyons, and danger.

And a sprig of evergreen.

That image had stuck with him. Its needle-leaves moistened with dew drops. *Too much Reverend Peter*, he decided.

He raised himself from the sofa where he had fallen asleep. He felt hungover. *Just exhausted*, he told himself. *But sober, thank goodness.*

His phone was ringing. It was still dark out. He squinted at the clock: 5.10 a.m.

'Hello?' he slurred. He listened. He asked the female voice to repeat what she had said. 'No, not me,' he replied to her question. 'But I'll call the parents. What's happening?' He listened. His stomach plunged. He became sardonic, for lack of a better alternative. 'That should give them time to get to the hospital, anyway. All right. Thank you.' He hung up.

He walked to the kitchen window. Pulled open the curtain. Just a shiny square of onyx. He would have given a lot of money to see sunshine or hear birds singing, just then. He found a crumpled packet of cigarettes on the kitchen counter. He was wearing a white T-shirt and his trousers from the day before. His back hurt. He lit the last smoke from the packet and leaned against his kitchen counter.

'Damn,' he said aloud.

It was 5.19. He would wait until at least six before calling Roddy Binns's parents. They were divorced. Who would he call first? The mother was a drunk, he remembered; a voluble Liz Taylor type, in furs; she would get hysterical. He would call the father first, he decided – tall, unsmiling Peter Binns – and let him manage the mother. Then he would hand all this over to Macrae.

He went to his computer and opened his email. Eighty-four messages since the previous night, with increasingly alarmed subject lines.

Is this true what I'm hearing
Epidemic in School
CLOSING HARROW???

He opened only one marked high priority:

Last-minute but Urgent Meeting of Essay Club, Tues 7pm.

It was from Dr Kahn, of course, inviting all the eleven members of Essay Club to a last-minute meeting for that night; with no explanation, but a subject, and a speaker:

Andrew Taylor, Upper Sixth, The Lot (Fawkes), it read. *The Truth About the Lot Ghost.*

Fawkes's eyes widened at this title. But he realized why they'd chosen it: there was nothing more to lose by being coy; they did not need to duck the headmaster any more. Fawkes had already been fired. Andrew had already been removed from school. It *was* inviting trouble to announce Andrew's plan to be at school. But, perhaps, no one on this email would notice: Ronnie Pickles and the headmaster were not advisers for Essay Club, he observed wryly. He noted, further, that Dr Kahn had not changed parentheses-Fawkes to parentheses-Macrae. By rights, now, Macrae should be the one to attend the meeting; to listen to, and to support, a resident of the Lot in the prestigious act of reading his essay at Essay Club. But when Fawkes scanned the TO list, there was no Macrae.

Good. Macrae might have made trouble for Andrew, and who knows, might have sought to bar Fawkes from attending the meeting.

But there was another contact on the list that caught his eye.

Alan Vine

Damn again. Dr Kahn had merely sent the note to the standard Essay Club list. She should have pulled Sir Alan's address. With this note she would be announcing Andrew's whereabouts to the last person they wanted to know.

Fawkes started a pot of coffee. He felt a growing sense of misgiving.

Of course you feel that – you've just received a phone call that one of your students – former students – is terminal.

Fawkes stared at the black square of window. He felt ... nothing. Worse than nothing. Yet he could not turn off that ongoing, ever-present channel of observation and rhetoric that ran in his head like a ticker tape:

Death, real death, doesn't inspire. It doesn't move you to elegies; not right away. First it drags you down, into inaction and despair.

Poor Roddy.

He tried to rehearse in his mind what he would say to Roddy's parents. But he felt a gnawing sensation, a nastiness that would not go away. It grew, as if the apartment were filling with a bad smell.

Wait

He had had this sensation before.

Adrenalin surged in Fawkes's exhausted body. He felt that same *presence* that had terrified him and Andrew days before in his study, upstairs. He scanned his living room, looking for something; some sign of it. But he saw nothing to threaten him. He instructed his rational mind to take control, override what he was so clearly feeling with his senses, when it caught his eye. He almost overlooked it. A few weeks before, it would have been the most natural thing in the world to see, sitting next to his television, on the console.

A blue bottle of gin.

Two-thirds full. The same bottle of gin he had so wilfully thrown away a week prior. He had enclosed that bottle in a double-layered black plastic rubbish bag, with many other bottles, and taken it to the collection point on the landing. The maintenance man had almost certainly collected it and carted it away long since.

In other words, it had no business being in his living room.

Yet there it was, sitting there, stubby and expressionless, like a little dwarf of infinite patience, waiting for him. Fawkes's heart throbbed. He was left alone with it. He could do whatever he wanted. There was no one here to see. It was 5 a.m. He would have plenty of time to sober up, for later. Plus, he'd been sacked! No more obligations! He could sleep it off and still have time to make it to Essay Club. Piers Fawkes felt a presence. It was poised, leaning forward, watching in devilish delight.

Fawkes crossed the room and seized the bottle by the throat.

25

Essay Club, Part II

THE HILL BUZZED at nightfall.

THE DAY HAD been almost entirely useless. Classes were held, true. But it seemed like a repetition of the day after Theo Ryder died, weeks prior; the boys full of rumours and unanswered questions. Only this time it was worse. The beaks merely went through the motions. Any wild rumour or false bit of gossip, introduced however arbitrarily, became cause to stop class and discuss what everyone wanted to discuss, which was the rumour of a TB outbreak in the Lot; the rumour that school was closing; the rumour that four students had gone to hospital and would soon be dead like Theo Ryder. In the small classroom spaces, sneezes brought severe glances; coughs could cause ejection from class. (*You'd better go back to the house and see Matron, Seabrook. You don't sound well.*) The queue in Dr Rogers's sickbay filled the waiting-room chairs and strung halfway down the stairs. Most distressingly, *no one was even bothering to deny the rumours*. Which could only mean, of course, that the worst and wildest of them were true. Harrow School – as the school gossips were happy to repeat – was shutting down.

In the headmaster's office, the telephone call Colin Jute had been waiting for came a little before three in the afternoon. It was from a doctor at Royal Tredway Hospital. The news was good – at first. *The boys' tests are negative.* Rhys Davies and Andrew Taylor were free of the mycobacterium tuberculosis. The headmaster rose, elated, standing at his desk, ready to hang up and take action: to send word around that the crisis had been averted; there was no danger; no risk to the other boys; no need to close the school for the first time in its history. He felt a flush of victory.

But the doctor seemed to be reading from notes, and he was not done. He informed the headmaster that the condition of the two Harrow students in treatment – Binns and Vine – was deteriorating. Jute sat back down. The parents had already been informed, the doctor said; but he assumed that the school would be interested. *Of course*, Jute replied. *Yes, quite.* To his credit, the headmaster felt several moments of pure sympathy before hanging up the phone and wondering what the hell he was going to do.

If those two went, that would make three dead students.

God, it would be national news.

He went to his calendar, and felt a pang of dread. He had dinner in London, *that evening*, with the governors. It began at six (his car would be there shortly); their quarterly review of the finances with the accountants, followed by a meal. What horrible timing. He reached for the plastic binder with the financial statements. They seemed remote, meaningless. *Then again*, he thought to himself, *perhaps this was a good thing, an opportunity.* Yes, it could be a lucky stroke, in fact . . . if things got ugly, which they very well might, he would need the governors' support. He would need to appear to manage the situation – *not of his making* – with clarity and strength. Right. He would call the key governors now – his 'core four', Hovey, Gorensen, Brothers and Jeffery – and prime them; then use the occasion of the dinner to put things in context, to prepare the governors, *proactively* . . . Jute began scribbling notes for himself. He called for Margaret and asked for the mobile numbers of the core four. Then he would shower; change; get battle-ready. He had just enough time.

HOURS LATER, AS Colin Jute's car swerved through Piccadilly traffic to the columned portal of the Cavalry and Guards Club, throngs of Harrovians began returning to their houses.

They climbed the slope from the dining hall in clusters, buzzing with excited chatter. Anyone watching might have assumed that these were students returning from a long holiday, energized to be back together, to tell the jokes and anecdotes they'd been saving that they knew would amuse their friends. Yet this show of camaraderie came not from long separation, but from nerves. From gratitude that they had survived, that the school had not been shut down; and while more disaster and bad news might arrive tomorrow, it was unlikely anything more would happen today. Time to spend several unsupervised hours in the houses doing absolutely no work and burning off their copious nervous energy. Sixth Formers mentally calculated their beer allowances. Shells took inventory of celebratory sweet supplies. A kind of *fin de siècle* giddiness overtook them. They would have fun tonight, as if it were their last together.

There were exceptions. Four boys checked their watches, ducked the curious glances of their peers, and headed to their rooms to change their clothes. These boys, all Sixth Formers, were not missed in the common rooms; they weren't the hell-raisers anyway. They hurriedly slipped off their greyers and pulled on the thicker striped trousers. They strapped the black silk waistcoats over their white shirts and black ties. They slid on tailcoats, adjusted the flaps behind them, and gave their hair an extra combing. Then, from the various directions and houses across the Hill – from far-flung Rendalls, coming up the ivy-covered Grange Road; or clattering down the stairs from Headmaster's – they made their ways to the Classics Schools, for Essay Club.

The Reverend Peter walked with Fawkes. The priest carried a briefcase, which held a small booklet bearing the seal of the Diocese of Worcester; a Church of England prayer book; a bottle of water; and the soft green twig of a fir tree, snapped off and pocketed that morning during his 6 a.m. run. Fawkes walked upright, with an aspect that very nearly resembled self-esteem. When he had found a bottle of gin mysteriously at hand that morning, he had struggled – heart thrumming with desire as if some naked and very available woman had just minced into the room – but he had defeated the urge and poured its contents down the drain, his nose wrinkled half in disgust, half in regret.

The two men – Reverend Peter in his clerical collar, Fawkes in a tie – arrived at the Classics Schools, the lights of far-off London at their back, and opened the broad door to Mr Toombs's Latin classroom, lit by candles, with only a few faces around its oval table. Out of eight boys they saw four – Antoniades, Askew, Wallace and Christelow – and out of three staff advisers, they saw two. Dr Kahn igniting the last of the candles. Mr Toombs laying out the silver goblets. Wallace, with his slouch, peeled the plastic wrapper off a new bottle of Madeira and prepared to pour.

Fawkes hung there in the doorway. 'No Andrew?' he guessed.

Dr Kahn shook her head.

'Isn't Andrew one of the chaps who was ill?' noted the lanky, forelocked Rupert Askew in his sleepy Sloane drawl, from his seat at the oval table. 'Maybe he *can't* come.'

'He's coming,' Fawkes replied.

'Is that a good thing?' persisted Askew, looking from face to face. 'There are a lot of rumours. About him in particular, I mean.'

'What sort of rumours?' asked Mr Toombs.

'Well, that he brought the disease with him from America. Basically, he killed Theo Ryder. And now these others too . . .'

'That's quite irresponsible!' Mr Toombs interrupted. 'Nothing but gossip.'

'Sir, you asked me what the rumours were!' Askew defended

himself. 'And it's not just me. That's why Harris stayed away from tonight's meeting.'

'And Turnbull, and the others,' added Christelow. 'They were talking about it at supper.'

'It can't be true, can it?' said Mr Toombs. 'Piers?'

'It's not true,' said Fawkes. 'Andrew is not ill. He was tested.'

'Andrew is leaving,' announced Scroop Wallace as he leaned over the first goblet and filled it with Madeira.

'Leaving?' said Mr Toombs. 'Leaving school?'

'I emailed him earlier, about a lesson, and he said he wasn't doing it. When I asked him why, he said it's because he's being removed from school.'

'Do we have to stay, then?' asked Askew.

'Essay Club is a voluntary activity,' Mr Toombs replied tartly. 'Removed by whom?' he demanded.

'His parents,' Wallace replied. Wallace had a slight hunch and pasty skin, and when he spoke people had the shivery feeling he was manipulating words the way sadistic children toy with insects. He seemed to take cold delight in this news.

'They're frightened, I suppose,' offered Askew, knowingly. 'With all the disease and death in the Lot. It's only natural.'

'Are you leaving, too, Mr Fawkes?' asked Nick Antoniades.

Nick was head of Headland House, Fawkes recalled. *Sir Alan must have let something drop.* 'I am, yes.'

'Really, Piers?' gasped Mr Toombs.

Askew leapt on this. 'What – the school?'

'That's right.'

'This is all mad!' he laughed. 'Honestly, Mr Toombs – *why are we here*? The speaker's not coming, and even if he were, he's leaving Harrow. The masters in the club are leaving. No one here's even part of the school!'

'You're being extremely rude, Rupert. I'm seriously considering asking you to leave the club altogether,' lashed out Mr Toombs. Askew assumed a hurt expression. The other boys grinned. 'Our chairwoman has called a meeting. Until she says otherwise, Essay Club is on. Andrew wrote his essay at short notice, I'm told. In all – and especially given what I've heard here tonight – he deserves a few extra minutes . . .'

At that moment the door opened. The candles fluttered. Andrew Taylor stood in the doorway with a bleary expression, hair flattened on one side, holding a sheaf of papers.

HE FELT IT at once. Almost as soon as he walked into the room. That full-of-water feeling. That living pressure, that surface tension, so strong it almost ejected him forcibly from the room. He felt them on him: eyes. Even though he was not in position yet, he felt those eyes staring across the table, drilling into the spot – at the head – where he would soon be sitting, in a high-backed chair, with its fan of blond-wood spokes. It was as if those eyes were ahead of time: already fixed: an inevitability. He felt them as he gripped his pages, as he turned sideways to slip past Christelow, as he greeted Fawkes with a nod and noticed the Reverend Peter with a raised eyebrow, as he heard Mr Toombs say *and here we are very good of you to come Andrew I was just saying what short notice you received for your preparation* as if they were words spoken from a boat deck high above, and he was sinking into dark water . . . but not yet. Somewhere in the murk stood Dr Kahn, watching him – aware and empathic, here among the jostling boys.

He edged to his seat but did not raise his eyes as he did. The boys settled down. Mr Toombs made more polite remarks, something about a *swansong very sad to hear about your departure it feels as if we had just got to know you and were very glad to have you among our number.* Andrew was surprised that at least one voice – OK, two – let loose a modest but a clear *Hear, hear.* (Wallace and Antoniades. Unexpected.) *But at least we are able to partake in your essay . . . very fortunate . . .*

Mr Toombs's voice trailed off in order to yield the floor to the speaker. And that was he. Andrew shuffled his papers, then arranged them to catch the maximum of the candles' peachy glow.

he could not raise his eyes or he would see Harness

Harness was here

His pulse raced. What would happen if he did look? If he did greet those eyes? And whose chair was Harness sitting in? That empty one there, at eleven o'clock?

you know whose

He was glad he had written out the essay, instead of merely typing out notes – Dr Kahn had been correct – because without his script he would have been lost. His mind sloshed and spilled, like someone running with a bucket. Sleep deprivation had unbalanced him.

and that presence

He felt as if he were on a slope, tipping forward

into the figure; crouched, pounce-ready

Harness – he knew – glared at him. Harness no longer felt any resemblance of love, lust, or desire. Just hate. Harness knew that Andrew, Fawkes, and the Reverend Peter had come here to do battle. The room stank of it. The musk of a fight. And Harness was swelling his chest and limbering for combat.

I dare you even to extend yourself I dare you even to show yourself because if you do I will smash you

I know you are here to extinguish me but I have reserves you cannot underestimate ferocity and fierceness of life you know me too well to think you can

Didn't you see what I did to the girl to your friend

How could Andrew continue his pretence of normalcy, in the face of this hostility? Yet there was Mr Toombs, looking at him expectantly, with his pink cheeks and spectacles. Couldn't Mr Toombs, and the others, feel it as well? How could Andrew do something as refined as read aloud in such an environment? Like playing a violin recital on the prow of a rushing train. He felt nauseated, gripping the sides of the paper with his fingertips. He just wanted to crawl away, to sleep.

Andrew had watched the dawn come and had ended his essay abruptly. He had returned to his room in the Lot and packed his large suitcase. He lay there and thought of Persephone, tried to think about what the next day would bring for her – for them – but he could not project his exhausted mind into past or future any more. This tortured mental cycling lasted until mid-afternoon, when a fit of last-minute stage nerves attacked, and he frantically retyped the final pages of the essay. Printed, stapled and then, at last, napped . . . then an *oh-shit* wake-up . . . followed by a frantic run across the Hill, at 7.04 p.m.

Ahem.

The Truth About the Lot Ghost.

Lord Byron, he read, *fell in love with John Harness when the latter was what we would call a Remove*

The presence swelled. The others *must* feel it now, he was sure of it. He thought he saw Fawkes shuffle, suddenly uncomfortable, and Dr Kahn pull her shawl around her as if a chill had descended.

Andrew read, automatically. Homosexual love at Harrow. Lord Byron and John Harness. Their love letters. The jealousies, the sexual predation, followed by the swoons of Cambridge. He was aware of the discomfited fidgets of his Harrow classmates. Askew in particular twisted in his seat, searching, frantically, dying to meet someone's glance: *Can he really be writing about this? This is gay porn! Are we really sorry this fellow is leaving school?*

But Andrew sensed the presence fierce and close.

Eyes boring into him.

Teeth gritted.

Animal.

Waiting.

DO NOT LOOK UP

'Byron and Harness's affair at Cambridge was thrown into

sobering relief,' Andrew read slowly, as Fawkes had coached him, 'by the death of one of Byron's close friends, Charles Skinner Matthews, who – aside from being regarded as one of the most brilliant and intellectually daring of the Cambridge set – was the closest to an "out" homosexual that Byron knew. Matthews's death itself, in addition to being sudden, and therefore shocking, possessed elements of horror and scandal as well. While publicized as an accidental drowning in the Cam River, Matthews more likely had killed himself – a suicide, by gripping the weeds in the river bottom until he was overcome. This incident may have been the turning point for Byron and Harness. If the brilliant Matthews had decided he could not face life as a homosexual in England, how could they? He had executed upon himself the sentence of England's Bloody Code: homosexuality deserves death. It was enough to persuade them that England held no future for a gay couple, however they might cloak their true emotions as friendship.'

Hang in there.

Now came Mary Cameron, the sixteen-year-old prostitute, Byron's slutty, gritty, street-smart fuck buddy; and Andrew Taylor the essayist could not help but grin to himself because he could tell through his peripheral vision that Askew was hooked; almost open-mouthed. *Gay porn . . . now straight porn? What an essay!*

'After Harness left Cambridge, Byron struck up what we might call a "rebound" love affair with none other than a teenaged London whore, whom he bought from her madam – like someone paying the lease on a car – for twenty-five pounds . . .'

Byron impregnated Mary. Brimming with guilt over abandoning Harness to London and poverty, he intended to do the right thing by this waif: marry her. His friends were outraged. It was a stupid, impulsive move; they piled on the letters and advice to get rid of her; Byron refused; but Mary herself, confused, and acting on her own professional instincts, sat down one afternoon in the Durant Street hotel and chewed hundreds of sulphur match heads until she became ill, and aborted the foetus in a pool of blood. This was especially awkward for the doctor called to the scene because Mary Cameron at that moment was dressed as a boy. 'Byron had been disguising her, so that a normally socially unacceptable companion – a cockney hooker – could become, for lack of a better term, socially portable. He could take her with him anywhere, as long as he called her his cousin, sometimes even his brother.'

The marriage talk ended. But the sexual liaison with Mary Cameron didn't. Byron's poetry of these months spoke of tender, physical intimacy:

Can I forget – canst thou forget,
When playing with thy golden hair,
How quick thy fluttering heart did move?

the rage builds
a great fist

'All the while,' Andrew swallowed, fear nearly overcoming him, 'John Harness was aware of the liaison. But tricked by the swirling rumours, Harness was aware only that a mysterious young *man* had replaced him as Byron's consort. This gives rise in Harness to a murderous rage. This rage climaxed here at Harrow School, at Speech Day in 1809. Byron was staying – my research suggests – at the Three Arrows Inn, where the murder took place.'

Andrew could hear the breathing. It was wet and lungy.

'What precisely happened at the Three Arrows is, of course, impossible to know.'

Andrew afforded himself a glance at Fawkes. Fawkes stared, so frozen-looking that Andrew stammered and lost the train of the sentence. *They must feel it, too, now.* He looked around the table. All the other faces, uncomfortable

'What?' he asked, breaking his flow.

'Go on, Andrew,' croaked Fawkes.

Because the icy bath of the presence had touched them all – they were pale, rigid, all of them, shadowed over with death

The only thing to do was to keep reading and

NOT TO LOOK UP NOT TO LOOK AT THE SEAT ACROSS

'Due to the fact that certain original letters of Harness's were found at Harrow School,' he continued with monumental effort, now reading in a gale-force wind, 'it can only be assumed that Harness and Byron met at their old house, the Lot. There they had a confrontation in a basement cistern room, a former secret meeting place of theirs. Harness had returned to Harrow to confront Byron about his change in loyalties. Byron met Harness to try and stop his obsessive stalking once and for all. This argument resulted in Byron returning Harness's letters and, significantly, the carnelian ring that Harness had given Byron as a love token, a symbol of their union. In the aftermath of this fight, Byron goes out on a social call and leaves his mistress at the inn. John Harness, overcome by a jealous rage, seizes his opportunity.

'During Byron's absence, Harness steals to the lovers' room. He finds Mary Cameron and attacks her with his remaining strength. He manages to suffocate her to death. He has a moment of triumph: he has vanquished his rival. In this moment, carried away by his victory, he decides to leave a token: he pulls Byron's carnelian ring from his own finger and places it on that of the dead girl. Now Byron – and only Byron – will know who has committed this murder. (These are the days before fingerprints.) Yet he has a horrible surprise: the corpse is a woman's. Harness was expecting a male rival. Recognizing his mistake, he slinks off to die, unsure of whether he has killed his true rival, or some stranger who happened to have been in Byron's room by mistake.

'Byron returns. He is astonished to find a dead body in his room. He is stricken to find …'

ALMOST INEVITABLY – IT was an instinct – Andrew now raised his eyes to meet John Harness's. Andrew had to catch his breath. He had never seen such malice. A shapely nose with long, flared nostrils; thin lips; small, babyish teeth; high cheekbones and forehead. It was at once a face of dignity and intelligence, and the devil's own face, curled and singed with murderous, white-hot hate. Andrew felt a pang of tragedy; perhaps in some other world, John Harness might have blossomed. Yet here he was, still imprisoned by the purity of his own venom.

'… his own lover, dead upon the floor, strangled. He finds the token. He immediately understands. And his heartbreak is doubled, since he has lost two lovers now: one to death, another to the sickening betrayal of this act. His beloved John Harness is a murderer.'

Andrew met the eyes again.

The room plunged into cold.

Andrew … Mr Toombs spoke; nervous; his voice catching …

Andrew began to fade away, overwhelmed by those eyes.

'No records we could find ever accuse Byron of murder – and such a report, surely, would have survived history, given Byron's later fame and talent for scandal. Byron, in the moment, must have done the prudent thing and preserved his own reputation. He would have waited until the dark of night, dressed Mary Cameron in her women's clothing once again – her whore's clothing – and carried her through paths he would know well (didn't he compose "Lines Written Beneath an Elm in the Churchyard of Harrow"?) to Church Hill, and dumped her body there. The corpse would be found in the morning, in the spot very near to where our own friend, Theodore Ryder, was found … by me … earlier this school year …'

Andrew's voice cracked.

*

THE BOYS AND masters in the room later recalled hearing, at that point, a sound like an animal growling.

'Andrew.' Now it was Dr Kahn who spoke. She was warning him. But he heard it, too.

The growling

He looked up at the face

It was smiling; or was it snarling? Harness had risen from his chair. His teeth were bared.

You're in for it now

I am not the growling animal you hear

I have conjured him in time

You know whose chair I am sitting in

The door to Mr Toombs's classroom opened. A figure stood there – a real figure. Pale. Rumpled. Grey stubble on his cheeks. Face transfigured by misery; a stuffed black overnight bag on his shoulder. The nine seated figures in the room turned to the door. There Sir Alan stared back at them, eyes vague and watery. His glasses – usually as bright and sharp as a weapon on his face – were for once off-centre, greasy. His glance searched the room, then fell on Andrew.

'You're here,' he said, 'reading an essay.'

Fawkes stood, rousing himself from the spell. On instinct, he blocked any clear passage Sir Alan might have towards the head of the table. Dr Kahn pushed out her chair on the other side. The only way for Sir Alan to reach Andrew was over the table.

'You're here,' he repeated, his voice growing in volume and anger, '*reading an essay*!' The candles guttered, as if blown by the grieving father's breath.

Andrew saw Harness now, standing, crouching, ready to pounce

Or was it Sir Alan the two were one

'Persephone is making a sound, now,' Sir Alan lamented, his eyes streaming tears, 'like nothing a human should produce. It's a slow . . . gurgle. It sounds like air eking through a water pipe.

Which, in a way, is exactly what it is. You see, she is so weak,' he choked, 'she's so weak she cannot even spit out the blood and . . . secretions . . . in her chest. She can't even cough any more. I thought that was the worst. Expectorating her own blood. But the worst, I know now, is when she stops. The doctors have a name for this . . . *Mister Taylor*,' he spat the words with fury. 'They call it the death rattle. When the death rattle comes, they say, she has fifty-seven hours to live. On average. Fifty-seven! How would you like to spend two of them, coming back to tell my daughter to her face that you murdered her? Or better yet, how would you like to be locked away, as you deserve?' He fished a mobile phone from his pocket and thrust it in the air. 'Shall I call the Health Protection Agency?'

'Andrew was tested,' Fawkes said. 'He does not have tuberculosis.'

'Shut up, you ass,' snarled Sir Alan. 'I know what he did.' Then his voice quieted unnervingly. 'And you're here . . . reading an essay.'

The body language of the others in the room eased with this falling cadence; Sir Alan was calming down, they told themselves; he was rational. The room of listeners wished very badly for something to appear normal, if even for a minute. But they soon discovered it was just the ocean receding before a wave.

'*To hell with you!*' screamed Sir Alan, and he lunged across the table. And Andrew Taylor saw him

John Harness in midair; John Harness an inch from his face; John Harness, in a shocking, final trump – oh the irony, young Mister Taylor, you who wished to defeat your enemy with *a story* – Andrew saw Sir Alan Vine fly across the table, at him; and in that flight

Vittoria Corombona

The barking strangling sunken-cheeked killer on the hill

The limber pale lover

Harness overtook Andrew's body, making him gasp as a man does plunging into arctic water. Wind swept through the open door. The candles flickered, and went out.

26

Death Rattle

IN THE DARK they heard coughing. It was prolonged; it made your throat itch to listen to it. There was a shuffling. The bang of a chair moving. Fragments of voices: *Can anyone . . . ? Should we light the candles or just . . . ?* Finally came a decisive scrape as Mr Toombs's chair pulled back. After a few seconds, a snap brought on the harsh classroom lights. The students blinked at one another, still in their seats. Dr Kahn had kept to her post. Fawkes had moved to the head of the table, to defend Andrew. Sir Alan had crawled across the table in his fury, but now he sat with his bottom resting on the table end, his feet dangling into the speaker's chair, leaning back on to the table, on one arm; an exhausted warrior. He stared at the shallow space between him and the blackboard. Andrew was gone.

'Good, he managed to get away. What were you going to do? Throttle him?' Dr Kahn accused, from her chair.

Sir Alan did not respond. He sat in a daze. Fawkes searched the space for Andrew and satisfied himself that the boy had escaped. He turned, ready to reprove Sir Alan, but he no longer saw rage in the puffy face, only collapse. The man's anger at Andrew had been, in a way, his last expression of hope, that there would be someone to blame, some action still to take. Now, deflated, it was clear this illusion had been stripped from him. Fawkes felt a stab of sympathy.

'I'm sorry,' Fawkes said.

'Sorry?' Dr Kahn sputtered indignantly.

Fawkes continued. 'Persephone is a wonderful girl, and a friend. I wish there were something I could do.'

Sir Alan flinched, as if these kindnesses stung him. He spoke softly, almost to himself, and with bitterness. 'You don't know anything.'

But Fawkes had already spun around. *Of course there was something he could do; what was he doing, standing there?*

He searched for the Reverend Peter at the table, among the other dazed members of the Essay Club.

'It's time,' he said. 'Come on!'

THE TWO MEN clambered back up the hill to the High Street. The Reverend Peter spoke excitedly. 'Piers,' he said. 'Piers, I don't know if you shared those sensations?'

'What?'

'It distinctly seemed as if there were something in the room with us.'

Fawkes winced. 'I know.'

'Have you experienced that before?'

'Unfortunately, yes.'

'I don't how to describe it. It was *negative*, wasn't it? Clammy. All over you, as it were.' The priest shuddered. 'Not a happy feeling.'

'No, not happy. You heard Andrew. Harness is a murderer.'

'And you think this person, John Harness, is responsible for the others being sick? Sir Alan's daughter, and the boys?'

'I do. Or I've gone mad. Which at this point seems a distinct possibility. But that would mean you're mad, too.'

'Yes. But it is the role of the clergy to join parishioners in their suffering.'

Fawkes glanced at the Reverend Peter sidelong. Sarcasm under pressure. Indeed, he liked the priest. They hurried around the bend in the High Street, past Headmaster's House and the Old Schools. 'It's all up to you now, Reverend Peter. Are you ready?'

'I hope so.'

'Don't hope. Be.'

'Jesus Christ is the arbiter of such conflicts. I am only his representative. But His power is absolute.'

'That's encouraging,' said Fawkes.

A voice called behind them. The Reverend Peter came to a halt.

Fawkes went ahead a few paces before stopping. 'Come on,' he ordered, crossly.

'But it's Judy.'

They turned. Behind them, on the High Street, Dr Kahn bustled, waving something in the air. They waited for her. She seemed to move in slow motion. Urgency tugged at Fawkes. *Come on, come on*. He felt that something terrible was imminent, and that every second he let pass might be ruinous.

'I'm coming with you,' she called, out of breath. 'Are you going to perform the exorcism?'

'House blessing,' corrected the Reverend Peter. 'Do you need to rest?'

'No, no,' she puffed. 'Look. I found these.' She held out a wad of crumpled white printer paper.

'Never mind those,' snapped Fawkes.

'They're Andrew's essay. I found them on the walk up the hill,' said Dr Kahn. 'He's come this way. Maybe back to the Lot.'

'OK, good. He can join in, if we ever get there,' said an exasperated Fawkes. 'We have to start the ritual, right away.'

THEY REACHED THE Lot after a few minutes. Music and television blared from the house into the street. The corridors echoed with ball-playing and shouting. The place seemed to thud with noise. *And Macrae thought he would tidy it up; get it under control.* Fawkes smiled bitterly to himself.

'Right. What do we need to do, Reverend Peter?'

The Reverend Peter chewed his lip appraisingly. 'Where is the main room? The centre of the house?'

'This way.'

They pushed into the long, narrow common room where Fawkes had held his house meeting on the first night of school.

The Reverend Peter appropriated a disused upright piano as his workstation. He placed his bag on its top and removed four items: his grey-bound booklet, his water bottle, a small brass crucifix and, to Fawkes's surprise, the twig of a fir tree, five inches of white and spongy stem with vivid green needles.

The Reverend Peter's air became more formal. 'You are petitioners with me in the blessing of this house,' he explained. 'Do you believe in Jesus Christ, the Son of God the Father Almighty?'

Fawkes and Dr Kahn exchanged glances.

'I'm a Jew,' said Dr Kahn. 'So no.'

'I'm an atheist.' Fawkes winced. 'I thought you were going to . . .'

The Reverend Peter ignored them. 'Do you accept His authority to cleanse this house of any defilement, to cast out the evil one and all his minions?'

There seemed only one answer to this, and Fawkes and Dr Kahn, affected by the priest's seriousness, stood up straighter and answered together: 'I do.'

The Reverend Peter nodded. *That was better.* 'I will perform a blessing on this house, especially all those places, Piers, which you feel have been most affected by the spirit. I will need you to be the guide. Judy, if you would please assist me. If you would hold the water and the evergreen, please.' She took the bottle of water. He held his hand over it. 'We thank you, Almighty God, for the gift of water. Over it the Holy Spirit moved in the beginning of creation. Grant, by the power of your Holy Spirit, that this water be sanctified to be a sign of your dominion over all that it might touch. Amen.'

The Reverend Peter peered at them over his glasses.

'Amen,' echoed Fawkes.

'This is now holy water,' pronounced the Reverend Peter. 'Judith, in every room we enter, I would like you to dip the evergreen in, then sprinkle some of the water about. Can you do that?'

She nodded.

'Right!' He smiled, and pushed his glasses up his nose. 'Let's start right here, shall we?' He picked up his booklet. The three of them stood in a tight triangle, feeling both silly and, somehow, important, listening to the boys' games pound the floorboards, and their electronic dance music throb, a storm of distraction whirling about them.

'Lord,' began the Reverend Peter, in his well-bred tenor, 'I cover myself and everyone around me with the blood of Jesus. I cover Piers with the blood of Jesus. I cover Judith with the blood of Jesus.' Fawkes watched Dr Kahn for signs of irony, but her face was grave. 'I cover this home with the blood of Jesus. By the power of His blood, I break off every power of the kingdom of darkness, for this home, for each of us, and for Andrew Taylor. Please sprinkle, Judith.'

'Hm?'

'Sprinkle now. The holy water.'

'Oh, right. Like this?'

'That's the idea, very well done indeed. Where shall we go next, Piers?'

'Upstairs,' he said. 'Andrew's room. Maybe he'll be there.'

They moved to the stairs, the Reverend Peter carrying his crucifix and booklet, Dr Kahn bearing the water bottle and dripping twig. Fawkes remained on edge. He was forgetting something critically important. He knew it, but could not put his finger on it. A clock ticked in his chest, and it was frighteningly close to buzzing. *Those papers – Andrew's essay*. Dr Kahn, as usual, had found the right track. But where did it lead? Fawkes, in the frenzy of the pounding music and the pressure of the ritual, could not locate this misplaced clue, so he merely led them up the narrow stairs with a frown.

THE FIRST THING Andrew felt was a nagging twinge in his throat. He coughed and hacked at it: *Surely this must come out somehow.* He felt a warm trickle, a clot of something form in his lower throat. He was about to hawk up this ball and spit it out . . . when a moment of self-awareness came on him.

Stop. Wake up.

He was still in the Classics Schools.

The candles had blown out. Confusion swirled around him. Yet Andrew knew one thing with certainty.

Harness had made him sick.

Heat pulsed in his forehead, flushed his cheeks. *Fever.*

You're sick. And if you spit in here, with ten, eleven others, you'll make them sick, too.

Andrew covered his mouth with his hand, and fled for the door in the dark.

Outside a cool evening awaited. The perspiration on his back and neck turned icy. His body quaked. He staggered through the darkness. Harness intended to kill him now. He had tried seduction, tried to lure him, but Andrew had resisted. And so Harness had seized him like a beast, a snake sinking fangs into him, clinging to him and weighing him down, waiting for him to tire; a predator making a kill.

Get as far from the Classics Schools as you can, he thought; *get away from people. You're infectious.*

He climbed the stairs to the street. His breathing came heavily. When he reached the top, he stumbled. He pulled up a trouser leg and found his calves and ankles had swollen: taut, puffy, dragging beneath him like bags of fluid.

What was happening to him?

The thoughts came with pure, primitive panic. *He had no time.*

Sir Alan said Persephone had only hours to live. She would be a corpse, Roddy, too, if he did not do something now.

Andrew leaned against a building and coughed again. He spat blood onto the pavement. He went faint. In this swoon – *it must have been just in his mind, subject to the fever, or to the exhaustion of writing all night, because how could this be real* – he perceived the High Street as it would have been on the night of his essay – in 1809. The night of the murder.

No concrete, no pavements, no paved roads. A narrow dirt road, with ruts from carriage and cart wheels, and beaten firm by horses' hoofs and human feet. A few lamp-lit windows. And beyond their feeble haloes, darkness. Here the great night hung over the Hill; it slithered between the trees; it dripped. It was here Lord Byron had carried Mary's body and dumped it.

Asphalt again. A car swooshed past.

The pain in Andrew's throat increased.

He understood, suddenly, what Harness was doing to him.

He was forcing Andrew to endure the journey from health to death, to experience that same, slow, consuming disease that Harness had suffered. Only Andrew would live it – die from it – in a single evening. He reached up with his fingers and touched his face; felt the ridge of his own cheekbone, and traced it with his fingertip. The fat had melted away. The sores grew in his mouth. The fever burned his cheeks.

Harness was going to kill him. He was going to kill all of them.

All of them?

What if I give myself to him?

Wasn't that the idea that had occurred to him before? And Fawkes had dissuaded him. But Fawkes was not always right. Fawkes did not know about dead Daniel Schwartz, about the overdose, about rising into the sky alone in a balloon, and being left behind and feeling in your churning stomach that you deserved *were fated* to die, too. Fawkes did not know about your father selling the canoe; or about *being through*. Fawkes, in his selfish way, loved himself; could not bear to part with himself. Could not know how Andrew might *just know*, with certainty, that he did not belong, and would never belong.

The idea grew ever more clear.

If I give myself to Harness then maybe he'll leave the others alone. I'm what he wants. Just let him know he could have me, if he gave the others back.

Andrew propelled himself forward on the mossy brick pavement, leaning against the plane trees. His breath came in gulps. His muscles scarcely obeyed his commands. His flesh had been devoured away.

He was emaciated.

He might not have the strength to make it to the Lot. He saw a car come around the bend and pause by the light at the crest of the Hill.

Andrew flung himself into the road, holding up his hand. The headlights were blinding.

'Can you . . .' The rest of the sentence died on his lips. *Can you give me a ride, just a few blocks up?* The pain in his throat was excruciating – a dagger stroke. But worse, perhaps, was the look of shock on the driver's face. He was fortyish, fit, wearing an exercise tank top, heading home from the gym. He started to respond to Andrew, then recoiled. The driver saw a gaunt youth, cheeks thrusting from wilted skin; dark hair over a starved, angular face. The boy had the appearance of something freshly exhumed. But what truly frightened him was the eyes. They were sunk in their sockets. They stared out at him with a kind of dull desperation; they wanted things from him, yet they knew asking was futile; they were going through the mere motions of survival. The figure mumbled. It was wearing some odd, old-fashioned coat. The driver slammed the stick into neutral, let the car ease down the gradient a few feet – away from the figure, who had lurched into his headlight beam, and then, when the vehicle had pulled clear, gunned the engine. As the driver put distance between himself and the figure, he glanced back. Was he dreaming? He dismissed the notion of calling the police or even an ambulance. Instead he would speed home, move quickly to his own door, and lock it tight.

'STOP, STOP,' INTERRUPTED Fawkes.

The Reverend Peter regarded him quizzically. He had been reading in a strong voice, trained by years of projecting into the back corners of chapels. They stood in Andrew's nook-like room. The desk contained the debris of Andrew's burst of research earlier: stray printer paper with circlings and underlinings. Beside the wardrobe lay a large duffel bag, unzipped, stuffed with some hastily packed items.

'We're in the wrong spot,' Fawkes said, frowning.

'The ritual calls for the principal rooms in the house to be blessed,' countered the Reverend Peter. 'You did say the spirit had appeared to Andrew here . . .'

'I know,' Fawkes admitted.

'Well, Piers, make up your mind,' Dr Kahn said.

'The basement,' he replied, finally uncovering the answer that had been nagging at him. 'The cistern room. When we uncovered it – when I uncovered it – that's when the real trouble started for Andrew. It's where the spirit is strongest. That's where we can drive him out.'

'It was their hiding place,' Dr Kahn agreed. 'Byron and Harness,' she explained to the priest.

Dr Kahn and Fawkes looked to the Reverend Peter for approval.

'All right.' The priest sighed. 'We'll just finish this prayer, shall we? *Lord, how many adversaries I have*,' he continued. '*How many there are who rise up against me.*'

'*Peter.*' Fawkes raised his voice in impatience. 'Now.'

*

THE WORKMEN HAD begun to repair the hole. With the anxiety oppressing the school, and with the headmaster's threat hanging over Fawkes, any historical interest in the hidden cistern room had been set aside for the needs of short-term morale. The stretch of basement corridor was littered with building materials and tools, stacked on paint-spattered groundsheets that lined the floor. A stack of boards would constitute the new stretch of wall. Plaster in a tub would fill the gaps. Trowels and sandpaper were ready to smooth it over. While they waited to begin, Reg had found a fortuitously sized square of wood panelling and had affixed it with epoxy over the hole leading to the cistern.

Andrew felt his breath coming shallower and shallower. He had to squint through his fever and occasionally shake his head to refocus on his surroundings. Whether by luck or by virtue of the shadowy zone he inhabited, he saw no other students as he climbed down to the basement, stopping every few steps to rest against the wall and listen to the sound of his own breathing. *The popping*. He did not have the energy to feel afraid any more. He merely experienced the exhaustion, the desire for relief – a cold compress, a cool bed ... or something else. Death. Up to now it had been an abstraction, something that happened to grandparents, not to you, not in a damp basement stairwell in England.

By the time he reached the basement corridor, sweat slicked his face. He tugged feebly at the wood panel. It would not budge. He lay down next to it, on the paint-stained sheet. He closed his eyes and rested.

Maybe he would die right here. Alone.

Persephone and Roddy. They were dying alone, too. Only they did not know the way out. He, at least, saw the exit. He understood, or guessed, that if he surrendered himself to Harness, the others might go free. Harness had wanted him all along. Harness was hungry. Let him devour Andrew. Here was, perhaps, his sole gift: his ability to understand and solve this riddle.

After a moment, he tried again. He wrapped his fingertips around the top of the wood panel, then threw his weight backward and pulled the board free. He managed to thrust his legs – bone-thin, his trousers now flopping like sail canvas – into the hole. On instinct he propped the board back into place behind him. He was not sure how he descended the ladder. He was not sure if there was a ladder. He might have been borne into the gloom by the glowing white arms of Harness, his white angel in the blackness. He did reach the bottom, though, and felt the damp stone under his fingers, the carved gutters running into the cistern's hole; the sandy grit, cold and unappealing. He eased himself to the floor and lay there. *He had made it*. The cold felt magnificent, a salve on his fever. Even if the ridges of the stone dug into his skin. Even if it was dirty.

He reached out to see how close he was to the edge. *The cistern was full*. It brimmed with cold water, shimmery, welcoming. *Of course it did*.

He closed his eyes. He could not move any more. He lay on his back, enjoying the peace. The silent, sensationless void of the cold room.

That was when he heard it.

Hrr hrr hrr hrr

Hrch

The noise rose from his own gullet.

Hrch

Sir Alan had said the words. *The death rattle*. The sign that there was no return, that the slide to death had begun. He felt its pull.

Hrr hrr hrr hrr – inhale.

Hrch – exhale.

His breath had become a feeble bong. A poor exchange of gases. There was very little of him left.

Millimetre by millimetre, Andrew raised his body. He pushed himself up on his elbows. He thought he might vomit from the effort. He thrust out one brittle arm, and raised himself on it like a tent pole. He remained there for a moment, poised, nearly fainting, and then, like a statue toppling, he fell into the water.

THE CISTERN WATER enveloped him with a sigh.

HIS FEVER WAS relieved.

Andrew Taylor stood waist-high in the chilly River Cam, his feet in the muck.

It was midsummer. He was drunk. He was naked. A glorious bright blue sky blazed above him. John Harness splashed a few feet away. This was a swimming hole they had found – another in a long list of their hideaway spots. Andrew's body had been restored. His skin was full again – goose-bumped from the cold, and from excitement.

Harness. He is showing me the reason he came back

He and Harness had never kissed before; only chaste pecks that could have been confused with friendship. *Well, not really*. But they could not have been confused with lust. But now, the alcohol made it inevitable, and it was just a matter of waiting; his whole body reached out, through the air, it seemed, towards Harness. Andrew had never seen anything more gorgeous: blue eyes against the fair hair and the white skin, pale and shapely; he seemed a kind of river god, stirring from marble; Andrew wanted to own him, to consume him. Harness stepped towards him and their faces met in a kiss so hungry they nearly bit each other. Andrew pulled away. He felt something under his hand, some flotsam in the water, and he raised it, water dripping away, and held before his eyes: a late June blossom, round and white with a black rim, the shape of a fingernail. A petal, the pure coinage of summer. Fragile, fresh, delicate and good.

he had seen it before

He looked in Harness's eyes and now saw there what would come.

That sunny protected spot in the Cam vanished. Time summoned him somewhere else.

and this is where it all led

He was in a cramped room in London. There was a bed, and a small chest, and a wardrobe with one hinge broken. This was all John Harness could afford. Who knew what time it was, day or night; it might have been four, five in the morning; the death watch had been continuous. On a little table, a candle nursed a tiny flame, a mere bead of light. On the bed, Harness's jaw moved in that random gyration that preceded death. His white-blond hair was shaggy, unkempt and uncut. His cheeks had sunk to starving hollowness. His chest emitted the death rattle. No one was there, except this young man, expiring. The candle, eventually, sputtered out and the room went dark. No one relit the candle. The death sound continued on. But by the time the dawn rose over London and the horses' clopping and voices of the day got under way, its rays, filtering through the shutters, lit on a corpse.

Praise the LORD with the harp; play to him upon the psaltery
and lyre
Sing for him a new song; sound a fanfare with all your skill
upon the trumpet.

The voices pulled Andrew from the scene.

Andrew was aware of the water now. His limbs, in it. No longer fevered. He was swimming, but in a narrow space. He knew where he was. The cistern. He was free of his disease. He had survived! Some chanting from a handful of voices – amateur, and off-rhythm, yet booming and strong – filtered through to him. He felt the keenest desire to be with those voices.

But then he saw Harness before him. Harness's hair floated in the dirty grey-brown water – all the rain that Harness himself had brought that autumn. Together they swam in it. They were still locked together in struggle. Harness's face grew fierce. His eyes were angry, it was true. But just as much, Andrew realized, they were confused and frightened. John Harness had not known the person he had killed – and now he did. He had not understood the wrongs he had committed – and now he did. And he had not grasped – here, in his prison, in this cave, outside and underneath time – that he was truly dead.

Those eyes were now comprehending it all.

It was Andrew's doing. But also the work of these words and poems that rang in the well water around them. Fawkes and the Reverend Peter and Dr Kahn had arrived. They were performing the house blessing. Andrew might be saved.

He gathers up the waters of the ocean as in a water-skin; and stores up the depths of the sea.

Harness's face twisted. The prayers seemed to enrage him. He reached out a in the murk, gripping Andrew's arm. In return, Andrew kicked his feet wildly – those wingtips, heavy, water-sodden, impossible! – and in a final burst of effort, pushed himself to the surface. He gasped. One deep breath.

The voices hesitated – had they heard him? Andrew filled his lungs to cry out.

Harness reached out again and pulled him down.

Andrew choked on the cold water. He flailed with his arms and legs, and struggled to reach the surface. But his tailcoat and thick trousers became a kind of wet parachute, dragging him under the water – and Harness's grip was irresistible. The bubbles ran out of Andrew's nose. Panic racked every cell. He clawed at the sides.

And then he remembered.

What if I give myself to him?

Andrew released his grip on the craggy cistern walls and felt himself sink. He held his hands up so Harness could see them –

free, no longer fighting. Andrew met Harness's gaze one final time. *He understands.* The fierceness slowly went out of those piercing blue eyes, and by degrees, they faded into the murk. Harness was gone.

Andrew had won.

Water poured into his nose and mouth. He felt himself sinking deeper into the black water. Exhaustion seized him and he succumbed to it.

THE THREE COMPANIONS heard the sharp gasp. They exchanged a glance. The presence had been so powerful here, they expected any sudden sound to come from *it*. But there was another explanation for this disembodied noise. Fawkes said it first.

'My God, Andrew's there!'

He began ripping at the wooden panel. He needn't have – it came away in his hands. They had not brought a torch, so Fawkes fought his way blindly into the hole, kicking at the broken plaster with his heels, and lowered himself into the darkness. He dropped, stumbled, and fell over backward. The ground was hard, and slick. The Reverend Peter followed (more athletic, he had a better landing). Scraped, but unharmed, they let their eyes adjust to the darkness. And for a moment Fawkes could not comprehend it: the cistern was full. It had been nearly empty before, drained except for a foot of rusty run-off and debris. Yet here it was, sloshing over, like a creek swelling under heavy rains. An arm, and a white hand, protruded from the murk.

'That's him!'

They squatted, then heaved. Pulling a human being in wet clothes from water was hard work. They grew soaked as they scrambled; they scraped their knees against the stone. Finally Andrew cleared the water.

Oh my God he's not moving

Fawkes's mind reeled. He almost did not hear the Reverend

Peter saying something practical, something urgent. Fawkes found himself pushed to the side, to witness the priest pumping the boy's chest. A few desperate minutes later, the Reverend Peter stood, a dark silhouette, staring down at the figure ... in triumph? In despair? *Is he all right?* Fawkes flung himself forward, his shoes squelching, and pulled the wet body to himself. He held it. He squeezed it to him. He could not let this one go. He could not. He began to speak to the boy, eagerly, but choked on his words. Andrew's flesh had gone a kind of fish-belly grey, seemed to be slicked with the dirty cistern water. His eyes stared forward. But the expression on the boy's face is what stopped Fawkes. Instead of showing the panicked horror of the drowned man, Andrew's lips, in death, had parted and curled, very slightly, at the corners; as if he'd had a secret whispered in his ear, and it had made him smile.

Epilogue

LORD BYRON LAY on his deathbed. Around him stood a munitions officer in gleaming white breeches and a red coat, as well as several Greek soldiers wearing mournful expressions (these latter were Shells, heavily made up with big black moustaches).

After a few moments of dialogue and a pregnant pause, the comforting figures froze in a tableau. Byron stood. Dusted himself off. (The audience tittered; it was a comical touch, to puncture the moment.) He stood up and came downstage. The lights tightened around him. The audience in Speech Room hushed, prepared to give the actors one last burst of attention. Under the blanket of darkness, Lord Byron recited, in a calm, cool tone, a final spell:

The dinner and the soiree too were done
The supper too discussed, the dames admired.

Byron's eyes winked at one section of the audience, centre left, as if he were tempted by some of the girls he'd seen there over the course of the evening. But he moved on.

The banqueteers had dropped off one by one –
The song was silent.
And the dance . . . expired.

He cast another glance around the room, fully in control. Then he turned. Slowly and deliberately, he climbed back into his place centre stage, amid the peering forms of the Greek soldiers, and under the munitions officer's concerned gaze.

'The last thin petticoats were vanished, gone,' declared Lord Byron, with a wan gesture at the sky. 'Like fleeing clouds into the sky retired. And nothing brighter gleamed through the saloon . . .'

The lights narrowed on the stage tableau.

'Than dying tapers,' he said, dreamy now, reclining into death. 'And the peeping moon.'

The spotlight faded and . . . was extinguished.

The applause in Speech Room was polite, even warm, though from his spot in the back row, Fawkes wondered if it amounted to a sigh of relief. Piers Fawkes had not scandalized the crowd with his potty mouth and vulgarity, or included X-rated references too raw for the grandmothers in attendance. No, for Fawkes it had been a rather conservative affair, befitting the stack of thin trade paperbacks arranged on the card table in the corridor on the way out, the ones with the oil painting of Byron on the cover along with *The Fever of Messolonghi* (a title he had come to despise) scribbled across it in what was meant to be a nineteenth-century-inky effect. Tomasina's idea. Seven pounds ninety-nine from Barking Press, with a blurb from Andrew Motion. Not bad, in all. Still, Fawkes, in his sports jacket, sank down into his seat. While he had been the guest of honour for drinks in Colin Jute's office with the governors, the evening was really for the students, and the audience said so with their applause. Cheers for the thirteen-year-old Greek platoon and their comic relief officer with the pillow-stuffed belly (Fawkes could not resist applauding; he liked his own broader jokes; and the boy's performance had been winning); grateful applause for Hugh; huzzahs for the ladies, especially the battleaxe Lady Melbourne, an unexpected audience favourite.

But the real roar came at the end, for Byron. The actor now stood at the front, his curly hair gleaming with sweat, gobbling up the attention. One section of Speech Room rose in enthusiastic applause – girls squealing in that unattractive way – as well as Sir Alan Vine and the Headland boys. Byron made a gesture, as if to rip off his clothes. The young males in the audience thundered; nervous laughter followed. Byron blushed, then coyly unbuttoned his Regency coat. The effect was anticlimactic, since Persephone Vine was of course still wearing a shirt, and had strapped down her breasts in a very tight athletic bra; even she was not going to flash her tits to three hundred parents and students in Speech Room.

Fawkes saw a middle-aged couple, sitting one row in front of him, look confused. The wife leaned over to another couple nearby. Fawkes could partly read her lips and suspected he knew her question: *I know it's really a girl, but who is she? What's all the excitement about?* The reply, he could partially hear over the curtain calls: *She's one of the ones who was ill.She and the other boy survived.* Woman Number One shook her head, moved; *hard to believe, that poor girl*, Fawkes read in her expression; and the woman applauded harder. Fawkes had had enough. He ducked through the row and out by a back exit, into the December night.

Once there, he did not quite know what to do. The right thing would be to stay, mingle, drink in the attention, store it up for later, thank his hosts and former employers. But then there would be the awkward goodbyes. That feeling of everyone else having someone to go home with, somewhere to go, but him. And there was Persephone. Looking at her, and the rest of the cast, up close, was knives to him. The missing face ... well, it was best just to avoid the whole scene. He lit a cigarette, circled around Speech Room, and started down the hill.

'Sir,' piped a voice behind him.

It was the tiny form of a Shell in his straw hat. He squinted up at Fawkes in the glare of the street light.

'Hello.'

'You're Mr Fawkes.'

'I am.'

'Are you still teaching here?'

'No, I've left.'

'Why?'

Why? Fawkes asked himself. *Because I was fired. Because I was a drunk. Because I battled the inexplicable, when no one asked me to. Because I lost precious things that did not belong to me.*

'I'm pursuing other opportunities,' he said drily.

'Sir?'

'Never mind. Piss off.'

Fawkes dug his hands in his pockets and restarted his journey, then reproached himself – hadn't he vowed to be better than that? He stopped and turned, but the boy had vanished.

An old sense of panic gripped Fawkes. Where had the boy gone? Who – what – had Fawkes been speaking to, out there in the darkness? He stood, bewildered. Then a giggle caught his attention. He turned again, and saw that the Shell was watching him, and had been joined by a friend: another tiny man, with pale skin, long white fingers, in his white shirt and black tie and bluer. The two regarded him with undisguised, gleeful malice, exchanged a whisper, and giggled again. He supposed he deserved it. They turned their backs to him and resumed their journey. Fawkes noticed that the two boys were holding hands. He watched them, surprised: their fingers intertwined as they walked away, one of them actually skipping. It was a delightfully innocent sight, in such a cynical, rowdy, bullying environment. *A young friendship, born at Harrow: a good thing*, he reassured himself. Yet Fawkes found a familiar fear pulsing through him. He watched them, until the two straw hats vanished into the black.

Acknowledgements

I AM LUCKY to have attended Harrow School for one year. It was an enriching and transformative time for me; one for which I will be forever grateful. It is unfortunate that Andrew Taylor's experience at the school, in circumstances similar to mine, was less happy. With some reluctance I felt it necessary to represent accurately Mr Taylor's time at Harrow, not my own.

Without the support of my mother, Martha Evans, this book could not have been written. Exceeding my wildest hopes, she offered to be my guide into literary, social and medical history, and gave me the tireless, cheerful commitment that only my mom can offer; wearing her expertise lightly, and always making it fun.

I am grateful to Dr Eric Leibert and Dr Rany Condos of the NYU Langone Medical Center for their generosity, patience and wit in answering my many questions about TB and its treatment.

My agent, Simon Lipskar, and editor, Sally Kim, worked hard to bring this book to life. An author couldn't ask for a more gifted, dedicated team.

Debts for other kindnesses: Jonathan Smith, the Witteveen/Quirijns family, Judith Lee, Rob Munk.

Sources for this book include *Byron: Child of Passion, Fool of Fame* by Benita Eisler; *A History of Harrow School* by Christopher

Tyerman; and accounts of John Keats's death by his friend Joseph Severn.

My wife and children tolerated much caffeine abuse and many sunny days spent indoors in order for this novel to be written. They saved me, and it, a thousand times. Always to them, my deepest thanks.